"A waking dream, at once powerful and subtly sinister."

—Clive Barker, *New York Times* bestselling author

"Jonathan Maberry delivers a perfect, suspenseful, edge-of-your-seat tale that will keep you riveted! . . . Jonathan Maberry is always my go-to author for awesome!"

—Sherrilyn Kenyon, #1 *New York Times* bestselling author

"With *Glimpse*, Jonathan Maberry carries us into the fertile liminal zone between waking and dreaming. Monsters dwell there, but so do some unexpected heroes, and none is more unexpected than the tragically damaged Rain Thomas. . . . She's a poignant creation, and it's impossible not to root for her as she makes her way through this wonderful (and wonder-filled) nightmare of a book." —Scott Smith, *New York Times* bestselling author of *The Ruins*

"Jonathan Maberry is a shape-shifter of a writer, able to get into his characters so deeply that we never doubt his truth for a minute."

—Charlaine Harris, #1 internationally bestselling author

"Jonathan Maberry—a master of his craft—has written something exceptional with *Glimpse* . . . a relentless and seductive book with real bite, and real heart. Rain's courage inspires, and Doctor Nine will haunt our dreams." —Rachel Caine, *New York Times* bestselling author of the Great Library series

"Award-winning author Jonathan Maberry hits it out of the park with his latest chilling tour de force, *Glimpse*. He channels the best of Stephen King and Peter Straub. . . . Raw and beautiful, detailed and explosive, here is a story that will haunt you long after you close the book."

—James Rollins, *New York Times* bestselling author of *The Seventh Plague*

ALSO BY JONATHAN MABERRY

NOVELS

Dogs of War

Kill Switch

Predator One

Fall of Night

Code Zero

Extinction Machine

Assassin's Code

The King of Plagues

The Dragon Factory

Patient Zero

Joe Ledger: Special Ops

Dead of Night

Fall of Night

The Wolfman

The Nightsiders: The Orphan Army

The Nightsiders: Vault of Shadows

Ghostwalkers: A Deadlands Novel

Bits & Pieces

Fire & Ash

Flesh & Bone

Dust & Decay

Rot & Ruin

Bad Moon Rising

Dead Man's Song

Ghost Road Blues

ANTHOLOGIES (as editor)

Joe Ledger: Unstoppable
(with Bryan Thomas Schmidt)

Nights of the Living Dead: An Anthology
(with George A. Romero)

Aliens: Bug Hunt

Baker Street Irregulars
(with Michael Ventrella)

Hardboiled Horror

Kingdoms Fall

Scary Out There

V-Wars

V-Wars: Blood and Fire

V-Wars: Night Terrors

V-Wars: Shockwaves

Out of Tune Vols I and II

The X-Files: Trust No One

The X-Files: The Truth Is Out There

The X-Files: Secret Agendas

ALSO BY JONATHAN MABERRY

COLLECTIONS

Whistling Past the Graveyard

Wind Through the Fence

Joe Ledger Special Ops

A Little Bronze Book of Cautionary Tales

Beneath the Skin

Strange Worlds (audio)

Tales from the Fire Zone (audio)

Darkness on the Edge of Town (audio)

Hungry Tales (audio)

The Sam Hunter Casefiles (audio)

GRAPHIC NOVELS

Wolverine: Flies to a Spider

Punisher: Naked Kills

Captain America: Hail Hydra

Marvel Zombies Return

Black Panther: Power

Black Panther: DoomWar

Black Panther: Klaws of the Panther

Mavel Universe vs the Punisher

Marvel Universe vs Wolverine

Marvel Universe vs The Avengers

Bad Blood

Rot & Ruin: Warrior Smart

V-Wars: Crimson Queen

V-Wars: All of Us Monsters

Age of Heroes

JONATHAN MABERRY

GLIPSE

ST. MARTIN'S GRIFFIN
NEW YORK

Published in the United States by St. Martin's Griffin, an imprint of St. Martin's Publishing Group

Excerpt from *Lamb: The Gospel According to Biff, Christ's Childhood Pal* by Christopher Moore, copyright © 2002 by Christopher Moore. Reprinted courtesy of HarperCollins Publishers.

Excerpt from *The Encyclopedia of Magic and Alchemy* by Rosemary Ellen Guiley copyright © 2006 by Rosemary Ellen Guiley is used by permission of the author.

The "Monk's Story" interludes were previously released in short story form as "Mystic"; first published in the anthology *Peel Back the Skin* by Gray Matter Press, 2016.

www.stmartins.com

The Library of Congress has cataloged the hardcover edition as follows:

Names: Maberry, Jonathan, author.
Title: Glimpse : a novel / Jonathan Maberry.
Description: First edition. | New York : St. Martin's Press, 2018.
Identifiers: LCCN 2017043682 | ISBN 9781250065261 (hardcover) | ISBN 9781250136329 (ebook)
Subjects: | GSAFD: Suspense fiction.
Classification: LCC PS3613.A19 G58 2018 | DDC 813/.6—dc23
LC record available at https://lccn.loc.gov/2017043682

ISBN 978-1-250-20953-5 (trade paperback)

Our books may be purchased in bulk for promotional, educational, or business use. Please contact your local bookseller or the Macmillan Corporate and Premium Sales Department at 1-800-221-7945, extension 5442, or by email at MacmillanSpecialMarkets@macmillan.com.

First St. Martin's Griffin Edition: March 2020

10 9 8 7 6 5 4 3 2 1

This one goes out to mothers everywhere.
You wind all the clocks.
You keep the monsters away.
And, as always, for Sara Jo.

ACKNOWLEDGMENTS

Special thanks to Catherine Rosenbaum for star charts and astrological information; and Edmond Angler, Kim Sandoval, Isaac Terrazas, Maritza Garcia Boak, and Elías F. Combarro for help with Spanish translations. Thanks to Claudia Cleary, Chris Newton, Sara Pinkman, Dr. Nancy Martin Rickerhauser, Veronica Sapp, Rebecca Lane Beittel, Haley Carlson, Tammy Rose, Sarah Stark, Bruce C. Davis, and Joe-la Dowdy for medical advice. Thanks to my assistant, Dana Fredsti, who is my superhero.

PART ONE

HIGHER POWERS

All that we see or seem is but a dream within a dream.

—EDGAR ALLAN POE

All that really belongs to us is time;
even he who has nothing else has that.

—BALTASAR GRACIÁN

CHAPTER ONE

It's like that sometimes.

It starts weird and in the wrong place.

This did.

Rain Thomas went to bed on Thursday and woke up on Saturday. She had no idea at all that someone had stolen a whole day from her until she arrived twenty-three hours and forty-eight minutes late for a job interview.

The interview did not go well.

CHAPTER TWO

Her alarm clock always sounded like an outraged cricket. It yelled her awake and then seemed to dodge her flailing hand until she finally caught it and slapped it silent. Bastard. She patted the bed next to her, looking for Joplin, but he was gone. He almost never stayed the night. That was the arrangement. He lived two doors down in an identical brownstone walk-up, and last night, let's face it, had been a booty call. She'd called him this time. It worked out to about fifty-fifty on who called whom. Great sex, some nice holding, and then retreating to separate corners.

That was fine. Rain preferred to sleep alone. *Sleep* being the operative word.

The warm lump by her feet was her dog, Bug, a mixed breed of rat terrier, Cavalier King Charles, Chihuahua, and god knew what else. She was small, cute, loyal, and semi-hysterical. Bug liked to crawl under the covers and burrow into the darkest, warmest spot on the bed.

3

Rain hovered on the warm edge of slumber, wishing she could roll over and drop back down. There was a dream she wasn't finished with. She tried to swim deeper, even though it was dark down where the full dream was swimming. Dark and a little scary.

But it was important. She was sure of that.

Against her will, the day coalesced around her. Her apartment was a little icebox on the fifth floor of a Brooklyn brownstone that looked like ten thousand others. The steep sets of creaking stairs were her gym membership. She wore pajama bottoms, socks, and a sweatshirt to bed but she was always cold. Even in summer. The landlord didn't turn the heat on until the end of October, and when he did, it sounded like a cokehead monkey was beating on the pipes with a hammer. What little heat leaked out of the radiator didn't have the enthusiasm to reach out to any other part of the room. No one was allowed to have a space heater. Fire hazard. Sneaking one in was the best way to get evicted. The upside was that the cockroaches didn't like the cold, and most of them stayed downstairs in the laundry room.

Fun times.

The apartment was on West 238th Street in Kingsbridge, several light-years from the encouraging footfall of gentrification. She had one room that was half the size of her mother's walk-in closet, with a kitchenette in the corner and a bathroom in a cubbyhole so small that she had to squeeze between the toilet and sink to get into the shower. The windows were nailed shut, and it looked exactly like the kind of apartment they'd put in a movie if they wanted to show how freaking depressing someone's life could be. Joplin's flat was a two bedroom with a full kitchen, which he'd inherited from his dad and had turned into his art studio. Sometimes she went over there, but it was every bit as cold, and he was a slob. A gorgeous slob, she had to admit, but one who hadn't evolved his social skills past his dorm room days at art school.

Rain rubbed her face with her palms and then glanced at the clock. 6:49.

"Shit," she said. The interview was at nine thirty all the way in the city.

She had every intention of jumping to her feet and going full whirlwind through her morning routine. Bathroom, shower, clothes, makeup, out the door, bagel and coffee on the 1 Train.

4

That was the plan.

Why bother? asked her inner voice. *You won't get it anyway. They'll do a background check and you'll be out on your ass.*

It was a familiar voice—the part of Rain's mind that ran a constant disapproving commentary on everything she did. It was one of several voices that vied for attention inside the untidy mess of her brain. One of the legion of counselors she'd sat with over the years suggested the label of "parasite." That fit. It lived within her and knew everything about her, but it had no interest at all in her well-being, though it was slippery and sly and often pretended to be the voice of her common sense, her better angel. As if.

Rain tried hard, every single day, to ignore that voice. Sometimes she managed, but it was persistent, relentless, and it knew all her secrets.

She put her face in her hands and tried not to cry. Not because her life was so hard. Her life had always been hard. And not because she couldn't remember the dream, even though she felt she *had* to. No. Rain Thomas cried because this was another day when she wouldn't score some rock and smoke her way off the planet. Another day. It was day number one thousand one hundred and six of not using, and it hurt every bit as badly as day one. She hid behind the closed doors of her palms and waited for the tears. Waited. But they didn't come. Not that morning. It wasn't a relief, though, because she knew they'd show eventually. They always did. People patted her on the back for getting her shiny pink three-year coin from Narcotics Anonymous. They told her she was strong. Joplin told her she was tough as Supergirl.

The hell did he? The hell, in fact, did anyone know?

Bug, disturbed by her attempts to get up, wormed her way from under the blankets, stuck her black nose and brown eyes out, and peered at Rain. There was a flutter of blankets from the dog wagging her crooked little tail.

"Good morning, fuzzball," said Rain thickly. Bug wagged harder, but her eyes cut to the night table where a Ziploc bag stood next to the clock.

"You want your morning cookie, don't you?"

A more enthusiastic wag.

Rain took a crunchy treat from the bag, broke it into three small pieces, and placed them on the mattress. It was a ritual. If she didn't do that, Bug would not emerge from the bed at all. Now she wormed her way on her belly like a World War I soldier sliding under barbed wire strung across no-man's-land. She took the first treat. Moved farther. The second. The third. By then she was completely out of bed and lay there, stretched to her full length, which wasn't much. A tiny body spotted with black, white, and brown, a tail that had been broken before Rain adopted her from the shelter and which perpetually canted to the left.

"Mommy has a job interview today."

Bug wagged her tail with great enthusiasm. Rain's cheering section.

"Think I'll get it?"

Bug sat up, hoisted a leg, and began licking her own crotch.

"Gosh, thanks for that note of encouragement," said Rain. She braced her palms against the edge of the mattress and pushed up against the gravity of her need. She stumbled across the cold floor, squeezed into the bathroom, and tried to make herself look like someone worth hiring. Worth trusting.

That was going to take a lot of makeup.

CHAPTER THREE

Rain fed Bug, got undressed, turned on the shower, tested the temperature mix, pulled the curtain over to keep from getting any water on the floor, and sat down on the toilet with her feet resting on the warm pile of socks and jammies. Her bladder was so full that it hurt, and it occurred to her that life was pretty sad if a good pee was likely to be the highlight of her day. Physically, emotionally, and spiritually. She reached for a magazine but realized she hadn't brought her reading glasses in with her. Sighed, put the magazine down. Kept peeing.

The shower curtain billowed out over the edge of the tub, spraying her with water that was still cold. She yelped and jerked back and then pushed the curtain back in place. The droplets on her leg felt like ice water. It always took so long for the hot water—such as it was—to crawl up five flights. Rain fished for the hand towel that hung over the sink and rubbed the water off her skin. The drops, cold as they were, left red spots on her skin as if she'd been sprayed with boiling water. Not blisters, but very bright and red. She frowned at them and watched them fade.

She kept peeing. It was turning into a marathon.

A few seconds later, the shower curtain whipped out again. Faster this time and the cold water slapped her from shins to breasts. Stinging cold. Not a trace of heat. Rain shrieked and punched the curtain over the edge of the tub, cursing at it as her entire body erupted into gooseflesh.

"You son of a *bitch*," she snarled.

The curtain rippled as if the cold water was somehow creating a wind in there. Rain glared at it, daring the plastic to move again. It was a pretty curtain, covered with Van Gogh's *Starry Night*. Swirls of blue and yellow and black. She'd bought it after winning twenty-five dollars on a scratch card, and she thought Joplin would approve. Buying it had been rare indulgence for someone who counted pennies, and a case could be made that it was the prettiest thing she owned. She and Joplin had broken it in by making love in that shower, her standing with her hands braced on the wall, him behind her, the water hammering on them as they moved together. Right now, though, Rain was ready to tear it from the rings, stab it with scissors, and stuff it in the recycle bin.

The curtain hung for a moment, gently rippling, as behind it the water still ran cold. There was no warmth at all in the bathroom, no plumes of steam to indicate the presence of a single goddamn drop of hot water from the goddamn boiler in the goddamn basement of this goddamn pile-of-shit building.

Rain tried to squeeze her bladder empty, but there was still more. How? She'd had a single cup of tea before bed last night. How could she, or any human being, pee this much?

She was reaching for the paper when she saw the shower curtain began to blow outward again. Not a lot . . . just a puff. With a growl, she slapped it back.

"Don't," she warned, pointing a finger at it.

It hung straight, trembling only with the beating of the shower water.

And then it moved again.

Harder this time. Faster. Rain growled again and slapped it back hard.

And then she screamed and jerked backward, half falling off the toilet, hitting the wall, recoiling as far and as fast as she could from the curtain.

No. From something on the other side of the curtain. Her slapping hand had *hit* something. It felt like . . .

A *hand?*

She hung there, leaning away from the toilet, the tub, the curtain. Part of the curtain hung over the edge now, and water ran down, forming a pool on the worn linoleum. Rain was afraid to move, to breathe. Her heart fluttered like a rabbit's—too fast, too hard, hammering at her chest as if it wanted to break free.

"Joplin . . . ?"

No answer.

"Joplin, if that's you playing some kind of stupid joke, I'm going to kill you."

Nothing.

"I'm not messing with you. This isn't funny."

The curtain billowed slowly, and Rain stared at it, unable to blink, too frightened to turn away. She knew that it wasn't Joplin. He had his faults, he wasn't always the warmest guy, but he wasn't this mean.

Bug came creeping into the bathroom and stared at the curtain. All the hair along her spine slowly stood up, and she bared her tiny fangs. That scared Rain even more.

"Who's there?" she asked, knowing it was a stupid question. If anyone answered, her world was going to break apart. But no one could answer. She'd reached in to turn the water on, leaning a head and shoulder past the edge of the curtain as she set the water mix. The tub had been empty. Of course it had. She'd have known if there was someone in there.

Of course she would.

Of *course.*

Bug suddenly yelped and ran from the bathroom. Rain could hear the dog's nails skittering on the floor as she crawled under the bed. Her place of safety.

That made it worse. Bug, small as she was, would stand up to the neighborhood pit bulls. She snapped and snarled at the gangbangers who hung out on the corner down the street. She was a rat killer.

Now her terrified whimpering filled the apartment.

It's him, whispered a voice, and for a moment, Rain couldn't tell if it was inside her head or inside the bathroom. Her heart jumped sideways in her

8

chest. The curtain continued to move as the water pounded on it, the drops popping on the thick plastic. The starry night swirled.

There was no one in her shower. There couldn't be. No way. And yet she stared, waiting, knowing that she had felt something. She had. She had. She had.

It's not him, she told herself. She did not say his name. Not now. Not in a moment like this. No way. God, no way. *Please, please, please, no.*

She tried to force herself to be real, to be logical. What was the sane choice? The obvious choice? How could it really be a hand? That was impossible, that was stupid.

But . . .

It had felt like a hand. Her fingers were splayed when she'd hit the curtain. She felt the impact, felt the different points of it. Palm and fingers and thumb. As if someone timed a slap to hers. As if someone had been waiting in there, watching her somehow, seeing her there on the toilet, naked, peeing, shivering with the cold. And then had pushed the curtain, knowing she would push it back. Timing a slap to meet hers. Playing a game. Playing with her.

"If someone's there, I'm going to kick your ass!" she yelled. It sounded stupid, even to her own ears. She was one hundred and ten pounds of naked nothing. And he was . . .

What?

She realized with a start that she knew it was a he. The hand had been much bigger than hers. Harder.

It's not him. It's not him. It's not him.

"I'm going to call 9-1-1."

The curtain moved. Slightly. Was it only the water moving it? Was that all it was?

That's when she saw the shadow. Blended in with the swirling skyscape of Van Gogh's tortured night was something else. A tone, a darkness that didn't fit in with that painting. There was someone *in* there. Standing just behind the curtain, not moving. But there.

Rain was absolutely frozen into the moment, her flesh smashed against the tiled walls, heartbeat rising and rising to a panicked crescendo. Part of her mind tried to tell her that this was it. She was going to get raped and killed. When they found her body, she would be naked and covered in

9

piss and her own blood, and that's what the cops would tell her mother. That's what her grandmother would hear on the news. That's all anyone would ever know of her. Ex-junkie murdered in her fifth-floor walk-up. Another piece-of-crap person added to the statistics of "Who gives a damn?"

That's what the parasite told her.

The only warmth in the whole world was a small line of pee that trickled down the inside of her left thigh.

"Please," she begged.

The shadow didn't move.

The curtain rippled once more, harder than before, and more water spattered on her right leg, all the way to the hip. The water was warm now.

She saw the first curl of steam rise like a snake above the shower rod.

"Please," she said again, a thick whisper almost without volume.

The swaying curtain stopped moving and hung straight.

It took every ounce of strength that Rain had to push off the wall, to raise her arm, to extend a hand toward that curtain once more. She knew it was a stupid thing to do. She should run. Get out of the bathroom, pull the door shut, get to the kitchen, grab a knife, make him earn whatever he took from her. Cut him for doing this to her. Die fighting instead of . . .

The curtain did not move at all. Rain stared at the shadow. It wasn't moving, either.

Nothing moved in the bathroom except the snakes of steam that twisted and wrestled up by the vent to the fan that hadn't ever worked.

"Please?" said Rain, and it came out as a question this time.

Nothing.

It took everything she had to stand up. Her legs buckled at once, and she sat down hard on the edge of the toilet and then slid off onto the floor. By pure reflex, she snapped a hand out to catch herself, but she missed the edge of the tub and caught the curtain instead, jerking it, tearing it off half of the rings. It whipped and twisted and fell with her. Hot shower water pelted her, pushing her down to the linoleum as steam billowed.

There was no one in the shower stall.

No one at all.

CHAPTER FOUR

She did not talk to herself while she got cleaned up and dressed. Rain was too embarrassed in her own eyes to pay attention to her thoughts. Embarrassed and scared and . . .

No, those adjectives were part of the conversation she didn't want to have.

Bug stayed under the bed and would not come out even for treats.

Rain busied herself with doing everything quickly, efficiently, precisely. It was the way she used to do things when she was drunk or high and knew—or thought she knew—that people were watching. *I'm not a junkie. Look how well I fold my laundry. Look how straight I walk down the street. See, I'm taking the train like a regular person.*

She studied herself in the mirror. She was thin bordering on skinny. Wavy brown hair, ordinary brown eyes, pale skin, a good complexion. Her best features, she thought, were her lips—full—and nose—small. When she'd been a girl, people always said she had beautiful eyes. Large and expressive. That was before seven years of using drugs. Now her eyes had a shifty quality. It was hard for her to even meet her own gaze in the mirror, let alone other people's. There was something about her now, even three years clean, that made people nervous around her.

As always, she turned away, unable to see the disappointment on her own face.

She had to reach under the bed and pull Bug out to put her leash on, but then the dog yanked her out the door and down the stairs. Once outside, Bug bravely peed on everything she could, pooped twice, peed some more, and then tried not to be led inside. After pulling, coaxing, cajoling, and threatening, Rain finally picked Bug up and carried her back upstairs.

"I'll be back in a few hours," Rain told the little dog. "It's okay, everything's fine. There's no one here."

Bug gave her a withering look and crawled back under the bed.

Rain looked at the bathroom, at the torn curtain.

"Shit," she said.

She fetched duct tape and used strips of it to reattach the shower curtain. She also used towels to mop the floor, Clorox spray to clean the toilet seat, and too much soap and hot water to sponge away the memory of her own stupidity. Or paranoia. Or whatever. She kept her mental thesaurus shut as she soaped and rinsed and dried. She did not narrate her life as she dressed and applied her makeup. Shoes that were good for walking and would look nice in a job interview, and a small bag that looked like real leather. She'd placed the folder with her résumé by the door so she wouldn't forget it. The clock above her tiny dining table told her it was time to go. She slid some treats under the bed for Bug and heard tentative crunching as she headed for the door.

Every single stair in the building squeaked in a different key of weary complaint. In the foyer, she caught Mrs. Grundy from 304 stealing Mr. Allyn's newspaper. He lived in 107 and was always complaining that kids stole his paper. Rain knew the truth and made eye contact with the old woman as she tucked the *Post* into her ratty blue bathrobe. It was an open secret, and even when caught, Mrs. Grundy acted as if no one saw what she did.

"Haven't seen you in a while," said Mrs. Grundy.

"I saw you yesterday," said Rain.

The old lady looked momentarily confused, then began climbing the stairs, one hand pulling on the rail and the other pressing her robe closed around her prize. Rain wondered how many steps Mrs. Grundy would have to climb before she forgot meeting Rain today. Or had she already forgotten?

The building was filled with oddballs and castoffs. No one was an actual friend of hers, but there were a few who Rain didn't mind saying hi to. Mrs. Grundy was old, and local rumor had it that she used to be a porn star back in the seventies, but Rain didn't think that was true. It was too much like the kind of thing people said to make the neighbors sound interesting. The woman who lived in 211 was widely believed to be a drug mule, and Joe Garrick, in the apartment across from Rain's, was supposed to be in witness protection. She wondered what stories they told about her. People knew she went to NA meetings. They knew she rarely had anyone over. What did they make of all that? Who did they think she was?

She managed not to consciously think about the bathroom until she was on the 1 Train. It was a long, rocking, rattling trip to Manhattan, and with nothing else to do, all she had time to do was think. She shared a bench seat with a sad-eyed old Latina woman. Every seat on the train was full but there was no one standing in the aisles. More like Saturday commuters than Friday. Rain was aware of that from a distance the way most people are aware of things, but she put no actual thought on it.

For the first ten minutes of the ride, Rain sat, purse and folder on her lap under her clasped hands, eyes looking at nothing in particular as she replayed everything that had happened that morning. It was all lurking right below the surface, and it still made her shiver. She would have bet her entire new welfare check that there was someone behind the curtain. She'd *felt* his hand. She'd seen the shadow of him back there.

The fact that no one had been there was almost scarier than if there had been. Rain thought she was past all that kind of bullshit. The fantasies and hallucinations. Being crazy. Crack was a gentle high, but it wasn't psychedelic. When she wanted to walk straight out of her mind, she dropped N,N-dimethyltryptamine—DMT. Or smoked it; but the pills always flipped the switch faster. Either way it was a rocket-ship ride to elsewhere, and it worked every time. Her favorite dealer, Bone, called it "Void," and that was a good-enough name, and they described the effects as a "tourist high." Not because it was favored by actual tourists but because once it hit the bloodstream you were no longer in your own country. Rain agreed with that.

Some of her friends were afraid of Void because when it was in full swing, it broke apart all understanding of reality. The so-called real world was suddenly false, its laws suspect; while the other world was incredibly and insistently real. More real. Way more. There were new physical laws, new languages that only travelers to that land understood—and when she was there, Rain did understand it; but not once the high wore off. Coming back and coming down was like what she imagined dementia would feel like. She was aware that she had lost parts of her intelligence, her memory, her clarity and was now in a reduced "lesser" state of consciousness.

On the day she got out of the hospital after giving up her baby, she took her first trip to that far-off place. She never wanted to come back, because there was nothing real or solid or beautiful back here.

It wasn't the distortion of reality that ultimately made her switch to crack. It was the grief of losing that enhanced insight. On that level, she could talk with Noah, she could understand where her dead lover was and what he was experiencing. On that level, they could be together, and their baby was always with them. Only there, though, and never here. Crack did not allow her to visit that place, but it took away her ability to care that she could not stay there.

Since then, though, she'd had a few DMT flashbacks, but they were quick, and even when they were firing she knew what was happening. So, no, this wasn't that. And she didn't think it was a flashback at all, because she'd been high for so long that she knew every flavor in that box of chocolates. The jittery coke high, the mellow weed high, the floaty XTC high, and the dreamy take-me-away high of good crystal meth. This wasn't like any of them. This felt more like her mind was slipping a gear. Rain had some experience with that, too. For the first eight weeks of each rehab, it had felt like her brain was a computer streaming five different movies at once, and none of them in English. She'd screamed her way through a lot of long nights in several different hospitals and knew what those fantasies were like.

What happened this morning just made her feel crazy.

Her heart still wanted to race out of control and she had to fight back the tears. She knew what they told her every time she went to a meeting, that being clean didn't make you anything but a junkie who wasn't currently high. Alcoholics were always alcoholics, and addicts were always addicts. All a clean day meant is that you worked the program that day. Tomorrow was another battle. And your body would never forget that it *wanted* to be high. That demon was always there, and the fight had to be fought every day.

"Please," Rain said again, whispering it aloud to give it power but saying it quietly so no one could hear.

Even so, the old Latina lady next to her turned and looked at her. She had the most comprehensively wrinkled face Rain had ever seen. She wore a pair of glasses hung around her neck on a colorful beaded chain and had a dark mole on her forehead exactly where an Indian bindi would be.

"*En realidad el fuego nunca se apaga. ¿Sabes?*" she said.

Rain's Spanish was only okay. She could get along but the woman spoke very quickly, and it took Rain a second to run it through her mental translation circuits. Something about fires? No, about fires not going out? Or never going out?

Something like that.

"Sorry—?" said Rain, then added haltingly, "*Yo no entiendo.*"

The woman studied her for a moment and there was a small, almost knowing smile on her thin lips. Then she said, "*Él le habla a su mamá.*"

That went past too quickly and she didn't know what it meant. She dug a phrase out of a back closet of her memory. "Um . . . *por favor, habla mas . . .* um . . . *despacio.*" Asking her to repeat it slowly.

"*Hay oscuridad, y le está a apagando su luz.*"

"*Yo no comprendo.*"

The old woman's smile flickered, and she turned away to look out the window at the nothing passing by. Rain studied her for a moment, replaying the words, trying to sort them out, but they didn't make any real sense. She was half sure the woman said something about someone looking for his mother, but there was no context. *Who* was looking for his mother? Was the woman talking about her grandson, maybe?

And the other comment made even less sense as Rain pieced it together. Something about darkness smothering light. Like that. She almost asked, but it was pretty clear the woman didn't speak English. Or didn't want to. Besides, Rain knew she'd better go over the stuff for the interview. She turned away, opened the folder, and then began fishing in her purse for her reading glasses.

Which were not there.

"Ahhhh . . . *shit!*" she cried, and several people turned around to look at her. People on trains always look annoyed, and when you did something loud or unusual, the annoyance turned into open hostility. Or maybe it was contempt. Either way, Rain immediately shut down into herself, muttering apologies, looking contrite, feeling stupid. She searched her purse again. And again. The glasses still refused to be in there. She looked around as if expecting them to be floating there in the air. "*Damn* it."

She slapped her purse down on her lap and seethed for a minute and then picked up the folder again, opened it, and squinted at the papers. Her résumé and the details she pulled off the company website. She could read UNCLE SAM TAX SERVICE because it was in large block letters. The rest was a smear that looked like it had been dunked in water. Rain bent toward it until her nose was almost touching the pages. That helped, but not a lot. The fact that her eyes were getting bad was something she'd been trying to ignore.

A light tap on her right shoulder startled her, and Rain almost growled at the interruption, but it was the old woman. Her face was creased into a smile so wide it made her eyes almost vanish into wreaths of wrinkles. It made her look like a kitchen witch, or one of those Russian nesting dolls. And her eyes—the sadness in those eyes seemed bottomless.

"*¿Por favor* . . . ?" she said as she lifted her own reading glasses from around her neck and held them out, the colored chain swaying.

"Oh, no," Rain said immediately, "I couldn't."

The woman paused and then in creaking English said, "Please, for *his* sake."

His? Rain figured it was some kind of Jesus reference. She looked at the glasses. They were old-fashioned, with horn-rims and a tiny hairline crack along the side of the left lens, but the woman looked so earnest and so clearly happy to be able to help.

Rain really needed to nail this interview because her shit heap of an apartment, her groceries, and her prescriptions for migraine medicine were, inconveniently, not going to pay for themselves. The tax-preparing job was something she knew she could do. Rain was always good with numbers and with deciphering things like word problems and math codes. When she was banging her dealer, she helped him work his numbers and manage his stock. Not something she could put on her résumé, but it was what it was.

The woman moved the glasses an inch closer, repeating, "*Por favor.*"

"Okay," said Rain, "just for a few seconds. Thanks so much."

The woman pressed the glasses into her hand and then folded Rain's fingers around them. The woman's hands were as fragile as bird bones and as cold as ice. Almost creepy, but mostly sad. Rain was twenty-six, and this woman had to be at least sixty years older. None of them looked like easy years, either. The woman nodded and kept nodding, her eyes cutting back and forth between her and the glasses.

Rain smiled awkwardly and nodded back as she raised the glasses and put them on. The chain drooped under her chin, and she felt a little silly. But, damn . . . she could see. When she glanced down at her résumé, the words were sharp and clear. Sharper and clearer, in fact, than they ever were with her drugstore glasses. She raised her head and looked around. Everything was clear. It was weird, because without glasses she could see things clear after about six feet, but closer than that everything became progressively blurry. But now, it was all crystal clear. It was kind of freaky, because Rain couldn't remember ever seeing the world with that much clarity. Or that much depth.

"Wow," she said. "These are great. I can see everything."

The woman laughed as if Rain had just told her a great joke. She touched Rain's arm. *"Muy bonita."*

Very pretty. Rain wasn't sure if that was a reference to the world as seen through the glasses or a compliment. Rain nodded as if she understood, then bent to study her notes. The train rumbled along, and the old woman turned away, seemingly content to study her own reflection in the dirty glass. Rain read through the papers. The thin crack in the left lens was a minor distraction, with the sliver creating a tiny distortion. Not too bad, though, if she concentrated mostly on her right eye.

Rain went through the job requirements and some notes she'd printed out about recent changes in the New York State tax codes. It was dense stuff, but she was able to navigate it. Last night she'd downloaded several copies of a blank tax form and practiced filling them out, inputting different income and deduction amounts. Those papers were in the folder, and she went through point by point to check her math. Although she was a high school dropout, Rain had taken and aced her GED and had snuck into some accounting classes at NYU. This was something she could do and do well, if she could only catch a break and get the job.

A scream jolted her out of her thoughts, and she caught a glimpse of a little boy go pelting up the aisle, shrieking with laughter. She turned by reflex because he was so loud, so cute, and running too fast.

Then she stared. Frowned.

The aisle was empty.

Rain leaned out and craned her head to see where the kid went. He looked familiar, with brown hair and eyes and rosy cheeks. She'd seen all that in a flash through the one slice of tilted lens in the borrowed glasses. The kid was quick. He ran by and then must have ducked down somewhere out of sight.

But as she looked, she felt her smile beginning to falter. Where *had* the kid gone? No one seemed to be looking down or over their shoulders. And no one else had reacted to the scream of laughter, even though it had been as loud and piercing as a seagull's cry.

Which is when Rain's mind replayed the sound.

It was a sharp scream, no doubt. But was it a shriek of laughter? Was that really what she'd heard? The more it echoed through her head, and the more the aisle remained stubbornly empty, the more that cry sounded like something else.

It sounded like a scream.

Rain took off the glasses and turned to the old woman. "Did you just see that kid . . . ?"

Her voice trailed off.

The seat next to her was empty. Rain blinked in surprise. She was in the aisle seat; the woman would have had to squeeze past her to get off. She touched the plastic seat beside her.

It was cold.

Rain looked down at the glasses she held in her other hand. They were there. Beaded chain, crack, horn-rims, and all. But there was no one seated next to her at all.

"I—" she began to say, but had nowhere at all to go with it.

She got up and walked quickly along the aisle, peering down behind every seat back, looking for anyone crouched down and hiding on the floor. There was no little boy on the train. No old woman, either. Not on that car or on the cars in front and behind.

She returned to her own car.

"What?" Rain asked quietly. Asking it of the day, of the moment. She stood with her feet wide to brace against the swaying motion of the motor, one hand gripping a metal upright, and yet she felt as if she were falling, falling, falling.

CHAPTER FIVE

People on the train kept looking at her, then looking away when she met their stares, and Rain realized that she'd become the *Other*.

That was a therapy word one of her shrinks tried on her. It was something different from the parasite. It was an external, social thing. The Other was the person who so clearly did not fit into the acceptable pattern of a group of strangers that it immediately unified them as "the people who are not the other." She'd seen it enough times with madmen and loud drunks and people who talked to themselves. She'd been part of the group at times, and she'd been the Other. Like now.

The Other was different from the Predator. That was when someone was clearly or possibly a threat. Gangs, moody types in long black trench coats, teenagers in hoodies, sweaty men clutching suspicious parcels. The Predator made everyone afraid but did not bond them into a unified group. Only the Other did that, and there was no coming back from it. Once the group has classified you as some kind of freak, then you will be the freak for the rest of your shared experience. In this case, the length of the commute to Manhattan. And the problem was that being under the social microscope tended to make people act weirder. Back when Rain was using, she'd realize that people were looking at her in judgment and she would give them something to validate their opinions. Sometimes she was openly provocative, sometimes loud, sometimes she'd yell at them.

Not now. Not since she'd gotten clean. The recovering did not have those bullets in the chambers. Normally she'd try to smile her way out of it, do the kind of comical wasn't-that-weird thing that begs for readmittance to the group. It never worked, and often felt as desperate as it probably looked.

Today, though, she didn't try for anyone's approval. She was too afraid. Not of their rejection but of them being right. Maybe she was the Other for real. Weird, wrong, broken. Off.

Slipping.

Slipped.

When she reached her stop, she fled the train and hurried through the station and up the stairs. Not once did she pause to notice how thin the crowds were for a Friday. She was running a little late as it was, and the tax office was nine blocks away. The day was cold, but she was sweating. Not because of the train but because of everything else. The bathroom, the old lady, the kid, that scream. The glasses that now hung around her neck.

CHAPTER SIX

"I'm here to see Mr. Javers," Rain told the woman at the front desk. "Lorraine Thomas, I have a job interview this morning."

The woman—who was short, plump, and pretty—smiled up at her with all the warmth of a pit viper. "You're late," she said.

Rain glanced at the clock on the wall above the short woman's desk.

"Um, I was told to be here at nine. It's only eight fifty."

The woman's smile got wider and colder. "Yes."

"So, I don't—"

"Your appointment was for 9:00 a.m., Friday the tenth."

"Yes, and—"

The woman cocked her head sideways and positively beamed at her. "Do you know what day it is today?"

"Of course I do," said Rain, trying hard not get angry. "It's Friday the tenth."

Instead of replying, the woman took a Kitten-A-Day calendar, one of the kind that comes with its own plastic stand, turned it around, and nudged it an inch toward her. There was a cute little orange tabby kitten completely wrapped in loose pink yarn. Above the picture was the day and date.

Rain stared at the date, then at the woman. "I . . . don't understand . . ."
"You're a little late, sweetie," said the woman, her eyes twinkling.
"Wouldn't you say?"

CHAPTER SEVEN

Rain stuffed the folder in the first trash can she found on the street. She had one flicker of momentary regret at having tossed away a copy of her résumé printed on expensive cream-colored paper, but did not feel like fishing it out of the can. She was too pissed, too embarrassed, and way too confused.

She pulled out her cell phone and stared at the time-and-date display. Checking the time was something she did fifty times on the way here, but it never occurred to her to check the date.

How was it Saturday? Seriously, how?

And what had happened to Friday?

She started to walk but stumbled. The sheer weight of everything pushed her against a brick wall and held her pinned there, gasping and staring at a world that did not make sense. Last night was Thursday. No way she was wrong about that. She remembered sitting at her desk, studying for the interview. The TV had been on, and all the Thursday night shows were on. She and Joplin had watched Trevor Noah, and his show ran Monday through Thursday. She didn't DVR it. Last night was, goddamn it, Thursday night, and today should have been, goddamn it, Friday.

Except it wasn't.

Her phone clock said it was Saturday. Google said it was Saturday. The copies of the *New York Post* on the shelf at the kiosk outside the tax office said it was Saturday. The crowds on the train. There hadn't been enough people. The street traffic was light. Busy, but Saturday busy, not Friday rush hour busy. Everything and everyone seemed to scream at her that this was real and the only wrong part of this was her.

Rain almost called Joplin to tell him about this and get him to confirm that he had been there last night. Thursday night. She went as far as going to her recent calls list, but she didn't punch the button. What if he said that he'd been there Thursday night and not last night? How would he react if she told him that Friday was gone?

She knew exactly how he would react. He'd assume she was using and pull back. Joplin may have been a college party boy a few years ago, but he was a drinker. He never took drugs and didn't even smoke weed because he said it screwed with the way he saw light and color. He didn't even drink while he was working on a canvas, and on nights when she opened up and told him about her years getting high, he was always distant. That stuff shut him down. No. Calling him would be a mistake. He was the guy she slept with, but he wasn't her boyfriend, and after six months of mutual booty calls, he didn't seem to be interested in changing the arrangement.

Rain stayed there for a long time, leaning against the wall because she was too afraid to step away from anything as real and solid as those dirty bricks. The cars that moved past became blurs of color; so did the people. Outlines and details lost their specific shapes and instead became smears of noise and movement around her. It was like the way words smeared when she tried to read without glasses, except right now it was everything. Rain felt her eyes burn, but no tears fell; instead the burn turned to stinging pain as if the tears were crystallizing and all those sharp edges were cutting into her. She was outside, but there didn't seem to be enough air to breathe, no matter how much she gasped. Her fingers and toes tingled and went cold.

Panic attack, panic attack, she thought, but even thinking the words made everything worse. Giving it all a name goaded it into taking hold of her.

Shutting her eyes didn't help. Not much. Not enough. The afterimages spun past her on the movie screens of her memory. The smell of her own perfume was suddenly cheap and it nauseated her. Rain tried to swallow, but her throat worked and worked and accomplished nothing.

A voice spoke to her. It said, "*Él le habla a su mamá.*"

Rain's eyes snapped open, knowing the voice. The old lady from the train. She looked, turned, scanned the street.

But of course the old lady was not there.

Rain touched the glasses that hung around her neck. She fumbled with them, put them on, hoping to find clarity that would make some sense of the moment. The hairline crack flashed with reflected sunlight as she put them on. The cars in the street still moved with sickening relentless constancy, but they were in sharp focus now. That made no sense, because she was farsighted, not nearsighted. Nothing else made sense, though, so Rain accepted it for what it was. She looked down at her hands, saw that her skin was fish pale. Her purse was on the sidewalk between her feet, and she didn't remember dropping it. People walked past, and a few of them cut her looks. *The Other*, they seemed to snarl. It was as if she were becoming the parasite that lived in her mind.

There was the blare of a horn, sharp and close, and Rain turned to see a little boy go running into traffic not twenty feet from her. Running fast, heedless of the danger. Running with blind panic. Running away from . . .

From what?

What did it matter?

It was *him*. The same little boy. Same clothes, same face. Only . . .

Was he the same? She wasn't sure. On the train, the boy looked to be nine or ten, but here he was smaller. The face was the same, even the clothes, but this kid couldn't have been more than five. Younger brother? If so, what the hell was going on?

The kid jagged left as if avoiding someone and cut right across the street.

"No!" cried Rain, breaking into a run.

Cars rushed toward the boy. Cars slammed on their brakes, tires screeched, horns howled, and Rain screamed as she ran out to catch the boy. A UPS truck shot past her, and Rain had to jump backward to keep from being crushed. A heartbeat later she lurched forward again.

The boy was gone.

Cars were stopped all around her.

Her. Not the kid. She stood in the center of the street, and everyone was focused on her. Honking, yelling, cursing at her. There was no boy anywhere in sight.

A man leaned out of his car window and yelled, "The shit's wrong with you, you crazy bitch?"

"Did you see the kid?" she demanded, pointing. "The little boy?"

"There's no boy, dumb-ass," said the driver. "You high or something?"

Rain flinched back from those words. If she had a knife, she'd have cut the man. Or herself. Or everyone.

The cars kept honking, even the ones where the drivers could have driven around her. She was the Other, and they were all mad at her.

"Get out of the freaking way!"

Ten voices seemed to yell that all at once. Rain felt pummeled by the sounds, the voices, the everything. She took a step toward the opposite side of the street—where the little boy *should* be, but wasn't. Then she stopped and backed up, retreating as if shoved away. She bumped into someone and whirled around to see a tall man standing right behind her. He was scarecrow thin, and he was smiling at her in ways that didn't fit the day or the moment.

"You look lost," said the man. "Let me help." He reached out to touch her. To take her arm. His fingers were long and pale and he had very thick, dark nails. His black suit was immaculate, but his tie . . . there was something wrong with it. The silk hung limp and red and wrong somehow. It glistened wetly, but almost looked like a tongue, like a piece of meat.

No, she told herself. *It's not skin. Don't be an idiot. It's a tie, and you're having a goddamn panic attack. Get out of the street. Move, move, move, move . . .*

"Let me help you," said the man in a voice that was soft and unctuous and yet familiar. Did she know him?

It's him, whispered a warning from deep in her mind, and Rain could not tell if it was her *own* thoughts or the parasite trying to confuse her. *It's Doctor Nine. Run. Get away from him.*

"Take my hand," said the tall man. He had very red lips that framed small, white teeth, but he wore sunglasses that hid his eyes. In all her dreams, Doctor Nine's eyes were hidden, and she was terrified to know what he hid behind those opaque lenses.

No, don't touch him. Move, move, move . . . get away. Run before it's too late.

Rain recoiled from the man, cast a wild look at the cars, and then broke into a run. She was wearing the wrong shoes for it, and from the first step, she felt needles of pain in her arches and ankles and insteps. She dodged around the tall man, reached the sidewalk, caught a sign pole like a drowning person grabbing at a scrap of driftwood. Held on. The metal was cold and hard and real. Cars still honked at her, but the traffic began moving again. Slowly, reluctantly, resentfully, but steadily.

When she turned to see if the tall man had followed, he was nowhere in sight. Like the little boy and the old lady, he had faded away. Or stepped through a crack in her broken mind. She had no idea where he went. Maybe he went back to Friday.

The thought was so ridiculous that she snorted out a laugh.

Which became a sob. Rain put her forehead against the cold metal pole and held on for dear life as everything she understood about today upended and sank slowly beneath the waves.

CHAPTER EIGHT

As she walked, Rain tried to make sense of a day that did not want to be made sense of.

She stopped in a Starbucks for coffee, found a seat in a corner, and sat staring into her cup for a long time. The train, the boy, the old lady, the job interview, the lost day . . . ? It was like tuning in to a movie halfway through. Or joining a conversation that had been under way so long it was hard to pick up the thread of what everyone was saying.

In some ways this was familiar to her. She often felt like she was observing her life rather than actually living it. It was a side effect of having deliberately become a passenger rather than the pilot during all those years being bullied by her mother, being a slave to crack and DMT, drifting along with the orchestrated routines of rehab, and participating in the predictable structure of Narcotics Anonymous. All of that had collectively prepped her for observer status. Even when she dreamed, there was a part of her that was aware she was dreaming and sat on the sidelines to watch, like a fifth-string player at a school lacrosse match. Dreams were usually more real to her than her actual life. In dreams, everything and anything was possible. In life . . . not so much.

So, was this all a dream?

She closed her eyes and tried to determine if she were actually asleep. The dream from last night was still there, hovering right below the surface. Rain kept her eyes closed and tried to move toward that dream, pulled by an instinct that the dream and what was happening today were connected. What, then, was the dream? The details were so hard to lure to the surface. There was something about . . .

Fire?

Was that right? No, it wasn't like something was *on* fire in the dream; not like a building burning down. No, it was something else. A place? Maybe. Probably. A fire *something*. Burning with beautiful light. There was more to it. She was positive. Only a few seconds ago, she knew something. She was *in* the fire. Not burning. Walking. Dancing? In the fire? In fire? It didn't make sense.

I was there all night, she thought. Thinking that flipped a switch on and off very fast. It was like peering into a darkened room and then there's a microsecond of light and afterward you try to remember the things in there. Rain had only glimpses of it, like the afterimage of the sun when you looked at it and looked away. Burned onto her eyes, but fading.

A nighttime street, glistening as if after a summer rain. Buildings rising on either side and stretching away up a long hill. Neon and LED lights burning, swirling, changing shape as if they were alive. Brighter the higher up on the hill. She wasn't on the hill, though. She stood at the very bottom. Down on the boundary. No. On *Boundary Street*. An actual street with that name. She stood among the shadows there. Not alone, but she couldn't see who else was there. Sometimes she could see them. Some of them made her cry. Some made her sick. One of them made her scream, but she hadn't dreamed of him last night. Or at least she didn't think so.

She looked up the hill to where all the beautiful lights glowed with strange promise. They were magical to see. Or maybe it was that they were actual magic. It was a dream, so that could go either way. People danced up there. And laughed. And sang along with the music that spilled out from the open doors of nightclubs.

She saw all of that in a glimpse. Saw it and understood it, knew it. Felt it. Maybe she caught so much of it because it wasn't the first time she dreamed about that place. Though when she was awake it was so hard to hold on to any specific memories. Sometimes when she was on the train, the rocking motion would coax her to the edge of a doze and she'd hear the music and smell the perfumes and colognes and cooking smells and incense and . . .

And see the faces.

People she didn't know. People she did know. Some dead people. People Rain was absolutely sure she needed to know. A few who scared her in very good ways. A few who scared her in really bad ways. Their faces swirled around her like the crystal patterns in a kaleidoscope. Many of them danced, and it made Rain want to dance, too. She used to dance, back when she was little and the world was still painted with fresh colors. She'd been good at it, too. Almost a prodigy. Good enough to go pro when she grew up. She'd danced and danced, and that was her cure-all. When young Rain was dancing, it was like everything made sense, or maybe it was that nothing else mattered. When she was younger, she could dance her way out of any bad mood. When her best friend's family moved to L.A., Rain danced it all out. Her hurt, the loss, and the grief, too. All of that became part of the dance.

Somewhere along the way, she stopped dancing. The music became muted and off-key, and the colors of the world faded and peeled, revealing uglier colors beneath. It was like what happened with her mother—she used to dance, too. And stopped. Forever stopped.

Rain wanted so badly to dance again. She knew that it would cure her, fix her, repair the broken parts inside. However, she was positive that dance was a gift, and she had squandered it, ignored it, let it wither and die. She could read the disappointment of that in the faces she saw. They knew.

He knew, too.

He. Him.

He hated her and hated that she used to dance. That thought came into her head, and not for the first time, though she did not understand what it meant. Not on a conscious level, though she knew with certainty that it was true. He was like that.

The man of my dreams, she thought with more intense bitterness than she felt for anything in her world.

Rain never had an imaginary friend when she was a little girl. No, what she had was an imaginary enemy. He came to her in dreams and, sometimes, she thought he came to her while she was awake. Came and whispered things. Bad things that, at first, she'd been too young to understand. As she got older and wiser and saw the world as it was, Rain understood.

The enemy never once spoke his own name, but once, during a session, a therapist had asked about the phantasm. It had been during a session in one of the rehab centers her mother had sent her to—was it the fourth one? The sixth? Not the last one, that was sure, because Rain had checked herself into that one and Mom never even came to visit. Maybe it was the fourth one. The therapist had been walking her through the minefield of her childhood, and Rain told her about the man who came and whispered to her and sometimes climbed into her bed and lay next to her, cold as a corpse, damp and smelling of rot.

"Does he have a name?" asked the therapist.

Rain hadn't wanted to say that he did. *Saying his name gives him power. Saying his name calls him.* Those thoughts flicked through her mind that day in the therapist's office.

And yet she said his name anyway. Unwanted, unbidden, the name came out of her mouth without permission, as if the words were crawly bugs and her mouth wanted to spit them out.

"Doctor Nine," she said.

She said it then and she said it now. The name hung burning in the air both times. It was nailed to the moment in a bad way. Crooked and awkward and ugly.

"What does that name mean to you, Lorraine?" asked the therapist.

Rain hadn't answered. The therapist asked again, and again, and finally put some edge into it. "Lorraine, why do you call him Doctor Nine and—*Oh!*"

That's when the therapist's nose had started to bleed. It was a bad nosebleed, too. She couldn't stop it. The blood ran thick over her upper lip and down around her mouth and in between her lips. The therapist gagged and yelped and ran for the little bathroom. Rain sat there and did nothing except listen to the coughing sounds from the bathroom and look at the pattern of bright red dots spattered across the floor.

It's because you said his name, thought Rain at the time. *He doesn't like it. You're not allowed.*

They took the therapist to the emergency room. Rain never saw her again. She never heard what happened to her. The new therapist gave her meds and asked her about her mother and never mentioned Doctor Nine at all.

Doctor Nine.

Rain had no idea why she called him that except that it was his name. One of his names. What she did know was that Doctor Nine had been in that dream, in the fire-bright place in the dream. Every time she began to turn to look at something else magical and bright, she'd catch a glimpse of him out of the corner of her eye. Each time she would turn, and he would not be there. Even in the dream, Rain didn't think she was imagining that he was there. He *was* there, but he'd slipped away to hide inside a shadow, because he didn't want her to see him. Yet.

Not yet. He wanted to watch her and watch her looking for him. When she caught those glimpses, he was always smiling. She knew that about Doctor Nine. He never, ever laughed but always, always smiled. A big, wide, white smile. He had red lips and very wet teeth and he loved watching her.

"Doctor Nine," she said again, spitting the words into the empty morning air. "Fuck you."

"What?" asked a stranger's voice, and Rain opened her eyes. It took a moment for her to remember where she was. A Starbucks in the city. The dream flew away like a balloon that had not been properly tied. Gone.

She shook her head at the stranger, and he gave her a look like he'd pegged her as another New York crazy. One of the Others.

Rain sipped her coffee and winced. It was ice cold.

She got up, threw the cup away, and went outside into a misty drizzle. It was a weird morning, and it was like the day started off by stripping its gears. Rain rubbed her eyes, not yet realizing that her trembling fingers were painted with magic.

CHAPTER NINE

The kid on the skateboard rolled down the wet Brooklyn street, moving in and out of traffic, onto curbs and back to asphalt with the seamless and uncomplicated flow of creek water following the path of least resistance.

He wore torn blue jeans, an ugly thermal hoodie that was four sizes too big, a stained New York Yankees baseball cap, and a bright blue waterproof backpack that was the only new, clean, and undamaged item he owned. He'd stolen it two days ago. Even his skateboard was junk, with mismatched trucks and a cracked deck.

The backpack was heavy, and it rattled with every irregularity the wheels rattled over.

As he rounded one corner, he saw that there was a line of big black birds on the telephone wires. A murder of crows, he thought. It was a phrase he had learned from a television show. He turned his board so that he skated with his back to the birds. It might work. They weren't looking for him. They didn't know he'd escaped again. Not yet, anyway.

Just in case, though, he stopped at every building on the block, ran up the stone steps and loitered inside long enough to sell the idea that he was delivering something. Flyers, maybe. In the third building, there was a stack of printed ads from one of the big-box stores, and he stole it, used a Filipino butterfly knife to cut the twine, and took it with him. He made sure to leave a few at each building so his stack would diminish. He also made sure to spend exactly the same amount of time in each building.

Even the one where he picked the lock on a specific mailbox and left a small, shiny windup pocket watch nestled in among the letters.

Then he delivered the remaining ads to the other buildings and skated away into the drizzle. The nightbirds watched him, but they did not see his small, secret smile.

CHAPTER TEN

Rain walked without paying any attention to where she was going or even glancing at the names of the street signs. The drizzle had stopped, but the sky was still overcast. The old woman's glasses bounced on their chain, tapping against Rain's chest in time to her feet, and that awkward metronome was all she thought about. Or tried to think about.

She wanted to call Joplin, but he was probably painting, with his moody Miles Davis music turned all the way up and his ringer turned off.

Moving fast and on autopilot was her way to keep the panic away. To force the monsters back into their box, to slam the lid down, wrap it in chains, fumble the locks into place, snap them shut. That was the process. The box was real to her, in its way. It had been something another of her shrinks had taught her—to create a kind of Pandora's box that would contain all her evils, her fears, her rational and irrational terrors, and a lot of the memories of the terrible things she had done and which had been done to her. The box was very full. The shrink suggested she name it, to claim it as her own, and she remembered the title of an old Grateful Dead song she heard once—"Box of Rain"—and that's what she had named it. The Box of Rain contained so much of her, because fear, doubt, self-loathing, addiction, need, and other similar qualities seemed to define her; it was appropriate they would reside in a box with her name on it.

So Rain crammed all the emotions that were crashing around in her head and heart into the box. It took effort. It cost her, as it always did. She knew it was a temporary measure and not a permanent solution. Not by any stretch. The panic monster wasn't so much trapped in the box, as it used it as a nest. It *waited* there. It did not allow her to lock it away, and it liked the taste of her pain too much to wander far.

It was her feet that brought her back to herself. They were killing her.

Why is it that cute shoes are so evil? Trying to answer that saw her down two more blocks.

Finally, she stopped and leaned on another signpost for a moment, lifting one foot for a few seconds, then the other as she looked around. The street was in shadows because the buildings on one side were taller than the other and they blocked the sun. It was colder here and, she realized, empty. There were some houses and a few stores, but everything was closed. On a Saturday?

Rain limped over to the closest store, but the windows were grimed to a gray opacity, and there was an unhelpful sign on the door with a little clock that said BACK AT 2. The note was old and weather-stained. Above the store was a sign:

MORT'S MEATS

The picture beneath the words was a silhouette of a big, hulking fat guy with heavy shoulders and a dripping meat cleaver. The stink of dust and something gone very bad a long time ago clung to the outside of the place, so Rain moved away. Who the hell would ever have bought meat at Serial-Killers-R-Us?

Another store farther along the street had a window filled with clocks and watches and a sign with the kitschy name Time Management. The window glass was dusty, and every single clock was stopped. All at different times. There was no one inside, and the place had an empty, abandoned look.

No one's paying attention to time, she thought. Then she grunted and replayed that. It was the kind of oddball half joke that often occurred to her, but at the same time it felt . . .

What?

Strange? That wasn't it; or at least it was too obvious.

No, thought Rain, the thought had been accurate. Though accurate *how* was beyond her. Friday was gone, so there was that. On impulse, she looked at her phone, at her call log, text messages, and emails. There was nothing from Friday, and that was weird in itself. She never went a day without at least some kind of spam mail. And her calendar was set to send her notices about every NA meeting in her part of Brooklyn. Plus her pals from the meetings, Yo-Yo and the two Bobs, sent her snarky Facebook memes, stupid cute animal videos, pictures of very hot guys, like that. But there was nothing. The last incoming email had been from 11:41 on Thursday night, telling her that she needed to log in to her PayPal account using her email address and password. Typical scam trying to steal her information. The laugh was on them because Rain didn't have a PayPal account and she knew every money-grabbing con in the book. All junkies did. No emails, texts, or links after that. Nothing.

The clocks in the window were dead, their hands frozen. Except for one, a grandfather clock with Roman numerals but no hands at all.

Someone stole its time, too.

She had a momentary and inexplicable impulse to put on the old lady's glasses as she stood there in front of all those quiet clock faces. She almost did, but after telling herself that it was stupid, Rain turned away.

The houses on this block were quiet and some of the doors were boarded up. Old boards, though, with lots of frayed handbills flapping on them, crisscrossed and overlaid, and graffiti tags in elaborate colors. Rain walked to the corner and looked up and down the side streets. They were empty, too. There was a rubble-strewn lot where a house had burned down recently and runoff from old rusted pipes ran red into the gutter. It looked like the rubble was bleeding.

"You are an idiot," she told herself, but her voice sounded too loud.

She discovered that the GPS app on her cell couldn't get a signal. *Of course it can't,* she grumped. *Why would a single woman lost in Murder Alley need a goddamn signal?*

Rain walked down a side street, looking for a sign, but there wasn't one. Very helpful. A sound made her turn, and she saw a cab turning behind her to go down the street she'd just left. Rain's hand shot up and she yelled for it, but the cab kept moving, and by the time she ran to the corner, it was turning again at the far end of the block. Seeing it vanish like that somehow felt like a statement, though Rain wasn't sure of the exact wording. Something along the lines of "The universe doesn't give a shit about you."

The day was so quiet, and when she stood still and cocked her head to listen, the sounds of traffic were distant, muffled, and hard to locate. Orienting herself was a challenge. How far had she walked? Manhattan was an island and the streets made sense. All she needed to do was find one street sign, and she could figure everything else out.

She walked for several blocks and found nothing, so she cut down some side streets, hoping to get lucky. No signs, no people, no open stores. A coldness began forming in the pit of her stomach. None of this made sense. This was New York. It was *never* quiet and *never* deserted. She wanted to take her shoes off because her feet hurt so bad, but the pavements were filthy and there was a lot of broken glass and trash. Above her, the sky darkened, and she saw, with mounting despair, that denser rain clouds had gathered. Even as she stared up at them, the first cold, fat drops fell, slapping her cheeks.

"Really?" she demanded of the sky. "*Seriously?*"

There was a distant growl of thunder and then as if that—or her reproachful questions—flipped a switch, the rain began to fall. She turned and ran, looking for a doorway in which to hide, but the rain chased her, caught her, drenched her. It was cold. So intensely cold. Icy fingers wormed their way beneath each layer of clothes, touching her skin, stealing her heat. A covered alley ran between two boarded-up stores, and she ran into it. It stank of garbage and excrement and other smells she did not want to label. More of the rainwater discovered cracks in the rows of planks someone had erected to form a roof, and cold droplets ambushed her as she moved from one end toward the other. It seemed somehow brighter at the far end of the alley, as if the shower was localized and on the other street the sun was still shining. Or maybe it was the artificial lights of a store. Anything. Rain moved through the shadows, tripping occasionally, her fingers reaching for the mossy walls for support.

It seemed to take forever to reach the other end, and as she approached, she saw that it was raining there, too. The light did not come from the sky.

At the end of a thousand years of darkness, the alley spilled out into another street. It was the glow of headlights. She stared. There, framed by the walls of the alley's mouth, half-veiled by the falling gray rain, stood a car. It crouched there on the glistening black asphalt, with smoke curling up from the tailpipe and steam hissing from the hot skin of its hood. Four-ways pulsed like a heartbeat, urgent, steady, alluring. Nor was it a late-model car. This was an old '57 Chevy painted a flaming scarlet with broad yellow lines running from tailfins to headlights. On the front fender, painted in a swirl of fiery letters traced in black, were three words.

The Red Rocket

There was a sign on the grille from one of the car companies. Like Uber or Lyft, but Rain did not recognize the logo and right then did not much care. The driver, just a shadow within the vehicle, looked at her through the water-beaded glass of the side window. The rain was coming down in sheets now, smashing onto the roof of planks, finding her, drenching her, leeching away the last bits of warmth in her skin, making her fingers and toes burn.

The driver yelled to her. "Licensed car service, ma'am! Need a ride?"

She almost said no. Almost ran back the other way.

She did neither of those things. Instead, Rain burst out into the street, ran the eight short steps to the cab, jerked the door open, and literally dove into the back seat.

"Get me out of here," she begged. She was a tangle of too many arms and legs and not enough room, but she clawed her way onto the bench seat.

The driver turned to look at her, but all Rain saw was the shadowy outline of a head and shoulders and the glowing tip of an e-cigarette through a smoky blue haze.

"Where to?" he asked.

She looked around. "I don't even know where I am."

The e-cigarette tip flared bright as the driver drew on it. A dog ran across the street directly in front of the car, throwing a feral snarl at the machine. The driver punched the horn, and the mournful Doppler wail chased the dog away. The windshield wipers slashed back and forth like the frenetic scythes of maddened reapers.

Rain turned to see if the dog was all right, but it was gone. Instead, she saw a man standing on the same corner where she'd last seen the animal. He was tall and wore a black suit. He held the curved handle of an umbrella in one hand, and the black silk dome completely hid his face.

Somehow Rain knew that the man was bald and that he was smiling.

"Drive," she said again. Softly, urgently.

"To where?"

"Anywhere. Christ, just *drive*."

The driver gave two seconds of a penetrating stare, then he nodded, turned, and hit the gas. The car tore holes in the storm.

CHAPTER ELEVEN

It took Rain a while to gather up all the disconnected pieces of herself and clumsy them back into something resembling an adult woman. All things considered, it was not a grand success. Her clothes were soaked, and there were stains on her skirt and jacket from the disgusting trash in that alley, and she was sure some of the stains on her shoes were never going to come out. A homeless person wouldn't mug her for anything she wore. The rain had soaked her all the way down to her underwear, and she felt violated by it, invaded. She was a mess. When she checked to make sure she had enough money for this ride, she found that there was water in her purse. She fished out a couple of soggy fives and a few ones that lay like debris amid the flotsam of her lipstick and eyeliner.

"Any survivors back there?" asked the driver.

Rain's first reaction was to tell him to go screw himself, but she didn't. "Jury's out."

The driver laughed. He had a good laugh, and he didn't laugh too much, too loud, or too long. Rain judged people on how they laughed, and when, and grudgingly gave him a couple of points.

Lightning flashed blue-white, and a heartbeat later, deep thunder boomed with such shocking force it set off car alarms along the side of the street. The heavy rain intensified to a downpour that blurred out the street signs and washed everything in a featureless gray.

She fished for her brush and tried to make sense of her hair while covertly checking out the driver. He was a light-skinned black man. Thirty-something. Very thin, with a crooked nose that had probably been broken and set badly. He wore a ball cap backward on his head. There was a logo on the cap—a bald eagle clutching an American flag hovering over the featureless tan-colored outline of Iraq with OPERATION ENDURING FREEDOM stitched above it, and below that, the word VETERAN. The hand resting on the top of the knobbed steering wheel was missing most of the little finger, and there was something wrong with the skin on his arm. It was mottled pink and brown and as uneven as the cheese on an overbaked pizza. Burn scars? Probably. It wasn't hard to connect those scars with that hat. Rain didn't ask him about it, though. She had her own history with the war in Iraq. Noah had been burned, too. Burned and . . .

Don't do it, she warned herself. *Do not do that.*

Rain tried not to think about the boy she had loved for such a short time before he went to off to die in a desert she couldn't find on a map. Trying not to think about him was part of how she stayed straight. Most of the time, she succeeded. Not always, though. And even now after nearly ten years, it still stuck knives into her and twisted them very, very slowly.

Noah.

Beautiful Noah. Lost Noah. Blown out of her life by a roadside bomb, trapped in a burning Humvee. Gone before Rain had a chance to tell him that she was pregnant. His death had made it easier to let her mother talk Rain into giving up the baby. Giving it away like unwanted junk mail.

Rain turned away, not wanting to see the embroidery on the driver's hat. Instead, she looked out at the storm as the car sliced down a side street, paused for a second at the corner, and then plunged into the cross-cutting traffic of the avenue. Horns blared and tires squealed wetly, but the driver just poured on the gas and trailed twin streams of pale smoke from his nostrils. The smoke smelled of cinnamon and mint. Weird, but not bad.

"Safe," murmured Rain aloud, and a moment later, her conscious mind realized she'd said it. She played back that word in her head and wondered what she meant, why she said it. *Safe?* The whole day had fallen off its hinges. No, it was worse than that—she'd blacked out and *lost* a day. Friday was gone. Completely gone, without even a smear of memory left behind. Even on her worst days using crack she hadn't lost an entire day. Hours, sure; clarity and perspective, no doubt; but not a whole damn day. She was broke, and she was losing her mind. Hallucinating. Seeing people who weren't there. The old Mexican lady, the little boy, and that creepy guy. No way seeing imaginary people equaled being safe.

So . . . *safe?* How was she safe?

She fished for a tissue, but everything in her purse was wet. In panic, she grabbed her phone and pushed a button; the screen came on, but there were still no bars.

"I'm sorry," she said, "but do you have any tissues?"

"Sure," he said and handed back a small box of Scotties. She plucked several out, wiped her eyes, blew her nose, and then used more to blot her phone dry. Then she remembered the glasses, and she wiped and dried them, too, and put them on. The inside of the car became much clearer. It was a very clean vehicle, despite the vape smells. The ID card on the back of the seat said that the driver was ALEXANDER STICKLEY. The photo looked old because the man who smiled from the picture looked much younger, his nose was straighter, and there were no visible burns. The face in the picture smiled at her. A safe smile, and again she mouthed that word.

Safe.

CHAPTER TWELVE

Despite everything—instincts, common sense, a life lived as a woman in New York, and every horrific news story she'd ever read—Rain fell asleep in the back of the car.

It was warm, the car's suspension turned the potholes into a cradle-rock rhythm, and the song the driver hummed sounded more like a lullaby than old rock 'n' roll. She closed her eyes for a moment and immediately sank down.

She fell through shadows into dreams, and into that part of the dreamscape where memories lived, untarnished or unvarnished by the years.

It was ten years ago and she was sixteen again. Heavily pregnant, waddling through Central Park. Her due date was the day after tomorrow, and she felt unbearably ugly. Everything hurt. None of the TV sweetness of pregnancy had any relevance to her experience. She did not glow. She was not looking forward to the big day. She was not buying baby clothes or decorating a room for the happy little bundle.

None of that.

All the paperwork was done except for her signature. Rain's mother had seen to that. It was a process Mom had started on that awful, awful Thursday seven and a half months ago. A one-two-three punch that nearly killed Rain. Or maybe it had killed the parts of her that mattered. She could remember the whole timetable of the day she learned she was pregnant. It was the worst day of her life. Well, so far.

At 10:17 on that terrible morning, Dr. Sharon Bernstein had told Rain that she was pregnant. Six weeks at least. It was a punch to the head but not entirely unexpected. When the gynecologist asked if Rain could estimate the date of conception, the answer was right there. The night before Noah left to join his unit and ship out to the Middle East. The one and only time Rain had ever had sex. One time. The pill had helped her with bad cramps, but it hadn't stopped one little bastard of a sperm from doing its job. She would be sixteen when she gave birth. A baby having a baby, as so many people later pointed out to her, starting with dear old Mom.

1:55 that afternoon. Rain had come home and hid in her room, composing a hundred different versions of an email to Noah. The messages were all over the place. Wildly passionate and joyful, but reading like the trash romance fiction they were. Straightforward and practical, lacking all emotion. Pleading, apologetic, desperate. She had managed to compose one that sounded pretty good, and then the phone rang.

3:05. It was a call from a woman Rain had never met. Noah's older sister, Michelle, who lived in Queens. Telling Rain something. Words that stabbed her. Words that blinded her and stole the light and tore screams from her. Something about a land mine in Iraq. An IED. Improvised explosive device. Words about the truckful of soldiers. All dead except one. Not the right one. The rest of them had been burned. More words after that. About Noah. About them—whoever *they* were—sending the body home. Words about funeral arrangements. Closed coffin. Arlington, maybe. Words that spilled onto the floor.

3:20. Rain remembered falling but not landing. She didn't remember them taking her to the hospital. Her brain rebooted itself when she was in the ER, and then all she could do was scream. Until they gave her some drugs.

The drugs helped. Diazepam. Very nice.

11:30 that same night. Mom and Dad sitting with her after they brought her home from the ER. Someone had given her parents a sheaf of pamphlets about grief counseling. As soon as she was alone, Rain tore them up.

Sitting on the couch in the living room. Dad on one side, saying almost nothing except meaningless little things that were supposed to be comforting, but weren't. Mom holding her hand, but without warmth, without really touching her. It was like holding the hand of a mannequin at Macy's. Cool and plastic. Mom talking without taking a break.

"—it's for the good of everyone . . ."

"—it's the best thing for the baby . . ."

"—you're too young . . ."

"—why ruin your life?"

"—it's not like he was going to come back and marry you . . ."

"—I'm not saying it's God's judgment, but what did he expect? Raping an underage girl . . ."

Dad had made one attempt to counter that point. He looked up statutory rape on the net and read, "In New York State, a person who is under age sixteen but older than thirteen years old can consent to sex with a person who is no more than four years older." Rain had been fifteen when she slept with Noah, and he had been eighteen.

"Technically it was legal and—" he tried to say, but Mom had silenced him with a glare so ferocious that Dad said nothing else the rest of the evening.

Mom returned to her litany, telling Rain that she could not raise a baby. Not and stay in school. Not and have a life. Not and blah blah blah. On and on until Rain, still deeply in shock over the call from Michelle, nodded.

That was then. As she walked through Central Park, she reviewed the timetable, able to remember it all with a cruel clarity. They weren't things she could forget.

Since then, it all proceeded with clockwork precision. Every detail had been arranged by Mom. The right doctors, the right hospital, the paperwork to give up the baby to the people at a reputable adoption agency. After the actual birth, Rain knew she would never see her baby again.

Nor did she want to.

Except when she did.

Although she was a minor, her signature on the last forms was required by law. Not even someone like Rain's mother could force her to give up the baby, which is why she said, "It's your choice, Lorraine. It's your choice." Over and over and over again, day in and day out.

That had been the worst day of her life.

Central Park was where she always went to think. Rain lumbered heavily along the winding footpaths in the park beneath a sky that was a startling blue. But, true to the depressing poetry of her life, there were gray storm clouds peering with bad intent over the eastern skyline.

A colored streamer caught her eye, and she turned to watch it flutter. It was one of several that unwound across the sky, twisting like dragon tails, painting the day in colors of saffron and red and white. Each stream was attached to a tall bamboo pole that swayed above the trees. Rain stopped and stood looking up at them. It was then that she heard a voice speaking or chanting in a low, almost inaudible mumble. A bass voice, and the sound of it rolled through the air and changed the texture of the moment. Rain recognized it as some kind of Buddhist chanting, like what she'd heard at school when they showed videos of world religions. She couldn't understand any of the words, but the sound of them lulled her to the edge of a softness of mind. A nice place, especially when the world around her was so hard.

After a few moments, she began walking again, following the path under a small hill and around a line of shrubs to where it ran past a field. At least a hundred people sat cross-legged on colored mats. They were arranged in a half circle around a group of five monks in reddish-yellow robes. Four of the monks sat on a long red mat, and the fifth, older than the others by many years, sat in the middle of their line on a small stool. Everyone was chanting in harmony. Rain wasn't sure if it was a song or a prayer, but she liked the sound of it. The gathered people were a mix of races and ages; some in loose yoga clothes, others in ordinary clothes. What unified them, though, was the tranquil lack of expressions on their faces. As if they were all asleep and dreaming the same dream.

Rain could feel the peaceful power of all of this pulling her. She even took a step toward them, but then the weight of everything else in her life planted her there, rooting her to the spot. Tomorrow or maybe the next day, she was going to have a baby. Have it and then give it up.

Noah's baby.

The thought of it tore her apart, ripping her right down the middle, cleaving her heart. On one hand, this was part of Noah; it was the very last part of him she would ever have—*could* ever have—and giving it up would be like erasing him from her life. That was so horrible that it kept her awake all night, except on those nights when she cried herself into a kind of daze where she felt drunk with grief, and from there toppled over into sleep filled with nightmares. Doctor Nine lived in those dreams, and ever since that terrible Thursday, the monster had been in her dreams nearly every night. Waiting for her when she closed her eyes. Grinning at her with his wet teeth, hiding his truth from her behind his dark glasses.

Have your baby, he would whisper. *Keep it and watch what I'll do. Watch the child sicken, and coarsen, and become like you. Beautiful outside and spoiled inside, like a wormy piece of fruit. That's what you are, sweet Lorraine. Filled with sickness and darkness and ugliness. Keep your child and together we will guide him through the kingdom of filth and rats.*

It was grandiose, she knew, and half of his dialogue was probably cribbed from old horror movies and novels, but that did not change the fact that Rain believed everything Doctor Nine said. *Keep the child and destroy him in doing so*, whispered the doctor. *Kindness is a knife, and I will teach you how to cut.*

On the other hand, the counterargument was to give the baby up for adoption and let other, cleaner hands take it and raise it.

Raise *him*. Even though Rain had never asked about the sex of the baby, she knew it was going to be a boy. Somehow she knew. Just as she knew the boy, her little Dylan, would grow up to look like Noah. And that would kill her.

Give Dylan up to save the baby and save her own heart and soul. Keep him and ruin both lives. The choice seemed clear, though it broke her heart every time she worked through the calculus of cold logic. She was sixteen and a schoolgirl and nothing much of a student. Her parents had open contempt for the unborn baby. It was an inconvenience of mammoth proportions to their family. Not to mention an embarrassment. A century ago, Rain knew, she would have been sent away to a distant relative until the indiscreet birth, and then she would return, sans child, to resume her life as an affected maiden of the house. This was not that time, but the inbred addiction to social scandal was still there in her mother's eyes. Less so in her father's, but there was less of most everything else in him.

She thought these thoughts, rooted to the spot, but as she did so, her body swayed as if the prayer was a song. As if she were still a lithe girl who danced every day. Rain felt the pull of it. Not of music tempting her but of her own legs needing to find music, real, remembered, or imagined, so that she could dance. And in doing so, she would somehow be able to whirl and leap her way out of the bullshit of her life. Dance had always been her escape, and now, when she needed it most of all, it was taken from her by cramps, a swollen belly, ruined balance, dizziness, and everything else that came with pregnancy.

Still, despite all of that, she swayed, eyes closed, dancing in her mind. Then, abruptly, the baby kicked inside her belly. It was hard, too. Real force. Almost as if the little boy wanted to dance, too.

That was a stab through the heart and, sick in soul and body, Rain spun away from the crowd and the monks, needing to leave right now.

And she bumped into another monk, who stood a few feet behind her.

The monk stepped back, bowing, smiling. "Pardon, miss," he said.

"No," she said quickly. "That's all me."

He shook his head but did not directly reply to that. Instead, he nodded to indicate her stomach. "Soon."

"Yeah, I guess," she said.

The monk nodded, looking happy. Though whether it was because the meditation event seemed to be going well or because he liked babies, Rain couldn't tell, and didn't much care. She gave him an awkward smile and mumbled something about having to go as she moved to walk around him. The monk stepped into her path. It was a gentle move, a shift of his body, but it stopped her.

"Please," he said and raised his hands, palms out as if to show her he was no threat.

"What?" she asked with enough New York attitude creeping into her voice that the monk's smile flickered.

He gave another nod to her stomach and reached one hand a few inches forward. "Please?" he repeated, pitching it this time as a question.

Rain stiffened. Ever since she started to show, people had tried to touch her stomach. Women did it all the damn time, in stores, on the street, in freaking Starbucks. It was weird. Why did people think it was suddenly okay to touch someone just because they were pregnant? How did that happen? She was sixteen, so groping someone her age was kind of weird to begin with, but touching her stomach felt wrong. Besides, she didn't want to hear anything that people wanted to say to her. All the good wishes and advice and personal stories about their own pregnancies. None of that.

Now there was a Buddhist monk wanting to touch her.

Rain wanted to tell him to go to the pond, fill his pockets—if he even had pockets—with rocks and jump in. A nasty comment rose to her lips.

And yet she nodded.

Rain had no plan to do that, no idea she was going to, until she did it. The monk searched her eyes with his. He had very dark brown eyes, but there were small flecks of gold in there. The eyes looked a lot older than the face they looked out of. The face was maybe forty, the eyes were so old she couldn't even guess. They were deep and, despite his smile, there was a lot of sadness in them, as if they had looked too closely at the world and seen it for exactly what it was. How could he still smile? She wondered.

He returned her nod and touched her stomach with a flat palm, fingers wide. Those ancient eyes closed for a moment, and he held his head at an angle as if listening to something.

The baby kicked again. And again.

His smile flickered for a moment, and he opened his eyes and gave her a brief, doubtful look. He cut a look to where his fellow monks sat, and Rain saw that they were looking at him. Or maybe at her.

The baby kicked once more, and the monk withdrew his hand. There was no trace of a smile on his face now, and he looked serious, even grave.

"This is a special one," he said.

Rain just looked at him.

"He is important," continued the monk. "He is not the flame, but he will strike the match. Do you understand?"

"Yeah, sure," said Rain acidly, "he's a baby. Who doesn't love a baby?"

The monk's smile tried to return, flickered, faded. "Listen to me, little sister," he said. "You are his mother. You must do what is best for him."

Rain wanted to punch him. She wanted to run.

"What do you think I'm *trying* to do?" she demanded. She yelled it so loud the whole crowd of meditators jerked and twitched and looked at her. The chanting stopped. "Don't you think I *know* what's good for the damn kid? I'm not a complete idiot. I'm not actually cruel, you know."

The monk was taken aback and tried to explain, but Rain turned away in anger and disgust.

"No," she snarled. "I don't want to hear it. Not from you and not from anyone. I know what I have to do."

She walked away as fast as she could, nearly running, wheezing and crying and growling as she headed for the nearest exit. Rain looked over her shoulder to see if the monk was following, but the man stood there, looking shocked and horrified, one hand raised as if he were about to call after her. She quickened her pace because there was nothing else he could say. He'd already said enough.

Still looking backward, she suddenly collided with someone entering the park.

"Oooof!" she cried and lost her balance, turning, falling stomach-first toward the ground.

Powerful hands caught her in an awkward bear hug, one hand around her chest and accidentally cupping a breast, the other clamped around her belly.

"I got you," gasped the man she'd run into.

He helped her upright, moved his hands from breast and belly and touched her arms, steadying her. Dizziness swirled inside her head like a dust storm. She gasped, gagged, and grabbed onto him for support.

"Are you okay, young miss?" asked the man.

She looked at him. He was a stranger and yet vaguely familiar. Maybe someone she'd seen in the neighborhood, or the park, before. He was a middle-aged white man, tall and very slim, dressed in a dark suit, red tie, white shirt. There were faint stains on his shirt and his tie looked damp, as if he'd spilled something on it. He wore very dark sunglasses and an old-fashioned fedora. He smiled down at her.

"I—" she began, gagged again, took a breath, and gave it another try. "I'm fine. Thanks. Really, thanks. You saved me."

"No," he said mildly. "Not at all."

"I'm serious. I . . . I guess I wasn't looking where I was going."

He released her and took a small step back, nodding to her protruding stomach. "Babies," he said wistfully. "A blessing and a curse, am I right?"

Rain snorted. "You're not wrong."

She walked away, left the park, crossed the street at West Ninetieth and did not look back again. Her stomach ached from where the man had caught her. There was a sharp, deep sickness that hadn't been there before, and the thought that being caught while falling had done some kind of damage stabbed her flesh with needles of ice.

When she reached the corner of Ninetieth and Columbus Avenue, Rain stopped and fumbled her cell phone out of her purse. She punched in a number and waited through four rings before it was answered.

"Mom," she said in a hoarse, ragged voice, "I'll sign the paper."

It was then that her water broke.

. . . and it was at that part of the memory when Rain woke up from her dream and was back in the car driving through the storm.

CHAPTER THIRTEEN

Rain stayed awake after that.

Even so, memories of that day, of the look on the monk's face, of everything that happened seemed to crowd into the backseat with her.

She was about to ask where they were, but the car turned a corner and Rain realized they were on Forty-Second Street. The Port Authority Bus Terminal was up the street. Had she told the driver to take her here? She honestly couldn't remember. The car drifted over to the curb, and the driver put it in park. Rain leaned forward to see how much the fare was but grunted in surprise because it was turned off.

"Um . . . is this some kind of flat fee thing," she began, immediately defensive, "because I don't—"

"No charge," he said.

Rain narrowed her eyes. "What? Why?"

The driver half turned, and as Rain leaned forward to talk to him, she could see that he was disabled. From the abdomen up he was whole, but below that there were prosthetics and straps and levers to allow him to operate the gas and brakes with his left hand while he steered with his right. The mechanics were so comprehensive it looked like he'd been built into the car, or that it had been built around him. Rain had no idea how the man got out of the vehicle, or how he walked at all.

"Why are you giving me a free ride?" she demanded.

Alexander Stickley studied her for a three count. "Why not?" he asked, and then he smiled. There were more burn scars on his neck and face, and she could see a small square lump under his shirt over the man's heart. Some kind of monitor or other medical device, probably. Whatever had happened to him had been terrible. Only his eyes and mouth seemed untouched. His eyes were dark but kind, and he had a nice smile. Warm. "You looked like you were having a bad day."

"You didn't have to stop for me in the first place, you know," she said.

He shrugged.

"You didn't have to do this," she added, nodding to the zeroes on the trip meter.

"Most people don't have to do most things, I guess," he said. "Besides, I've had me some bad days, too."

Rain nodded and dug into her purse for a few dollars to use as a tip, but when she offered the money, he shook his head.

"It's all good," he said.

"At least get yourself some coffee or something. . . ."

"Tell you what," said the driver, reaching into his shirt pocket and producing a business card. "How 'bout you just call me if you ever need a ride again."

"I usually don't take cabs," she said.

"Car service," he corrected, then patted the steering wheel. "Me and the Red Rocket got nothing better to do, and we both like getting people to where they need to be."

"'Red Rocket'? I saw that painted on the fender." She had to smile. "This doesn't look like much of a rocket."

He grinned. "She'll fool you. She looks slow, but not when she wants to be fast. This ol' girl can outrun sundown if she has to."

That made Rain smile.

"So if you don't need a ride," said the driver, "give the card to a friend."

Rain almost said that she didn't have very many friends, but she already felt pathetic enough. The truth was that she had friends, but how many of them could afford to take cabs, either? The few friends she had went to the same Narcotics Anonymous meetings she did. They were like her, debris washed up on the shores of their own lives. Poetic, but also true.

She took the card.

All it had was a word and a phone number. She read the word aloud. "*Sticks?*"

"Oh, yeah. That's what people call me."

"Because of—" she began, her eyes flicking toward his metal braces. "Sorry, I didn't mean to—"

Sticks smiled and shook his head. "It's all good. That's not why they call me Sticks. I used to be a drummer. *Wanted* to be a drummer. I carried sticks with me all the time, and I'd bang on anything. Turns out you need talent, though, and I guess I didn't get that gene. Got the nickname, though."

"Okay, Sticks. Thanks."

"Any time," he said, and as she jerked open the door, he added, "Kind of tough to be out in the storm."

Rain paused, catching something in his eye and something in his voice that made her think that his comment had nothing at all to do with the weather. They studied each other for a moment, then he nodded and she nodded back. Saying something in some kind of subliminal code Rain could not yet decipher, but which she knew was both true and important.

"Thanks," she said.

"You take good care."

She got out but paused before closing the door. "Do you still drum?"

"Not much anymore, no."

"I used to dance. Before . . ."

"Before what?"

"Before life."

Sticks considered for a moment, then nodded again.

The rain had slowed to a drizzle now, and she hurried over to the entrance, paused, turned, and waved to Sticks. He nodded, put his e-cigarette between his teeth, put the Red Rocket in gear, and drove slowly away.

"Safe," she said once more. And then she shivered, because on some level buried down deep in the soil of her soul, Rain knew that she was not safe for anything but the moment. *Safe* was a word she didn't really believe in. Not for a long time, and certainly not today. She looked up at the afternoon sky as the dark clouds parted and bright blue sparkled there, spilling clean light down on her. The day whispered to her that the storms were over and it was all going to be pretty.

She didn't believe in that, either.

INTERLUDE ONE
NARCOTICS ANONYMOUS MEETING

St. Jude's Catholic Church
Thirteen Months Ago

"Hi. My name is Rain, and I'm an addict."

They all said, "Hi, Rain!"

Depending on the night, the place, the weather, the latest disaster on the news, or the content of what the last person shared, the tone of that response could vary. A lot. Usually the members of the meeting tried to sound cheerful, inviting, inclusive. Sometimes they sounded like a bunch of zombies. And there was a lot of room for variation in between. Tonight was a happy crowd.

Rain knew that some of it was because people liked to see someone like her get up and share. Because she was young; and because she was pretty, though in a mild and unchallenging way. A supporting character in a TV show way. Besides, no one in any of these chairs had a right to sneer, and they all knew it. Every single one of them had walked away from a train wreck of their own making. Failed marriages, failed attempts at college or school, failed relationships, failed expectations, failed lives. That they were here was a sign of hope but not proof of a cure. They were always going to be addicts. That was how it worked. No matter how many years they were clean, no matter how long since they last used, the hunger for it would be there. Rain knew that some of them had gone from four-year chips back to zero. Some never made it past six months before hitting reset.

Rain didn't share that often, and when she did, sometimes it was a straight fifth-step of admitting to God—or whoever—to herself and to another person the exact nature of her wrongs. There was enough in that inventory for it to unfold in chapters over weeks. She never sugarcoated it. Not anymore. Not after her breakthrough during her fifth month clean of this current two-year run. That had been her big moment of telling the worst of it. The group had applauded her, and some of them were crying.

Tonight was different.

Tonight when she got up to share, it wasn't exactly about the stuff she'd done wrong but about what might have been if she'd made a better choice. It was a ninth-step meeting, about trying to make amends to the people she hurt.

"I know that's what we're supposed to talk about," she told the crowd, "but I can't. And it's not that I don't want to make amends, I really, really do—but I can't. The person I hurt most was my son."

A couple of heads nodded. Those of the group who knew some of this story. Others leaned in, interested. Even the faces of the generic people on the inspirational posters on the walls seemed to be listening.

"You see," said Rain, "when I was fifteen, I got pregnant. Nine years ago. First time having sex, too. I was on the pill because of my periods, and I thought that was good enough. They told me the pill was 99 percent effective. Go figure. My boyfriend was eighteen, and he was going off to fight in Iraq. He never got much of a chance to fight, but he died over there. I turned sixteen while I was pregnant, and because I was still a minor, because the baby's father was dead, and because my mother convinced me that I was going to ruin my life if I kept the kid . . . I gave him up. Even with all that, I gave him a name. A secret name only I knew. One I whispered to him while he was still inside of me. One I only ever said aloud once, when I saw him for a split second before they took him away. He looked right at me. I know, newborns don't see well and all that, blah blah blah. I'm telling you that he *saw* me. We had this moment, you know? And I whispered his name. Just that one time. Then they took him away." She paused. "I mean . . . I *let* them take my baby away, and I never saw him again except in dreams or when I was high."

The audience was silent, watching her.

"By the time my water broke, I'd convinced myself that giving him up was the only right thing to do, you know?" continued Rain. "I mean, I read all the pamphlets, went to the counseling sessions, heard the statistics, received the full pitch. A teenage girl who was never the sharpest knife in the drawer anyway couldn't provide the right care for a baby. Right? Not like a married couple who couldn't have kids but really wanted one. Even at sixteen I could do that kind of math. My mother hated the baby because it was something that created a kind of scandal, and she thought it would get in the way of me pursuing a career as the greatest dancer in the history of ballet. That was her damage. Complications from my birth screwed her out of her own ballerina agenda, and now here I was trashing my chances of her living through me. Mom never went through a sympathy phase or a supportive phase while I was pregnant. She went right for the 'get rid of it' and 'get on with your life' phase."

The moderator, a fat black woman with orange hair, tried to catch Rain's eye and maybe gently steer her back to the point of the ninth step, but Rain was already moving there.

"But," said Rain, "I'm not here to talk about how I messed up my parents' lives. That's a different story for a different day. No, I wanted to talk about the one person I hurt who never had a chance to defend himself. Not my dad, and not poor soldier boy Noah." She shook her head and fished for a tissue in her jeans pocket, found it, dabbed her eyes. "The person I hurt most is the person I can't ever directly apologize to."

She could still see that tiny, pink face. Those eyes, so awake. Dylan. The name meant "ray of hope" or "ray of light," and that's what he had been for her. The only ray of light in the growing darkness of her life. Dylan. The only hope she knew.

"I only saw my baby for a moment," said Rain, "and then he was gone."

CHAPTER FOURTEEN

The drizzle had stopped, and there was the slightest hint of blue up there, though shifting curtains of clouds were trying to hide it.

Once she got home, Rain opened her door with great caution and whistled for Bug, who came running like a bullet, jumping and wagging and whining and nearly turning herself inside out. Still in the hallway, Rain reached in to snatch the leash off the hook beside the door, pulled the door shut, and went downstairs with Bug. She wasn't ready to face her apartment yet.

Her neighborhood was in no way scenic. There were brownstones, there were a few grubby stores, there were abandoned apartment buildings, there were crack houses, there were empty lots. There wasn't a spot of green anywhere except weeds sneaking up through cracks in the concrete or plastic bags fluttering eternally from telephone wires.

Rain and Bug passed a little old Japanese man pasting handbills on the windows of closed businesses. He was crooked and withered, wearing a sweatshirt that was too big for him, ugly khakis, socks, and sandals. He glanced at her and then away, and for a moment she thought she recognized him. Two different partial memories played tug-of-war in her head. Wasn't there a Japanese guy living in Joplin's building? She thought there was and maybe this was him, but she'd never had a good look at the guy, and he kept his face away as he worked as if he didn't want her to see his face now.

The other memory was an older one of the monk in Central Park. But that man had been about forty, and this man looked ancient. Not the same guy, she decided, but there was a quality about him that triggered this encounter to that older one. Bug wagged her crooked tail at the man and gave a happy yap.

"Hi," said Rain.

The man stiffened but did not look at her. Embarrassed? Shy? She couldn't tell. She studied the handbill he'd posted. It was the same as others she'd seen all over the neighborhood.

Gomen'nasai

"What's that mean?"

The man's body began to tremble and his shoulders hitched.

"*Gomen'nasai*," he said, then he gathered up his handbills and tape and ran away. Not walked. Ran. Rain stood watching him, totally nonplussed.

Overhead, the sky was filled with dark birds that circled and circled. There was no blue up there anymore. Feeling depressed and confused, Rain turned and walked back to her building.

CHAPTER FIFTEEN

Alyson Creighton-Thomas sat alone in her a big Central Park West apartment designed for a family.

Her husband, Bryce, was not home. He didn't come home very much anymore, and when he did, it was when Alyson was scheduled to be out. She knew he'd been there by what clothes were missing or by what mail was gone from the desk in the study. There was never a note from him. They had gotten past the note phase, and long past the texting phase. Now they were ghosts haunting the apartment where they once lived as husband and wife.

Across the living room, past the lovely furniture and the acres of white carpet, the TV screen swirled with motion even though the sound was turned all the way down. Alyson watched a group of children stand at a stretching bar under the stern eye of a matronly ballet teacher. She watched as the children performed onstage for clapping parents. She watched as a small, slender, dark-haired girl ran across the stage and leaped into the air, one leg leading, the other following along a perfect horizontal line, executing the *grand jeté* with fluid grace, then landing, turning, rising up on the tip of her pointe shoe, twirling and twirling. Then another leap, an *emboîté*, then a powerful *entrechat*, and another. On and on.

The DVD was eight hours long, and she was midway through her second watching this weekend. Her five hundredth since her daughter had started going to meetings. The five thousandth since that fucking baby was born. That wretched, squealing, worthless piece-of-shit baby. That bastard. That fucking bastard.

Vodka was her wingman and her confessor. Pills of so many useful kinds were there to show her the way to the end of each day. A Xanax or a Zoloft or an Amytal were Sherpas that would guide her from couch to bed and back to couch.

When her phone rang, she almost didn't answer, because she seldom did that anymore. It was the house phone, and it wasn't near the couch. Getting up meant finding her cane, which had fallen down out of sight between couch and side table. It meant struggling up, something that embarrassed her even when she was alone. She let it ring through, not willing to spend the coin of effort.

The caller left a message, and the landline base station had a speaker function. She sat and listened to Mr. Alan Javers complain to her that he had tried to do Alyson a favor by agreeing to interview her daughter. "But she blew off the interview and then has the audacity to come in a day late. Frankly, Alyson, my receptionist said that Lorraine looked—and I'm quoting here—'kind of out of it and didn't know what day it was.' I mean, I'm all for helping you out, and I genuinely appreciate the business you've sent my way over the years, but . . ."

There was more, but Alyson stopped listening.

Kind of out of it and didn't know what day it was.

The words seemed to be repeated in her head but by a different voice. An old and familiar voice. One that always spoke the hard truths to her from the shadows of her mind. *She's using again.* A week ago, Alyson would have been on the phone, cane or not, to screech at her daughter for falling off the wagon. A month ago, she'd have demanded that Rain go in for tests. Six months ago, she would have already started the paperwork for another trip to rehab.

Now she did none of that.

Instead, she had a sip of vodka. Then she took a Xanax and washed it down with more vodka. On the screen, the brown-haired little girl danced and jumped. Alyson did not know if she was watching her daughter's recital or one of her own.

CHAPTER SIXTEEN

Rain and Bug and stopped at the mailbox. There was the usual half ton of bills, two magazines—*Entertainment Weekly* and *Rolling Stone*—something that made Rain stand there frowning at what lay under the mail. She took it out and turned it over in her fingers.

It was a pocket watch. Small and delicate, with a long silver chain and a clear crystal cover over a yellow face set with Roman numerals. The hands were stopped at three minutes to twelve, and there was no second hand. Rain turned it over and saw that there was a slot for a windup key on the back. Rain searched the mailbox for a key, but there wasn't one.

"What the hell?" she said, trying to understand how it got there. Joplin wouldn't have left it. He didn't have a key to her mailbox. The watch was pretty, though, and it felt good in her hand.

Bug stood on her hind legs to sniff the dangling chain. She barked happily at it.

"Weird," said Rain. She stuffed it into her pocket, closed and locked her mailbox, and climbed the stairs with her tail-waggy little dog.

The dog stopped wagging as they approached their apartment door. Rain felt a chill race up her spine as she thought of what had happened that morning. She stood outside for almost two minutes, dredging up the nerve. It had been a long, bad day, and she felt empty of courage.

Bug did not scratch at the door the way she usually did when they got home. She wasn't eager to get inside, either. Great.

Finally, Rain took a steadying breath and unlocked the door.

The first thing she did once they were inside was go straight to the kitchen and grab the biggest knife in the rack. It was a bread knife with a fat blade and a sturdy black plastic handle. Bug scuttled behind her as

Rain crept toward the bathroom, steeled herself, and pushed the door open with her foot, the knife raised to strike.

There was no one inside.

The Van Gogh shower curtain hung there, pretty and unmoving, but the memories of that morning came back at her with such reality that she began to sweat inside her damp clothing. She tightened her grip on the knife, reached out a quivering hand to take hold of the curtain, and then whipped it back. She totally forgot that it was held up with duct tape and did not slide along the bar. Instead, the plastic tore from the remaining rings and the bar itself popped out of the socket. The released tension flung it at her, and Rain fell back against the edge of the doorframe with the bar and the curtain hitting her in the face. She fell with a bone-jarring jolt, lost the knife, and sprawled on her back halfway into the bedroom.

The tub was empty.

Of course it was empty. No strangers. No mad rapists. No junkies breaking in to steal her stuff. No Doctor Nine. No anything. Because of course there was nothing. It was all in her head. That's what she told herself. Which is a good thing to say when you're fighting fears, but a bad, bad thought to be alone with.

It's all in your head.

She dared herself to say the rest of it. The parasite in her head accepted that challenge. *It's all in your head because you're crazy,* it told her. *You cooked your brain with drugs, and now you are nothing but damaged goods, sweetheart.*

You're nothing but damage.

You're nothing.

Bug cringed and whimpered by the open bathroom door and then suddenly peed all over the floor. Rain kicked free of the curtain, shoved the bar away, covered her face with her hands, and completely lost it as the whole day smashed down on her.

CHAPTER SEVENTEEN

When Rain clawed the pieces of herself together, she cleaned up the dog pee, then went into the kitchen and counted the cans of dog food. On her last trip to the market five days ago, she'd bought fourteen large cans, one for each day. She gave Bug half a can in the morning and the rest at night. She counted the remaining cans and did the math. The can for Friday was not there. It should be, but it wasn't. Like the day, the can was missing, too. When she checked her birth control pills, the Friday dose was likewise gone.

How did that make sense?

Either she was awake on Friday and took her pill, fed the dog, and did the other Friday things, or she didn't. If she did, why couldn't she remember any of it? If she didn't, then . . .

There was really nowhere to go with that. If she had slept all the way through Friday, then wouldn't Bug have peed and pooped on the floor? She checked everywhere, but there was nothing except what she'd just cleaned up in the bathroom.

A faint tremble began deep inside her. It had nothing to do with how cold the room was. Bug, sensitive to her mood, whined softly and leaned against her. She picked the tiny dog up and cuddled her. "Mommy's not crazy," she promised, knowing it was a lie. Bug, true and perfect as ever, wagged her crooked tail.

Rain kissed Bug and fed her, then bundled up in what she thought of as her "slob" clothes and went out in a hunt for food. She wore old dance tights, a hoodie she'd borrowed from Joplin and never returned, no makeup, and a scarf that was about a mile long. Protected against the rain and guys cruising for easy meat, she ran out into the night.

As she passed her mailbox on the way out, Rain remembered the little windup pocket watch, but she'd left it upstairs. How the heck did it get in there with her mail? Tomorrow was Sunday, so she'd have to wait until Monday to ambush the letter carrier. Seemed so weird to leave it without some kind of note.

"Add that to the day," she said to the empty foyer as she went out.

She spent money she couldn't afford to order Chinese takeout. The restaurant charged too much for delivery and there would be a tip, so she always got it herself. She called Joplin to see if he wanted to come over and help her eat it, and maybe help her piece together what was happening— the glasses, the kid, the old lady, the lost day—but her call went straight to his voice mail. She hung up without leaving a message.

On the way back, she stopped outside a dance studio and looked through the window at the little girls doing ballet, wishing she could shed her skin and let the little girl inside go running and leaping to join them. They were all smiling, happy in their exertions, joyful in the mechanics of their routine. Rain ached to dance, to have the freedom to try it again. She even went inside and stood in the waiting area to watch.

Watching was nice.

For a while.

There were always memories lurking beneath the surface. Her own and ones that she had borrowed from her mother. Alyson Creighton-Thomas used to dance, too. Mom had been really good at it, a rising star. Once upon a time her mother had been a candidate for "featured dancer" in the New York City Ballet. That was a lifelong dream and every indication was that it would happen, and from there maybe even prima ballerina. Friends of her mother often said that she had the talent, the determination, the beauty. She had everything.

Except that at nineteen, Mom had gotten pregnant. Just like Rain, there had been one overly energetic sperm that had fought its way across the no-man's-land of regular birth control pills. A sperm that had beaten all the odds, found the egg, created magic. And if it had been only a baby, Mom might have taken a year off and then worked like a demon to get back in shape and back onto the stage. Other dancers had done that. However, her mother had been in labor for more than twenty hours when the doctors discovered that the baby's oxygen supply had been disrupted by a prolapsed cord. They did a C-section, and even though the family could afford the best doctors—always the best for the Creighten and Thomas families—things went south. Mom's femur was fractured. Not common, but not an unknown thing, either. The damage was severe, requiring surgeries, pins. And then a staph infection swept in and brought sepsis with it. More treatment and another surgery.

Even nineteen-year-old dancers rarely make it all the way back from that. Rain's mother did not. She could walk, but there was a limp. On damp days, she had to use a cane or not go out in public. She stayed home on rainy nights. She could still dance, but only at weddings, and always with care. Ballet was out of the question.

That had been how Rain came into the world, like a driver of an out-of-control car smashing into innocent pedestrians. Her mother had lost her one chance. Rain and her father—because of his energetic sperm—thereafter shared the roles of the villain in an ongoing drama.

The twist was that her mother had enrolled Rain in dance classes nearly as soon as she could walk, and then became the worst possible stereotype of a domineering, hypercompetitive stage mother: bullying teachers, sneering at other children, waging war with other mothers. Somehow, though, it hadn't spoiled the dance experience for Rain. All she ever wanted to do was dance, and if Mom made that possible, that was fine. From about age eight onward, Rain understood, though, that her mother was trying to live vicariously through her. Whatever. That didn't matter much to Rain until her own pregnancy and her own delivery-room disasters.

After that? Without dance to bond them, they might as well have been strangers who barely noticed each other on the street. The level of warmth was about the same. Maybe a little less.

She gazed with longing at the dancers.

The instructor gave her a quick but guarded smile, clearly not recognizing her as a parent of any of the kids and not sure if she was a perspective student. Rain shook her head to indicate that she just wanted to watch. The instructor nodded, but there was a look of doubt on the woman's face. That happened a lot when people looked at Rain. They knew there was something wrong with her, something off. It was a bit of *the Other* that Rain knew always lived inside her.

When the woman wasn't looking, Rain stole three dance magazines from the table, shoved them into the bag with the Chinese food, and left. She had a stack of them in her closet, and she could kill an entire evening looking at the pictures and remembering the feel of the lifts, the leaps, the turns and twists and . . .

"God," she said, catching sight of herself in a store window. "You're so pathetic."

Bug greeted her with more enthusiasm than Rain felt she deserved—dogs were great for that. She checked the bathroom and under the bed. Nothing.

Then Rain realized that her ringer was off and she'd missed two texts. One text was from a collection agency—why on earth did they think she would respond to a text after all the calls she'd dodged?—and the other was from Joplin, who said he was going to be staying at his sister's place in the Village overnight and would call her tomorrow.

Rain looked at Bug. "Men suck, don't they?"

Bug gave her an enthusiastic wag. Rain gave her a cookie.

Rain wrapped herself in two quilts and binge-watched old episodes of *Dancing with the Stars* while she ate the Chinese food. Bug crawled under the blankets and kept Rain's feet warm. Rain ate everything she bought and felt fat and bloated and disgusting. But happy, too. And satisfied in a twisted way that she understood but had never been able to explain to her shrink. She knew that other women would get it, even women who weren't like her.

The bathroom door was closed. She got up three times and went in to check it. She took the knife with her. Bug did not accompany her. Each time, the bathroom was empty, and each time, that wasn't a comfort. She retreated to her nest of blankets, pressed her feet against Bug, and started another episode.

When her phone rang, she shrieked like a startled seagull. Bug leaped up and her muffled barks were loud, even under the covers. The ring seemed incredibly, weirdly strident, and for a moment Rain was afraid to look at the screen display, knowing that it would be *him*.

It wasn't. Nor was it Joplin. Instead of a name on the screen there was an icon of a yo-yo spinning on its string. Rain punched the button and lifted the phone to her ear.

"Yes?"

"Hey, girl," said the caller.

Rain closed her eyes and exhaled with relief. "Hey, Yo-Yo."

Yolanda Jablonski—Yo-Yo to everyone since she was in third grade—said, "You okay?"

"Huh? Sure, I guess. Why?"

Yo-Yo popped chewing gum. "You like totally blew us off yesterday."

Yesterday.

"Oh, shit, I'm sorry," Rain said quickly. She had promised to meet Yo-Yo and go to the NA meeting Friday evening, then go to the diner afterward. However, that—like everything belonging to Friday—had been blanked from her life. "Everything got messed up."

There was a pause. "When you say 'messed up' . . . ," said Yo-Yo slowly.

Here it goes, thought Rain.

"No," said Rain quickly. "It's not that. I didn't use."

"Girl, you'd better not be lying to me."

"I'm not." As she spoke, she broke open the fortune cookie that had come with the food. The little slip of paper read: *Life's too short to spend so much of it on your knees.*

Yo-Yo said, "Look, I just left the late meeting. Not at the church—the place near me. I got a text from the gang and the Bobs said they're heading over to the diner and want me to meet them. I said I'd call you. Why don't you come with? We can get pancakes. You cannot say no to pancakes. That's not allowed."

"I . . ."

"Hot maple syrup and way too much butter."

"Yo-Yo, I—"

"C'mon, Rain," said Yo-Yo, "just do it, okay?"

"I just ate. I'm stuffed."

"Stress eating has no calories. Fifteen minutes," said Yo-Yo. "I'll meet you outside your place."

The line went dead.

Rain set the phone down and looked around her apartment. It was ugly and small and cold, but it was her place. Until that morning, it had been her safe place. She cut a look in the direction of the bathroom.

Had been.

Then she remembered the little watch and went looking for it, found it on the floor by the hamper. It was such a delicate thing. There was no way to wind it, and she wondered if the keyhole on the back was used for that purpose. No key, though.

"That's about right," she said and put the watch on the bedside table. She put on fresh clothes—jeans, a royal-blue hoodie, and sneakers—and grabbed her everyday purse. It was big enough for her to put the knife, wrapped in a dish towel, inside with the handle up so she could grab it.

For what? asked her inner parasite, mocking her. *Stay home. If you go out with your friends, you'll tell.*

"Shut up," she said out loud.

He'll hurt you if you tell.

Rain did not answer, aloud or in her thoughts. Instead, she picked up the big bread knife, shook her head, and slid it back into its place in the butcher-block holder. Too big.

She took a steak knife with her instead and went out into the night to meet her friend.

INTERLUDE TWO
NARCOTICS ANONYMOUS MEETING

St. Jude's Catholic Church
Thirteen Months Ago

"There's more to the story, though," said Rain. She paused to take a breath, aware of how this was making her feel. Sharing was supposed to be a liberating experience, but her whole body felt tight and sore, and there was a fluttering inside her chest. "I've never really shared this part of it. Not in any of the meetings I've been to."

Some of the people in the audience perked up, interested now.

"You see," said Rain, "it was never an easy pregnancy. I mean . . . the baby was always healthy, but I wasn't. I got sick early on and had all kinds of problems. Infections, colds, circulation issues. Couple of times I blacked out and fell, tore some muscles. There was some internal bleeding. I kept getting dehydrated. Stabbing pains in my uterus, and all the other stuff. My blood pressure kept going up, too, and I had all sorts of heart problems. Arrhythmia and palpitations. Then I was diagnosed with preeclampsia. It was a mess. *I* was a mess. They kept telling me that I was young and strong and that the baby and I would get through it okay. My parents have money, and they made sure I saw all the best doctors."

The room was very quiet, but it felt too hot. Rain used her sleeve to wipe sweat from her eyes.

"Then my water broke. I panicked. Not because I was afraid of the process of giving birth but because I thought I'd do it wrong. That I'd somehow fail at something as natural as this."

The women in the room were staring at her, and Rain thought she could tell which of them were mothers and which weren't. There was a different energy in them, a different light in their eyes. Not necessarily a love light. It was more like the campfire glow of veterans from the same war. After all, everyone here was an addict, and their life choices had to have stained the lives of their kids. Had to.

Rain cleared her throat. "And I was afraid of what was going to happen after I gave birth. I was there to deliver the baby and then give it up for adoption. They hadn't even told me the sex, though I always knew— somehow knew—that he was a boy. A little boy. Noah's little boy. My little boy."

Dylan. She whispered it inside her head. *Sweet little Dylan.*

"I'd signed the papers," she said softly. "Taken the pre-birth counseling. I knew my parents would never want or love the baby. They are not . . . *warm* people. I'd been a disappointment to them long before I ever became a teen pregnancy statistic. Long before I ever began using." She shrugged and tried to play it as no big thing, but some of the older women in the audience gave her looks of disapproval. As if to say, *Own it.*

"I did not have the courage or the optimism to fight to keep my baby," she said, and saw some nods from the ones who understood. "I want to apologize to my baby, and I wanted witnesses to that. I needed people to understand that I was doing what I thought was right. That it wasn't me betraying my baby. That . . . I . . . I . . . oh, God . . ."

She did not feel her knees buckle, did not feel them hit the floor. There was no pain in her chest. People were suddenly rising, coming at her in a wave, and she was terrified. *They know now. They know what I did, and they're coming to make me pay.*

That was her thought as the darkness washed over her face and she fell into a big black hole.

Fell.

Fell.

It was not the first time Rain Thomas died.

CHAPTER EIGHTEEN

She saw Yo-Yo standing by a parked car, cigarette between her fingers, studying the world with calculating eyes.

Yo-Yo stood hipshot, with one arm across her waist and the elbow of the other resting on it, with the hand holding the cigarette folded back. She stood like that a lot, watching, knowing she was being watched, her eyes filled with challenge and bad promises to anyone who messed with her. Yo-Yo was nearly six feet tall, and a three-way racial split of Greenpoint Polish, Manhattan Heights Dominican, and the Chinatown in Flushing. Most people who looked at her guessed she was either black or a mix of black and Puerto Rican. She never corrected them. Her family tree was complicated, and Yo-Yo wasn't wanted by any of them.

She was ostensibly Rain's sponsor, though she preferred to call herself a "coach." Sometimes she was that, and sometimes she was a bully, and sometimes she was an ally. Yo-Yo had her own stuff, though, and Rain knew that just because her friend had five clean years didn't mean she was less a junkie. They would always be addicts. Always.

"Girl," said Yo-Yo, shaking her head, "you look like shit."

"Gosh, thanks."

Yo-Yo took a last drag and then flicked the cigarette away and chased it with an exhalation of blue smoke. Then she reached for Rain and pulled her into a hug. Yo-Yo was a hugger. Not with everyone, but with a certain few. Rain and the two Bobs. The four of them. The charter members of the Cracked World Society. That's what Gay Bob named it. It was a reference to an old Leonard Cohen song, about how it was okay that there were cracks in everything because without them the light couldn't get in. Straight Bob gave everyone a T-shirt once, but they were ugly and no one wanted to wear them. Not even Straight Bob.

"What's going on with you?" asked Yo-Yo.

"Bad couple of days."

"*How* bad?" asked Yo-Yo, leaning on it.

"I already told you, it's not that. I *haven't* used."

"Then what?" demanded Yo-Yo. "You break up with the boy toy?"

"His name is Joplin. And, no. Besides we're not an actual couple."

Yo-Yo made a face. "Yeah, yeah, just the longest running series of booty calls in the history of no-obligations, can't-commit sex."

"Stop it."

"He's got a nice ass, though," said Yo-Yo philosophically. "Really nice ass. If you ever kick him to the curb, I'd be happy to console him."

"We're not a thing. He's free to do whatever."

"Uh-huh," said Yo-Yo. "Well, if it's not painter boy, then what is it? You look like you got mugged and they weren't nice about it."

Rain tried to smile but it felt like a wince. "Close enough. Tell me, can life mug you?"

The taller woman snorted. "We're a couple of users going to meet a couple more users, and we all met in NA. Is that a serious question?"

"No." Rain looked around. The storm had stopped hours ago, but it was cold and muggy and the streets still glistened wetly. "It's been really weird lately, you know?"

"Weird how?"

Rain shook her head. "If I'm going to go over it, I need coffee."

They began walking. Most of the brownstones in her neighborhood were only half occupied, so only a few windows were lit. Rain felt the empty ones watching her. Cars moved up and down the street, their tires making hissing sounds on the wet asphalt. Yo-Yo had longer legs but she walked with a mincing step because she had on shoes that looked good but didn't feel good. Rain had no trouble keeping pace with her.

The usual neighborhood suspects loitered in doorways, hoods pulled up, hands in pockets, heads tracking to follow everything that moved. Some of them nodded to Rain; one guy called out a crude comment to Yo-Yo, but she fired back a suggestion that he go do something that was improbable, obscene, painful, and which involved close relatives and live-stock. The other gangbangers cracked up and gave their friend playful—but hard—punches and shoves, all of them accepting the fact that the tall black woman had clearly won that exchange.

A kid on a skateboard rolled past, his back turned to them and a hat pulled down low to cast his face in shadow. He wore a backpack that rattled with musical metallic sounds. Rain watched him, but the gangbangers ignored him as if he wasn't there.

Rain and Yo-Yo passed a long wooden fence that had been erected in front of the building that had burned down the previous month. Even after all this time, there was a heavy stink of wet charcoal and burned plastic. People had posted all kinds of posters and handbills on the wood, gluing, stapling, and tacking them up. A lot of religious ads for a new local church called the Lamenting Apostle, which Rain thought was a great name for a nineties post-punk band but a stupid name for a church. There was an hysterical spray-painted scrawl warning *The Shadow People Are Coming!*, and Rain figured it for either the rantings of one of the many, many local nutjobs or some kind of in-crowd code for something like an off-the-radar rave. There were ads for mattress blowout sales, a store that sold discontinued medical equipment, a company that bought any kind of gold, and a bail bondsman. There was a cluster of letter-sized *Have You Seen Me?* posters. Each one of those showed an unsmiling face, and Rain wondered why people didn't put smiling pictures on that stuff. Then she thought maybe people wouldn't scramble to find people who looked happy. She was almost past the sad array of pictures when she suddenly jerked to a stop and stared at one. It was a color picture of an old woman with a heavily lined face, sad eyes, horn-rim glasses, and hair pulled back into a gray bun.

Rain touched the picture and murmured, "What the . . . ?"

Yo-Yo walked three more steps before she realized what had happened, then turned and came back. When she saw the picture she said, "What's wrong? That one of the old broads who lives in your building?"

"No . . . I . . . wow, this is so weird."

"Everything's 'weird' to you today."

"It really is," insisted Rain. "But this is . . . well, this doesn't make any sense."

"What doesn't?"

"Yo, I know this woman. I mean, I saw her. *Talked* to her."

"Oh, damn, I didn't know she was a friend," said Yo-Yo quickly. "I'm sorry, girl."

"No, you don't understand, I met her today. This morning. On the train."

Yo-Yo frowned at the handbill. There was no date to say when she went missing and the paper was weathered by more than one rainfall. "I don't think so," she said. "These pictures have been up here for a couple of weeks."

"Not this one. It can't have been," insisted Rain and quickly related the encounter on the train. She dug a hand into her purse, rummaged around, and then brought it out, holding a pair of glasses. "See? They're the same. Look at the lens. See that little crack? It's exactly the same."

"Oh . . . shit," murmured Yo-Yo, taking the glasses. She cut a look at Rain. "This was today?"

They looked from the picture to the glasses in Yo-Yo's hand and back to the picture. The paper was stained by exhaust fumes, tattered by days or weeks of weather.

"That's some freaky-deaky shit right there," said Yo-Yo, handing the glasses back, almost forcing them into Rain's hand.

"What does it mean?"

"The hell should I know?" Yo-Yo pulled her cell phone out of her pocket and took several photos of the handbill, making sure to get clear shots of the old woman's face and zoom images of the glasses; then she took photos of the text. There wasn't much. *Have You Seen Me?* and a name, Dolores González; and below that a phone number with a Manhattan area code. They called the number and leaned together to listen to it ring. Six times, eight times. Ten. No answer.

Yo-Yo tore the handbill off the wall, folded it, and put it into her pocket.

While they stood there, too confused to say much, a big, old-fashioned car came rolling down the street, its windows so dark that they couldn't see who was inside. It slowed as it passed, creeping by as Rain and Yo-Yo turned to look at it. Then it moved along, picking up speed as it went. The car turned at the corner and was gone. The two women stood and looked at the empty corner. They both shivered, but neither noticed the other doing it.

"Come on," said Yo-Yo, taking Rain's hand. "Let's go find some light."

It was an odd bit of phrasing, and Yo-Yo paused, frowning at what she'd just said. Rain nodded, though. It made sense to her.

They hurried through the dark.

INTERLUDE THREE
NARCOTICS ANONYMOUS MEETING

St. Jude's Catholic Church
Thirteen Months Ago

Rain wondered if she should scream.

That seemed like the kind of thing someone should do when they fall off the edge of the world and plummet into the big dark. A scream. To let someone know how far she was falling.

She didn't scream. Couldn't. You need breath for that, and Rain did not think she had any. Not anymore. Her chest was still, her lungs sagging, her muscles going . . .

Dead?

Yes.

That was it, and she knew it.

Rain understood what that felt like.

It wasn't the first time she'd fallen like this. Though, admittedly, after all the bad things she had done over the last nine years, it was probably true that she was falling from a lesser height. The first time she'd been sixteen. She hadn't had enough time to rack up many sins. She'd slept with Noah once and never again. With the pill, she should never have gotten pregnant. But look at that—a miracle. Almost a virgin birth. There should be wise men and gifts and singing animals. Or something like that. There should have been a star in the sky.

As there had been when she died nine years ago.

It had been so bright, that star. Not stationary but pulsing. Steady and true.

A bright, shining star that burned above her in the darkness. So bright. So beautiful. Clean and pure. She'd remembered that.

That first fall had been on the day she had Dylan. Everything had gone wrong. The doctors later told her that it was an amniotic fluid embolism that resulted in cardiac arrest. Something Rain had never heard of. Something no one figured was a real threat in a healthy young girl.

She'd died with her baby still in her.

The doctors had cut Dylan out, but a C-section takes time. They had to use the paddles to bring her back. There were lights, too. Big ones. Like flashes from nuclear explosions, filling every part of her with light. If she had been awake, she would have been terrified that the electricity would have hurt her baby. The doctors had an answer for that, too. The jolts went in a straight line, directly to her heart. They did not touch her baby. That's what they said.

Rain knew they were wrong.

Dylan had felt those blasts. They'd done something to him. In that same moment, the pulsing light she saw changed. It became much more intense. Like a laser. No, like a searchlight in all that blackness.

Searching and finding her.

That's what saved her.

Her baby's soul, his heart light, was so bright, so steady that it showed her the way. It was what drew her up and gave her a direction in which to swim. And she had swum.

Up and up and up, gradually becoming aware of the pain as her nerve endings reignited. Aware of the indignities and violations of them cutting into her, stretching her wide, taking the baby.

In the darkness, Rain had felt him go. Felt him taken away. Felt the cold bite as they cut the umbilical cord.

It was the worst thing she had ever felt. For a moment, just a moment, she had almost stopped swimming. Almost let herself drift down into the painless, bottomless darkness.

She didn't, though.

Dylan had called her back. He wanted her to be alive. She'd followed him back from death.

That was then. Nine years ago.

Now she was falling into darkness again, but there was no heart-light to show her the way.

There were the drugs they shot into her. There was the false light of defib machines. Those were the things that brought her back. Not coaxed her, not led her. They dragged her back.

Inside of all the noise of EMTs and doctors and nurses and machines, there was her mother's voice, clear as day, maybe talking to a doctor, maybe on the cell phone to a friend. Saying, "God help me, but maybe it's for the best."

She woke in the hospital three days later and felt the total absence of Dylan. The complete and utter aloneness. And the knowledge that two years into being clean, all her escape hatches—LSD, VOID, crack cocaine—were all welded shut.

That was thirteen months ago. Rain had gotten out of the hospital, gotten well, gotten stronger, went back to meetings, lived her life. She did not use, but God oh God how she wanted to. And Doctor Nine was always there, just beyond her line of sight, waiting, smiling, patient.

CHAPTER NINETEEN

There were several diners in that part of Brooklyn, with names like Lucky Pete's, Stella's, American Dollar. But this one was just the Diner.

That's what it had on a neon sign above the door. As far as Straight Bob was concerned—and he purported himself to be a serious expert on diners from sea to shining sea—it was a classic example of the type. A big wraparound counter with a break in the middle for the entrance to the kitchen. Red Naugahyde covers on the seats. Menu signs with white plastic letters on black felt. A row of hot plates for coffeepots. Ancient miniature jukeboxes at each booth, though none of them had worked for as long as Rain could remember. The singles on offer were for the latest releases by David Bowie, Prince, Whitney Houston, Michael Jackson, and Amy Winehouse. Like that. No one who was still alive. Rain knew that wasn't intentional, but it worked out that way. Sometimes she thought it was retro cool, and sometimes it was just plain creepy.

The Bobs were seated at the big booth in the back. Yo-Yo slid in next to Gay Bob and Rain sat across from them.

"Wow," said Straight Bob, giving Rain an up and down, "what's with you? You look like shit."

"You're one to talk."

"I always look like this," said Straight Bob. "What's your excuse?"

"Been a weird day," said Rain.

"Good weird or bad weird?" asked Gay Bob, but before Rain could answer, the waitress appeared. She did that. One second she wasn't there and the next she was.

Her name was Betty, and it was Straight Bob's assertion that all diners should have a waitress named Betty. Or Babs. Maybe Brenda or Bernadette. Something with a B. This one was a Betty, and she was every bit as much a classic as the diner, with mountains of frosted hair sprayed into submission, a huge matronly bosom, half-moon glasses perched on the bridge of too much nose, and really good legs for a middle-aged woman who was on them all day. Couple of pins on her uniform—cats, dragonflies. Once in a while she'd switch them to something seasonal. Christmas tree or a Halloween jack-o'-lantern. Lipstick in a medium red shade that was never sexy or pushy, and a perfume that wasn't expensive but nice to smell.

"Getcha?" asked Betty, holding up a pad and pen.

"Coffee," said Yo-Yo, but Betty gave her a "no shit" look. "And pancakes with hot maple syrup, bananas, and walnuts. Oh, and bacon. Crisp. I don't like it limp."

"None of us do, honey," said Betty, and Gay Bob grinned and held a fist out for a bump. Betty withered him with a raised eyebrow, and he took his hand back. Betty turned to Rain. "And for you?"

Rain was about to order an omelet and then realized that she'd burned through most of her budget on the Chinese food. But Gay Bob came to her rescue.

"Dinner's on me tonight, kids," he announced. Gay Bob had money from a slip-and-fall lawsuit, and he liked spreading it around. Everyone at

71

the table tried their best to pretend to say no, but they caved very quickly. Rain ordered her omelet with mushrooms and spinach, turkey sausage, and potatoes. Straight Bob ordered a second short stack, having already finished the first. Straight Bob had a comfortable belly and liked to keep it entertained.

Betty went away, and Straight Bob held up a hand for silence until they heard the waitress bellow the order through the little serving window.

"Nice," he said.

Straight Bob and Gay Bob were regulars at the local meetings. They were completely different from each other in virtually every way except that they were both Bobs. Not Roberts, Robs, Bobbies, or any other variation. It was a thing with them. Just like Rain was not Lorraine or Lori. She was Rain, a name she'd started calling herself in kindergarten.

Straight Bob was short, round, balding, mildly pedantic, and kind. He was a knower of things. He knew about diners, about trains—real and HO scale—classic cars, folk music, the history of guitars, the complete biographies of each of the Beatles, Beat generation literature—he could recite "Howl" from memory—and dozens of other subjects. Rain sometimes wondered if he was somewhere on the spectrum. He had moderately good social skills when he wasn't going through one of his increasingly frequent bouts of depression. He was obsessive with learning everything about any subject that interested him; and it was important to him that he knew more about those subjects than anyone else.

Gay Bob was a completely different physical type. He was tall, lean, muscular, and a fitness freak. He had a great body, and Yo-Yo once confided that if Gay Bob wasn't gay she'd have "climbed him like a rock wall." Rain could appreciate that. Gay Bob had a waist as narrow as Joplin's but shoulders a mile wide, but he wasn't bulked up like a muscle freak. More like one of those Olympic swimmers. Great skin, too, gorgeous blue eyes, and a smile that made people of both orientations want to disrobe. Not that he played on that much. He wasn't exactly celibate, but he wasn't actively on the hunt. He worked as a bouncer at Pornstash, which was a glam bar for the leather crowd, and on his off hours, he was trying to be a novelist. He wrote decent song lyrics, but his prose—those sections Rain had been allowed to read—was god-awful. Gay Bob thought he was writing a novel that would be short-listed for everything from *The New York Times* to the Pulitzers. Rain was a lot less sure about that.

Both of them were train wrecks, though, for whom the meetings and, more important, the Cracked World Society was as much social as survival. Gay Bob was sixteen months clean from a five-year-long fight with painkillers. He'd been hooked on OxyContin after his slip and fall, and the addiction had cost him a longtime relationship and a good-paying job as a fitness coach. His depression was less obvious and more insidious than Straight Bob's, because Gay Bob had more practiced social skills and could convince nearly everyone, and sometimes himself, that he was cool, collected, and ready to move forward with his life. Rain had spent a lot of nights taking long and directionless walks with him, talking about different kinds of highs and how much easier it would be to step off the sobriety ledge. She knew how close to that edge he was.

For his part, Straight Bob had gotten into speed and graduated to cocaine. At meetings, he spoke with that unique pride of the recovering addict of how he'd put $350,000 up his nose over the years. It cost him his marriage, a good job as an actuary, and all meaningful connections with his two grown children. He was not invited to family gatherings, and even his Christmas and birthday presents were returned unopened. He'd been in and out of rehab eleven times but was now closing in on his one-year chip. However, he saw a therapist three times a week following a court mandate after his last near miss with suicide.

Both Bobs were struggling. So was Yo-Yo. So was she. Being in recovery did not, and could not, mean that there was true recovery at the end. It doesn't work like that. The addiction was hardwired into each of them, and often a dangerous depression lurked like cancer beneath the skin. It was one thing to be brave and righteous at a meeting, but then they each went home to the wreckage of their lives. Rain knew that it sometimes felt like it would be easier to stop trying to repaint the walls and just burn the house down. Depression was always there, and sometimes it was a more devoted companion than anyone else. Sucked, but there it was.

Betty brought the coffee. Rain cupped her hands around the heavy white porcelain mug, holding it close to inhale the warm vapor.

"Rain, my dear," said Straight Bob, "are you going to tell us why you give every indication of having been dragged by your heels down a flight of stairs?"

They all looked at her.

"Believe me, guys, if I tell you what happened to me today, you'll think I'm crazy," she said.

Gay Bob made a face. "Too late for that, sweetie. In terms of sanity, your ship sailed a long time ago, hit an iceberg, caught fire, and sank."

Yo-Yo punched his arm. "Don't joke."

"Who's joking? I mean, let's face it, none of us are wired all that tight."

Rain shook her head. "No, I said it wrong. If I tell you what happened, you'll think I've been using."

"*Have* you been?" asked Straight Bob.

"No. But I want to," said Rain. "After the day I had . . . I really want to."

They sat with that, each of them afraid of the statement, each of them nodding because it was inarguable.

Gay Bob gave her a sad, sweet smile. "Then I guess you'd better tell us about your day."

CHAPTER TWENTY

She told them everything.

Almost.

She did not tell them about Doctor Nine. Or mention him in any way. Everything about him was edited out. She started with thinking there was someone in her shower and ended with the missing persons poster and the glasses. Yo-Yo produced her phone and let the Bobs scroll through the photos of the old woman. They all did a close inspection of the glasses in the pictures and the glasses Rain handed to them. Yo-Yo produced the folded handbill and spread it flat on the table. It was at that point that Rain saw the expressions on the faces of the Bobs change from tolerant acceptance of a troubled friend to confused disbelief to a final acceptance of the inexplicable.

Straight Bob held the glasses up and studied them from every possible angle.

"They're the same ones," he declared, and everyone nodded.

"How, though?" asked Gay Bob. He tapped the handbill. "I mean, isn't it more likely that the storm made this look older than it is?"

"No," said Rain and Yo-Yo at the same time.

"No way this went up today after you saw her," he declared. "I bet it's been on that wall for weeks. Maybe a month."

"Well," said Yo-Yo, "doesn't that mean that they *found* the old lady after this was posted? If Rain saw her on the train this morning, then she has to be back. People go missing and get found all the time, especially old people. Maybe she's senile or has, like, dementia or something?"

"I was sitting on the aisle seat," said Rain. "She would have had to get up past me."

"And you only saw the boy out of the broken part of that one lens?" asked Straight Bob. He picked up the glasses and put them on and clicked his eyes back and forth. "There's a little distortion because that piece of lens is out of true, but I don't see anything weird."

"I did," insisted Rain.

"My eye keeps trying to focus on both sides of the crack," mused Straight Bob. "Uncomfortable. Maybe the old lady was okay passing them on because they were broken."

Rain shook her head.

Gay Bob took them next. "Let me look." He looked around, winced, and removed them. "Wow . . . total distortion. It's a great way to get a cheap high."

"If you don't mind migraines," suggested Straight Bob.

"So basically a cheap high for masochists," mused Gay Bob. "I know people."

He handed them to Yo-Yo, who recoiled as she put the glasses on and took them off right away. "Ouch! Felt like my left eye was being spooned out of my head."

Rain took the glasses back and held them. "So what's it all mean?"

Gay Bob cocked an eyebrow. "Why don't *you* put them on? Tell us what you see."

"Don't," blurted Yo-Yo. Everyone turned to her. "I . . . sorry. I just don't think you should."

"Why not?" asked Straight Bob.

"I . . . don't know. It creeps me out, is all."

Rain put them on anyway. There was no real pain, but her left eye had trouble focusing. She looked around the diner and saw Betty pouring coffee for one of the mechanics, the cook reaching out to set a couple of plates on the counter. Normal stuff. A woman with curly black hair, dressed in a soiled nurse's uniform, sat in a booth off to the left, away from everyone else, discreetly nursing her baby under a blanket. Two hipsters were looking at something on an iPad and snickering. All completely normal. No little boy, no old woman.

No Doctor Nine.

She took the glasses off and put them back into her purse.

"Okay," she said, "so maybe this is me being crazy, or maybe it's a flashback from my old Void days. It still doesn't explain how I missed all of Friday. It's like Friday didn't even happen for me."

No one had an answer for her, and that ended the night for them. They were talked out but hadn't gotten anywhere. The Bobs looked confused; Yo-Yo still seemed oddly nervous, though she tried to pass it off as the effects of a long day and a crazy story and some PMS. Gay Bob had paid the bill, and they headed toward the door. Outside, the heavy humidity had coalesced into a dense fog.

"Swell," complained Yo-Yo.

They filed out with Rain trailing, and as she reached back to pull the door closed behind her, Rain caught the eye of the nurse with the baby. The woman had very green eyes. Cat green. A slow smile formed on the nurse's face. All Rain could see of the baby was a single tiny pink hand reaching up to grab the frilly ruff around the edge of the reclining seat.

Rain paused, looking from the smile to the hand to the smile and back to the hand. It may have been a trick of the light, or of the distortion of the heavy glass in the front door of the diner, but that little hand seemed to be clutching the ruff so hard the dimpled knuckles were white. The nurse brushed black curls from her forehead, then bent and arranged the covers so that the hand vanished from sight. As she did that, she never stopped smiling.

"You coming?" asked Yo-Yo, breaking the spell of the moment. Rain blinked and looked back. The nurse was looking at the pale screen of an e-book reader.

Rain almost told the others about what she thought she'd seen, but didn't. She'd already told them too much, and her friends, cynical and wary as NA veterans often are, were already giving her strange looks. So she left it. Trick of the light, she thought, end of a bad, crazy day. Only that.

She turned away and hurried to catch up with her friends.

INTERLUDE FOUR
NARCOTICS ANONYMOUS MEETING

St. Jude's Catholic Church
Eleven Months Ago

"Hi. My name is Rain, and I'm an addict."

They all said, "Hi, Rain!"

"I guess most of you know I've been away for a while. I think about half of you were here when I last got up to share. That was a show, right?"

A few people laughed. Not real laughs, though.

"For those who weren't or who don't know what happened," Rain said, "I had a heart attack right here on this spot. Yup, there was me actually dead. Right here." Rain moved to where her body had fallen. The newbies in the crowd craned forward as if they could somehow see the ghost of her crumpled body there at the feet of the living woman who'd gotten up to share. "But the funny thing is . . . it's not the first time I died."

Every pair of eyes in the place snapped toward her.

"When I had a heart attack here," said Rain, "the lady who used to run this meeting did CPR and then the EMTs came and shocked me back. The first time, though, there was a light and I followed it. That's what saved me. Not the doctors. That light. I think the light was my baby."

In her head, the parasite snickered in a voice that sounded more like Doctor Nine's. The hinges on the Box of Rain creaked. A pin drop would have sounded like a piece of heavy pipe crashing to the ground.

Rain turned to her friends. Yo-Yo turned away, looking embarrassed.

Straight Bob studied the hands he had folded in his lap. Only Gay Bob stared straight at her and nodded. A small nod, but there. It helped. Rain took her lifelines wherever she could get them.

"I think the light I saw," Rain began awkwardly, "was my baby's heart. Alive. Beating. For me. I know it sounds goofy. It sounds like I was tripping, but no. I wasn't using back then. Not yet. Not while I was pregnant." She sniffed and fished for a tissue, wiped her nose. "I think it was my baby, the baby a monk in Central Park told me was *special*. A baby that I was supposed to take care of. I think it was my baby calling for his mother. For me. Calling me back from the dark. Helping me find my way back to being alive."

She blotted the tears in her eyes.

"And I came back. Wasn't easy. I'd already gone a long way, you know? I came back for my son. My baby saved me. My baby brought me back. Don't ask me how because I don't know, and I don't think it's some Disney happy ending shit. This wasn't a Hallmark special. It's not the feel-good movie of the season. 'Cause you know why?"

There were too many tears for the sodden tissue.

"Because you know how I repaid my baby for saving me and pulling me out of the dark?" She looked around, and she knew her eyes were wild. Her heart hurt in her chest, but not like she was having another heart attack. No, it hurt because it was breaking in a fresh, new place, cracking off from the fragile spots where it had begun to heal. "I still gave my baby up for adoption. After all that, I gave him up."

She looked out at the faces. Saw shock, saw horror, saw those who nodded because they saw that ending coming.

"I saw my baby for one second. It was after my heart attack, after the C-section. They revived me, but I was still half-dead. Everything was messed up. Too much noise, people yelling, my mother staring at me. Don't know why they hadn't thrown her out. Maybe they forgot she was there, or maybe seeing her was more of me being screwed up. Everything was broken and wrong. The only thing I remember with perfect clarity was my baby. He was still there. They hadn't taken him out yet. Maybe it was because it all happened so fast. My mother later told me that the nurses had taken him away before I ever woke up. They all said my baby wasn't in the room when they revived me." Rain took a breath, held it, blew out her cheeks, and shook her head. "I know he was there. I *know* it. No one will ever be able to tell me different. I saw my baby open his eyes and look at me. We looked at each other. Do you understand? We *saw* each other. And . . . and . . . I gave my baby a name. I told him his name."

Yo-Yo and the others exchanged confused glances and then turned back to Rain.

"We had that one moment. I never told anyone else that I named my baby. No one. And I won't mention his name now, either. It's a secret, and I've kept it all these years, and I guess I'll always keep it. I don't expect anyone else to understand why that's important. It's mine to know." She paused, sniffed, tried to smile. "I used to think that if I ever met him again, no matter where he grew up or even if the people who raised him never told him that he was adopted, that he would know who I was. And I'd know him. All either one of us had to say was his name. And he'd know. Even if the adopting parents gave him a new one and raised him as someone else. He'd know and I'd know. That was part of our secret. We'd both know. I made that promise to him. In that one moment, I gave him his true name and made that promise. Then they took him away while the doctors were still not sure if I was even going to live. I saw my son for one second. One fucking second. And then he was gone."

Rain stood there, trembling, as naked as a person could be.

"I got out of the hospital three days later. I never saw my son again," she said. "The day I got out was the day I started using."

CHAPTER TWENTY-ONE

They stopped by Straight Bob's car to finish talking. As always, the group lingered past the point of useful conversation. Rain knew that the others were as reluctant to go home to empty apartments as she was. That's how it worked. Companionship was a kind of drug; you take painkillers until the pain stops.

Gay Bob was telling a story about a tourist who came into Pornstash to use the bathroom without knowing what kind of bar it was. The tourist was from somewhere in the Bible Belt and apparently thought he'd stepped into one of the outer rings of hell. "He stood there twitching and twisting, needing to pee so bad he was ready to burst but terrified of going into the bathroom. Not sure what he thought would happen. Maybe he figured we'd gangbang the straight out of him or something."

"Probably thinks you can catch being gay from a toilet seat," suggested Yo-Yo.

They all laughed, though Rain's attention was split, as she saw the nurse come backing out of the diner, pulling the stroller. A car idled at the curb, but it was blocked by a parked panel truck. All Rain could see was the back of a man in a black topcoat bend and take the baby from the stroller and wait while the nurse collapsed the device. The man held the baby oddly, though, using his hands to cradle it but keeping the baby away from his body. She'd seen some people do that before, of course; people who didn't know how to hold a baby. This looked different; and even though she couldn't see the man's face, there was a sense of revulsion in his stiff posture. As if he did not like touching this child. Or any child. The nurse took the baby from him and cuddled it, then disappeared as she ducked into the car. The man put the folded stroller in the trunk, then vanished as he walked around to the other side. There was a *chunk-chunk* of doors closing. A moment later, the car rolled quietly past where Rain and her friends stood. She stared at it. It was the same old-fashioned car that had driven slowly past her and Yo-Yo earlier.

Rain tapped Straight Bob's arm. "What kind of car is that?"

Straight Bob stared at it, eyes wide, mouth agape as the car went past. "Holeeee shit. That's an absolutely mint Cadillac Series 80 V-12 Fleetwood-bodied town cabriolet. A 368-cubic-inch engine and 150 horsepower."

Gay Bob nudged Yo-Yo. "I think he just came in his pants."

"Maybe I did," said Straight Bob, leering at the car.

"Hey, wait a sec," said Yo-Yo. "Rain, honey, isn't that the same one we saw earlier?"

"I think so," Rain agreed. "I mean, how can there be two like that?"

The car vanished into the pale gloom, whipping curtains of heavy mist around it like something out of a horror movie. They all stood watching the empty street as if expecting something else to happen. There was nothing left to say about anything, so they shared hugs and split. Gay Bob jogged off. Straight Bob drove home alone after having his offer of a ride declined by the women. Yo-Yo walked with Rain because her place was that way.

When Straight Bob's taillights faded into the mist, Yo-Yo gave a sad shake of her head. "You heard what happened, right?"

"No, what?" asked Rain.

"His ex-wife's getting remarried. She's moving to Akron, and the youngest son is going with her."

"Oh, shit."

"And you know the older one hasn't spoken to him in like forever."

They glanced back at the empty night where Straight Bob had vanished.

"Getting worried about that boy," said Yo-Yo.

"Uh-huh," agreed Rain, though she was worried about all her friends.

The two women began walking. "Tell you something, girlfriend," said Yo-Yo philosophically. "When you get weird on us, you really bring game."

"Gee, thanks."

Following a long, thoughtful silence, Rain asked, "Hey, Coach . . . how worried should I be right now? With Friday and all that stuff today?"

After a few steps, Yo-Yo said, "It's something to think about. Maybe talk to someone about."

"Yeah, maybe," said Rain. "I can't help thinking about it, but I don't know how to think about it. Does that make sense?"

"Nothing makes sense tonight," said Yo-Yo.

Rain was about to reply when Yo-Yo suddenly slowed and pointed.

"Hey, is that Joplin's building?" she asked.

Up ahead, the lights inside the mist had changed, shifting from the distorted hues of headlight white and brake-light red to a dark purple that pulsed and slashed back and forth. It took Rain a few more steps to realize that the color was a blend of the blue and red of emergency lights.

Police lights.

And ambulance lights.

CHAPTER TWENTY-TWO

They ran as fast as Yo-Yo's shoes would allow, and with each step, forms appeared and defined themselves in the mist. The hulking shapes of police cars and an ambulance. Crowds of people. Whatever was happening centered around the brownstone where Joplin lived, two doors down from Rain's. She tried to find him in the crowd, but he wasn't there, and panic sparked in her chest.

She got her cell out and punched his number and got voice mail. "You've reached Scot Joplin. One *T*, no relation. I'm either not here or not all here, so leave some words and numbers and I'll get back to you."

Rain turned away, pressed a palm to her other ear, and half bent to find a bubble of relative quiet in all the din. "Joplin, I'm outside of your place and something's happening. There are cops and ambulances and all that. I hope you're okay. Please give me a call as soon as you get this."

As she hung up, she remembered that he was supposed to be in the city for something related to his paintings, staying at his sister's. She hoped so.

Rain and Yo-Yo drifted to the edge of the crowd and stood watching as a pair of burly EMTs carried a stretcher out of the front door and down the steps. The wheels dropped down, and the EMTs rolled it toward the ambulance. No one seemed to be in much of a hurry. Strapped to the gurney was a black rubber body bag.

"Ah, jeez," breathed Yo-Yo.

The EMTs passed within ten feet of them. Rain stared at the body, at its shape, and at its length.

"God, Yo, I think that's a kid," she murmured.

Yo-Yo gripped Rain's wrist. "Someone you know?"

Rain tried to think if there were any kids in Joplin's building. She barely paid attention to her own neighbors and couldn't come up with many faces or names or identities of the people here.

"No," she said. "No, I don't know . . ." Her sentence drifted off. Neither of them said another word, though, as they watched the EMTs load the body into the back of the ambulance. The crowd also fell silent as they, too, saw and understood what was happening. As the doors chunked shut, one EMT, a woman, looked over her shoulder in Rain's direction. Rain stiffened. The woman looked almost exactly like the nurse from the diner. Same face, same black curly hair, same cat-green eyes, same dark red lipstick. It was unlikely, even impossible. It couldn't be the same woman. Except that Rain knew it was. Just as she knew who it was.

It was *his* nurse.

It was her. The woman who had . . .

Rain's mind ground to a halt, gears stripped, engine blown, tires flat.

The nurse.

Long ago, after Rain had given birth to Dylan, after the terrible trauma of that birth. After the surgery and everything else, she'd had that one dream. Or hallucination. Or vision. Or . . . had she actually seen it? Doctor Nine and this woman, the doctor's nurse, holding her baby. Holding Dylan. Taking him away. Doing things to him. Owning him.

On impulse, Rain removed the old woman's glasses from her purse and slipped them on, angling her body so that Yo-Yo wouldn't see what she was doing. The EMT was gone from sight, though, having gone around to the driver's side of the ambulance. Rain scanned the crowd, not knowing what she was looking for or if she was doing anything at all except feeding her own parasite. There was a clatter behind her, and she looked over her shoulder to see a kid get onto a skateboard and roll away from the lights and crowd. She recognized the backpack and tried to remember where she'd seen him before. Earlier that night? A local kid? She wasn't sure. Some small thing, almost a thought, tickled her, but it was gone in an instant and she turned away.

The crowd looked like every other crowd gathered to witness pain. They might have come from central casting for any TV or movie scene of people watching a fire, a cleanup after a drive-by, or something like this. Death. The faces were mostly blank, and in the strange light, everyone's eyes looked black and as dead as mannequin eyes.

Out of the corner of her eye, through the slice of glass on the outside half of the left lens, Rain saw something that caught and held her interest. On the far side of where the emergency vehicles were clustered, a man and boy stood near the edge of the crowd. They were about a yard away from the next closest person, as if they did not want to be part of a crowd, or as if they could not be. A crazy thought, but it popped into Rain's head.

The man wore dark glasses despite the fog and the night.

The boy stood with his head bowed as if looking at something on the ground in front of his feet. She couldn't see his features at all, and the flashing emergency lights splashed him in red and blue over and over again. He looked to be about ten. The same age he'd appeared to be on the street in Manhattan that morning. If it was even the same boy. If that was even possible.

Looking through the cracked lens made Rain's head ache. She felt a tingle in her nose and touched her nostrils, expecting to see blood, but there was nothing.

The boy suddenly looked up and turned this way and that, searching the crowd. He did not look directly at Rain, but she could see that he had a strange expression on his face. Confusion was part of it, but there was a feral anger that was palpable. The round face was dirty, bruised, and hostile. There were greasy food stains on his cheeks and shirt as if he ate like an animal, rough and selfish and too fast. There was something else, too. Even though Rain did not get a good look directly into the boy's eyes, there was a light there. Small, faint, flickering. But there.

Still there, murmured one of her inner voices.

On the heels of that whisper, Rain thought she could hear the chains on the Box of Rain begin to groan as if something bad inside was trying very hard to get out. Or was nearly out. She shivered.

"Yo," she breathed, "do you see that guy with the kid?"

Yo-Yo glanced at her and then followed the line of her gaze. "What guy? Oh, wait. The tall man wearing sunglasses?"

"You see him?"

"Sure, why?"

Rain grabbed her friend's wrist. "Do you see the kid?"

"Sure, but . . . hey, *ow!*" Yo-Yo stiffened. "Wait that's the kid you've been seeing?"

Rain's mouth went totally dry, and her heart beat so hard and fast that it made her feel like she was going to faint. Or have another heart attack. The man placed his hands on the boy's shoulder. He wore thick winter gloves even though it wasn't cold enough for them. He smiled and turned away, pulling the little boy after him. They were gone from sight in an instant.

Yo-Yo started forward as if she were going to follow him, but Rain caught her by the elbow and pulled her back. "Don't."

They looked at each other, and instead of asking why, Yo-Yo nodded.

Then she frowned. "Hey," she said, "your nose is bleeding."

CHAPTER TWENTY-THREE

It wasn't a bad nosebleed, but it took time and ice and patience to stop it.

Yo-Yo escorted Rain to her apartment, but when Rain told her that it was okay, that she didn't need to stay, her friend left with only a small pretense of opposition. She apologized for flaking out, but Rain all but shoved her out the door. They both needed to be alone, to end the evening, to go process it all and make decisions about what they understood and believed. Rain got all of that and so, it seemed, did Yo-Yo. The nosebleed was slowing anyway, and it was late.

Bug was freaked out by the smell of blood, and she danced and barked and got in the way. Eventually, the dog calmed and watched with great interest as Rain went through the familiar steps of dealing with a nosebleed. Rain sat up straight with her head tilted slightly forward; she used her thumb and forefinger to pinch the soft part of her nose shut. When it slowed even more, she got an ice pack and pressed it to her face with one hand while pinching with the other. She held it all in place for ten minutes, timing herself by the clock on her phone. When she removed the pack and unpinched her nose, there was no renewed flow.

"Good," Rain told Bug. "See? Mommy has it all covered."

Bug wagged her tail and went over to stand beside her empty food bowl. Rain fed her, then got cleaned up. She opened her laptop and clicked one of her playlists on iTunes. Beyoncé began singing about kicking some guy's ass for being a two-timing dick. Rain did the dishes and looked around for something else to do. It was a small place, so there wasn't much room to putter, but she kept at it because doing mindless busywork like straightening magazines and watering her two anemic houseplants was better than thinking about the little boy in the body bag.

It was like trying not to think of elephants.

Harder. Worse.

The man with the dark glasses leered at her from the shadows every time she closed her eyes. She wanted the boy, the one with the man, to look at her, but he never did. Not down on the street and not in her imagination. Who was he? *Why* was he showing up in her hallucinations? Or visions . . . or whatever they were.

She'd started having terrifying visions before she even started drugs. They were one of the reasons she got high in the first place. The first one came to her while she lay in her hospital bed and watched the steady swirl of activity on her floor through the window. She hadn't had a window like that in her real room, but she did in the dream. If it was a dream. Through it, Rain could see the nurses' station and one of the elevator doors. In the dream, she was very sick. Not merely tired and sore from the long hours of labor, the heart attack, the C-section, and the rest. No, in that dream, Rain was dying, wasting away and nearly gone. As she lay there fighting to breathe, trying to stay alive, she watched the people beyond the glass; saw how alive they were. Working, talking, laughing. Each of them with a future. All of them ignoring her.

Then a doctor in a white lab coat walked past. He was tall and thin and wore . . .

. . . black . . .
. . . sunglasses . . .

The doctor stopped and turned slowly toward her. He was smiling. Of course he was. Doctor Nine *always* smiled. He gestured to someone Rain could not see, and a moment later, a nurse stepped into view and stood beside him. His nurse. *The* nurse. Black curls and green eyes. She carried a newborn in her arms. The baby was naked, still smeared with the red viscous muck of delivery. He was squirming and crying—screaming, really—but no one else out there seemed to notice or care. No one turned to look at the baby or at the nurse, who was holding him like he was hers. Doctor Nine stood apart, his smile flickering into distaste every time he looked at the infant.

"No," whispered Rain.

The doctor cupped a hand behind his ear, his face contorting like a mime pretending to listen. Comical in all the wrong ways. His expression encouraged her to speak up, to repeat herself.

"*No!*" she cried.

His smile got wider.

"*Let me have my baby!*" wailed Rain.

The doctor looked surprised and pointed from her to the screaming baby and back, eyebrows rising above the rims of his sunglasses in inquiry, as if to ask, *Is this yours?*

"Please, give me back my baby. I didn't mean to . . . I don't want to let you have him. Please," she wept, "I take it back. Let me have my baby. . . ."

The doctor turned to the nurse and gestured for her to give the baby back. She looked at him and then at Rain. Without taking her eyes off of the teenage girl in the bed, the nurse bent and licked the child's face. She did it slowly, unrolling a wide, pink tongue and drawing it across the baby's face.

Rain screamed.

The nurse continued to lick, her tongue flicking and slurping up the blood, cleaning it all from the tiny child's cheeks and nose and forehead and . . .

Rain's throat suddenly locked tight as a fist around the next scream. With each lick, as the blood was cleaned away, the child's *features* vanished, too. Soon there was nothing left except skin that was as smooth and featureless as a lump of plastic. No . . . it was the unhealthy pallor of a worm.

The scream burned in her chest, needing to spill out, needing to shatter the window glass so she could grab her baby and . . .

The smooth pallor changed with a final lick across the lower part of the baby's face. Instead of nothing, now there was a long, curved, red line. Like a wound, except that it did not bleed. Worse, it opened to reveal teeth—tiny and white and wet. The lips of the wound became the lips of a new and alien mouth. A familiar mouth, though in miniature. The baby—her baby?—smiled in perfect harmony with Doctor Nine. Exactly the same except for scale.

The rest of the baby's face was still blank, and all that Rain could see was that dreadful smile.

Doctor Nine touched his fingers to his lips and blew Rain a kiss. He turned away and nodded for the nurse, who lingered a moment longer, her lips smeared with blood and mucus. Then she licked the gore from her lips and swallowed, her eyes fluttering as if the taste of it drove her to the edge of orgasm. Then she, too, turned away, taking the baby with her, leaving Rain to finally release that scream.

She felt her heart break. She felt her hope for her child crack and fall away in brittle pieces. That's how she thought of it. Hope as a fragile and vulnerable thing, cracking apart. Not all of it, though. If it all went, she wouldn't have felt anything or cared at all. A little hope remained, and it was as sharp as broken glass. It cut into her heart and did not budge except to cut deeper.

The drugs she had been taking when she had that dream, the ones prescribed for her by caring doctors, kept her trapped, and it replayed the dream over and over again.

Hell must be like that.

When they released her from the hospital, Rain went looking for a different kind of high. Anything that would take her mind completely out of gear. Void did it, but there were dangers there, too. Crack was her salvation for a lot of years. Now she was clean, and she had no defenses at all for the dreams when they came.

And the dreams came every night.

CHAPTER TWENTY-FOUR
IN DREAMS

Rain often dreamed of a little girl named Bethy. She was sure there had never been such a child in her own life. Only in dreams.

That night, she dreamed of Bethy again. It was a kind of dream she often had, unfolding in sections, like chapters in a book. If she woke up, the dream would be waiting for her when she fell asleep again. Not always the very next night, but soon. Inevitably, soon . . .

Bethy sat awake nearly all night watching Millie die.

She thought it was quite beautiful. In the way spiders are beautiful. The way a mantis is beautiful when it mates and feeds. If her sister thought it was something else . . . well, so what? Bethy and Millie had never seen eye to eye, not once unless Bethy was lying about it. Bethy was a very good liar. All it took was practice. It was a game they had started playing just a couple of hours after they all got home from camping. Mom and Dad were already asleep in their room, and Bethy had convinced Millie that it would be fun to stay up and pretend that they were still camping, still lost in the big, dark woods.

Millie thought that would be fun, too. Millie was easy to lead, though she truly had a completely different sense of what was fun. Millie thought Poké-mon was fun. Millie liked her Barbies unscarred and her Ken dolls unmelted. Millie liked live puppies. Millie was blind to the sound of blood, the song of blood.

Bethy said that they could pretend that Doctor Nine was going to come and tell them spooky campfire stories. Dad's big flashlight was their campfire. Millie, sweet and pretty in her flannel robe with the cornflower pattern, her fuzzy slippers, agreed to the game even though she thought that Doctor Nine was a dumb name for an imaginary friend. Well, to be fair, she truly did think that Doctor Nine was imaginary and that Bethy had no actual friends.

The clock on the wall was a big black cartoon cat with eyes that moved back and forth and a tail that swished in time. Millie loved that, too. She called it Mr. Whiskers and would tell time according to what the cat said. "Mr. Whiskers says it's half past six!"

Mr. Whiskers was counting out the remaining minutes of Millie's life, and wasn't that fun, too?

Bethy looked at the clock and saw that nearly an hour had gone by since Millie had drunk her warm milk. Plenty of time for the Vicodin to enter her blood-stream through the lining of her stomach wall. If Millie was going to get sick and throw up, it would have happened already, but . . . nothing, and that was good. It kept this tidy. Getting her to take the pills had been so easy. Once mashed with a hammer from the cellar, the powder was easy to dissolve. It was no matter if it made the milk a little lumpy, as Bethy had brought big cookies upstairs as well. Cookies to dunk in the warm milk. Just perfect. Millie had swallowed all of it. Bethy only pretended to drink hers.

Now it was time to watch and learn. Bethy took out her diary and her pen and sat cross-legged on the floor and watched.

That was how the Bethy dreams always started. There was more, but by the time that dream ended, Doctor Nine was outside waiting for the little girl to leave her dead sister's body behind, go downstairs, and join him.

Rain dreamed of Bethy many times. Of the little girl with the curly black hair and cat-green eyes. A girl who was born innocent and became . . . what?

A monster? Rain had no idea what Bethy had become. If she was a monster, Rain did not yet know what kind. She was sure, though, even deep inside her dream, that the dream was a true story. And that it had happened years ago. And that now the little girl was all grown up.

Rain groaned in her sleep. She reached under the covers and pulled Bug up to her chest, clinging to the small dog for dear life.

CHAPTER TWENTY-FIVE

The skateboarder scraped to a stop outside of the apartment building. This was one of the newer ones, with a well-lighted entrance, good locks on the heavy glass front door, and a video camera.

The boy smiled. He didn't care about any of that.

He walked up the steps and paused for less than two minutes to pick the lock, then he slipped inside. It was a good lock, but he'd learned all about locks. About any kind of mechanism, really. Locks and clocks, those were his favorites.

The lock on the mailbox was a piece of cake, as it had been with the others. He opened it in twenty seconds. There were still letters there, which meant the man who lived here hadn't picked up his Saturday mail. Good.

The boy shrugged out of the backpack, opened the flap, and sorted through the dozens of windup pocket watches to find the right one. The watches were of different sizes and made from different materials. Each had a small vial nestled in between pins, gears, cogs, and springs. The face of the clock was parchment yellow, with Roman numerals inlaid with onyx. The boy took a tiny key from a ring in his pocket, inserted it into the slot, and turned it very slowly and carefully until the hands were set at three minutes to midnight. Then he removed the key, held the clock to his lips, closed his eyes, and breathed on the crystal face.

Then he put the clock into the mailbox, closed the door, reengaged the lock, and went out into the night. He paused for a moment to glance up at the video camera. He smiled at it even though it did not, and could not, see him.

It wasn't time for that kind of thing yet.

He kicked the skateboard down the steps, jumped down to land on it while it was rolling, and vanished into the night.

There was so much more work to do.

CHAPTER TWENTY-SIX

Around one o'clock, when she woke up to go to the bathroom—knife in hand and a ten-pound fierce hound at her heels—Rain saw something on the floor and bent to pick it up. It was the card the car driver had given her. Sticks. It must have fallen out of her pocket. Rain took it with her into the bathroom and dropped it in the trash can. While she sat on the toilet, her eyes kept cutting toward the trash. After she was done, she walked out of the bathroom, stopped, and turned around. Then she went back and fished the card out of the can and leaned against the doorframe, looking down at it.

The word *safe* kept echoing faintly in the back of her mind.

"Stupid," she said aloud and threw the card back into the trash.

At 3:18 in the morning, she got out of bed, walked over to the bathroom, took the card out of the can, and carried it with her back to bed. She was asleep when she did this and in the morning was mildly—but not entirely—surprised to find the card on the nightstand.

Once she was in bed, though, Rain sank deep and fell into a dream. It was not more of the Bethy dream. No, this was different. This dream was about her.

She was on the dark side of Boundary Street, looking up the hill to where the bright lights glowed with promise. There was so much color up there, and it wasn't cheesy ad-driven color like Times Square or gaudy trash color like Las Vegas. This was different. These lights always looked magical. Healthy, if that was a word that could be applied to artificial light.

Cars moved along Boundary Street, some cruising slowly and others going fast. There were motorcycles, too. A whole bunch of bikers rolled past, their engines growling like bears. She counted fifty bikes, all gleaming chrome and metallic reds and blues and greens. Most of the riders were guys with cutoff sleeves, extravagant beards, muscular arms inked with dragons and impossibly busty women and flaming skulls. Cliché stuff and some cruder art that Rain knew were prison tattoos. A few very tough-looking women rode with them, not as backseat luggage but on their own bikes, with their own colors and ink. They all wore the same emblem on the back, the silhouette of the Grim Reaper riding a chopped-down Harley, the scythe strapped across his back. The reaper's bike rode atop a swirling tornado. In an arc above the image was the gang's name—The Cyke-Lones. One of the riders, a really hunky guy with a shorter, neater beard and sunglasses despite the darkness, turned and looked at her. Even though Rain had never met him, or even heard of this club before, she knew his name. He called himself Boulevard Shark. It was a stupid name, she told herself, but she didn't believe it. He was so insanely hot that Rain's thighs rubbed and twisted together while she slept, because he reminded her of someone she knew back when she was using. She'd made it with that other guy a few times, and though he wasn't really kind to her, he was less unkind than a lot of the other guys she knew.

The bikers thundered past and then, two by two, turned the corner. Not heading up toward the light but seeking the shadows on the wrong side of Boundary Street. Rain stood on the curb and watched them go, feeling the bass rumble of their engines behind her sternum.

Rain touched her chest and was surprised to realize that she still had the old reading glasses. She put them on and gasped. In the sliver of glass on the left lens formed by the crack, the colors around her were different. They were brighter, richer, and there were so many tones and shades that she couldn't identify. In the dream, the number of primary colors expanded to include some that she knew she would never be able to remember or explain once she woke up. Also, she could hear the music better with the glasses on, as if seeing the light connected her to *something bigger and more profound. The colors that filled the air and pushed back the shadows were part of the same thing as the music. And she realized that it was Music, not music. Capital M because it was a proper noun. A name of a living thing. This sound was completely and genuinely alive, and it owned its own name.*

She stood on the dark side of Boundary Street and heard the Music roll down the hill and speak to her in its voice. It was so . . . aware of itself, as if ordinary music had been played so long, so well, with such insight and profound artistry that it had developed consciousness and identity. It made her smile and it made her tremble all the way down to the soles of her feet, as if her aching feet were begging to move.

To dance, as she used to dance.

And then Rain saw a figure standing in the shadows a dozen feet away.

Not the enemy. The boy.

He stood at the very edge of the spill of light. She could see his face and shirt and the scuffed toes of his sneakers. He was a beautiful little boy. Six, maybe. The same age he'd been on the train but younger than when she'd seen him on the street. With brown hair that was a mix of waves and curls, and brown eyes filled with sparks of gold. He was skinny, though. Way too thin. Starved. And in his dark eyes there was a haunted, desperate look. Rain's heart ached for him. She wanted to take him out of those shadows, hold him, help him find . . .

Find what?

Home? His parents? What?

The boy smiled at her. Or tried to. He winced at the effort, and tears jeweled his eyes. His face was completely smooth, like porcelain, and in that moment, in a flash of insight, Rain knew that this boy did not know how to smile. He never had. Not once.

Not since that one horrible smile when the nurse licked it onto his face.

Rain knew the boy could not smile. She knew why. Because Doctor Nine stole all his smiles. That thought, unowned by any of her inner voices, came and went. It was an absurd notion, and yet Rain knew that it was absolutely true.

Suddenly, a long-fingered hand, white as bone, with nails like talons, reached out of the inky shadows and clamped hard on the boy's shoulder. The grip was crushing, and those spiked nails curled downward into the tender flesh. The boy cried out in sudden pain, his knees buckling with terror and a grimace cracking that porcelain face.

"Help me!" he shrieked—and then he was gone, jerked backward into the shadows, which twisted and boiled with unnatural shapes. Impossible shapes that were not at all human. The boy's despairing wail tore through the air and then faded, faded, as if he were being dragged a long way back. Rain tried to run after him, but she was frozen to the spot, though whether by magic or terror or shock she couldn't tell.

That cry drove a knife through her, and even as she stood there, gasping as if she had run, her heart pounding dangerously close to rupturing in her chest, she heard the echo fade.

Help me? Was that really what he said?

The echo faded from the night, but it was there inside her head. What he had screamed as he was taken was not two words but three, and it had been that last word, that single word that finally dropped her to her knees.

What he'd actually screamed was this . . .

Help me, Mommy.

CHAPTER TWENTY-SEVEN

Rain woke with a screech that made Bug yelp in fear.

She sprang out of bed, fists balled in horror but ready to fight, eyes bugged wide, skin burning, heart jackhammering. Bug stood on the bed barking ferociously, turning to look for something to bite. Rain backed quickly away from the bed, retreating from it, fleeing from it, hating it for what it had just done to her. Those three terrible words haunted the air, burning in her ears and in her mind.

Help me, Mommy.

The boy's eyes had been like those of beautiful lost Noah, whom they had to bury as charred bones in a box. Noah the soldier who hadn't even known he was going to be a father. Noah, whose ghost probably haunted a desert on the other side of the world. This boy looked so much like him. The same eyes. Exactly the same.

Rain felt herself collapsing, first bending at the waist as if punched and then sinking to her knees on the cold floorboards.

"No," she whispered. Begging the world and the lord of dreams to take away that sadistic set of images. She toppled forward, catching herself on her balled fists.

Her bed stood empty, the sheets and blankets rumpled and hanging down. Pale morning sunlight slanted through the window and trapped her in a yellow square on the floor. The sunlight was the warmest thing in the world, and Rain raised her head, lifting her face into it. She wanted to call someone, needed to tell someone, to anchor what had happened to the real world by sharing it. But who? Yo-Yo would freak out and would probably think herself justified to stage some kind of intervention for Rain. Who did that leave? Her parents made it pretty clear they were done with her, distrusting her latest attempt at recovery even though it had lasted this long. They never answered their phones, and Rain was certain they were screening their calls. It's possible her number was even blocked. That was something Mom would do. Dad . . . who knows? He might call her back, but he'd want something for it. Besides, if she told them this, it would only convince them both that their judgments had been right all along.

No help there. No hope there.

Who else? Who did that leave? Her shrink would want to be paid for the patience he'd have to exert. Rain had no other friends beyond the Cracked World Society, and they had their own damage. And there was nobody in this building who gave a lukewarm shit about anyone else. The nice ones were all crazier than she was, and the rest orbited the real world at enough of a distance to avoid even casual collisions.

The sunlight was beautiful, and she closed her eyes. The face of the little boy was still there, but it was fading, like a picture on a subway wall as the train pulls away. Such a beautiful little face.

And Noah's eyes looking out of Dylan's face.

It took a lot for Rain to stand up. It cost her dearly to leave that square of sunlight and the warmth it afforded her. She did it, though; pushing with her fists against the floor like some ancient and ponderous statue flexing its heavy limbs as it came to life. It took that much effort. She stood for a moment, swaying on the edge of passing out. The room around her rocked like a tilt-a-whirl, but she kept her fists balled and set her jaw and demanded that it stop spinning.

It did. Reluctantly. Slowly.

The bedside clock told her that it was 6:57.

She called Joplin and got his voice mail. She left a quick message. "Call me!"

It sounded weak and needy, and she hated herself for leaving it. Then something occurred to her. A weird thought. When she trusted her feet enough to walk the few steps to the nightstand, she found that the card was there. She picked it up and looked at the name. Alexander Stickley. Sticks. Bug sniffed the card and wagged her tail. Rain tried to understand why, of all people in the world, she would call a guy who worked for a car service.

She called anyway.

Sticks answered on the third ring.

CHAPTER TWENTY-EIGHT

Yo-Yo is awake again, hours earlier than she planned. The dream won't let her sleep in this morning.

There is a suffocating thickness to the darkness around her bed, and she wants, needs, must run from it. But she can't. She knows that. You can't run from some things. Not in the real world. Even Yo-Yo, the dreamer, knows that, has always known that, just as she knows that dreams are part of the real world. Well . . . these kinds of dreams are. There is sunlight on the other side of the blinds and curtains, but Yo-Yo is afraid of it. Sunlight shows the truth, and what if she could see her dream in that unflinching light? Would it force everything from her dream to be real? Would it open a door and let them walk right in, see her, own her?

She wants a weapon, a defense against the darkness and what it contains. A torch, pitchforks, a crowd of angry villagers to chase the monsters. In the pernicious darkness, she craves a weapon against her fear and what it wants to do to her.

There is only one.

A needle, a knife, a pen with which to cut her skin and let the corrupted wine of terror spill out onto paper.

In her alien darkness, Yo-Yo lets her fingers crawl along the floor beside her bed until they find the pen and the notebook. Hastily she snatches them off the floor and pulls them into the bed with her, against her chest, against the hammering of her heart.

The darkness is bigger now, thicker. It smells of old sweat and oily rags. She doesn't turn on the bedside light, because she knows it offers no protection, even against the darkness. When you turn on the lights, the dark things just hide behind chairs and under the bed frame. They don't really go away.

She holds the pen and pad to her like a sword and shield, and with them in her hands, her terrors take a small half step back.

Yo-Yo doesn't need lights to write. Her hand knows the way; the pen point knows her notebook too well to need the path illuminated. The writing is the act of counterattack. Yo-Yo knows this. She has beaten back a thousand monsters with it and trapped them on the page. A stack of tattered and rubber-banded notebooks surround her bed like barbed wire.

In the dangerous dark, Yo-Yo writes. A poem. She may or may not ever read it. Knowing that she has written it is enough. Knowing that she has fought back is enough.

In the past, it has been enough.

Until now, it has been enough.

She writes.

Doctor Nine
Is as thin as a bone.
He is a scarecrow
From a blighted field.
He is handsome
In the same way
That a scythe
Is beautiful.
And he smiles
But he never
Ever
Laughs.

And he never
Ever
Laughs,
But he always
Smiles.

CHAPTER TWENTY-NINE

Sticks was already in the diner when Rain walked in, seated at a booth in the back.

It wasn't the Diner, which always closed from midnight Saturday to seven on Sunday morning for cleaning. Rain had arranged to meet Sticks at American Dollar, which never closed, and certainly not for a thorough cleaning. It was the quintessential greasy spoon, and it attracted a mixed crowd of graveyard shift cops, delivery truck drivers, and fringe dwellers who never seemed to be anywhere else except diners like these. Once in a while the priest from the women's shelter was there in the morning, slipping Jack Daniels into his coffee and staring at nothing at all. Nobody else ever came here unless they had bad directions.

A pair of metal cuff crutches stood against the wall between Sticks's booth and one of those claw machines that had an Out of Order sign on it and was filled with dusty stuffed toys.

"Pardon me if I don't get up," he said with a grin.

"Um, sure, no problem," Rain said as she slid onto the cracked green vinyl seat across from him. "Thanks for meeting me. Sorry to call so early."

"I was up," he said, shrugging it off.

In the slightly yellow diner light, Sticks looked sickly and frail, and his burn scars were a darker red against the brown of his skin. He sat with his hands cupped around a mug of coffee that was softened by a tiny drop of milk.

A waitress appeared as if by magic. The name stitched over her left breast was Bernadette, and she wore pins shaped like wiener dogs.

"Getcha, hon?" she asked. Rain wondered if all diner waitresses were related. Or maybe they were fembots programmed with the same software and scripts.

"Um," said Rain and cut a look at Sticks.

"I already ordered," he said. "Short stack and crisp bacon."

"Sounds good," said Rain after a quick mental inventory of the cash in her purse. If she skipped lunch and had cereal for dinner, there was enough to cover his breakfast, too. Rain figured she owed it to him for meeting her.

The waitress went away, taking with her the scent of the kind of perfume they sold in gift packs at the drugstore. The kind that came with lotions and powders, all for under ten bucks. The kind kids gave their moms for Christmas and thought it was something special. Bernadette wasn't wearing a wedding ring, but that didn't mean much. She could still have kids. It wasn't likely she'd have bought that scent with her own money.

Sticks sipped his coffee and studied her. "Why me?"

Rain waited until her coffee arrived, and she loaded too much sugar and cream into it before she answered. "I . . . don't actually know."

Sticks waited for more.

"Look, yesterday—" Rain began, faltered, took a breath and a sip, and tried again from a different direction. "What were you doing on that street yesterday? When I came out of that alley, your car was right there. Why?"

Sticks looked down at his cup for a moment, then shrugged as he glanced back up. "You wouldn't believe me if I told you."

"Try me."

He smiled. "You can run faster than me, so if this freaks you out, you don't have to worry about me chasing you."

Rain did not smile.

"Okay, then," said Sticks, "but it comes with backstory, okay?"

"Most things do."

"Weird backstory," he amended.

"Most things do," she said again. They studied each other for a moment and he nodded.

"Here goes," said Sticks, blowing out his cheeks. "First, I guess, you got to know something about me. When I was kid, I used to have dreams. Special dreams. My grandma says most people have a little touch of it, but some got more than others. Some people have too much of it, and it messes with their heads. Drives them nuts. I guess if I was a painter or writer, I could work it out better, but I'm not like that. I'm not artistic, so I don't have a way to—what's the word? Channel? Yeah, I don't have any way to channel it."

Rain cocked her head to appraise him. "Are you talking about visions?"

"Dreams, visions, whatever. Sure. Not useful stuff, like I can't tell you tonight's lottery numbers. Wish I could. And I didn't predict that my Humvee was going to roll over an IED. My grandma—Grammy, we called her—could see things a little better sometimes. She'd always know who in the neighborhood was going to die, who was sleeping with who, who was knocked up. Like that."

"Was she a voodoo priestess or something?"

Sticks snorted. "Grammy was a Baptist church lady who worked at a box company in Queens."

"Oh. Sorry. That's me being stupid."

He waved it off. "Grammy was different from most folks, though. Not in every way, but in some ways. Like I'm different." He paused. "Look, two nights ago, I had a dream about driving the Red Rocket in a part of the city where I'd never been before, which is weird because there's nowhere in the five boroughs I ain't been. Nowhere. I was hacking before I went into the army, and I took it up right after they cut me loose from the VA hospital. Other than being a soldier and a summer working at Action Burger in senior year of high school, I never had any other job. I love driving, even in city traffic. I been all over the country, and I used to take these long wandering nowhere drives. No map, no GPS, no plan. I'd just get in my car and go and see where the road took me, you dig?"

She nodded. "Sounds scary."

"It's not. It's great. You drive into someplace strange and there's no one to guide you or make connections for you and you just *deal* with it."

"Why?"

Sticks looked surprised. "Why not? Anyway, in the army, I was a driver. Pretty good at it, too, no matter what I was driving. Then I drove over an IED and this happened." He raised a scarred hand to touch his melted face.

"I lost someone that way," said Rain softly. "An IED, I mean. In Iraq."

Shadows passed across Sticks's face, and he nodded. "Yeah, you couldn't take two steps over there for a while without tripping one. I lost a bunch of friends, including all the guys in my vehicle. Still feel like it's maybe my fault for not spotting it. I was behind the wheel. That's another story, and it's my shit to process. I don't blame driving for what happened to me, though. I always feel better behind the wheel. My car, the Red Rocket . . . it's like it's me, you know? When I'm rolling along, I'm not crippled. I'm whole. So when I say that I know every street in New York, I'm not joking. I could win any quiz show on it. In my dream, though, I was in a part of the city that I'd never seen before. No street signs, no nothing. Understand something, though—I *knew* the names of those streets. The main one, where I guess you ran *from* when you went through the alley, that's Boundary Street. The one that I parked the Red Rocket on was Misery Street."

Rain sat up like she'd been jolted by ten thousand volts. "Wait . . . what? Go back. Did you say *Boundary* Street?"

"Yeah." He studied her with narrowed eyes. "Why?"

"There's a Boundary Street in *my* dreams, too."

They sat with that for a long few moments.

Sticks shook his head slowly. "I looked it up on Google Maps, and there's nothing. I mean . . . there are Boundary Streets in other cities, but not here in New York. Weird, right?"

"Yeah," she said, shifting uncomfortably. "But I'm confused. Is this still your dream or someplace you've actually been to?"

He sipped his coffee and set his cup down thoughtfully. "A bit of both. I go there in dreams a lot. More lately, though. Boundary Street and, um, other places. But yesterday I found myself driving—actually driving—on those same streets, and they are not in New York. No goddamn way."

Rain nodded. She understood that part of it, though she could not begin to explain it.

"So I pull around the corner and stop," continued Sticks, "because I kind of feel like that's where I'm supposed to be. Crazy as shit, I know. I was there for five, ten minutes when it starts to rain, and suddenly I get all excited and know that the person I'm waiting for is coming."

The whole diner felt suddenly very cold. The waitress came with their food and set the plates down without a word, put some silverware setups rolled in cloth napkins down next to each, and went away. Rain almost— *almost*—used the interruption to bolt and run, because she knew with sudden and absolute certainty what Sticks was going to say next. But she was trapped in the moment, waiting for him to finish it. But he said nothing.

"This is *nuts*," said Rain, her mouth completely dry.

"Yeah, it is," said Sticks. "I wish my Grammy was around so I could tell her, but she's in a nursing home now. Dementia. Sometimes she knows me, but most times she doesn't. I wish I could tell her about this, though." He paused. "Now it's your turn. You're not as shocked or freaked out about what I said as anyone else would be. I can see it in your eyes, and I think it's why we're both here right now. So . . . you want to tell me why you called this morning?"

Rain wanted to cry but instead she smiled. "Okay," she said, "but it comes with backstory."

CHAPTER THIRTY

Gay Bob is awake. The dream won't let him sleep.

The dream is vivid, as real as if he'd lived it. He waits for it to fade, wanting this one to pale itself into half memory and then dissipate like morning fog. His good dreams always do that, and he wants this one— not good at all—to be equally elusive.

It remains. It refuses to budge. It hovers like a wasp at the front of his mind, threatening to sting. Wasps can sting over and over again and not die.

He laughs out loud, hoping the sound of his laughter will make him feel silly and self-conscious about having a nightmare. Nothing is so potent a weapon as a cynical metropolitan gay man's dismissive laugh. That is his belief.

Except this morning.

The cynic is powerless in the face of the truly inexplicable. Faithless by experience, Gay Bob nevertheless has faith in this dream, and that makes him sweat. His T-shirt is pasted to his chest and ribs and back. His dark hair is cold rat tails against his neck and forehead.

Around him, like fortress walls, are his precious books. He looks at their darkened shapes, willing Heaney and Joyce and Márquez and Szanto to stand up for him. He reaches out and touches the stack nearest to his bed. Castro and Galeano, Neruda and Matthiessen. But his guardians are still sleeping, none of their dreams invaded as his had been.

Gay Bob is afraid.

The dream won't back down. It stands there, grinning at him with its thin red lips and sharp white teeth, and it reaches for him with long and trembling white fingers.

He can't make it go.

"Fuck!" he snarls at the darkness. His heavy curtains are pulled, and he loathes the lines of sunlight trying to cut their way into the room. He knows he can't let his day start without doing something about his dreams. That's how it works. That's how he keeps balanced. Reaching over, he swats the touchpad on his bedside lamp, and there is a pale pool of yellow light around his head and shoulders. Without knowing why, he gets out of bed, stands up. His hands are in front of him as if he is ready to fight. He is powerful. He's boxed and wrestled and knows some kung fu. He's been in a hundred scuffles growing up gay in the inner-city school system, and he's fought his way through some outright brawls at Pornstash. He's never lost a fight. Not since he was fifteen, and not even close in his adult life. He breaks people; they don't break him.

But he is alone now, and it isn't that kind of fight.

He looks around the room. Looking for the enemy. Looking also for a weapon—a club, a sword.

He sees his weapon of choice. His face accepts the smallest of feral smiles. In three long strides, he's at the desk and punches the button to fire up his laptop. The screen light glows icy blue, and he is still smiling, although tightly.

Gay Bob has strength he doesn't know he has, and it has nothing to do with the moves he learned in all those sweaty gyms and dojos. He has other kinds of strength, unknown and largely untapped.

He sits down at the computer, and as he does so, he's aware of turning his back on the darkness. Not for a moment does he believe that the dream was only that. Gay Bob isn't stupid, and he isn't naive enough to accept that reality is the only truth. His cynicism is of another species altogether.

The computer finishes loading, and he caresses the surface of the track pad to put the cursor on the icon for Microsoft Word. A blank page opens, white and pure and sympathetic.

He writes.

Gay Bob always dreams in text. Even when there are visuals, some part of his mind is describing them. He's always been like that. His is the mind of a natural writer, born to no other destiny. He has scores of discs of dreams and fragments of dreams. It doesn't matter that no one else likes what he's written. He loves it all because writing is what makes him feel alive. It's what keeps the demons at bay.

Nothing that he's written before, though, is like this.

As he begins typing, the dream takes a new form, a new style. And he knows that he has crossed a line, crashed through some kind of ceiling, become—somehow—a different kind of writer. This story is proof of that unexpected and powerful evolution. It is the firstborn of a clutch of new stories that he knows, without doubt, that he will write. It isn't magic realism or literary fiction or social drama.

He writes a horror story.

It's a true nightmare, too, of the old kind before TV and movies told us what to dream. It is a nightmare of primal fears, of elemental forces.

Gay Bob knows that if he can write it out then he can trap some of its essence on the page, reducing it, diminishing it. He hopes.

And so he writes . . .

They blew into town on a Halloween wind. The Mulatto drove the big roadster, and the nurse sat in the back next to Doctor Nine. The glittering towers of a great city rose like spikes of diamond in the evening gloom. Flocks of nightbirds troubled the air above the car, following where the doctor went. Always following. Always hungry.

A green sign above the road announced the exit to the Brooklyn-Queens Expressway.

Doctor Nine's smile was a cold knife slash across his pale face. Without haste he reached forward and touched the Mulatto's shoulder.

"Take that exit."

The Mulatto nodded and crossed the lines toward Brooklyn.

"Something . . . ?" asked the nurse.

"Oh, yes," said Doctor Nine. "We need to make a house call."

The Cadillac drifted down the exit ramp, silent as the wind. The night followed like a hungry pack of dogs.

Gay Bob stares at the screen, his eyes red with exhaustion and still troubled by the dream. Writing it out should have defused it, but somewhere in the back of his mind, he is afraid that writing had struck a match and held it to the wick.

He clicks on the option to file and it presses Save As. It asks him for a file name. He types: *Fire Zone.*

He sits for a long time and stares at the name.

Gay Bob turns off the computer and crawls back into bed, pulls the blankets high and tight. In three minutes, he is asleep.

He wakes nine minutes later.

He stands on the sill of the open sixth-floor window of his apartment building. He is naked, cold, shivering, dripping with sweat. His cry is small, lost in the night. He shifts, and his bare foot crunches on something. He looks down.

There, on the sill and on the floor behind him, are round pills. OxyContin in all its varied colors and strengths. White tens, gray fifteens, pink twenties, all the way up to the glorious, delicious green eighties. Hundreds of them. A lifetime's worth of them.

Enough of them.

Too much of them.

There for him.

Gay Bob screams. Trying so hard to wake up. But he is already awake.

CHAPTER THIRTY-ONE

"I was raised in the city," Rain said. "In a big apartment on Central Park West. My dad's a financial advisor, but he wasn't much a part of my life. You know the expression 'married to his job'? That's him. Not sure if he actually loves my mother, and I'm not sure why they stay married. It's not like they fight or anything. They don't do much of anything, at least not together. Dad spends most of his time at work, and Mom is always out running some kind of celebrity event. She's a fund-raiser for all these worthy causes—saving this old theater, saving that historic house, saving after-school music programs. Important stuff, I guess, but she didn't do much to save me." Rain stopped and cocked her head, listening to that. "God, how whiny was that?"

"It's all good," said Sticks. "Let it come out the way it wants to come out."

She thought about that, nodded, continued. "I used to write in my diary that I lived in a haunted house, except that it was me who was haunting it. I was the ghost. I didn't say much because no one seemed to want me to. We lived in a big apartment with more rooms than we needed. We had a cleaning lady in three times a week, but she only spoke Russian and never said enough for me to pick up much. Hello, goodbye, like that. Or she'd hold up something off the floor and shake it at me and growl, 'Yours?' Like that. There were no other kids in our building, and I went to one of those private schools where we had to wear stupid plaid skirts and sweater uniforms and they called us *Miss*. Not even *Ms*. I was Miss Thomas to all the teachers and just Thomas to the other girls. No boys at all. Not after sixth grade. Girls. Most of them were from families a lot richer than ours. And that's weird, being the poorest rich girl in a school where there are daughters of millionaires and, I think, a couple of billionaires. Only two of us took public transportation to school. The rest had drivers."

"Sounds rough," said Sticks, and she gave him a sharp look.

"Don't make fun."

"I'm not, actually," he said. "Sounds like you spent a lot of your time being ignored. That can't feel good."

"I guess," said Rain. "Anyway, so there's me, Little Miss Nobody mousing my way through a life even *I* didn't care about. Then I met Noah. He was working at a Starbucks, and we started talking, you know, the way people do. Talking about nothing just to talk. The weather, movies. Like that. He was funny, though, and smart. He smiled a lot. He had a good face, if you know what I mean?"

"Good outside or good inside?" asked Sticks.

"Both," said Rain quickly, then paused and thought more about the question. "Mostly inside. I mean, sure, he was nice looking, but that isn't what made me start liking him. He wasn't fake."

"Nice."

"Noah was a few years older than me," said Rain, "and he thought I was eighteen. I didn't tell him how old I really was until once when we ran into each other by accident on the subway and I was in my school uniform. He kind of freaked because I was fifteen and he was eighteen. But by then, it was pretty clear that we both felt something. I know I did. Bigtime, too. First love. Cue all the Disney cartoon animals and corny music."

"Don't do that," said Sticks, and she cut him a quick look.

"Don't do what?"

"Don't take something big and make it small. This Noah sounds like he was a good guy."

They studied each other for a long moment, and then Rain nodded. "That's the sort of thing Noah would have said. So, yeah, Noah and me . . . we started going out. I convinced him that it was cool, that he wasn't doing anything wrong by going out with me. After all, he was only three years older. He had some issues with it for a while, and when we, y'know, *made out* for the first time he was really awkward about it. But according to the law, we were totally legal. Hell, with most guys I'd have had to beat them away with a baseball bat, but Noah was so proper. He wasn't ever just trying to get laid. He didn't try to pressure me into anything, not hand jobs or blow jobs or anything." She paused. "I'm being crude."

"You're telling the truth, and I'm a grown-up, Rain. We're cool."

She nodded. "There was another complication, though, and it kind of accelerated things for us. Noah told me that he had enlisted in the army right before he met me and now he had to report. His Starbucks gig was him making money before he had to head off to basic training. We had that clock ticking all the time. The night before he left . . . I told him I was in love with him. I expected him to push me away, but he said he loved me, too. That he had for a while but didn't have the nerve to say it. That was a rough night. I mean, it was beautiful because I'd never been in love before, but we both knew he was leaving the next day. We held each other, and kissed and . . . well . . ." She shrugged. "He was very gentle about it. Very loving. It was really beautiful. It was an act of love, not us just having sex. Does that make sense?"

"Yes," Sticks said quietly, "it really does."

"He left next day, and even though he wrote all the time and emailed and called when he could, I never saw him again. He went from basic to some kind of special training thing, and then his unit was shipped to Iraq. It happened all so fast. Months, I know, but it felt like seconds. It all blew by. He went to Iraq and then he . . . his Humvee . . ."

She shook her head. It took her a long time before she could even try to talk. Sticks waited patiently, his eyes calm, his burned hands loose around his coffee cup. The waitress refilled the cups.

Rain told Sticks about discovering she was pregnant, about finding out Noah had been killed, about giving up the baby. She told him all of it. About getting lost in drugs, about going in and out of rehab. About getting clean and working the program.

"How's this get us to Boundary Street?" he asked.

"It's part of it," said Rain. "At least I think so. While I was getting high, I began to have visions. They were as vivid as dreams, but I'd get them sometimes while I was awake. Strange people and places. Not all bad, but the bad ones were really bad. I . . . can't tell you all of it, though, and don't ask me to. I can't, and you have to accept that, okay?"

Sticks said, "Okay, but if you ever decide you want to tell me *all* of it . . ."

"Sure. Not now, though," said Rain. "Here's what I can tell you, though."

She told him about meeting the little monk in the park, about the horrors of her birth, about dying during the birth and following the bright light back to life, about dying again during an NA meeting. She told him about the nurse. Some instinct told her that she could mention the nurse, that it was allowed, where naming Doctor Nine was not. She told Sticks about seeing the boy on the train and on the street. She told him about the old lady and the glasses. She told him everything she could without ever mentioning Doctor Nine's name.

"Now," she said after a heavy pause, "the problem is that I don't know how much of this is some kind of flashback, actual psychosis, or whether the universe is broken."

Sticks wiped his mouth. "Holy shit, girl."

"I know."

"I mean, *holy* shit."

"I *know*. So . . . am I crazy?"

He shook his head. "You have those glasses with you? Can I see them?"

"No, after my friends tried them on last night, I decided to leave them at my place. They creep me out."

"Yeah," he said. "Look, this kid, is he real or not? What's your gut say?"

It took so much for her to answer that. She couldn't even look at him when she answered. "Yes," she said in a hollow little voice.

"Then what's it mean? The glasses, the freaky-deaky nurse, you losing a whole damn day? What do you think it all means?"

Her fists were balled on the tabletop. "I think it means that those glasses are showing me the truth. I think it means that my son is out there, that I've been seeing him. And I think—God help me—I think he's in real trouble."

Sticks leaned forward. "What *kind* of trouble?"

She slowly raised her eyes. "I think monsters are after him," she said.

CHAPTER THIRTY-TWO

Straight Bob got up from the computer and staggered toward the bathroom. He was sobbing, making small mewling sounds, spilling out words that made no sense. Denials, accusations, outrage, apologies. All to himself.

He was naked, and his thighs and belly were pasted with semen and drops of blood. His forearm muscles ached, and his penis blazed with friction burns. He had no real idea how many times he'd jerked off during the night. Five? Eight? More? Even after his body was completely spent, he kept working at himself to get hard again, his right hand moving relentlessly, his left squirting Jergen's hand cream all over his crotch to lubricate things, though after a while it did nothing but create a layer of paste.

His heart hammered from the exertion, from the stress. From passion.

On his laptop, the images still played, rolling from one video to the next to the next to the next.

A nurse seducing a patient.

A nurse swallowing the enormous cock of a hunky doctor.

Two nurses driving each other wild with a strap-on.

A nurse giving a priest a hand job while he read last rites over a dying woman.

A nurse . . .

A nurse . . .

A nurse.

Always a nurse.

All night, a nurse.

Straight Bob could not stop himself from downloading the videos to his hard drive, creating playlists, running them, making himself hard, forcing himself to come, screaming each time. Sure that the nurses were performing—not *for* him, but *on* him.

The nurse.

They all looked the same. Even though there were different porn actresses in each video, they all looked the same. A nurse with dark curly hair and cat-green eyes and a wicked red-lipped smile.

He leaned against the sink, cold porcelain against his thighs, and stared at his face in the mirror. Not understanding. Hating himself. Feeling as if the world was falling off its fasteners, tilting, sliding down the wall to crash to bits.

"Please," he begged his own image.

In the other room, a new video started.

A visiting nurse paying a house call.

"No," he begged.

A minute later, he was back in his chair in front of the laptop. Weeping, pleading. His hand moving and moving and moving while the nurse did what she did and smiled directly into the camera. Looking at him.

Seeing him.

CHAPTER THIRTY-THREE

The Cadillac pulled to a slow stop across the street from American Dollar.

The engine growled like a hungry dog. Rain fell, but it fell through the car and spattered on the street below, the angle of descent only slightly troubled by the passage. No one on the street glanced at the car, though one old woman, newly come from church, touched the crucifix that hung on a chain beneath her blouse.

The driver let his hands fall onto his lap, and he sat there as still and unmoving as a clothing store mannequin. Except for his eyes. They were milky and dusty, and they roved up and down the street. Up and down, up and down.

Behind him sat three figures. The doctor. The nurse. The boy.

One was smiling. One was laughing. One was weeping.

On the radio, an orchestra was playing *Totentanz*, a lugubrious piece by Franz Liszt. On the floor of the car, between the doctor's polished shoes, were pieces from a broken clock.

He looked at the boy, who was there, and then not there, and then there again.

So very like Doctor Nine.

"Soon," said the doctor.

The boy caved forward and put his face in his scarred and dirty hands.

PART TWO

THE FIRE ZONE

Real magic is not about gaining power over others:
it is about gaining power over yourself.

THE ENCYCLOPEDIA OF MAGIC AND ALCHEMY
ROSEMARY ELLEN GUILEY

I have you fast in my fortress,
And will not let you depart,
But put you down into the dungeon
In the round-tower of my heart.

And there will I keep you forever,
Yes, forever and a day,
Till the walls shall crumble to ruin,
And moulder in dust away!

"THE CHILDREN'S HOUR"
HENRY WADSWORTH LONGFELLOW

INTERLUDE FIVE
THE MONSTERS AND THE INFANT

They sat together in the dark.

The baby. The doctor. The nurse. And near them a chorus of watchful shadows.

Not a total darkness because even the monster needed some light. To see by. To covet by.

The baby was still tiny. A newborn. Unable to speak. Pink and round and tender. His fat little feet pedaled the air above where he lay, as if practicing for running away. The monster knew he would try that one day. Run away.

They always tried to run away.

The light showed that, too.

The nurse rocked the cradle and hummed a tune that had no structure, no order. Her eyes were filled with ugly thoughts, and she kept licking her lips as if hoping to find a trace of something. Juice, perhaps. Or sweat.

The monster sat beside the cradle and watched the little fingers paw and slap and grab at the things that hung from above. The stubby little fingers could almost reach the hairy white sac of spider eggs that wobbled near one torn edge of the web. The mother spider watched the boy, as the monster watched the boy, and their hungers were not dissimilar.

In the dark, the baby screamed.

In the dark, the nurse rocked and sang.

In the dark, the monster smiled.

CHAPTER THIRTY-FOUR

Yo-Yo woke from a short, bad nap. Her stomach hurt. Something she ate, maybe. Or some bacteria cooking up something nasty in her system. Whatever it was, it hurt.

She showered and dressed and went to the first meeting she could find. It was all the way down at a place next to the Dunkin' Donuts on Neptune in Coney Island, a few blocks from Seagate, and most of the people there were strangers. She sat and listened and did not speak. She didn't dare.

While she sat there listening, she played with the small windup pocket watch some prankster had slipped into her mailbox. It didn't work, and she had no way to wind it, but it was pretty and she rubbed its glass face with her thumb, using it like a worry stone.

When it was over, she left without having coffee or cookies. There was another meeting near there, on the other side of MCU Park, where the Cyclones played minor-league ball. Again, she sat and listened, needing the company of others of her kind but not wanting to share with them.

There was a third meeting all the way over at a Methodist church near Bergen Beach. And another one in Briarwood. Then one in Corona. There was always a meeting somewhere.

Yo-Yo moved like a desperate nomad through Brooklyn, going to one meeting after another. In all that time, she never said a word to anyone except meaningless hellos and goodbyes. All that time, her heart felt like it was breaking inside her chest.

Why did I write his name down?

That question burned in her mind. She'd written his name in her poem, and Yo-Yo knew with absolute certainty that he did not like it.

No, not at all.

CHAPTER THIRTY-FIVE

Their coffee went cold in their cups. Rain and Sticks stared at each other and didn't notice. They'd been there a long time, but no one else needed the booth; the place was mostly empty.

Bernadette came over with a pot, saw that the cups were still full, shrugged, and walked away without comment. The storm was still brewing outside, with winds whipping abandoned pieces of the Sunday paper along the street and chasing everyone indoors. A few raindrops splatted against the glass in brief squalls, but the big downpour was still to come. It had turned twilight dark out there.

"Monsters," Sticks said at last.

"Monsters."

"Are we talking monsters like . . . what? Child abusers? Human traffickers? Like that?"

"No. Actual monsters. Supernatural, I guess."

"Like vampires and werewolves and demons and that shit?"

"Maybe," said Rain, studying the new lines that were now etched onto his face. "I don't know what other word to use."

Sticks looked around the room as if answers were likely to be posted on the walls, then he glanced back at her and shook his head. "Got to admit that I don't know where to go with that."

"Like I do? I mean . . . Christ, we're sitting here having a conversation about monsters and neither of us is joking. And it has to do with the baby I gave up for adoption ten years ago."

"How?"

"I don't know. Look, Sticks, I've always had weird stuff going on in my head. I've logged more hours in therapy than you've had hot dinners. Not kidding. But how do I find a set of rules for how to deal with all this? I don't trust my own head, and I don't know if anything's real."

"Except that you believe this is happening," he suggested gently.

"Yeah, except for that." She cocked her head. "Do you believe in the supernatural?"

Sticks used one unburned finger to slowly trace the edges of the burns on his other forearm. "You know that saying about there not being any atheists in foxholes? You dig what that actually means? It's all about when you're slammed up against the shit and you start wondering all about those Sunday school lessons on salvation and redemption. Don't matter what church you ever been to, don't really matter if you ever *been* to church, but when the air's filled with live fire and RPGs are tearing your friends to dogmeat and you're strapped to your chair in a burning vehicle, you'll find God. By any name, you'll find someone or something to pray to, and you'll pray with your whole damn heart. I knew some guys who were always hard-core don't-believe-in-no-damn-thing-and-religion's-all-a-joke, except they were praying and crying while they lay there, out of fresh magazines, bleeding, the medic lying with his own guts out, and fucking Al Qaeda coming out of holes in the desert."

"Is that faith or desperation?"

"Don't make much of difference," said Sticks. "I lost God growing up and found Him over there the first time I found myself in an active combat zone. Lost Him again when it cooled down, then really hooked on when I woke up in a mobile surgical station about to get evaced to a burn center. I prayed to Him so hard when I was waiting on news about the other guys in my Humvee, begging God to let them be alive. Kicked the son of a bitch to the curb when they told me I was the only one who didn't go home in a flag-draped goddamn coffin. But then I had a shit ton of conversations with Him while I was waiting to find out if I'd ever walk again. I prayed, I offered deals. I told God I'd devote my life to trying to help the families of every man who died when I rolled over that mine. I would have done anything, taken back every bad thing I ever done to wiggle a toe; and I knew—*knew*—I was talking to someone and they were listening."

Rain said nothing.

"Faith can be a bitch, though," said Sticks. "Especially if you start to believe that maybe God isn't the actual 'all,' you know? Like when you start believing that there *is* something out there in the dark and it wants to hurt you and God doesn't have your back. First time I saw the bodies of innocent little kids killed by Al Qaeda, I kind of lost the whole 'the Lord will protect you' thing. So do I believe in God the same way my grammy does? Or how she used to before she lost her mind? Nah. All that church and gospel stuff never worked for me, but it don't mean there ain't something out there. Something bigger, stronger, whatever. Something that's working the engine, something that's driving all of this through time and space. So . . . yeah, Rain, I guess I believe in the supernatural. Just don't ask me what it is."

She nodded, accepting that. "Then there's another part of it. Dreams I've been having about a place I go to, and . . . I think it's somehow related to where you found me yesterday."

His eyes changed, sharpened, and his muscles stiffened. "What place?"

"I . . . don't know its name. I almost know it, but it keeps slipping away when I wake up. It's real in my dreams and maybe, in some insane way, it's real when I'm awake, too."

Sticks licked his lips, and she saw that there was a faint but definite tremor to his hands. "Rain, this place . . . tell me one definite thing you can remember. Any detail."

Rain tried, but every time she looked inside, the details seemed to vanish like debris in roiling dark water. All she could catch were the tiniest of glimpses. "Fire," she said uncertainly. "There's something about fire . . ."

Sticks sat back heavily against the seat and stared at her with wide, unblinking eyes. "Holy shit," he murmured.

"What? What's wrong?"

"Look," he said slowly, "I don't want to sound all creepy here, but I've being having dreams, too. Wild ones. They started when I was in the VA hospital."

She tensed. "What *kind* of dreams?"

He licked lips again. "It's about a place that's up the hill from Boundary Street. Even though New York doesn't have a lot of hills. I'm not even sure it's *in* New York. It's like this place is in every city, if that makes any sense at all."

"It does," she said in a whisper. "You're saying you've dreamed about the same place?"

"I think so."

"That's impossible."

He laughed. "How can we have a conversation about freakazoid glasses, vanishing old ladies, and a monster nurse and you think dreams are suddenly the weird part?"

"I know, but it's just that this is all . . ." She gave up trying to find the right word because there probably wasn't one. So she asked, "Do you know what the place is called?"

"I do," he said. "At least I know what it's called in *my* dreams. When I go there, it's called the Fire Zone."

Rain almost screamed.

CHAPTER THIRTY-SIX

Gay Bob stood naked in the bathroom watching the toilet flush.

He lost count of how many times he'd flushed so far.

Once for each pill. It was like throwing roses on a coffin, and he mourned each and every pill as he dropped them one at a time into the bowl. He knew that he should have flushed them all at once, but he couldn't.

He.

Could.

Not.

There was something about the ceremony of dropping each one, of denying each one, that kept him tethered to the world. He expected to feel more powerful each time he pushed the handle and saw the swirl of water take each tablet out of his life.

His mind felt like it was burning with a fever, or something worse. The heat and the pain made it so hard to think. A fragment of him, though, stood to one side as if watching this all on a movie screen; and it was that small part of him that kept wanting to shout out the necessary questions. Where had the pills come from? Who had put them there? Why would anyone do that? If it was a prank, then why spend so much money? What was wrong with him that he was taking this as some kind of normal?

A lot of questions. Those and others. However, that small part of him had no voice. It had no more chance of engaging the rest of him than a theater patron had in opening a dialogue with the actors on the screen. He was merely a witness to a bizarre story unfolding around him, with him as the central character. Protagonist or victim, it was hard to decide.

So many whys kept flooding the spectator version of him.

The rest of him stood over the toilet, dropping the beautiful little pills into the churning water of the toilet bowl. Doing that—the act of picking up a pill and dropping it—felt like he was carving off pieces of his own flesh and flushing them. The process diminished him, moment by moment, pill by pill, flush by flush. And yet he couldn't break his own rhythm. It was a task assigned in hell, and he knew that once committed he had to see it through.

It took a long time.

It took such a long damn time.

He was only awake for part of it. For the rest, he was elsewhere. Not asleep. He was simply not there.

INTERLUDE SIX
THE MONSTERS AND THE BABY

They played together in the dark.

The doctor, the nurse, and the baby.

Special games that they devised together.

Sometimes it was a poking game.

Not with the doctor's finger. Oh, no, that would not do at all. Touching baby skin was nasty. It would be better to stick his fingers into hot coals. That would burn less. And those kinds of burns would heal. If he were to touch the baby's skin, the burns might never heal. Babies are pure and filled with hope. That was a lesson the doctor had learned long ago. With other babies.

No, the doctor preferred to use a stick. Or a pencil. Or a rolled-up piece of paper. Anything that was on hand. Anything that was easy to hold and fun to poke with. A chicken bone was always nice, especially if there was still some meat and gristle on it; a little fat, maybe some blood. The chicken did not have to be cooked. Sometimes he let the nurse pick something. She liked sharp toys.

The baby was so much fun when they played the poking game. He screamed with such a high, sweet, piercing scream.

CHAPTER THIRTY-SEVEN

Rain grabbed his hands and held them. Squeezed them.

"God!" she cried. "The Fire Zone. Yes. That's the name. I've been trying to remember it, and it's been killing me that I can't. But now that you said it . . . *yes*. A thousand times yes. Please, though . . . tell me about it. About how you see it. Tell me anything."

Sticks did not pull his hands away. He held on, smiling, looking both scared and relieved. "It's big," he began. "It's like a big part of the city. And it's always night there. Or maybe that's because I only go there when I'm sleeping at night."

"It's always night," she said, nodding, knowing it to be true as soon as she said it.

Sticks's eyes became unfocused as he looked inward instead of out. "There are these big clubs. Huge ones, and the music they play is alive. I mean they played it alive."

"They call it Music," she said, "with a capital *M*."

"I've been dreaming about this place ever since I was in the VA hospital. I couldn't wait to go to sleep because when I'm there, when I'm in the Zone, I'm not crippled. I can walk."

"I dance in my dreams," said Rain.

He nodded. "Me, too. Everyone dances there. Not all the time, but in the clubs—"

"—and on the streets," she cut in. "In the parks. People love to dance there."

"They do. Snakedancer leads them. He's the dance master in the Zone."

She said, "I can almost remember the names of the clubs. I can see them in my mind, but they're hazy. There's a big one, huge, with colored lights making crazy patterns on the white walls outside."

"That's Unlovely's," said Sticks. "That's my favorite place."

"Mine, too," she said brightly. "It's safe there."

He frowned at that. "Safe? No . . . I don't think so. Safer, maybe."

They thought about it and nodded at the same time. "Safer," she agreed. "Then there's the one with the 3-D animated tornado outside."

"Café Vortex," supplied Sticks. "And the little one by the park. The Crippled Dwarf. I'm not allowed in there. That's only for . . . for . . ."

"Invited?" she suggested. They paused for a moment.

"Invited," he said, but he wasn't sure. "We're not invited. Not like that. We're what the people in the Zone call refugees. But the other clubs are open to anyone. There's another big one, but I haven't been in there. It scares me."

Rain thought about it and asked, "With a big red neon hand outside? Torquemada's, maybe? Is that a real name?"

"It is," he said. "I looked it up after the first time I dreamed about it. Tomás de Torquemada was the guy who pretty much ran the Inquisition. He tortured and killed people in the name of God. Witches and such."

"So what's that make the club? An BDSM joint?"

"No. It's a dance club. I'm not sure why they picked that name. Clubs are like that, I suppose, even in the Fire Zone."

"Yes," she said, "but it's definitely not safe."

"No."

"In my dreams," said Rain, "I know I want to go in there because that's where the best dancers go, but like I said, I'm not a dancer anymore."

"I saw you running yesterday," he said. "You moved pretty damn well."

"It's not the same thing."

He gave her a look. "You're telling me that you can't even party dance? I find that hard to believe."

"I can't dance anymore," she said, putting enough claws in it to stop that part of their discussion.

He didn't argue. Instead, they talked about it for half an hour, trying to pull more details out of what they remembered, and feeding off half-remembered bits from each other. She had some of it and he had some, but apart from the clubs and the Music, none of the other details were shared. Mute, faceless dancers who dressed in colorful leotards and danced and danced to try to save their souls. Types of music with odd names like "othertone," "ultrafusion," "demitrend," "musica morbifica," and "suicide blues." Rain knew that people left their real names behind and took strange nicknames; but it was Sticks who came up with some of those new identities. A DJ named Oswald Four, a bartender named Brutal John, a pharmacologist who called himself Doctor Velocity, an ancient and wizened repairman named Caster Bootey who Sticks said was kind of like Yoda.

"He always says cryptic shit that you know is important," said Sticks, "but which don't make much sense. I think maybe it's like Zen, where you have to puzzle your way through it 'cause if you don't figure it out, then the answer won't mean as much."

Eventually, they talked themselves out and fell into a mutual silence, smiling at each other. The smiles faded.

"Well," said Rain, "either we're both completely out of our freaking minds or we're going to the same place."

"In dreams," he corrected. "Only in dreams."

"Maybe," she said. "We were both on Boundary Street."

Sticks winced. "Okay, but that place scares the shit out of me. I never want to go back."

"Even if that's how you get to the Fire Zone?" asked Rain. "For real, I mean. What if you *have* to cross Boundary Street in order to find that hill that goes up to the Fire Zone?"

"You want to know what happened when I got home yesterday?" said Sticks flatly. "I was sick as a goddamn dog. I threw up. I crapped my brains out. I even had some blood in my pee. I started feeling sick as soon as I stopped my car by that alley, and it got worse the whole drive to the Port Authority. I thought I was going to shit in my drawers in the Rocket. Made it to my apartment just in damn time, but it was close. And all last night, I had some of the worst nightmares I ever had. Do I want to go to the Zone again? Sure. In dreams. But no way am I ever going back to Boundary Street. No fucking way."

When Rain did not answer for a long time, Sticks's face fell. "Oh . . . shit. That's why you called me, isn't it? Aw, fuck, man. You want me to take you *back* there?"

"Sticks, I need to figure out what's happening to me. I need to find that little boy. Whether he's my son or not, I need to find him. He's alone and he's scared and he's in trouble."

Sticks leaned back from her. "And *we're* the rescue party? I don't want to be mean here, Rain, but we're a cripple and a crazy lady. If there are monsters out there, then how are we going to fight them? Seriously, tell me how."

"We have to try."

"The fuck we do," he said with real heat. "I fought my war and look what happened. I got nothing left to give. I drive a car and I live small and I got next to nothing, but I don't want to lose what little I got left."

"He's a kid, Sticks."

He took a breath, let it out. "He's not my kid. And there's a real good chance that, taking into account all the drugs you said you took, he's not your kid, either. Maybe he's not even there. You even said it, Rain—maybe this is all you flashing back or losing your shit. I don't know, but if you're auditioning for the remake of *Buffy the Vampire Slayer*, then I'm not volunteering to be part of your Scooby gang. That's TV shit. In the real world, the Big Bad chews you up and spits you out and grinds what's left into the pavement."

"Fuck you, Sticks," she said, but there was no emphasis in it. Rain slid out of the booth and stood.

"Wait," said Sticks, making a grab for her. She eluded him easily, fished in her purse for money and threw it down on the table. "Don't do this," he begged.

She looked down at him. "You had me for a moment there," she said coldly. "The Fire Zone . . . all of that. I thought you understood."

"I do," he insisted but then slapped his hand against his walking sticks. "Seriously, though, what can *I* do?"

"You could believe me."

He said nothing, and his silence lasted too long.

Rain turned and walked out of the diner.

INTERLUDE SEVEN
THE MONSTERS AND THE TODDLER

They ran together in the dark.

Well, not together. Not exactly.

The toddler ran, and the monster chased him.

The monster was fair about it. He always gave the toddler a lead, let him take a dozen steps, two dozen. Then he would run after him with his long, thin legs. The monster always caught the toddler. And even when he gave him a hundred steps, the toddler could only run so far. The cellar was big, but all the doors were locked, and the toddler had never learned how to climb stairs. Even if he could, there were monsters on the stairs, too. The Mulatto was there most of the time, sitting still and quiet and always watching. Or the nurse was there, her sharp silver knitting needles going clickety-clickety-clack. *Sometimes the stairs were covered with nightbirds, sitting five to a step, watching with dead eyes.*

It was fun, sometimes, to let the toddler keep trying to run, to keep looking for a way out or a place to hide. That was part of the fun. That was delicious.

CHAPTER THIRTY-EIGHT

Rain wanted to run.

Not run home. Just run. Any way. Far away. She wanted to outrun her life. She wanted to run so far that no one she'd ever meet would know her name. It was so tempting.

All she had to do was go. She could figure it out. Food, clothing. Whatever. She'd lived hard before and she could do it again, but this time without drugs. Without anything or anyone. It would be like she died here and was reborn somewhere else. Why not? After all, dying was easy. She'd done it twice already.

Nothing would feel more right. Nothing felt sweeter to her. Screw Sticks, screw Doctor Nine, screw his nurse, screw psychosis, screw LSD and Void flashbacks, screw NA, screw everyone. If she could have gotten a match and a big enough gas can, she'd have set it all to burn.

Halfway home, she stopped and looked at a bus that was rolling toward her. She could get on and go. To hell with whatever was back home. Her charger, her clothes, her laptop. Could she leave that behind? There had been plenty of times when she'd had less than she had now. No possessions meant no attachments. No obligations. There was a song lyric playing in the back of her head. Something about freedom meaning that you had nothing left to lose. Rain didn't know what song it was from. It made sense to her, though. Nothing left to lose and nothing left to care about. Things you owned also owned you. She'd read that in a book once.

The bus driver saw her and angled toward the curb. The door hissed open, and Rain took one step toward it.

"Anytime now, sweetheart," said the driver. He looked bored and disinterested.

Rain almost took that next step. Almost.

Almost.

Almost.

Bug was at home. Small, vulnerable, innocent. Bug needed her.

"Sorry," she said. "Wrong bus."

The driver gave her a quizzical look. "Only bus on this route."

"Sorry," she said again. "My bad. Sorry."

The driver's eyes lingered on her for a moment longer, and then he shook his head and pushed the button to close the door. The bus pulled away, and she stood there and watched it go. A pair of black crows flapped lazily after it. Another squatted on the roof of a liquor store across the street. Watching her.

"Up yours," she said.

The bird opened and closed its mouth very slowly as if taking a bite out of the moment. Thunder rumbled in the east.

Bug. Sweet little dog.

And Dylan.

The weight of the impending storm crushed down on her. Rain turned and walked away beneath clouds that sometimes rained on her and sometimes blew cold wind in her face. It was as aimless a walk as yesterday, but this time she was in her own neighborhood. The stores were familiar, their lights on, doors open, signs welcoming. After a fashion. This was still what Yo-Yo called the "closeout sale rack" of Brooklyn after all. No one had gentrified this part.

She kept trying to be furious at Sticks, but it took too much effort. It wasn't his fault, and she knew it. This was her stuff. Either her madness or her twisted reality or her horror show. Whatever. It was hers, not his. Not anyone else's.

So she went home. To Bug. To the emptiness. The bathroom was still empty. Of course it was.

She sat on the edge of her bed and removed the knife from her purse, feeling stupid now that she even carried it. Rain put it back in its drawer in the kitchenette, shucked off her clothes, put on sweats, and crawled under the covers with Bug. Raindrops began beating against the window.

Once upon a time, during a therapy session with one of the few shrinks who was not simply going through the motions with the inmates at the rehab center, she'd gotten a lecture about that. The shrink—and Rain had long since forgotten the man's name—said, "Rain, you think you're addicted to DMT and crack cocaine, but those are almost incidental. What you're really addicted to is guilt. And not actual guilt, because you feel guilty for things that were or are beyond your control. You borrow guilt, or maybe you've been told that the guilt is yours to own. It's not. I mean, seriously, how can you really be at fault for what happened when you were born? How can you be in any way genuinely responsible for the complications of her pregnancy that resulted in her being unable to dance professionally?"

Rain had argued with him about that. About her fucked-up karma, but the doctor wasn't buying.

"You blame yourself for what happened when *you* gave birth," continued the doctor, unperturbed. "You suffered an amniotic fluid embolism resulting in cardiac arrest. That is extremely rare and very dangerous. The fact that they were able to save the baby with a C-section and save your life, too, is frankly amazing. It's miraculous. Sure, there was some nerve damage, but that's a small price to pay for your overall health. You delivered a healthy baby, and you are a healthy young woman, even after your subsequent drug use. In previous sessions, you've said that you have proof that the universe is out to get you, but I don't see it quite the same way. And, although I am not a person of deep faith, I can't help but think that there are very positive forces at work in your life."

Later in that same session, Rain had tried to pin him down as to his professional opinion of what was going on with her. Were the voices in her head real or not? Was she crazy or not? Was there any hope for her or not?

"Hope," he'd said, coming at it very carefully, "is a tricky thing. Some people say that it's the most dangerous emotion, because it can encourage you to believe that things will get better than they are right now. Sometimes that's true, but sometimes it's not."

"Then what am I supposed to do?" she'd demanded. "Give up and accept that my life is shit and I'm shit?"

"No," the doctor replied, "that's not what I said at all. I said hope was dangerous; I didn't say it wasn't worth the risk."

He never really answered the question as to whether she was crazy or not. He'd given her some runaround about her facing challenges and needing to accept realities. She tuned out most of it even though the doctor, as shrinks went, wasn't a total waste of human tissue. What he had said about guilt and hope stuck with her. It should have been a comfort to her, but it wasn't.

She stared up at the cracked ceiling above her bed and wished she was dead.

CHAPTER THIRTY-NINE

Doctor Nine sat in the back of his car, eating an orange. He used a single black fingernail to slice through the skin, but he did not peel the fruit. Instead, he cut a wound in it, bent his mouth to it, and then squeezed so that juice ran cold and sweet over his lips and chin.

Only after it was sucked dry did he eat the orange. Bitter skin and all.

It was an experiment. The orange was real, and it took great effort to touch it. Easier, though, than it had been when he had tried it yesterday. Not as easy as it would be tomorrow.

Beside him, the nurse lay back, her thighs spread, rubbing at her naked crotch with furious fingers and laughing as she came. Her thighs and the seat were soaked, and the windows of the car were fogged.

CHAPTER FORTY

Bug began barking. Short, sharp sounds that knocked her back into wakefulness one jolt at a time. Rain rubbed her eyes and then looked into the small fuzzy face. Into liquid brown eyes. Bug was wagging her tail, needing to be paid attention to.

"Come here, you little monster," she said and pulled the dog to her, enduring licks all over her face. They lay there for a while, doing nothing but sharing warmth. Sometimes that was enough.

Then Rain got up, dressed, and took Bug out for a long walk, trying to exercise the night away and reclaim at least the physical feeling of normalcy. Bug had to sniff everything and left tiny drops of pee here and there, which Rain assumed was the canine version of text messaging with her friends. It was early, though, and the streets were mostly empty. A few of the neighborhood tough guys were out on their usual corners, and they nodded to her. One of them, a guy she used to buy rock from, tapped his pocket and raised an eyebrow, but Rain shook her head. They had that same conversation a dozen times a month. He always responded with the same knowing smile, as if he was saying, "Give it time, girl. You'll be back."

She hoped he was wrong about that, but she wasn't certain.

Back home, she gave Bug some treats, told her to behave, put some music on for company, then went downstairs alone and walked over to Joplin's building. A threadbare crow balanced uneasily on the telephone line, its beady black eyes fixed on her. She didn't like the way it followed her every move. Maybe the rain would chase it away. The sky looked ready to burst. Again. Lately the weather report was the same. Rain, rain, and more rain, with occasional lightning. And rain.

"I ought to change my name to Sunny and Dry," she told the bird. It fluttered its wings and dropped a big splat of white poop onto the ground near her feet. "Yeah, well, there's that."

She called Joplin, got voice mail, disconnected. Then she texted him to say she was downstairs and asked if she could come up. No answer.

Rain waited for about a minute before making up her mind.

"Might as well," she told the crow. It opened its beak as if it were going to caw again, but this time there was no sound. Rain shrugged, climbed the steps, pushed the door open, and stepped inside. The door did give a haunted house creak, but the foyer was unusually cold and smelled strongly of Pine-Sol. There were two dead roaches on the floor below the mailbox. Big black ones, sprawled on their backs. The names on the mailboxes were unfamiliar to her. Diaz, Conseco, Smith, Smith, Alensky, Hoto, Joplin of course, and others. She fished around in her head to try to come up with any first names she may have heard that might match those names. Was there an Esteban here? An Anita? Maybe a Stanley. Had Joplin ever mentioned any of them by name? She didn't think so. She debated going back to her apartment to write a note that she could tape to the wall here, but frankly didn't know what she wanted to say or if anyone would respond.

Then there was the *thump-thump* of feet on the stairs, and there was Joplin, jogging down to the foyer. He blinked in surprise and then smiled a big, warm, happy smile and came toward her, arms wide. He gathered her up, and she clung to him. Then she shoved him back and jabbed his chest with a stiff finger.

"I've been calling and calling you," she said. "Don't you ever listen to your messages?"

"Oh, yeah, geez, I'm sorry," he said. "I forgot to bring my charger when I went to my sister's place. Got home half an hour ago. I was heading out to get some paint." His sister, Lanie, lived in the Village. She managed an office and didn't do much to hide the fact that she didn't like Rain very much.

"Christ," complained Rain, "I really needed to talk to you."

He studied her, frowning with concern. Scot Joplin was thin, black-haired, and bearded but not in a hipster way. He had very pale brown eyes and a full, sensuous mouth. He wore a University of Pennsylvania sweat-shirt over jeans and ancient Chuck Taylors.

"Why?" he asked quickly. "What's wrong?"

"I came over because of what happened last night. The kid . . . ?"

"You heard about that? That was seriously messed up."

"I was here last night."

Concern clouded his face. "Here? Why? Did you know that kid?"

"No," she said and explained about coming back from the diner with Yo-Yo.

Joplin looked puzzled. "Maybe I'm sleep deprived, Rain, but am I missing something? If you didn't know the kid, why come over here now?"

"Why not come over? Somebody died practically next door. It's scary. Why's that hard to understand?"

Joplin thought about it, shrugged. "Okay. Sure. I guess I can see that. Freaked me out, too. I mean . . . why would a kid that young do something like that?"

"Something like what?"

He gave her a quizzical look. "I thought you said you and Yo-Yo were here last night."

"We got here when the EMTs were taking the body out. I don't know what actually happened."

Joplin pointed up the stairs. "Third-floor landing. Up there where the super's working on the ceiling and has everything torn out with the pipes exposed. Kid goes up there, wraps a plastic shower curtain around the big cold water pipe, climbs up on the workman's ladder, and jumps."

"He *hung* himself?"

"Yeah. How freaky is that?" Joplin scratched his bearded chin. "I heard the cops talking about it. They said he did it wrong."

"Wrong?"

"Tied the knot too tight. The one cop said that when they hung people in the old days, they had a little slack in the noose so that there was a jerk on impact that broke the neck and made it quick. Tie it too tight, though, and you just hang there and choke to death."

Rain went to the bottom of the stairs and looked up. She couldn't see anything, but she shivered anyway. "That's horrible."

Joplin said, "The cop said that the kid must have been hanging there for half an hour before he choked out. Said he must have had second thoughts or panicked by reflex or whatever, but there are all these marks on the wall from him kicking and scratching. It's nasty as shit. They'll have to paint it all out once they finish doing the pipes and ceiling. Glad I don't live on three." He paused and glanced up the stairs, too, then cut her a sideways look. "Which makes me sound like a heartless prick."

Rain said nothing.

He winced. "It's pretty sad. Little kid and all, I mean. I meant that stuff like this really turns dials on me. My cousin, Jimmy, committed suicide. He'd been busted for stealing cars in Des Moines, and his lawyer said he was probably going to do a year or two in jail. He was claustrophobic, and the thought of being locked in a cell drove him nuts. Even the two days he spent in county lockup before his folks bailed him out made him go nuts. Screaming and hitting himself. They took him to a psych ward for evaluation, and he spent a whole night in four-point restraints and a week under observation. He was climbing the walls by the time he got home, and then after what the lawyer said, he must have lost it. He went to this skyscraper, 801 Grand, tallest building in Des Moines, climbed twenty-six flights of stairs because he couldn't deal with elevators, broke into someone's office after hours, and jumped out of the window."

"Oh, God," murmured Rain.

Joplin shivered. "We were always pretty tight, Jimmy and me. Close cousins, you dig? I was thirteen when he, you know, did it. I can't get inside the head of someone who would do that to themselves. I had nightmares for years. Still have them every once in a while. Dreams of stepping out of a window, of falling, of seeing the ground rushing up at me and then trying to take it all back, trying to fly or something so that I wouldn't hit the ground. That's what I used to think about with Jimmy. I kept imagining what he was thinking as he fell. I mean, I can understand being so trapped and feeling no hope at all and wanting to end it, but actually *doing* it? No. That's nuts. That's way scary. I think maybe he felt that, too, on the way down. Witnesses said they heard him screaming."

Rain stepped close and gave Joplin a hug. He resisted at first, stiff as a board, but then hugged her back. They stood like that together for a long moment. Then Rain detached herself and glanced up the stairs.

"The boy from last night, does his family know why he did it?"

Joplin shrugged. "That's just it—no one knows who he is. Didn't live here."

"What did he look like?" asked Rain.

Joplin gave her a strange look. "You mean when he was hanging there? That's a creepy question."

"What? No, I mean in general. Was he white, black . . . ?"

"Oh. White kid, about twelve, I guess. Brown hair. That's all I know. I didn't see him, but that's what people said." Joplin put a foot on the bottom step. "Why? You think you might know something about him?"

Rain almost said no, because of course she couldn't know anything about this unknown boy. She said, "I don't know. Maybe. I saw a kid yesterday."

"In the building?"

She realized that the boy she'd seen outside had been the one watching the EMTs bring the dead kid out of the building. He was not the dead boy. And yet somehow they were the same in her mind. Like the younger boy on the train. All the same, impossible as that was. Even so, she nodded. "Around."

Joplin fished a crumpled business card from his back jeans pocket. "Here. This was under my door with a note saying to call if I knew anything. Guess they gave them out to everyone."

Rain held it close and squinted at it. *Detective Anna-Maria Martini.*

"Maybe I'll call." She changed the subject. "How'd it go in the city?"

"Good, I think. I have six canvases up at this café in the Village, and they said the owner wanted to talk to me, so I'm hoping it means he wants more stuff now, but I want to talk to them about putting more up. I borrowed a few bucks from Lanie to get more supplies. She knows the owner, so . . . here's hoping."

"That's great," said Rain with feigned enthusiasm. "Which café?"

"The Human Bean, on Avenue B?"

"Oh," she said, "yeah, sure." She'd gone into the Human Bean once, but it seemed pricey and affected, with people sitting in clusters of old mismatched armchairs and sofas, heads bent together in earnest conversations, probably about things that didn't matter to Rain. Politics and stuff.

"Started a new canvas the second I got home," said Joplin. "It's going to be a little different than the other pieces. Less representational, more suggestive but not straight impressionism or abstract. Somewhere in between. Taking a few creative risks."

"Can I see it?"

"I'll be back in a couple of hours. If you want to come over, I can make something. I have pasta and some spicy sausage, and I can pick up a bottle of . . ."

His voice trailed off and he looked embarrassed.

"I can drink wine," Rain said. "*We've* had wine together, remember?"

"Yeah. That was a long time ago, and I thought maybe it was, I don't know, not allowed."

"Wine's allowed. Alcohol is not my drug of choice."

He tried not to wince, failed, looked even more embarrassed. "Look, I need to go get my stuff. Yes or no on dinner?"

"Yes. And yes to wine, too. Something very red and very Italian."

"Cool," he said, looking relieved. They went outside together. Her apartment was to the left; the art supply store was eight blocks to the right. Joplin started to go, stopped, looked into her eyes for a moment. "Hey, are you okay?"

She actually laughed. "I had a weird day. Tell you about it over dinner."

"So . . . it's not what happened to the kid."

"Nothing to do with that," she lied.

He kissed her and left, and she watched him go. Joplin was sometimes distracted, occasionally flaky, often too much in his own head, and wasn't really her boyfriend. But he was pretty, he was kind, and he could kiss. Even his quick kisses were warm and deep and very nice. It was like some of the things he painted—filled with layers of unexpected depth and more genuine humanity than was evident from his semidetached social skills.

CHAPTER FORTY-ONE

Rain stood outside and looked up at the cloudy Brooklyn sky.

There was a lot of wind up there, tearing the edges off the clouds and whipping them around. The afternoon sun was only a rumor behind the masses of iron gray, smoky purple, and deep black. She saw that there were more of the ugly crows sitting on the telephone wires and rooftop edges.

Rain didn't like those birds. She'd always liked crows, but not them, and not the ones she'd been seeing around lately. They looked strange, dirty, feathers were dusty and dry and . . .

Dead.

The word was whispered inside her mind by a voice that did not belong to her parasite or anyone else she knew. It was the voice of a little boy. Simple, soft, talking the way kids do when they're explaining something from one of their storybooks.

They're his nightbirds. They always watch you. They want to steal your time.

She almost spoke a name. Her son's name. She almost asked the voice in her head if it was Dylan who spoke to her, but she didn't, fearing a trap. What if Doctor Nine was somehow listening to her thoughts? It was a confusing contradiction; she could think her son's name, but she couldn't use it when speaking to any of her inner voices. Sometimes she heard Doctor Nine speaking to her from the shadows of her mind. If he could do that, then how could she be sure he could not read her thoughts? Weren't they both the same thing, somehow? Or were there rules that she didn't know? If being insane even had rules. And if being insane was what this was.

Shhhh, whispered the boy.

Rain blinked and realized with a jolt that she'd been standing there with her eyes closed. Not looking at the birds at all. Just standing. Asleep or . . .

She glanced up at the crows and saw that there were six of them now, but she hadn't seen the new ones arrive. She glanced around and saw that a car that had been parked near her was gone and a beat-up Jeep was parked in its place, and yet she'd not heard or seen a thing.

Did I actually fall asleep just now? she asked herself. It was an absurd question, and a scary one. The birds cawed as if laughing at her.

"They're his nightbirds," she murmured, repeating what the boy had whispered to her. "They want to steal my time."

Only afterward did she realize that she had changed it from "your time" to "my time." Accepting it, taking ownership of it. She listened for more, but the boy's voice was as silent as if it had never spoken.

The crows on either side of the street cawed at her. A warning?

She almost shouted "Fuck you!" at them, but didn't. Instead, she turned toward the door to the brownstone. It still stood ajar. She had a powerful and—she admitted to herself—irrational need to see where the boy had died.

Rain went in.

The hall was empty, and as she passed the row of mailboxes, Rain brushed her fingers against the nameplate for JOPLIN. Then she climbed the steps. Each single step creaked in its own key. Shrill or sneaky, painful or plaintive. The first-floor landing was only half-lit, with two of the six overhead fluorescents gone dark and smoky. The disinfectant smell was stronger up here, but she could smell pot smoke and patchouli incense. There was a bundle of last week's *New York Daily News* tied with string and stained with coffee and urine. There were lots of greasy footprints and wheel tracks on the runner that led to the second flight of stairs, so Rain followed the path left by police and EMTs. She winced with each floorboard squeak, mentally rehearsing what she would say if someone appeared to ask why she was there.

As she neared the top of the stairs, Rain wondered why she was doing this. The kid who died here could not possibly be the one she'd seen standing in the crowd with Doctor Nine. How could he be? It was impossible. As she thought this, though, the conversation with Sticks came back to her with chilling clarity. *Christ, we're sitting here having a conversation about monsters and neither of us is joking.*

If monsters were real, then how was anything impossible? Or, along a parallel track, if she was insane, then how was anything too outrageous to accept?

Because there are always rules, whispered the same voice she'd heard outside. The boy.

"Please, please, please," Rain begged as if she were speaking to an actual person. "Tell me if this is you."

The boy's voice fell silent again. It had sounded different, much farther away, though she did not understand at all how that was possible.

The old building seemed to exhale a weary breath as she stepped onto the third-floor landing. It was colder up here, and none of the fluorescents worked. The white metal frames for them had been removed and stacked against one wall, the tubes still in place, and a pair of sickly yellow droplights hung from the exposed pipes. Boxes of new pipe, sheets of drywall, and a bundle of wooden laths were set against one wall, and a rickety wooden stepladder stood beneath the ceiling. All this work had been done since the last time she'd been to Joplin's flat, which was up on four.

The runner carpet was badly stained with dark, fresh blotches. Blood, she thought, and maybe shit, too; and her perverse memory provided her with the ugly information that the muscles of corpses went slack before rigor set in, during which things like the sphincter relaxed. Rather than disgusting her, the thought of the little boy hanging there with crap running down inside his pant legs was heartbreaking. It robbed the kid of even the pretense of dignity.

She stepped into the hall and walked slowly up to the spot where the boy must have died. There was one eight-foot section of ceiling that had been torn down, but only three feet of pipes were visible. What had Joplin said? The boy had hung himself with a knotted-up shower curtain? Why not rope or a belt? Why a shower curtain?

You know why, whispered the nasty voice of her parasite.

Rain tried not to imagine that the item the boy had used had been one familiar to her, that it had swirling colors she saw every day. That, too, was impossible because her curtain was still hanging in her bathroom, held up with fresh strips of duct tape. She'd seen it before she left home. Still there. Still there, so it couldn't have been here.

The ladder was positioned to the left of the door to apartment 3F. The door was closed, and a small silver Tibetan knot was nailed to the frame. Rain had seen it before, and Joplin said that the old Japanese guy who lived there lived like a hermit and seldom went out. He was the kind of guy who jumped at shadows and never spoke to anyone except to apologize, and he apologized for everything from being on the stairs at the same time to making eye contact. A frightened, sad little man who put a talisman against evil on his door and replaced it with a new one four times each year, on the two equinoxes and the two solstices. The current one hung askew, and Rain wondered if the boy had kicked it.

Probably. She wondered if the man who lived here was the same Japanese man she had seen putting up handbills around the neighborhood. Probably, though that didn't give her any insight into him.

A sliver of light escaped from beneath his door, and Rain saw a shadow of someone's feet. The peephole darkened for a moment, and she realized that the old Japanese guy was standing on the other side of the door watching her.

"It's okay," she said, loud enough for him to hear. The shadow vanished, and she immediately felt bad for scaring him.

On the doorframe and along the wall closer to the ladder were scuff marks by the dozen. Rain closed her eyes to shut out the image, but behind her eyelids there was a high-def video crafted by her parasite that showed small sneakered feet kicking at the wall, trying to find purchase on the cheap chest-high wainscoting, of toes and heels hammering as panic over-rode whatever hurt or damage had brought the kid up here. Signs of the cold lizard brain fighting against the less practical monkey mind to sur-vive all the way to the edge of the big black. The wallpaper was torn, the crown molding on the wainscoting cracked, rubber and dirt smashed onto the surface of everything.

She stood still and tried to figure out how to react to this. It had been more than whim that had brought her up here, she could feel that much, but sensing that did not bring with it an explanation for *why* she was here. None of this made sense, and Rain desperately wanted to ask someone for advice. Or feedback. Or something. Yo-Yo had been outside with her, but there was so much risk in telling her. And Sticks . . .

Sticks. What was he, after all? Not a stranger. Not really. He'd dreamed of the Fire Zone, too. That meant they were connected somehow. He'd saved her yesterday after she'd gotten lost. That had to mean something, didn't it?

"Yes," she murmured, and she regretted how things had ended between them. His number was still programmed into her cell. All it would take was to press a callback button. She touched the side of her purse, felt for the shape of her phone. Found it. Took it out. However, she did not call. Instead, she opened the camera and took more than three dozen photos of the hall, the pipes, the ladder, the wall, the floor. Everything. Doing that helped. It made her feel strong, even if only a little. It was her *doing* something. What did it matter if she didn't yet know why she took those photos or what she could possibly do with them? It was the right thing to do. Of that she had no doubt.

Rain put the phone back into her purse and turned.

A man stood in the shadows behind her. Tall, thin, pale, dressed all in black. Smiling at her from the darkness.

Rain screamed.

INTERLUDE EIGHT
THE MONSTERS AND THE BOY

They fought together in the dark.

The boy was used to pain. It was his oldest friend. Pain was nothing to him. Not physical pain, anyway. He wore his scars because they were what he had to wear. He ate the pain because it was the most frequent meal on which he could dine. He let it fill him and burn inside of him.

He even began to like the pain.

Some of the pain.

He liked the pain he got when he fought the monsters. The punches, the kicks. Even the whip. That was okay. Nothing the monsters could do to him would be worse than they had already done. After years of listening to them, of being taught by them, of sitting sometimes for days with only a flickering TV for company and news stories of horrors and wars and disaffection and hatred for entertainment, he knew that he had reached a limit. He had been taken as far out onto the edge as it was possible to go. There was only one thing they could still do to him and that was kill him.

But if they did that, then the game would be over.

And he would win.

That was a big moment for him, the realization that he did not need to escape his lifelong prison in order to beat them. He didn't need to find a way to the world he'd seen on the TV to be free. All he had to do to completely, thoroughly, and deliciously defeat the monster was to die.

That's why he fought them.

It was on those nights, after he had lost another fight, that the boy began dreaming about the Fire Zone.

CHAPTER FORTY-TWO

"Shhhh," said the figure, holding a finger to his lips.

Rain stumbled backward, her hand fishing for the knife, but it wasn't there. It was home, snugged into its place, and as useless to her as if it were at the bottom of the ocean.

Run! Screamed all her inner voices as the figure took a step toward her, moving from dense shadow into the piss-yellow glow of the first droplight. He was no longer smiling.

But it was not Doctor Nine.

This man was heavier in the arms and shoulders, a few inches shorter, with brutal eyes, a crooked nose, and lips that were bisected by a diagonal white scar. He wore a black leather jacket over an Everlast sweatshirt, dark jeans, and a pair of scruffy black Payless sneakers. From the edges of his cuffs and above the V of the sweatshirt, Rain could see tattoos. Not the gang or prison tats she'd seen on the Cyke-Lones in her dreams or the gangbangers in the neighborhood. No, these were different. They were faces. Small, pale, black and white but highly detailed. Photo-real. Grim faces filled with pain. Dark eyes watched her from the faces on his arms and throat, and with a sudden flash of intuition, Rain knew that he was covered with dozens—scores—of faces. Everywhere except his hands and his own face. Ghostly human masks that were strangely alive, living on his skin as if they could look out from their prison of flesh and ink and see the world.

"What do you want?" she snapped, hating the fear and helplessness she heard in her own voice.

The man looked at her with dark eyes that didn't seem to want to blink. "I could ask you the same thing."

And then she realized that she'd seen this man before. She fished for it and the memory came. Last night, at the Diner. This man had been sitting at the counter.

"Why do you want to know?" she said, putting as much challenge into her voice as she could squeeze past the choking fear.

"Do you live here?"

"What's it to you?" she asked with more defiance than she felt. Why hadn't she brought the damn knife?

"You don't live here," he said in a soft whiskey-rasp growl of a voice. He looked to be in his thirties; his eyes were a lot older than the face.

"How would you know where I live?"

The man put his hands in his jacket pockets, probably to show that he wasn't a threat, Rain figured, and walked past her. She turned and gave ground in order to keep distance, then watched as he went and stood by the ladder and looked up at the pipes as she had done a few moments ago.

"Saw you come out of your building and walk down here," he said.

"You were *watching* me?" she gasped.

"I was watching the street," he said. "Sitting in my car finishing my coffee. Saw you and your boyfriend. Saw him leave."

"He's not my boyfriend," she said.

"Whatever. Saw you standing there for like twenty minutes with your eyes closed. You high or something?"

"How about 'fuck you'?"

"Fair enough," he said and gave her a small grin.

The thought that she had been standing like a zombie for twenty minutes scared the hell out of her. She moved a bit closer to the stairs, needing to flee, but curiosity made her ask, "Why were you watching the street?"

"Wanted to see who came in and out of here."

"Why? You some kind of cop?"

"No," he said, "I'm a licensed investigator."

"Oh, yeah? Prove it."

He dug his wallet out of a back pocket, removed a business card, and extended it between two fingers. She hesitated so long that he stepped over to the sheets of drywall and tucked it upright between two of them. Then he retreated a few steps, crossed his arms, and leaned against the opposite wall. When she still didn't reach for it, he said, "The card won't bite and neither will I."

"People say that . . . ," she began and let the rest hang.

"Look, sister, it don't mean shit to me if you believe me or not. We're both trespassing here. The difference is I'm on the clock and you're not."

Rain kept well away from him and edged over to take the card. It was a cheap one, and it didn't say much. She could read it easily without her glasses. A name, *G. Addison*; a phone number and email address. Below the name was a single word: *Investigations*.

"What's the G stand for?"

"Gerald," he said, "but everyone calls me Monk."

Rain turned the card over, but there was nothing else on it. "Aren't you supposed to have an actual license?"

"I've got one, but why should I show it to you?"

She had no answer to that, so she said, "I've seen you around."

"I know," Monk agreed. "At the Diner. You were there last night with some people."

"Did you follow me? Is that what this is about?"

He grinned. "You need to get over yourself, sweetheart. Not everything's about you." Monk cut a look at the pipes. "Unless it is. Want to tell me why you came up here? Why'd you take all those pictures? I mean, I'm here on a gig, but you're—what? A tourist? A crime-scene junkie?"

She fumbled for something to say and grabbed an answer completely out of left field. "I blog about crimes in Brooklyn. It's, um, part of a community awareness project I'm doing for my MFA."

Monk studied her for three full seconds. "Bullshit."

"How would you know?"

"Because you're a terrible liar," he said. "And you're way too scared to be someone who creeps around crime scenes. At best, you're a first-timer; but my guess is that you're a civilian and this is all brand new. So let's circle back to why you're so scared."

"Well . . . you showed up out of nowhere. What do you expect?" Rain snapped.

He shrugged. "Look, let's understand something, okay? I mostly do skip-trace work, which is running down bail skips and—"

"I know what a skip trace is," she said irritably.

"Okay. Well, I kind of creep up on people all the time. Pretty sure that I've seen every possible reaction of surprise, alarm, upset, horror, shock, and fear there is. I guess I've become a connoisseur of that sort of stuff. When you saw me, you were afraid I was someone else, and that fried you pretty hard; but when I stepped out of the shadows and let you see me, your expression shifted. You went from being afraid of a particular some-one to a woman being afraid of being alone with a big, male stranger. I understand that second reaction. Women should be alert and cautious, because there are a lot of asshole men out there who have skewed the math in favor of fear being the most natural reaction for chance encoun-ters. It totally blows, and I know I'm a little creepier than most. I look like rough trade, and I *am*. I look dangerous, and I am. I look like I could hurt someone, and I can. I have. And if I tell you that you are totally safe around me, there's no reason at all you should take me at my word. You're scared but you're not stupid, and I can see in your face that you've had some shit happen to you. Maybe a lot, maybe only a little, but enough to make you suspicious, defensive, hostile, and dubious. All of that is fair, and no guy—not even the Dalai freaking Lama—has any right to tell you that you're overreacting or being unfair and prejudiced. As long as we have dicks, more muscle mass, and are still on the evolutionary bell curve where we're closer to cavemen than elevated beings, your fear is 100 percent justified."

Rain did not know how to respond to all of that, so she said nothing.

Monk smiled, and there was a sadness in his eyes she hadn't noticed before. "So," he said, "when I tell you that I can read your facial and body language and know that you were afraid I was someone else, I'd risk my next month's rent that I'm right."

Rain cleared her throat. "Did, um, someone hire you to find out what happened here?"

Monk's smile faded. "I'm looking for a kid from this neighborhood who ran away two years ago. Runaway. Left a note. He'd be about thirteen now. He was always troubled. Bad dreams, night terrors. In and out of whatever therapy his mom could afford. Kid started cutting himself and drawing pictures all over his wall with his own blood."

"Jesus."

"I know. No one was sure if it was a chemical imbalance, birth defect, bad wiring, or life just fucked him up. The woman thinks her ex might have done stuff to him while she was out working."

"Did you ask him? Her ex, I mean."

There was a flicker of something very dark and nasty in Monk's eyes. "We had a conversation," he said. "He convinced me that he didn't know where the kid was. This is one of those cases I keep coming back to, but there's been no trace at all. A shrink friend of mine said that his runaway note could just as easily be a suicide note."

"What did the note say?"

"'I lost all my time. The hands fell off my clock.' He used to draw clock faces on his walls. They never had hands on them. So, yeah, you can read a lot into that. None of it good." Monk must have seen something in her expression, because he frowned. "That mean something to you?"

She thought about the voice of the little boy who'd spoken in her mind. *They want to steal your time.* "It's nothing," she lied. "Look, Mr. Monk, I—"

"Just Monk," he corrected.

"Okay, Monk, I came up here because I saw a boy a few times yesterday and he seemed to be in trouble. I thought maybe it was him who'd . . . you know . . ."

"Yeah. Was it?"

"I don't know. I got here last night when they were taking his body out, and he was covered up. I never saw his face."

Monk nodded, reached into an inner pocket, and produced a four-by-six color photo of a nice-looking boy with brown hair and dark eyes. Unsmiling eyes and a mouth held in a rigid line. "This him?"

"No . . . I don't think so. Same hair color and all, but . . ." She glanced at Monk. "You said he'd be thirteen now?"

"Just turned."

"The kid I saw was maybe ten."

"Could you be wrong? Boy I'm looking for was small for his age."

"I only saw him for a moment a couple of times."

Monk sighed and ran his hand thoughtfully over his face. "My next stop after this was to go and look at the body in the coroner's office. Don't suppose you want to come with me? See if it's either of the kids we're looking for."

It was a repulsive, terrifying thought, and it sickened her.

She said, "Yes."

There was a creak, and the door to the old Japanese man's room opened a quarter of an inch, enough for them to see a sliver of a frightened brown eye.

"Go away." It was said very quickly, urgently, in a quavering voice.

"It's okay," said Rain quickly.

"Please," begged the old man. "Go away before . . ."

"Before what?" asked Monk.

The man flinched. *"Gomen'nasai,"* he yelped, and the door closed.

They heard the lock click, then there was the distinct sound of a deep, broken sob. Rain and Monk looked at the door for a moment and then at each other.

"What did he say?" asked Rain.

"It's Japanese," said Monk. "He said he was sorry."

"For what?"

Monk shook his head and turned away. He took a small glass vial from his pocket and knelt by the wet stains on the carpet. Rain had seen a million vials just like it; dealers used them for crack. It jolted her. But if Monk noticed her reaction, he showed no sign. He removed the plastic stopper, took a pocketknife from his pocket, flicked the blade into place, and then used the tip of the knife to scrape something off the carpet into the vial. He pressed the vial deep into the nap until some of the fluid oozed into it.

"What are you *doing*?" asked Rain. "God, is that the kid's blood?"

Monk replaced the stopper, stood, and held the vial up to study it in the bad light. The contents were yellowish red, and tiny flecks of debris floated in it. "I thought it was, but if so, it's mixed with something else. Piss, maybe, though the smell's wrong."

"Why the hell do you want that?" she asked, appalled.

He tucked the vial into a pocket and didn't answer her question. "Let's go," he said.

Monk headed downstairs, and after a moment, Rain followed. It was pouring when they came out of the building

"Swell," muttered Monk. "Just what we need. More goddamn rain."

"It'll stop eventually," she said.

"Could say the same about everything."

Rain shrugged.

"Hey, by the way, sister, what's your name? I never asked."

"You'll laugh."

"Try me."

"It's Rain," she said.

He laughed.

CHAPTER FORTY-THREE

"Got to make a couple of calls first to make sure we can do this," said Monk, lingering in the foyer of her building. "You can wait in my car if you want." He pointed to the old black Jeep Wrangler Rain had noticed earlier.

"I'll wait," she said.

"Suit yourself."

Monk called the morgue to make arrangements to view the body. He put it on speaker so Rain could listen. It seemed legitimate, and that dialed her tension down a bit.

"Okay," he said, pocketing his phone, "we're good to go."

He opened the door to go out but stopped when he saw that she wasn't following. He sighed. "Look, how about I give you the address and you can meet me there?"

"No," she said, "it's cool. Let me make a quick call first, okay?"

Rain called Yo-Yo, got her voice mail, and explained who she was with and where she was going. Rain also ran through the shower and shielded her phone while she took a picture of Monk's car and license plate. Then she stood under an awning while she sent it to Yo-Yo via text message. Monk looked amused, but when she looked at him, he nodded.

"Smart," he said.

"I—" she began, but faltered in embarrassment.

"You have good safety instincts, Rain," said the investigator. "Don't stop short. Take a picture of me, too. And of my business card. You don't know that I'm not a crazy ax murderer. Send enough information so that if I go all Hannibal Lecter on you, the cops will be able to find me."

She did.

Once they were in the car and driving through the downpour, Rain tried to get a better look at the faces on the man's arms and neck. She knew Monk was aware of her watching, but he didn't comment. Finally, she came right out and asked. "What's with the faces?"

Monk drove a couple of blocks in silence.

"I said, what's with the—?"

"I heard you," he said.

"And?"

"And it's none of your business." He wasn't brusque or mean about it, but he didn't leave a door open for more on that topic. Rain let it go. After a minute, Monk said, "So what's your real interest in this kid?"

"You wouldn't believe me if I told you."

"Try me."

She shook her head. "No. It's too freaky."

Monk gave her a sideways look, then nodded, and the rest of the trip was silent except for the patter of raindrops and the whisk of the wipers. They arrived at a large, blocky redbrick building that looked too old to be of use to anyone. Cars with official plates crowded the small lot, and there were two ambulances standing quietly side by side to the right of the entrance. Rain thought the place looked entirely appropriate for where they'd take people who'd committed suicide. It was cheerless, heavy, and oppressive. Monk parked in a visitor slot and they ran for the door, trying and failing to stay dry. Monk bought hot coffees from a stand in the lobby. That helped, but there was a chill worming its way through Rain's skin down to her bones.

They took the elevator down to the basement, where the lights were too bright, revealing old paint, cracks on the walls, suspicious stains. There was an intensely unpleasant medical stink to the air. A bored security guard sat behind an old desk reading a novel called *The Shadow People*. The title tickled at something in Rain's memory, but it flitted away and she didn't try to chase it. The guard, who looked like a retired cop, looked up as they approached.

"Hey, Monk," he said.

"'Sup, Slick." They shook hands, and Rain thought maybe Monk slipped the guard a folded bill, because the man slipped his hand immediately into a pocket.

"Little heads-up," said Slick, "Anna-Maria's in there with Doc Silverman. She won't be happy to see you."

Monk winced.

As they went past the guard, Rain asked, "Anna-Maria? Is that the cop?"

He looked surprised. "Detective, but sure. You know her?"

Rain briefly explained about the business card Joplin had given her.

"She's a good cop," said Monk. "But she's not the friendliest person you'll ever meet. It's all about the job for her. Doesn't like most people. Treats me like I'm dog shit on her shoe."

"Why?"

"Because bounty hunters like me don't have to follow the same rules and restrictions that tie her hands. I can kick a door without a warrant and all kinds of stuff. She resents me, and I guess I can dig why."

"Swell," said Rain. "This should be fun."

There were two women in the morgue. One was old, with a Bette Midler face, gray-red hair in a loose bun, a white lab coat, and sensible shoes. The other was a thirtysomething petite brunette with a lovely face spoiled by a stern, thin-lipped mouth. The younger woman wore a dark blue pantsuit over a white blouse. Marginal lipstick and eyeliner; no smile. Suspicious eyes.

"Monk Addison," said Detective Martini in about the same way someone might say *head lice*. Her lip even curled. "What do *you* want?"

"Nice to see you, too, Detective."

"You don't have business here, Monk. Get out."

Monk held his hands up in a "no problem" gesture. "I'm on a case."

"A case," said Martini, crushing the word with her disapproval. Then her eyes clicked over to Rain. "Who's this? Since when do bounty hunters have interns?"

Monk introduced Rain and explained where she lived and that she might have seen the victim. Martini gave Rain a more thorough evaluation and then asked to see her ID. Rain was already thinking that this was a bad idea, but there was no way to back out of the moment, so she produced her nondriver state-issued ID. Martini studied it, compared the photo to Rain, then handed it back.

Scowling with disapproval, Martini said, "Tell me exactly where you saw the boy."

Rain had prepared an edited version of events. She described the boy she'd seen and gave a vague description of a tall white man with dark hair and sunglasses.

"He was wearing sunglasses in the rain?" asked Martini.

Rain shrugged. "What can I say? He had sunglasses on. Maybe he didn't want people to see his eyes."

The detective made a face like she was sucking a piece of lemon. "Did you see the man strike the boy?" asked Martini.

"What? No."

"Did you see him inflict any injury?"

"No. It wasn't like that," Rain said quickly. "It was just a feeling I got when I saw them together. I got a creepy vibe."

"A creepy vibe," said Martini flatly. "That's it? That's all you can give me?"

"It's all I have."

Martini closed the notebook but didn't put it away. "Very well. I take it you're here to view the body for purposes of possible identification?"

"Well, I can't actually identify him other than saying if it was the kid I saw with that guy."

"Understood." Martini turned to the doctor. "Navah, would you mind?"

The doctor, who had remained silent and observant until now, stepped forward and offered her hand. "I'm Dr. Silverman. Thanks for coming in, Ms. Thomas. It's a brave thing you're doing."

Rain shook her hand, and there seemed to be more warmth in the medical examiner's hand than in the whole world. Rain wanted to cling to it.

"Have you ever viewed a body before?" asked the doctor.

"No."

"Are you sure you want to do this now? It can be unnerving."

Rain took a breath, held it, exhaled. "That kid must have been in hell to want to kill himself. If it's the same kid I saw, then maybe you guys can help figure out why he died. Why he needed to kill himself. Or maybe figure out what he was running from."

Martini, one eyebrow cocked. "What makes you think he was running?"

"Of course he was," said Rain. "Why would you kill yourself if you weren't running from something?"

The others exchanged looks, but no one answered the question. Without a further word, Doctor Silverman led them through the second set of doors.

INTERLUDE NINE
THE MONSTERS AND THE BOY

"Do you know what 'hope' is?" asked the doctor.

The boy was six, and this was a question he'd been asked dozens of times every month as long as he could remember. The boy watched TV all day and it was on all night, but he did not know the answer to the question.

No matter what answer he tried to give, there was a belt waiting. Or a big wooden spoon.

If he said nothing, it was the belt or the spoon.

Every time.

CHAPTER FORTY-FOUR

The room was very cold and very horrible.

The steel doors, the dissecting table, cameras, lights, all of it. Like it was in every cop movie, every morgue scene, every horror movie. Clean but not cleansed of every bit of misery that had passed through there. Rain could feel the hurt, the harm, the loss, the grief, the pain, the terror, the shock, and all the rest of it, as if all those emotions were spread like a veneer over every surface.

The doctor opened one of the metal doors, reached in, and slid a tray halfway out. The body was shrouded in a black rubber body bag, and Silverman glanced around at them before she touched it.

"You sure you're ready?" she asked Rain.

"No," admitted Rain. She nodded, though.

Monk stood close beside her, and Martini positioned herself on the other side of the slab. Rain guessed that the cop wanted to study her face. *Go ahead*, she thought, *have fun with that.*

Doctor Silverman unzipped the bag and gently parted the folds to expose the boy's face and upper shoulders. Rain was relieved to see that there were none of the big Y-shaped surgical cuts she'd seen in movies. As if reading her thoughts, the doctor said, "An autopsy is scheduled for tomorrow."

"Tomorrow?" asked Monk. "Not today?"

"It's the earliest available slot," said Silverman apologetically.

Martini snorted. "Murders come first, and this is Brooklyn after all."

The boy did not look like he was asleep. Nor did he have the waxed mannequin look people have in coffins at viewings. He was blue-white pale and looked empty. His hair was brown and looked almost translucent. His lips were parted to reveal dry white teeth, and one eye was half-open. The color was a dark brown covered with a milky glaze. The lips were faded to a dusty rose and looked chapped. The flesh around the boy's neck was bruised, but even the bruise had gone pale. The skin, though, had a horrible crimped look to it. Rain stood there, taking in the details but otherwise unable to move, speak, blink, or even breathe.

"Ms. Thomas," said Detective Martini, "can you identify this boy as the one you saw on the street and on the subway?"

"I . . . I can't be sure," she mumbled. "I need my glasses."

She reached into her purse and brought out the old woman's glasses. The doctor had a quirky half smile, as if surprised to see so old-fashioned a pair of glasses on so young a woman. The detective's expression was as cold and uninformative as a reptile's. Rain closed her eyes for a long moment, then opened them and looked at the body.

Everything that she could see through the unbroken parts of the lenses was exactly the same as it had been a few seconds ago. Every single detail. But out of the corner of her eye, through that sliver of disjointed glass, there was definitely something different. Something wrong. Her heart stopped beating as if an invisible hand had reached into her chest and crushed it. Her breath died in her chest, turned sour, turned to poison, because the boy she glimpsed through that sliver of glass was the same one she had seen before. The one from the street in the city. The one from outside. The one from the train.

The one with Noah's face and Noah's eyes.

The room, already cold, went colder still. It reached unreal numbers, became a kind of cold that could not be measured. A degree of killing frost that touched her heart, her soul, and threatened to crack her into a million jagged pieces.

Don't scream, she told herself, shrieking it inside her mind to drown out the sounds that wanted to burst from her constricted throat. *Don't scream don't scream don't scream don't scream.*

Everyone was looking at her. How much time had passed? Two seconds? Ten? More? Time had no meaning at all except that it was measured by the roiling breath trapped in her lungs.

Breathe, you stupid cow. Breathe or they'll know. It was her own voice, and the parasite, and all the others who wanted to own her mind but did not want her to be caught. The parasite spoke louder.

Breathe or they'll make you talk. They'll make you tell about him.

Him. Not the boy. Doctor Nine.

A fly buzzed in the air and landed on the crenelated edge of the zipper on the body bag. Its tiny wings fluttered for a moment, and Rain could see it wash its face with thread-thin arms. Then the fly crawled over the edge of the open flap and disappeared inside. A moment later it reappeared, walking across the bruised and icy flesh of the dead boy. The fly walked toward the thickest part of the ragged marks left by the knotted shower curtain and then stopped. No one seemed to notice it. Not the doctor, not the detective, not even Monk.

Did they not see it or . . . ? Or was it that they couldn't see it?

No. He only wants you *to see.*

The fly stood there, its multifaceted eyes seeming to stare up at Rain as if daring her—and her alone—to brush it away. As if saying, *Go on, girl. Touch this skin. See if you can chase me from it.*

Rain's hands were like knots of ice at the ends of her arms. She looked sideways through the cracked glass at the boy. Then she blinked and the face changed. It was a boy's face, but it was wrong. The dead boy was suddenly older. Not ten. Closer to twelve or more likely thirteen. There was the faintest shadow on his chin and upper lip. The signs of a puberty that had started before his life stopped.

No! She shouted the denial inside her mind. *This is not my son.*

And yet a voice—the boy's voice from earlier today—whispered to her. *Not yet, but it will be*, he said. *It might be. This is me if he wins. You have to do something, Mommy. He's almost strong enough now. He's almost able to come all the way through.*

Rain snatched the glasses from her face and nearly snapped the frames, putting them back into the dark safety of her purse. As she did that, she heard the detective's voice speaking as if from a great distance.

"Ms. Thomas, is this the boy you saw?"

"No." The word came out jagged and rough. The body on the slab no longer looked like the one she'd seen last night. It was a trick. An evil, sly, cruel trick, aided and abetted by the broken glasses. She cleared her throat, coughed, tried again. "No," she said. "No, it's not him."

The detective narrowed her eyes. "Are you sure?"

"Yes." She backed away from the table.

"No doubts?"

"This isn't him," insisted Rain. She wanted so badly to be anywhere else but here. She gave a violent shake of her head. "I can't do this."

Rain turned and fled the room.

CHAPTER FORTY-FIVE

Yo-Yo went into the stall of the bathroom down the hall from where the NA meeting at a neighborhood rec center was about to start. It was a dingy little cubicle and not particularly clean. She cleaned the seat, covered it with pieces of toilet paper, removed her jeans and underwear and hung them on a hook, and stood for a moment, not sure whether she needed to pee more than she wanted to throw up. Her stomach had been a mess for a week now. At first she thought it was the spicy Guatemalan food she'd eaten at a neighbor's birthday party. Several days of Tums and Pepcid later, she was beginning to worry that it might be something else.

The nausea bubbled and surged for a few moments, but then it settled back. Yo-Yo sighed, sat down, and stared at the inside of the closed door. There was a lot of graffiti scratched or inked onto it. Names, crude diagrams of oversized male genitalia, phone numbers, obscenities. The most recent stuff was written in black Magic Marker.

He's coming.

And below that was:

The Shadow People are always hungry.

It should have been meaningless to Yo-Yo, and yet it made her skin crawl. She looked down so she wouldn't see it. When she finished, she got cleaned up, dressed, and walked down the hall in time to see the meeting's coordinator stack the last of the folding chairs against the wall.

"Hey," she said, "what's going on? Was the meeting canceled? Is everything okay?"

The coordinator, a short Asian guy wearing a TRENTON MAKES—THE WORLD TAKES sweatshirt, turned and frowned at her. "You're Yo-Yo, right? That's your name?"

She was surprised, because this was the first time she'd been to this particular meeting. "Yes, why? How'd you know my name?"

His frown deepened. "I don't understand."

She walked over to him. "I asked how you know my name."

"I know, but I'm missing something here. You just told everyone your name."

"Everyone—who? I was in the bathroom."

He looked completely confused and wore a quizzical smile. "At the meeting. You were the first person to speak. You stood up, introduced yourself, and talked about your addiction."

Yo-Yo stared at him. "Bullshit," she said. "I was in the bathroom for five minutes. The meeting is supposed to start at five."

"It did."

"What are you talking about?" she demanded. "I mean five this afternoon. Now."

The quizzical smile gave way to irritation and then was immediately replaced by concern. "Look, miss," he said, "I have to ask. Are you using? Have you used today?"

"What? No, asshole," she snapped, "I was in the bathroom to pee. I was gone for five minutes and you're telling me this bullshit."

"Please calm down," he said, patting the air with both hands. "There's no need to yell. Do you want to call your sponsor? Do you have a cell phone? If not, I can let you use mine and—"

If he said anything else, Yo-Yo did not hear it. She stood there and stared past him at the big industrial clock set high on the painted cinder-block wall. It was a simple design with numbers instead of Roman numerals. The red second hand ticked past the black hour and minute hands.

Against all logic, all sanity, all possibility it told her that the time was ten minutes after six.

An entire hour was gone.

Completely gone.

CHAPTER FORTY-SIX

Monk caught up to Rain at the elevator.

"Hey, whoa, wait a goddamn second," he called as the bell dinged and the doors slid open. Rain ignored him and stepped into the car. She tried to block him from entering, but Monk pushed his way in. Beyond him, as the doors closed, Rain could see the detective and the doctor standing in the hall frowning at them. The doctor's face showed concern; the detective looked suspicious.

Monk stepped back from her as the car began to move.

"What was that all about?" he asked.

"I told you. I never saw that boy before. He's not the one I saw yesterday." Her words tumbled out faster than intended. "And I . . . I never saw a dead person before."

"And you want me to accept that's all it was?"

"Yes."

"Did I mention that I think you're a lousy liar?"

"I don't give a shit what you think."

Monk sighed. The doors opened on the first floor, and Rain got out, looked around, saw a ladies' room, and made a beeline toward it. She pushed through the door to find a small two-stall room and no one around. Rain banged open the door to the closest stall, kicked the seat up, bent over, and vomited. It came out in a rush, bringing up everything she'd eaten and so much fear and horror. It was so much and so hard that it hurt her stomach and chest and throat, and it didn't stop when her stomach was empty. She kept heaving and gagging.

He's almost strong enough now, the voice inside her head whispered. *He's almost able to come all the way through.*

Her stomach twisted again and again.

Then it was over.

She sagged backward against the stall door, gasping, pawing weakly at her mouth. Black flowers seemed to blossom in the air before her eyes, and her face was cold with oily sweat.

You have to do something, Mommy.

"God," she whimpered as she crashed in slow motion against the closed stall door, collapsing down over the pain of that word.

Mommy. Dear God.

Mommy.

CHAPTER FORTY-SEVEN

There was a tentative knock on the door, and Monk called, "Hey, you okay in there?"

"I'm in the *bathroom*," she snarled.

"Okay, okay."

Rain left the stall and tottered over to the sink, washed her face, and used handfuls of water to rinse the sour taste of sickness from her mouth. Then she dug in her purse for gum, found none, but located an ancient container of Tic Tacs and poured six of them onto her tongue. She smoothed down her clothes, ran fingers through her short hair, appraised herself in the mirror. In that bad light, she looked older than her years. She looked like her mother. Same slim dancer's build, same lines around her mouth and between her brows, same look of disappointment and disapproval. She turned away and went back out to the lobby where Monk waited.

"You okay?" he asked.

"I'm fine," she said stiffly.

"If you say so. C'mon, I'll drive you home."

"No," she insisted. "It's okay. I can take a bus."

"It's pouring. If you don't want to talk to me, then fine. But at least let me drive you."

Thunder shook the building and rattled the heavy windows.

"Fine," she said.

"Fine," he said.

They ran for the car, and once they were inside, Monk turned the heat on high. He popped the glove box and removed a pack of tissues. Rain saw the butt of a heavy automatic pistol in there.

"I'm licensed to carry," he said quickly. "There's a trigger lock on it."

"I don't like guns."

"I don't either," he said, and there was a deep bitterness in his voice that Rain did not ask about. He had his stuff; she had hers. They pulled out of the lot.

"What happened back there?" he asked after a few minutes.

Instead of answering, Rain asked her own question. "Why did you take a sample of blood from the carpet? You didn't even mention it to Detective Martini or Doctor Silverman."

"It wasn't for them."

"Then why?"

Monk drummed his fingers on the curve of the steering wheel for a few moments. "Remember you said that I wouldn't believe what happened to you?"

She nodded.

"I don't know that you'd believe me if I told you why I took the blood sample." He paused. "It's something I do. It's how I find the sons of bitches who hurt kids like that one."

"He committed suicide."

"Maybe he did," said Monk. "Or maybe there's more to it than that."

"But why the blood? What do you do with it?"

He gave her a completely humorless smile. "I'll make you a deal, okay? You tell me what's going on with you, and I'll tell you about what's going on with me. I'm willing to do that, but it's got to be all the cards faceup on the table. Otherwise, no deal."

Rain thought about it while they waited at a red light. She shook her head. "I can't."

Monk sighed. The light turned green, and he drove. "Then that's where we are," he said.

A couple of times on the drive back, Monk tried to start a conversation. Not about the boy. Idle chatter. Rain looked out the side-view window at the storm and gave one-word answers until he gave up. As they drove along her block, Rain saw Joplin go dashing across the street, a broken umbrella held ineffectually over his head. He vanished into his building.

Before she got out, Monk said, "Look, I don't know what's going on with you, Rain, but whatever's happening is bad. Believe me when I say that I can tell. You have my card. If you need help, call me. Day or night, it doesn't matter. I don't sleep a lot, so you can always reach me."

She said nothing.

Monk sighed and nodded, and she got out and ran for her door, but when she turned to see if he was still watching her, his car was gone.

CHAPTER FORTY-EIGHT

Joplin texted Rain as she was reaching for her front door.

U home? Come up?

She almost didn't reply. Rain was frazzled, scared, confused, and even more convinced that she was losing her mind. Going to Joplin's would mean passing that spot where the boy killed himself. Whoever that boy was.

She stood in the foyer and texted back:

Got to feed Bug.

His reply:

Feed her and then come over.

She typed:

Need to take a shower.

After a very slight pause, his reply came in.

I have a shower.

And then:

I have running water.
Happy to soap your back.

She didn't reply.

Instead, she went home, took Bug out for a quick pee break, fed her; then Rain changed clothes, then walked to Joplin's building, and slipped inside as quietly as a ghost. She climbed the stairs and lingered but for a moment on three, glancing at the ladder, the exposed pipes and the stained carpet.

You have to do something, Mommy.

"I'm sorry," Rain said softly.

She thought she heard a sound behind the Japanese man's door, but after a moment of listening, there was nothing else. So she climbed the last set of stairs and knocked on Joplin's door. He was smiling when he opened it. He looked at her, and an immediate expression of concern clouded his face.

"What's wrong?" he asked.

Rain shook her head. "I don't want to talk."

Joplin stepped aside to let her enter, then he closed and locked the door. There was music playing. Joplin preferred old stuff. French café music, old

Dylan and early Tom Waits, mixed with opera and some of Chopin's moodier pieces. An eclectic mix that put him in the right gear while he was painting. He reached for his iPad to change to a different playlist, but Rain touched his hand, and when he glanced up, she shook her head.

He took her in his arms and held her. He smelled of linseed oil and gesso and paint. But also of coffee and cinnamon and soap. Joplin put a finger under her chin and lightly raised her face, then he bent and kissed her very gently and very deeply.

She pushed his hand away, grabbed the hem of his black T-shirt, and pulled it over his head. He had a lean, wiry body without piercings or tattoos. All his artistic expression flowed from mind through arm into paintbrush and from there to canvas. Rain unsnapped and unzipped him, and he stepped out of jeans and underwear. He was already hard, and she took him between her palms, feeling his warmth and reality.

When he reached to undress her, she flinched, shook her head, and did it herself. There was a measure of control she needed to find, and she took her time removing each layer, then dropping them like autumn leaves around where they stood. He did not try to touch her until she took his hand and placed it flat between her breasts with his palm over her heart.

Then she took his hand and led Joplin into his own bathroom. He had a glass shower stall. No curtains. Nowhere for something to hide. When the water was the right temperature mix, they stepped in, slid the door shut, and did nothing but hold each other under the spray for a long, long time.

Then there was a longer time of tenderness. They touched each other as if it were for the very first time. Tentative fingers and hands and lips and tongues, discovering the curves and planes of each other. He came before she did, but that was okay. Rain wasn't in a race for any kind of closure. She needed the warmth, the connection, the clean intensity of what they were doing.

Later, after they had dried each other off with big towels and walked naked to his bed, they began again. Joplin kissed his way down the length of her and then settled with his hot mouth on her, his hands caressing her hips and stomach and breasts. He knew better than to touch the ragged scar from her C-section. He'd made that mistake once before. Now he respected her boundaries and her needs. There was no urgency, but even so, she clutched handfuls of his hair and cried out as she came.

In the past, it had been one orgasm apiece and then rest. Not that afternoon. Before her heartbeat had even begun to settle, he rolled onto his back and pulled her atop of him, and they moved as one up a long, long hill, and when they plunged over the edge, they did it together.

INTERLUDE TEN
THE MONSTERS AND THE BOY

They learned together in the dark.

On the floor and all around his dirty little cot were dozens and dozens of windup pocket watches. Doctor Nine sat for thousands of patient hours teaching the boy how to build the clocks. From parts of old, dead clocks, and also from scratch. The Mulatto brought in lathes and grinders and milling tools, and the doctor taught the boy the art of clockmaking. It was the only part of their time together that the boy looked forward to. Making things. Fixing things. Cogs and pinwheels and quartz crystals and springs. He was instructed to lay them out with care. He was required to know and name each piece, and to explain every function.

One evening, the boy asked, "What's so important about clocks?"

"Ah," said the doctor, very pleased with the question. "Time is a scalpel. It cuts with great delicacy at every life. It slices away bits of everyone's future. With each cut, there is less of a future."

"So what?" asked the boy.

"That is a very good question, my boy," said the doctor. "However, I will ask you a question first. What is hope? You know that word. Tell me what it means."

The boy, wary of tricks and traps, was careful. Even at seven he was sly. "That's when people think something good is going to happen."

"Close," said the doctor. "Hope is when they think something good might *happen. They aren't sure, but they hang so much of their lives on that slender little hook of chance."*

The boy said nothing, but he nodded because he wanted the doctor to think he understood. Real understanding, he had long ago learned, would come later, in

162

the long, quiet hours when he was alone with his thoughts. Or when he watched the world on TV and tried to understand what being alive in the world outside meant.

"Time is a scalpel," said Doctor Nine, "and hope is the whetstone that keeps it sharp."

The nurse laughed at that. Doctor Nine smiled.

CHAPTER FORTY-NINE

The only sign above the tattoo parlor's door said INK, but everyone in the neighborhood knew it as Patty Cakes's, after the woman who owned it.

A bell above the door tinkled as Monk pushed his way inside. Patty was there, a tiny switchblade of a woman with a retro purple Mohawk and lots of facial scars. She was half-Filipino and half-Chinese, who'd come to the States as a young woman, dragging a lot of personal baggage behind her, and had washed up there. She and Monk went way back, and it was her drill that had sunk the ink of half of his body art. The most photo-real of the faces were her work, and she was the only one apart from Monk who knew what those faces meant. And what they did to and for Monk. She cried sometimes when she was doing the art, and sometimes she screamed. Sometimes they both did. And a lot of times, they got drunk together and talked about places far away from there. Vietnam and Tibet, back alleys in Shanghai, and villages in Colombian jungles. Sometimes they talked about the Fire Zone, and sometimes they talked about Boundary Street. Sometimes they just got drunk together and clung to each other as the wheel of night turned. They weren't lovers. Patty called it being "soul family," and Monk could accept that.

She was doing cleanup on her tools and looked up to see what kind of expression he wore. She was intuitive and usually knew if they were going to have another bad night of ink and pain and blood.

Monk shook his head, though, and held up the small vial of fluid and debris he'd recovered from the carpet in the building where the unknown boy had died.

"That's not blood," she said as she held out her hand.

Monk gave it to her. He hooked a stool with a foot, pulled it over, and sat down next to the small fridge. "There's blood in it."

She shook her head. "Not much."

"Then what is it?" asked Monk.

She held the vial up to study it against the light. "Beer me."

He opened the fridge and took out a pair of Dagon beers from Myanmar. He popped the tops and handed one over. They tapped glass and drank. The beer was light, semisweet, and mildly hoppy. It was one of the few beers they could agree on. Patty Cakes liked IPAs that had real teeth, and Monk went the other direction toward hefeweizen. The beer was ice cold, and it went down smooth.

Patty removed the stopper on the vial and smelled it. "Huh," she said.

"What?"

"Not pee, either. That's what I thought it was going to be. Blood and pee."

"I know. So what is it, then?"

She replaced the stopper and set the vial down on her worktable. "I don't know. If it was straight blood, I could tell you something. I get a tremble off of this, but that's all."

They drank.

"Is Morty still in town?" asked Monk.

Morty Albertson was a biochemist who worked at an independent testing facility that had contracts with police departments throughout New York and northern New Jersey. He was an ink junkie and had full sleeves drilled by Patty.

"Yeah. He's been in here a couple of times. Trying to get me to do some art that I don't want to do. Something stupid."

"Stupid like what?"

"Two skeletons boning each other. His words. He wants it on his back, between his shoulder blades."

"Why?" asked Monk.

"Because he's trying to bang a Goth chick who works in his lab and he thinks that'll impress her."

"Is she fourteen and emotionally stunted?"

"No."

"Then it won't impress her."

Patty took a swig. "Which is what I've been telling him." She looked at the vial. "How fast a turnaround do you want on this?"

"Today."

"It's Sunday."

"Sure," said Monk, "which means he won't be bothered if he goes into the lab."

"On his day off?"

"Tell him if he does, you'll do the skeletons."

"I don't want to do the skeletons," said Patty.

"This is for a good cause," said Monk.

Patty frowned. "What cause? Was the kid who hung himself the one you're looking for?"

"I don't think so. Didn't really match the photo. I'm going to call Doc Silverman in a bit to see if she'll email me the fingerprint ten-card to see if she can put a name on the victim."

"If it's not your case, then why the rush on this stuff?" She tapped the vial with a bright blue fingernail.

Monk took a moment with that. "I met this woman," he said and told her about Rain Thomas. Patty listened without comment to the whole story.

"Is she a new client?" asked Patty when Monk was finished.

"No."

Patty cocked an eyebrow. "Someone you're interested in?"

He smiled and shook his head. "Not in that way, no. She's damaged goods."

"Isn't that your favorite flavor? You and all your broken birds."

"Knock it off," he said mildly. "This is different. There's something about her. She tried to fake me out by saying she was a crime blogger, but that was bullshit. Then she tried to play concerned citizen, and she couldn't sell that, either. Anna-Maria Martini didn't buy her shuck any more than I did. No, this Rain has some kind of personal stake with the dead kid. You should have seen her face when she looked at the kid on the slab. But here's the part that really caught me—at first she didn't seem to recognize the kid at all, and then she put on her glasses and did this weird thing where she looked at him out of the corner of her eye. Which was odd because the lens on that side was cracked. It was as if she was trying to see him through the crack."

Patty sipped her beer. "Why?"

"I don't know, but she went white as a ghost. She couldn't get out of there fast enough. Claimed she didn't know the kid at all, but . . ." He spread his hands. "On the way home, I almost got her to open up, but she wouldn't. Or couldn't. Tell you one thing, Pats, she's one terrified young woman. She has some grit and she has some skills at hiding it, but . . . well, you know me. I know what fear looks like."

Patty sighed and nodded. They touched glasses and finished the beers. Monk opened two more.

"And you think the stuff in the vial will give you an answer?" asked Patty after her first sip.

"Shit if I know. I got no 'in' to her. Depending on what I get from Doc Silverman and Morty, maybe I'll have somewhere to start."

Patty leaned back against her table and drank from the bottle as she studied him. She wore a thin tank top that was dark with sweat. Her nipples were visible through the material, and a pulse throbbed in her throat. She blew across the top of her bottle, making a high, sweet, flute sound. Her eyes saw more of him than anyone else ever did, Monk knew. He sat there and endured her appraisal.

"One of these days, you're going to get killed doing this kind of thing."

"What kind of thing?"

Patty shook her head. "I'll call Morty."

INTERLUDE ELEVEN
THE MONSTERS AND THE BOY

"Where's my mom?"

The boy asked the question a lot.

He already had the answer about where his dad was. The nurse had made him watch war movies and replayed the scenes where soldiers died. Never easy deaths. Bad ones. Saving Private Ryan, Hacksaw Ridge, We Were Soldiers, The Hurt Locker. *Dozens of others. Soldiers being shot as they stormed a beach. Soldiers being shot as they huddled in a big landing craft, dying with nowhere to run or hide. Soldiers being blown apart by gunfire, cannon fire, land mines. Soldiers dying alone in remote jungles. Soldiers crawling through burning deserts, dragging shattered limbs. Soldiers trying to stuff their intestines back into the ruins of their stomachs.*

Every time a soldier died on the screen, the nurse said the same thing. "Your dad."

Your dad.

Your dad.

Dead in a thousand ways. Always dead. Forever dead.

After a while when the boy watched those videos, he did not see the faces of the actors playing those doomed soldiers. He saw a kind-faced young man who looked like an older version of him. The same eyes, the same hair, the same face shape. Dying. Dad dying.

After a while, the boy stopped asking.

There were new movies after that. Sometimes only clips of scenes cut from a hundred films and TV shows. People—male and female—tying rubber bands around their arms and sticking themselves with needles. People smoking funny little cigarettes or huffing paper bags or dragging on glass pipes. People sniffing powder up their noses. People sticking needles under their toenails or between their toes. People taking little pills or eating mushrooms or eating strange candy.

The first time he saw the images, he was happy because the people looked so happy. Their eyes drifted shut, and they smiled peaceful smiles.

That changed quickly, though.

The nurse began adding scenes of these same people looking sick, emaciated, wasted, dirty, dying. Dead.

As the weeks passed, the videos stopped being about people in general and she showed him only scenes with women. Young women. Taking their drugs, getting high. That was part of it. The nurse also showed him some of the things they did to be able to afford their drugs.

He was seven when she showed him the first of those videos. It was how he learned about sex.

It was how he learned about his mother.

That knife never seemed to lose its edge.

CHAPTER FIFTY

Joplin fell asleep, but Rain only pretended to doze. When he was deep, she slipped out of bed, got dressed, and left.

On the way out, though, she paused to look at his latest canvas. It was a big piece, six feet across and five high. She stood staring at it for several long minutes.

His work was almost always moody, except when he was doing something on commission. When left to wander his own artistic paths, Joplin tended toward vaguely representational pieces in which realistic and recognizable human or animal subjects were contrasted by impressionistic backgrounds, with colors left to suggest mood and meaning.

Not this time. The current piece had no direct realism anywhere in it. Blocks of color, large and small, collided in a very abstract series of lines that suggested—however vaguely—a city street at night. Harsh lines of blended colors seemed to be cars moving at high speeds while rectangular shadows leaned drunkenly away as if the speed of the cars was warping the buildings. That was what dominated most of the painting, but there was something else, and that's what drew Rain's attention. Joplin had dabbed some pure white in the upper left, but he'd begun to smear and blend the edges. At first, Rain thought that the darker colors were polluting the white, but then she seemed to catch the meaning he was going for. The grays and blacks and blues and purples that surrounded the white were not closing in it, but rather it was like a light shining through all that darkness. If that was what he meant, then it was much more hopeful of a painting than it first appeared.

Hopeful, but not sentimental, she decided, because the white—the *light*, as she now thought of it—was so far away and there was so much darkness between the eye viewing the painting and that purity.

"It's like the Fire Zone," she murmured and then cut a quick look to see if she'd awakened Joplin. He slept on, though, his chest rising and falling, one arm stretched out as if to hold her.

He's beautiful, she thought, and something warm and secret and small seemed to ignite deep inside her. Something that wasn't passion, though the memory of that was still there. No, this was something else, and Rain recoiled from it because it was too close to something she'd felt only once and long ago.

She backed away from the canvas and forced herself to turn away from Joplin.

You're not allowed, whispered her parasite. *Doctor Nine will know, and he'll come and punish you both.*

She almost cried aloud.

Instead, she snuck away like a thief.

CHAPTER FIFTY-ONE

The man in the apartment on the third floor of Joplin's building was Asian, but he wasn't old. Not nearly as old as he looked. He looked eighty, but he was barely fifty. He felt a thousand years old.

His name was Yukio Hoto. Japanese by birth, though he had spent most of his life studying and teaching at Ki Gompa monastery in the Spiti Valley of Tibet. Hoto had devoted his life to Buddha's gentle teachings and to sharing the essence of that knowledge. Not proselytizing but sharing, encouraging, guiding. It had made him happy for a long time; it had fulfilled him and made him joyful, even after moving to the cynical streets of New York here in America.

The last ten years, though, had aged him. He looked like a man made of dust. Grief and guilt can do that to a person. His youth had been leeched out of him along with his hope.

I have failed, he thought, as he always did. *I am the enemy of hope.*

The other monks of his order tried to convince him otherwise, but he saw the growing alarm in their eyes. The fear. The despair.

I am the enemy of hope. I have failed.

He crept to the railing and peered over to see the young woman go down the last few steps and along the foyer toward the door. Tears burned in his eyes, but they felt cold and bitter.

That poor girl.

He remembered her from long ago, but he had no idea she had a friend in this building. He knew the artist upstairs had some kind of girlfriend, but Hoto rarely paid attention to the comings and goings here. He sat in his room and prayed for forgiveness and waited for the clock of his life to run out. How could he even begin to imagine that the child's mother lived nearby? Or that she ever came into this building.

A voice whispered to him. It came from nowhere in particular, but it filled the hall.

He's almost strong enough now, it said. *He's almost able to come all the way through. And he is sooooooo grateful for all your service.*

Hoto cried out and sagged back, crushed, stabbed through the heart at the memory of her sweet, sad face.

"I'm sorry," he said to the empty foyer. It was not in reply to the words. He hoped that Buddha heard him. He prayed that it was so.

Then a terrible thought occurred to him, and he turned and looked up at the naked pipes above the ladder. His lips parted in a silent "oh" and then slowly widened into an equally silent scream as awareness struck him like fists, like bullets, driving him back against the wall, a hand now clamped over his mouth.

INTERLUDE TWELVE
THE MONSTERS AND THE BOY

They built together in the dark.

Doctor Nine taught the boy how to make clocks. Very special clocks. With numbers on the front, a small crystal vial inside, and a keyhole in the back. The boy had seen clocks like that many times, when the doctor and the nurse took him to places where people were sad or hurt or dying.

"Why do it that way?" asked the boy. "Why a key?"

"Ah," said Doctor Nine, "that's the secret. That's what makes this all so much fun."

The doctor held up his own clock, the pocket watch one with all the hands. He turned it over to show that there was a keyhole in the back.

CHAPTER FIFTY-TWO

It was full dark when Rain got home.

Bug scolded her with sharp barks and yelps, but wagged her tail and accepted hugs and kisses. They went out together for a walk around the block, past the abandoned homes and burned-down stores and the drug dealers and the pain. Rain stopped by a Korean market that had closed a few weeks ago. The windows were boarded up, and someone had painted the same message Rain had seen on the wooden barrier near where the brownstone had burned down.

The Shadow People Are Coming!

The first time she'd seen that message, Rain had dismissed it as nothing. A rave notice or one of those needlessly obscure ads for a band that was about to drop a new CD. Not now, though. It occurred to her that the words meant something. Hadn't the guard at the morgue been reading a book about the Shadow People? She was sure of it.

On impulse, she opened the Google app on her phone and typed in *Shadow People*. A bunch of posts on different websites came up, including a Wikipedia page for Shadow Person that talked about how some people believed in living shadows. Apparently there were beliefs all around the world and back through history of creatures that either lived in the shadows or were some kind of living shadow. Depending on the source of the belief, these Shadow People could be ghosts, gods, demons, or supernatural entities who had no other designation and fell into their own category. There were links to podcasts about it, including the radio show *Coast to Coast AM* that Straight Bob listened to. All conspiracy theory stuff. On the other hand, there actually was a band called Shadow People, an ultra-dark heavy metal band out of Saginaw, Michigan. And a movie from back in 2013 about people watching haunted videos that somehow summoned evil beings.

Bug whined and tugged at her leash, but Rain was caught up in her reading. She found several websites that cited studies done in the 1960s and '70s about people in a sleep study who claimed to have encountered "shadow intruders." Some of the articles were weighted down with clinical explanations of perception distortions caused by sleep paralysis, narcolepsy, drug use, or sleep deprivation. Rain had to smile at that, however sourly, because she had suffered from all of that at one time or another.

Bug barked at her.

"Okay, okay," said Rain, reluctantly pocketing her phone. "Let's go."

The little dog did her best to pull Rain down the street and away from the sign. Rain did not notice the Cadillac parked on the other side of the street. Old, black, beautiful in an ugly way, with smoked windows. She had not seen it when she'd glanced across the street during the walk, because it was not always there to be seen.

CHAPTER FIFTY-THREE

Back home, they climbed the stairs, and Rain locked them in.

Bug went scampering over to the bed, dug her way under the covers, and did not make a sound. Rain took a very long shower in water so hot it nearly made her scream. If she could have stood it hotter, she would have dialed it up; but no amount of water could boil off the day. Her only regret was that she also smelled of Joplin's cologne and of their mingled body oils. She closed her eyes and thought about the feel of his strong hands moving over her last night, in the shower and in bed. He had a gentle, knowing touch, and they had made love enough times for him to be familiar with the landscape of her body. He knew the things that made her tremble and he knew the things she did not like. Joplin knew how to kiss, to bite, to caress. Rain felt heat blooming deep inside her, and she wished she had stayed with the artist. For more of him. For more of his warmth.

Optimism was not the emotional muscle that got the best workout from her, but she was starting to wonder if maybe it was time to stop barking at people when they called Joplin her boyfriend. Sure, he was weird and moody and sometimes got lost in his own head while he was working on a new canvas—but so what? She was weird and moody all the time. Joplin was a beautiful man, and he was a good man. He knew a lot about her past and her damage, and he never backed off, never flinched away.

She let the water rain down on her as she thought about him. And about the future.

Then the old, ugly voice in her head began whispering to her. Telling her that Joplin did not know *everything*, did he? He knew she'd been an addict, but he didn't know everything Rain had done to ensure her next fix, and the next, and the next.

"Shut up," pleaded Rain, pounding the side of her fist against the wall.

Tell him everything, taunted the parasite. *Tell him about the train, the glasses, the boy. Tell him about Doctor Nine. See what happens. Go on, see what happens.*

She beat the wall until her fist ached.

After a while—a long while—the parasite fell silent.

"Goddamn you," said Rain, though that might have been directed any-where. The parasite, Doctor Nine, the world, the truth. Anywhere.

She turned the water off, dried off, and dressed in the warmest clothes she had. Thick woolen tights and an oversized sweatshirt. Ugly clothes, but safe ones. Familiar ones. She put on thick socks and climbed into bed. Only when she was snugged under blankets did she realize that her ringer had been off all day. She checked her messages and found a slew of them. From Yo-Yo and from both Bobs. Eight from bill collectors, but she deleted those. One from her mother telling her that her mail was being forwarded. Cold and plain like that, no sending love or asking her to call back.

"Thanks, Mom," said Rain bitterly. Even so, she sent a thank-you text. Good thing text messages lack inflection, and she never added emojis when texting with her mother.

The messages from her friends were nearly identical. They were all skip-ping tonight's meeting and were heading straight to the Diner. That was good, because Rain was not in a mood to share with a roomful of people, many of whom were strangers.

She thought about this as she stared across the short, cold stretch of floor that separated her bedroom-cum–living room from the door to the bathroom and the door to the world. Her tiny place. Her prison cell.

"God, I wish I had some rock," she told the air around her. It was not the first time she'd said that. She said it in meetings sometimes, mostly to connect with the common hunger they all shared. She said it now because she wanted it so bad her brain hurt. She needed it to open a door in the floor that she could drop through and be out of her fucking life. Crack was the only thing that could blunt the edges and make the moment feel safe. Feel beautiful. She often thought about filling the tub, smoking a pipe, and then cutting her wrists so that the smoke would lift her up and carry her away into the big black without a whimper.

She could almost smell it now, sitting there in the gloom of a rainy evening. Outside, the storm bullied the twilight and made her building shudder. Inside, there was the memory of smoke, of bliss. Of escape.

Inside her mind, a voice murmured a single word from far, far away.

Mommy.

"It's not you, Dylan," she said bitterly. "It can't *be* you."

No answer.

Bug wormed her way out from under the covers and looked at her with doggie concern in her big eyes. When Rain didn't immediately pet her, Bug came and snuggled in against her hip and tried to lift Rain's hand with the point of a wet nose. Rain ran her fingers along the dog's neck.

"This is me falling apart," Rain told her in a voice that was far too reasonable. "That's all it is, baby. This is your mom finally losing it. There are no monsters. No Shadow People. There is no Fire Zone. There's no D-D-Doc . . ."

She stumbled to a stop, unable to say the name.

"He's not real," announced Rain.

Why not smoke a pipe? Just one. Why not? Her mind posed the questions as a possibility.

"Maybe," Rain said, putting it out there, nailing it to the moment. Allowing it to be a possibility and accepted the cold comfort it offered. It helped. It really helped, and for once Rain wasn't afraid of it.

Bug whimpered, and her whole body trembled.

Rain got her phone, plugged it into the charger, lay back with her body curled around Bug's. The plan was to close her eyes for five minutes, reset her brain and get her act together, and then get up and make some soup for lunch. It was a good plan. Simple and practical.

She closed her eyes and was gone within seconds.

INTERLUDE THIRTEEN
THE MONSTERS AND THE BOY

The monsters took the boy on trips.

They went to a hospital emergency room, and the boy sat in a chair and watched the nurse and the doctor talk to people who came hurrying in behind gurneys that were heavy with blood and pain. The actual doctors at the hospital never saw Doctor Nine, the boy was sure of that. Doctor Nine was a shadow in the room, a shadow in the eyes of the person on each gurney. The nurse was there, though. Sometimes she was dressed as a nurse, sometimes she was an EMT, sometimes a cop. Other times she was other things. She was always there, though. When no one was looking, the nurse would turn to the boy and smile. Sometimes she had blood on her lips and she would lick it off, very slowly and deliberately.

Doctor Nine followed the gurneys, and he always carried a clock with him. It was the only time the boy saw that particular clock. It was a pocket watch with big Roman numerals and a dozen hands that did not tell the time in any way the boy understood. Each hand had a wickedly sharp point.

Once, when he asked what those extra hands were for, Doctor Nine surprised him by answering.

"They are my scalpels."

"Scalpels for telling time?" asked the boy, confused.

"Oh, no, scalpels for taking time. For slicing it, cutting it off, and letting it fall. One slick—snikt!—and a moment falls to the floor. Another cut—snikt!— and a second is gone, or a minute. Snikt-snikt-snieckty-snikt! A moment of resolution. A kindly thought. A flicker of optimism or a better choice. Snikt-snikt-snikt. Thinking better of something, or pausing to consider, or—my favorite of all—counting your blessings. No, no, we can't have that. Snikt! And the moments fall, and my nurse gathers them up and we take them home. Pay attention and you'll see how it works. Think of it like a tree as autumn sets its leaves

175

ablaze. It is most beautiful before it enters symbolic death. That is beauty. It is like hope—it is at its most delicious when it is about to die."

The boy paid very close attention.

He watched and he learned how it worked.

Every time after that, when they went to cancer wards and hospice houses and homeless shelters and lonely rooms where people waited through the last ticks of the clock, the boy watched Doctor Nine capture moments and store them in his watch. Sometimes they were just that—moments, a fleeting half a heartbeat of time; on other days he would capture whole hours as people sat by deathbeds and realized that prayers were as hopeless a cure as drugs or surgery.

Doctor Nine and his nurse captured all of that time.

In the dark, the little boy worked on the clocks and thought about stolen time. Night after night after night after night.

CHAPTER FIFTY-FOUR

Monk drove back to the brownstone in Brooklyn where he'd met Rain Thomas. He had Joe Pass playing jazz guitar on the CD player, but he barely heard a note of it. He kept trying to understand what had happened today. Rain Thomas and the dead kid did not seem to fit together in any way that made sense. He knew she was keeping a lot of details from him, but he couldn't get a handle on what they were. He could tell a lot about her—from observing her and picking details out of the things she said. She had a junkie vibe, but not actively so. She had a grifter's vibe, too, but he didn't think she was working a con.

The storm had slowed to an intermittent drizzle, and people were starting to poke their heads out into the early evening gloom. He parked behind a car that was up on blocks, its wheels gone, engine stripped and dashboard torn out. It hadn't been there a few hours ago. The gangbangers around here worked fast. Monk was impressed.

He got out and looked up and down the street. Saw a few folks, studied them, watched them turn their heads and look away. People did that when he looked at them. Not always, but people with some kind of dirt they wanted to hide. Not that Monk looked like a cop; it was that people could tell he *saw* them. Saw and knew; saw and understood.

Fair enough.

He dug his hands in his pockets and braced for a moment against the cold wind. A rustling sound made him look up, and he saw a line of thirty or forty black birds on the rooftop above the building where the kid died. He couldn't tell if they were crows, ravens, or some kind of overgrown and underfed starlings. Ugly, whatever they were, and they were almost invisible against the dark sky. He stood there for a moment, watching and being watched. Hating and being hated.

"And fuck you, too," he said and went inside.

The foyer and stairs were empty, and the building seemed to sag under the weight of its own disappointment. As if it had tried to be a home to the people who lived there and had finally accepted its own comprehensive failure. Monk would not have been surprised to find that suicides were common in a place like this.

As he climbed the stairs, his skin twitched and itched, as if the faces tattooed on his flesh were wincing or trying to turn away. It was not the first time he'd felt that, or had the same thought about what the feeling meant. He was pretty sure he was right about it, too.

They know, he thought. *They see more than I do.*

Monk stopped on the third-floor landing. Everything was as he'd left it when he and Rain went to see the body. Same pipes, same ladder, same carpet. He stood there, wondering what it was he expected to find, or to see differently. He cocked his head and tried to listen to the hallway as if it could whisper something to him.

There was nothing.

Nothing he could see, at least.

After ten long minutes, he shook his head, turned, and left.

CHAPTER FIFTY-FIVE

Rain knew where she was.

The Fire Zone.

She'd always known, though it was nice to have the name. Better to have it. Safer.

Safer? Was that truly the right word? As Rain walked along the darkened streets, she chewed on it, tasted it, swallowed it. No. Not safer. Correct. That was the word, though she did not yet understand why that was the right way to think about it. What mattered most, she thought, was that she knew where she was.

The Fire Zone.

Rain looked behind her—down the hill to the dense shadows of Boundary Street.

"That's where I live," she said.

It's where you belong, whispered her parasite. *You're not supposed to be up here.*

"Kiss my ass."

Rain turned again and regarded what lay before her. She was nearly at the top of the hill, and the whole of the Fire Zone was spread out before her. Up ahead was a nightclub. The façade was rough-textured and painted a mottled white, towering above the waves of light that lapped at its base. It soared twenty stories upward into the sky and was crowned by a massive rotating laser cannon that fired a barrage of bright red and blue light into the night. At ground level, the revelers were bathed in the sanguine glow of a pulsing neon hand that was fifteen feet high and the color of arterial blood. Mounted to the left of the massive doors, the hand throbbed with the insistent rhythm of a passionate heart, the fingers splayed wide as if in pain, or in ecstasy.

Rain stopped in front of the club and looked dubiously up at the pulsating red hand and was suddenly jabbed by a splinter of memory from another Fire Zone dream. She had a vague image of people dancing. Not just club dancing but really dancing. With heart and passion, with art and insight. Moving together and alone, giving themselves over to a connection to the rhythm that went far deeper than talent and drilled all the way down into instinct. She closed her eyes for a moment to try to capture the image and bring it into clarity, and for a moment—a single, sweet, delicious moment—she saw the bodies. None at rest; all in motion. She saw the way they encountered the Music. Met it, accepted it, fought it, wrestled with it, flung themselves into it, absorbed it, drank it, and became it. It was too beautiful to be primitive, but it was nonetheless primal. Essential. She knew that she did not have the vocabulary to describe it to herself, though at the same time she knew that no one did. This was something undefinable and yet knowable. Like true art. Like love and passion. Like peace.

You're a dancer, whispered a voice. Her own? Her son's? *Go in and dance.*

"I can't," she said.

You must. Dance for your life.

"I'm broken," said Rain.

Everybody's broken. Everything is broken. Look closely, you can see the cracks in everything. That's how the light gets in.

She opened her eyes and realized that the voice had not come from inside her head. A man stood there. He was tall and lithe and nearly naked. Brown skinned and beautiful, with cat-yellow eyes and a smile that could melt chains and break hearts. Every inch of him that she could see was covered with intricate tattoos that flowed around each curve of muscle. The skin art seemed to move, but always out of the corner of her eye, never when she was looking directly at it. Rain realized that she knew this man's name.

"Snakedancer," she murmured.

He laughed to hear her speak his name, and he laughed when colors exploded without cause in the air around him. Dozens of other people came out of the night and began moving with him; dancing with him but without imitating his steps. It was like watching smoke—always changing and yet always smoke. Waves were like that, she thought, and fire. Always moving, never the same, and yet constant in important ways.

"Dance, little bird," said Snakedancer. He had an accent that she could not place. Some island, maybe. Or Africa. Or paradise. He seemed to be from a place where they understand joy. It was a country she had not visited for a long time.

She looked at Snakedancer and past him to the big translucent glass doors. Shadows of the people inside moved and swayed to the beat and the bass notes made the pavement beneath her feet shudder. She could feel it like a slow heart attack, pulsing inside her chest, but feeling wrong, hurting because she was not part of this.

The tall dance master reached out and tried to touch her face. Sadness flickered through his smile. "You need to dance," he said.

"I . . . can't," she said, fighting tears. "I used to, but not anymore."

"The dance never stops," he said. "Dance for your life."

And then he turned and gathered his flock, and they all swept through the doors of the club. For a moment, when the doors were open, she caught a glimpse of a massive room crowded with hundreds of dancers. Laser lights whipped and swept and stabbed, and the Music held sway over everything. Then the doors closed and Rain sagged back, feeling stupid and dirty and abandoned.

Brokenhearted, Rain turned and walked away as fast as she could. Across the street and along the broad avenue. Not back toward Boundary Street, but parallel to it. There was a park ahead, and she hurried toward it, avoiding the couples who walked hand in hand toward the sounds of Music.

At the near corner of the park was a tall metal pole wreathed in wrought iron ivy and roses, atop which was an antique clock. The glass cover hung open, and an old man stood on a stepladder as he studied the exposed gears. Rain stopped to look up at him. The clock was old, but the man looked so much older. Ancient. His skin was dusty brown gray, and she couldn't tell if he was Middle Eastern or black or Native American. His features seemed to be a little bit of everything. His hair had long since turned to a white frosting. He was dressed in denim coveralls, with tool belts crisscrossed like the gun belts of a western quick-draw hero. A red toolbox was perched on the top of the stepladder and rattled as he twisted and turned his arms to try to reach some awkward gear. There was a *clunk*, and the man leaned back, lips pursed in concern as he studied the broken clock. He tapped a wrench against one calloused palm.

"Well, that's not good," he said; then he seemed to sense her watching, and he turned to look down at Rain. "Hello, missy."

"Hi," she said. "Having trouble?"

The old man smiled. He had a wonderful smile. The kind of smile Rain wanted to stand closer to.

You could be near that smile, but the nightbirds could not. Doctor Nine could not abide the light of that smile. Not him, or his nurse, or any of the shadows he traveled with. Rain cocked her head as if to listen to that thought. It was a realization that came with no actual explanation, and yet she knew that it was the truth.

The repairman studied her, lips pursed. "You're asleep, aren't you?"

She blinked. "I . . . I think so . . . ?"

He nodded. "It's okay. A lot of people are asleep. Even some of my best friends. Some people having been sleeping for a long time now."

"This is a dream?" she asked.

"Well, sure, I suppose that's one of the things this is," said the repairman. He took a cloth from his pocket and began cleaning his wrench. There was a burst of laughter and noise as someone else opened the door to the club and went inside. The old man glanced at the club and then at her, nodding as he did so. Then he glanced at her and nodded again. "Ah."

"What?"

"You didn't go into Torquemada's." *Torquemada's.* Sticks had mentioned that name.

"How did you know?"

"Dream, remember?" he said. "Stuff like this happens in dreams. And people like me know all kinds of mysterious stuff. Isn't that how dreams are supposed to work?"

"I guess."

"Sure they are. All sorts of things like this happens in dreams. It's weird and it's strange, but 'weird and strange' are what grease the wheels of dreams."

Rain had no idea how to respond to that. The old man got down off the stepladder and placed the wrench with great care in the toolbox. There was a reverence in the way he handled the tool.

"Here's another thing about dreams," he said as he began folding his

181

cloth. "I know your name. It's Lorraine, but you prefer to be called Rain. That's fine. Rain's a good name."

"I—"

"My name's Caster Bootey," he said. "And don't make jokes. I've had that name longer than people been using it to talk about sneaking into each other's lives late at night. And, besides, it has an *e*. Bootey. That's me."

The name sounded familiar, but at the moment, Rain could not remember if she'd dreamed it before or if Sticks had mentioned it. Either way, it was okay.

"Hi, Mr. Bootey," she said.

"Caster will do."

"Caster," she said. "I like that. Do you, um, *work* here?" she asked.

He laughed, and he had a deep, rich laugh. Not a Santa Claus laugh or anything that comical. His laugh was more knowing than that. More grown up. Grown up and grown old. "Sure," he said, "I guess I do some odd jobs around the place. Fix the lights and suchlike. Been trying to fix this clock, but it's got some problems. Keeps losing time."

"Oh."

He gave her a sly glance. "You've been losing time, too, haven't you?"

"How'd you . . . ?"

"Dream," he reminded her.

"Oh. Right."

"You have, though, haven't you?"

She took a breath. "Someone stole Friday from me."

He nodded. "And what do you think about that?"

"I don't understand it," she said. "I don't know what to think about it. How can someone steal a whole day?"

"Happens a lot more than you think," said Caster, "though really people tend to lose their own time. Takes a bit of doing to steal someone else's day. That takes a bit of doing. It takes some knowing how."

"I lost a job because of it," she complained.

"Ah, well, there are always little sacrifices when these things happen."

Rain pointed in what she thought was the direction of Boundary Street. "Why'd he do it?"

"Why'd *who* do it?"

She began to say the name, but stopped and shook her head. "Him."

Caster made *tsk-tsk* noises. "You're afraid to say his name. Well . . . here's a secret. It's a big one and a good one, but it's free. This is the Fire Zone, Rain. If you can't say his name here, you can't say it anywhere."

"I—"

"Give it a try."

"If I do, he'd hurt you. That's what he does. He punishes me for saying his name."

Caster grinned and lowered his arms. "I'll take my chances."

She shook her head. "I . . . can't."

"Ah, well." He took a screwdriver from his back pocket, held the handle up as if it were a microphone, and yelled into it. "*Doctor Nine!*" It came out enormously amplified, and echoes bounced and crashed against all the walls and then fled over the treetops until the winds tore them to silence. Caster chuckled. "Doctor Nine's got no tricks to play on me. Not on you, either, missy. Not unless you allow it. People will always try to tell you different, but don't listen to anyone."

She gaped at him.

"You're going to catch flies like that, Miss Rain."

She closed her mouth.

Caster put the screwdriver away. "This is only a dream, so a lot of this isn't going to make sense. Right now, I mean. It's all going to make sense later. Your part, my part, Doctor Nine's part. All of it."

"My life is falling apart," said Rain. "Nothing makes sense."

"Actually," he said, "everything makes sense. Everything's part of every-thing. That's how it works, you know. That's the secret. Nothing and no one exists entirely in their *own* universe. Our lives overlap and touch and blend and merge and infuse. We share the same air. We share the same stars. Sometimes we share the same dreams—more than people realize. We share the same angels and, unfortunately, we share our devils. We infect each other with good and bad germs, you might say. Your mother gave you a bad dose—oh, yes, she did. You have the bug now. Your friends have it, too, and you're going to think they caught it from you. They didn't. Not really. And you didn't catch it from your mom. Not really. Not in the way you think. Not in the way *she* thinks. It more complicated than that, but also less complicated than that."

She stared at him.

He sighed. "And I'm pure confusing the living hell out of you, aren't I? Well, that's another part of how dreams work. This is *your* dream, Rain. Not mine. I always make sense in my dreams. You have different filters, do you understand?"

"I don't know."

"Think on it."

Around them and all through the park, fireflies burned in a thousand shades of green and blue and red. Caster held out a finger and one landed on it, tiny and lovely. He blew it away with a kiss. "The trick is for each person to find his or her own way to put the puzzle pieces together. You know almost enough now to make sense of it, Rain. Really."

"Nothing makes sense," she repeated, leaning on the words, filling them with anger.

"You believe that now, and that's part of the problem," said Caster. "As long as you think this is a mystery, then it'll be a mystery. As long as you think this is a war, then it's a war. As long as you think that you're help-less, then you'll be helpless. That's how it's always worked."

"That doesn't make sense."

"Give it time," said Caster, then he glanced up at the clock. "But not too much time. The clocks won't be broken forever."

"What?" she asked.

He turned back, and now there was no smile on his face. "Your time is coming, Rain. It's coming very soon. Your time is coming *back* to you. Time is never lost. It's being kept in trust and it will be given back, and you're going to have to decide what to do with it. Shhh, don't speak; lis-ten. *He* is alive in your life. You called him into reality the same way your mother did and so many others did, and do, and have done, and will do. He is easy to invite into your life, but he is a difficult houseguest to evict. You've made him comfortable, and he loves you so. He needs you so, and so far, you are becoming everything he could ever want."

"I don't understand any of that."

"You do, but you don't think you do." Caster took a hip flask from his pocket, unscrewed the top, and took a swig, then his smile crept back. Dimmer, but still a good smile. "Maybe it's time to wake up."

"None of this is making any sense."

"Yet," he said.

"What?"

The phone woke her up. And then Bug started barking.

CHAPTER FIFTY-SIX

He's almost all the way through.

It was that thought more than the ringing phone or her dog's high, sharp barks that woke Rain up. She fought against being awake because she did not want to leave the Fire Zone. She didn't want to lose her grip on those words. The phone won, though, and she fell back into the now. Bug hopped and danced on the bed. Rain pushed the dog aside, clawed for her cell, stabbed the green button.

"*What?*" she growled.

"Rain?" said a familiar voice. "Is it okay that I called?"

"Oh," she said, sitting up and rubbing her face with her free hand. "Sticks? Oh, yeah, sure. I guess. Bug, hush!" The dog stopped barking but watched her, crooked tail swishing back and forth. Rain coughed her throat clear. "Um . . . hi."

"Hi. Look," began Sticks, "I've been thinking a lot about this morning, and I hate how we left things."

"Yeah," she said. "Me, too."

"I'm sorry," said Sticks.

"Yeah," said Rain, "me, too. I've been going through some stuff lately. All that craziness I told you about, and some other stuff. I'm not exactly rewarding company for anyone."

"Maybe," said Sticks, "but what happened at American Dollar was my bad."

"No," she said, "and it's sweet of you to try to take the hit. I shouldn't have tried to pressure you about helping me."

"Okay, sure," said Sticks. "It's all your fault and you're a terrible bitch."

Rain burst out laughing. "God, I am so going to kick your ass."

He laughed, too, and when the laughter died out, the silence that followed hovered somewhere between comfortable and uncomfortable, as if neither of them knew which card to play next.

Rain said, "I dreamed about the Fire Zone again. Just now. I took a nap and I went there."

"Really?" he said at once, his interest immediate and intense. "What happened?"

She told him as much of the dream as she could remember. Torquemada's, Snakedancer, and the old repairman, Caster Bootey.

"Caster! That's great," said Sticks with evident delight. "I love him. Tell me, was he all cryptic and shit? Sounds really helpful but doesn't answer anything straight out?"

"Yes." She paused. "You do realize that this conversation is surreal, right? I mean like crazy we-need-serious-help surreal."

"No joke."

"What's it all mean?"

"I have *no* idea," admitted Sticks.

"It scares me. What if I am crazy after all?" she whispered.

"Then," he said, "it means I'm really part of your dream. I've been worse things to people."

"Me, too, I guess."

"Look," said Sticks, "I thought about things, and I made a decision. It scares the shit out of me, but it's something I want to do. Or maybe I need to do it. Not sure. But here goes . . . why don't I pick you up at your place tomorrow morning? Let's see if the ol' Red Rocket can find Boundary Street." He paused and then corrected himself. "We'll see if we can find a way to drive into the actual Fire Zone. Both of us. Awake. And together. How's that sound?"

She took so long fumbling for an answer, he asked if she was still on the line.

"That's great," she said, half lying. "Thanks."

"Don't thank me yet. We could both be doing something really fucking stupid."

She knew that wasn't what he really meant to say. Not stupid. He meant to say it was dangerous. She sensed that he was aware of it, too, and of her knowing it.

"Tomorrow," she said, and then she ended the call.

A few moments later, though, she received a text that said, "Outside your apartment 10 AM." Rain took a few deep, calming breaths. Allegedly calming. That was tomorrow and there was still tonight to get through.

He'll make you sorry if you say anything, her parasite told her.

"I know," she said aloud.

He'll hurt you if you tell Sticks about him.

Rain felt like she was next to nothing at all. Small, weak, poor, unloved, a failure. "Doctor Nine can't hurt me anymore," she said. "I've got nothing left to lose. I already lost Dylan. What else is there?"

Bug suddenly began barking. Not her playful bark or the challenging bark she used with other dogs. This was the abrupt high-pitched bark of immediate and intense fear. Rain looked down at her and then followed Bug's line of sight. The bathroom. The door was almost closed, the light off.

She had left the door open and the light on.

That's when she heard the soft, unmistakable sound of quiet laughter.

CHAPTER FIFTY-SEVEN

Rain stood there and stared at the bathroom door. Her legs trembled and her heart slammed over and over again at the inside of her chest. Bug kept barking, but she would not move an inch closer to the bathroom.

"No," she said as if saying it could make it so. As if that word could push reset on the moment.

I warned you, but you're too stupid to even listen.

The knife was in the strainer, and Rain began edging toward the sink, careful not to make a noise, not even a sock scuff on the floor.

He knows you were going to tell, said the parasite. *He knows. He always knows.*

Bug growled, but began backing away, crouching low to the floor. The bathroom door creaked. Ever so slightly. Half a creak. It could have been the building settling on its old bones. Rain knew that. It could have been an intruder breeze stealing in through a crack in the wall.

Sure. Bullshit.

Rain took another soft step toward the sink, and then a board creaked beneath her weight. She froze, staring at the door as if expecting it to whip open and vomit forth a tall shape with a pale, smiling face and only black pits where his eyes should be. Or maybe the nurse, grinning through her red lipstick, green eyes filled with malice and bad ideas. She did not dare move. Bug stopped making any sound and stood frozen to the spot, hair standing stiff. Rain's hand was stretched out, fingertips almost touching the handle of the knife. If she leaned she could . . .

Creak.

As she shifted toward the knife, the floor groaned beneath her again. Louder. The bathroom door moved, too. A half inch. Less. Enough to draw a faint cry from the hinges that was every bit as loud as the creaking floorboard. Rain hung there, needing the knife but afraid to make another sound in case . . .

Suddenly, every light in her apartment went out, plunging everything in shadows and stillness and silence. Rain stopped breathing.

Circuit breaker, she told herself, mouthing the words to give them reality.

Rain snatched at the knife, and the blade rasped along the wire mesh of the strainer. The handle was cold and real in her hand, and she brought it up, blade toward the bathroom, clutching it both hands, holding it like a talisman. Between her and—

And what?

Him? It?

The bathroom door creaked again as it moved another half inch open. She could see only shadows inside.

"I have a knife," she said, her voice unnaturally loud in the brown stillness.

Nothing. No sound at all. The bathroom door was five steps away; the door to the hall was six but in the other direction. One choice made no sense at all; the other was obvious to anyone but an idiot in a schlocky horror movie. She knew what she *should* do, but indecision pinned her in place. This was *her* home. Not his. Not Doctor Nine's. He wasn't allowed to be in here. No one was. Rain did not have much, but she had this apartment. Small and cold, with too few amenities and too many cockroaches, but it was hers.

The door creaked once more, moving an inch this time. Bolder. A statement, maybe.

"I'm not afraid of you," she said, trying to make the lie sound like a threat.

A voice answered her, but it did not come from the cobwebs in her head. It came from inside the bathroom. It said, "Yes, you are."

Rain stared, mouth open. It was real. It was a man's voice—*his* voice. He was here, speaking with oily sweetness from the bathroom. Bug screeched like she'd been kicked, and she vanished beneath the bed. Rain gripped the knife so hard her flesh squeaked on the handle.

"You're not real!" she cried.

"If I'm not real, little Lorraine, then neither are you."

"What do you want from me?"

Doctor Nine released a long, amused, nasty sigh filled with ugliness and appetite. "I already *have* what I want from you, my dear. You gave it to me, and what a sweet and lovely gift it was. So full of pink promise. As unspoiled as a fresh-picked peach."

"I didn't give you shit."

Doctor Nine's voice changed, becoming *her* voice, repeating her own words. "'I've got nothing left to lose. I already lost Dylan. What else is there?'"

Dylan.

Rain almost dropped the knife. Her skin seemed to suddenly be made of thin ice, fragile and ready to crack at the slightest touch.

"No," she whispered.

"Oh, yes," said Doctor Nine in his own voice. "And do you know how long I've longed to know that name? To know *his* name? Dylan. Such a delicious name. Ray. Of. Hope." He spaced out each word as if he were taking a small bite and savoring the taste.

In Rain's mind, the little boy ran screaming down the aisle of the subway train. "Please," she cried, "don't hurt him!"

"Hurt him?" Doctor Nine sounded genuinely surprised. "I would never lay a finger on him."

"Give him back!"

"Ohhhhhh, sorry, but you see, I can't. He's with us now. This is where he wants to be. With me. Always with me."

There was a new sound from the bathroom. A gurgling, choking, gasping, desperate cry and with it was the crinkly rasp of her plastic shower curtain. Then there was a heavy thud, a screech of metal as something pulled too hard on her curtain rod. Rain stood erect, the knife forgotten in her hands, listening to the soft, awful sounds of feet kicking at the wall. She did not dare close her eyes, because she knew what she would see. The pipes in the other building, the kick-marks on the walls. She already had imagined it with enough razor clarity to carve it into her mind as surely as if she'd stood and witnessed that boy step off the ladder and fall.

Fall but not far enough. Not all the way to the ground. Fall, but far enough for what he wanted to do. The thumps and kicks shook the thin walls.

Then Rain was moving. "No!" she wailed. "*Dylan . . . Mommy's coming! Dylan . . . Dylan!*"

She rushed the bathroom door, ready to cut Doctor Nine. Ready to slash and chop through the knotted plastic curtain. To cut the jerking body down. But as she reached out, the bathroom door slammed shut hard enough to rattle the glass in the windows. She skidded to a stop, beating at the door with one fist and chopping at it with the knife.

Then hands reached around her from behind.

Cold, damp, smelling of rot and dead fish and shit. One clamped onto her knife wrist, stopping her with the tip of the blade driven half an inch into the wood. The other encircled her waist, fingers splayed so that the little finger and ring finger were low on her belly. His weight leaned against her. So cold. So strong. She tried to turn, tried to fight, tried to move. Doctor Nine pressed himself against her. Rain could feel him. He was *real*. He was right there. She could feel the lean hardness of his body. Thighs like carved marble, a chest like a wall. She could feel him press his groin against her back. His cock was hard and immense, and even through the fabric of his clothes and hers, Rain could feel how cold it was. He leaned his mouth against her ear, and his breath was like the fetid breeze from an open crypt. He smelled of things that rotted but did not want to die. His tongue, wrinkled and clammy as a worm, licked a slow, wet line along the outer edge of her ear, tracing its shape.

"Thank you," he murmured. "Oh, my little Lorraine, thank you *so much*."

He pushed her against the door. It was a sharp, sudden shove that mashed her face and breasts and stomach into the wood with such shocking force that she felt flattened. Then the pressure was gone and she started to sag down.

But with a howl of rage, Rain whirled and chopped backward with the knife.

And cut nothing.

The room behind her was empty.

Almost.

There, on the floor where he had been standing, were maggots. Hundreds of them, clinging together to form the shape of two shoeprints. Then they burst apart and wriggled away in all directions. Rain screamed and ran for the hallway door, twisted the knob and pulled, and nearly tore her fingernails off when the door did not budge. The dead bolt was set, and the keys were in her purse. Rain spun and put her back to the door, the knife raised high to stab.

The lights came on.

The bathroom door was all the way open. That light was on, too.

Rain stood with her back to the door, eyes and mouth wide, pulse fluttering, trying to understand something, *anything*, about this. The metal rod above the tub was torn halfway out and sagged down. The curtain was gone. There was no body. There was no Dylan. There was nothing. In the bathroom or anywhere. The knife clattered from her hand.

"I'm sorry," she said, though her chest hitched and her voice broke over the words. "Oh, baby, I'm so sorry . . ."

A voice whispered to her from deep inside her mind. It was like a wind that blew through the empty rooms of her soul, past the Box of Rain, through a nursery that was never painted and a house that was never a home.

Why did you do it, Mommy? Dylan's voice was a little child's voice. Too young to bear the weight of the things that had happened. *Why did you tell him my name?*

Rain snatched up the knife and stabbed it down into the floor. The tip bit deep. She gave it a savage back-and-forth wrench, tore it free, stabbed again. And again. And again.

From under the bed, her little dog whimpered like a frightened baby.

CHAPTER FIFTY-EIGHT

Gay Bob kept writing. Wanting to, fearing it, needing it.

He had showered and put on boxers, but that was it. He had a pump pot filled with coffee, and he drank it boiled, black, and bitter. He had hip-hop playing very loudly and on random shuffle. He never heard a word of it, though. The last of the pills, a red one, sat on the edge of his keyboard.

He named it. Called it the Little Red Monster. In his fever of writing, of being only half-awake, he thought he could hear it whisper to him.

Don't write any more, it said. *You know he doesn't want you to.*

"Shut up," he told the Little Red Monster.

Listen to me, it insisted. *Swallow me. Let's go play where it's nice and safe.*

Gay Bob sometimes had to stop and punch his thighs with his fists until the Little Red Monster shut up. Or until the pain in his thighs screamed louder. Whatever.

He kept writing. About Doctor Nine and the nurse. About the Mulatto. About all the shadowy people who had driven in that big, black Cadillac over the years. Over the many, many years.

He wrote and wrote and wrote, and sometimes he simply stopped and nothing happened. He never noticed that two hours were gone from his life.

Two very important hours.

CHAPTER FIFTY-NINE

Rain wanted to pray, but she was pretty sure no one was up there listening.

Not that she had lost all belief in God—she had a smidge of faith left—it's just that she did not believe for one moment that the Eternal All gave a crooked damn about her. At some of the rehab centers and even among the NA crowd, there were plenty of people who shouted that God loves and God forgives and God looks out for all his children; but Rain had plenty of proof to the contrary.

It was getting late. Yo-Yo and the Bobs would be expecting her to meet them at the Diner soon. She didn't want to go, but she absolutely did not want to spend the rest of this night alone.

Then something occurred to her. One of those instinctive things that seemed to come out of nowhere but felt right. Kind of right. She sat on the edge of her bed and looked at the three business cards she had on her night table. Sticks, Monk, and Detective Martini. Picked one up. Called the number and waited through four rings before he answered.

"This is Rain Thomas," she said.

"Oh, hey," he said. "Hi. Didn't expect to hear from you."

"I didn't expect to call you."

"You did, though," said Monk. "What can I do for you?"

"How much do you know about the way that boy hung himself?"

A pause. "Some. Why?"

"He hung himself with a shower curtain, right?"

"Yes," agreed Monk.

"Did you see it?" asked Rain.

"The curtain? No, why?"

"Can you find out if it had a pattern on it?"

"Why?"

"I don't want to say right now."

"Look, Rain, if you know something about the case, then you should tell me about it. I can help. And I can run interference with the cops. Trust me."

"Can you just find that out and let me know?"

He said, "Only if you promise to tell me what's going on. No crap about blogging or Neighborhood Watch or any of that. The truth."

Now it was her time to pause. "Monk," she said, "do you believe in monsters?" She expected him to laugh. She expected him to make some snarky comment and hang up.

He said, "There are a lot of ways to answer that question. But, in general . . . yes, I do."

Rain closed her eyes. "Call me when you find out about the pattern."

She hung up, walked and fed Bug, got dressed, and went to meet her friends. She took the knife with her.

CHAPTER SIXTY

Monk Addison's cell phone rang as he was nosing his car toward home. When he saw who it was, he pulled to the curb but left the engine running.

"Doc," he said, "thanks for getting back to me."

"Monk," said Dr. Silverman, "what do you need?"

"Kind of an oddball request," said Monk, fishing a pack of cigarettes out of his pocket.

"Oddball? From you? I'm shocked."

"Yeah, yeah." He kissed a cigarette out of the pack and slapped his pockets until he found his lighter. "I'm calling about the kid we came and looked at today."

She paused. "Considering what happened, I'm not surprised you're calling."

"What, you mean because of Rain Thomas freaking out?"

"No, about what happened to the body."

"You lost me," said Monk. "What are you talking about?"

"Haven't you seen the news?" she asked, clearly surprised. "Someone broke into the morgue and stole the boy's body."

"*They did what?*"

"Stole it," she said, "bold as you please. In all my years, I've never heard of such a thing. Not in Brooklyn. Doing that is bad enough, but then to go and burn it all the way over on Lincoln Avenue is beyond—"

"Whoa, stop," insisted Monk. "Back up. You're saying someone stole the kid's body and then *burned* it?"

"Yes. They doused it with some kind of accelerant and set it on fire, right on the corner of Lincoln and Third. Whatever they used created an intense fire, because the body was literally incinerated, and it continued to burn despite the rain. There's nothing left but ash and some of the heavier bones."

"How'd they get the body out of the morgue?" demanded Monk.

Silverman described the few details she had, which were thin. The surveillance cameras in the hallway outside of the morgue had been on the fritz since the week before Christmas. Slick, the security guard, was on a pee break. There was a three-minute window for someone to enter the morgue, locate the body, remove it without stealing a cart, wheelchair, or gurney, and then vanish without being seen by anyone. The subsequent dumping and immolation of the victim was done with equal precision.

"Witnesses?" asked Monk. "At the morgue or on the street where it happened?"

"None the police have so far identified. Anna-Maria is understandably furious, and quite frankly, I'm pretty upset myself. Why do something like this? Was it malicious vandalism? Was it some kind of ritual thing? Personally, I'd love to see Anna-Maria put whoever did this in jail for a very long time."

"Shit," said Monk. "Any luck getting an ID on the kid yet?"

Silverman sighed. "None, I'm afraid. We're running DNA, but with a boy that young, it's unlikely there's anything on file. Might be more useful comparing it should anyone choose to step forward and claim to be a relative."

"Damn," said Monk, staring out at the night. "Listen, will you answer one thing more for me?"

"Okay, what is it?"

"The shower curtain he used to hang himself with . . . did it have a pattern on it?"

"That's an odd question," said Doctor Silverman, "but . . . yes. It did."

"What was it?"

"It was a clear plastic curtain, heavy grade, with a *print* of a painting. You've seen them. I guess they're popular with the college dorm crowd. There are a lot of these things. Monet, Klimt, Frida Kahlo, I even saw a Kandinsky once. This one, though, was Van Gogh. You know, the swirly one. *The Starry Night*, I think it's called." She paused. "Monk, why do you want to know this? Do you know something about this case? What are you into?"

"To be honest, Doc, I don't know what the hell I'm into."

He ended the call, flicked the cigarette out the window, pulled a U-turn, and drove back to the brownstone.

CHAPTER SIXTY-ONE

They met like mourners. Quiet, haggard, sad-eyed.

Rain saw Yo-Yo and Gay Bob first, but Straight Bob was crossing the street and arrived at the same time she did. Straight Bob was walking very stiffly and carefully.

"You okay?" asked Yo-Yo.

"Wasn't watching where I was going," he said without looking up. "I, um, walked into a fireplug."

They all looked at him, and he avoided looking back.

"Well, ouch," said Gay Bob slowly, the skepticism clear in his tone. "That's got to smart."

Rain looked them up and down. Yo-Yo was taking long drags on a cigarette like she was trying to burn it all the way down with each puff. Gay Bob looked like he hadn't slept in a month. "Okay," said Rain, "what's wrong with everyone?"

Gay Bob said. "Been a day, honey."

"Well, no shit," she said.

Straight Bob looked over his shoulder at the intense darkness. It wasn't raining yet, but they all knew it would. He shivered. "I don't want to talk out here."

No one argued, and they went inside, found their favorite table, and sat staring at anything but one another.

Finally, Rain couldn't take it anymore. "I don't know what's going on with you guys, but I've had a really, really fucked-up day. Want to know what I did this afternoon? I went to the morgue and looked at a dead kid. He hung himself last night in the building on my block. I saw them take him out. Yo-Yo was with me."

Yo-Yo's head snapped around toward her. "You went to the *morgue?*"

"That's kind of sick," said Straight Bob.

"That's kind of badass," said Gay Bob.

"*Why?*" gasped Yo-Yo.

"I know why," said Gay Bob. "You thought it was going to be the kid you saw on the train, the one you thought was maybe your son? Am I right?"

Rain said, "Maybe."

"*And. . . . ?*" demanded all three of them.

"It's complicated."

Betty arrived to take their orders but paused, frowning. "Geez, what's *with* you four? This is usually my happy table."

They mumbled through their orders but did not answer her. She shrugged and drifted off.

Rain turned to the others. "She's right. What *is* wrong with everyone? And if anyone says, 'Nothing,' I'm going to punch them."

Gay Bob tried on a smile. Yo-Yo's face was blank.

Straight Bob put his face in his hands and began, very quietly, to sob.

"Hey, *hey,*" said Gay Bob gently, putting a tentative hand on his friend's shoulder. "What's all this?"

Straight Bob's voice was small, far away. Lost. "I think I'm losing my mind."

Yo-Yo laced her arm through Straight Bob's, and Rain took his hand. They clung together like that. There was no judgment in any of it. They had all stood up in meetings and talked about the things they had done to feed their addictions; the bad decisions made willingly, the paths of self-destruction walked with careful determination. Yo-Yo had given hand jobs at ten dollars each to make money. Gay Bob once kicked two guys unconscious for a minor infraction at Pornstash and then robbed them in the alley behind the club. Rain had her own list of crimes. Stealing from her parents, stealing from friends by pretending to borrow money she never intended to pay back, running street scams on kindhearted strangers. Stealing meds in two of the rehabs. If she hadn't gotten into the last program, she knew for sure she'd have started giving blow jobs to truckers on the Jersey Turnpike, because that's what a lot of girls did.

When Straight Bob could manage—and it took time—he wiped his tear-streaked face but didn't look at anyone as he told them about the videos he watched. And the number of times he'd forced his raw and bleeding cock to stiffen, and how he punched his own groin over and over again when he could no longer accomplish even a marginal erection. He said that he passed out on the kitchen floor wearing a T-shirt and socks. He admitted to sitting in the shower for an hour, crying and thinking about how easy it would be to kill himself.

"What were these videos?" asked Yo-Yo quietly, bending to kiss his hand.

Straight Bob sniffed and shook his head. His face was red and swollen, and Rain worried about his blood pressure. "What does it matter?" he said. "It's not what I watched, it's that I couldn't stop. I. Could. Not. Stop."

"Tell us anyway," said Rain.

He shook his head, and they sat in silence with him. But eventually he told them. Every detail.

As he spoke, Rain felt like she was being punched back into the Naugahyde cushions of the booth seat. Beaten by his words. Destroyed by them. In her mind, the chains holding the Box of Rain closed rattled as something inside fought to escape.

The nurse.

The nurse.

Goddamn it.

The nurse.

CHAPTER SIXTY-TWO

Monk parked across from the brownstone and stood studying it for a moment, trying to read its façade like a poker player across a table from him.

The building knows, he thought. It was a strange thought, but not for someone like him. He went inside and slowly climbed the stairs. He was halfway up the second flight when he heard someone cry out in abject horror.

"Oh, Jesus! Oh, my God!"

It was a man's voice, and it was filled with unbearable horror.

Monk raced upward, taking the last steps three at a time. He wished he'd brought his gun, but as he reached the third-floor landing, it was clear he would not need it. No gun was going to help what he saw.

A young man with black hair and paint-spattered clothes leaned against the far wall, his beard flecked with fresh vomit, and more vomit was splashed on the wall and on his shoes. Midway down the hall, the rickety ladder lay on its side. Above it, swinging slowly from a rope attached to the exposed pipe, was a naked Japanese man.

The man's face was purple, his thick tongue lolled perversely from between slack lips, and his sightless eyes stared through Monk and through the wall behind him and on out into the big black nothing. The swinging body was covered with crude tattoos that looked self-inflicted, like wounds. Old and new, some crusted with blood. The tattoos were words, written in kanji. Monk could read the language well enough.

Watashi o yurushite.

Repeated hundreds of times.

Forgive me.

And across the hall, written in a different hand, were words in English.

They are coming!

CHAPTER SIXTY-THREE

"No," whispered Rain. She gripped the table to keep herself from falling off the edge of the world. Straight Bob sat with his head against Gay Bob's chest, heavy body quivering. "No, no, no, no, no, no, *no*. It can't be the nurse."

Suddenly, everyone at the table was staring at her.

"Wait, what am I missing here?" asked Gay Bob. "Rain, do you know something about this nurse?"

"Of course I do. She's always with *him* and—"

Rain screeched to a stop, horrified about what she had started to say.

"With . . . *who*?" asked Yo-Yo.

"No, I didn't mean that. I didn't say his . . . I mean, he isn't—" Rain babbled, trying to backpedal.

"No," snapped Gay Bob. "No more of your famous Rain Thomas evasive bullshit. You've *almost* told us about something more times than I can count. Don't look surprised; I'm a junkie, but I'm not stupid. Even yesterday when you were telling us about what happened in the city, you were clearly leaving stuff out. You've done it enough times. We all know you're hiding something."

Straight Bob and Yo-Yo nodded.

Run, begged her parasite. *Get out of here before he finds out.*

Rain sat with her back pressed into the cushions and her palms braced on the edge of the table. She did want to run, but her need to understand what Straight Bob saw in those videos was a more powerful and immediate force.

"This nurse," she began slowly, "she has curly black hair, doesn't she?"

"Wh-what?" gasped Straight Bob. "How could you possibly know that?"

"She does, doesn't she?" After a moment, Straight Bob nodded. "And green eyes?" asked Rain. "Bright green, like a cat's, am I right? They look like those color contacts, but they're not. It's her real color, but no one else has that same color."

Straight Bob gave her an accusatory look, as if he was offended that she could know something that was part of his fantasy world, however damaged. He nodded again.

"Her lipstick is always red," continued Rain. "Very bright and dark, like blood in a bad horror movie. Too red. She's about five-five or -six. Slim build, but busty."

"Yes, but Rain, how do could you possibly know what she looks like?"

"Because I've been seeing that evil bitch for ten years," said Rain.

"What?" demanded Gay Bob. "Where? And *how*?"

"I don't know how," said Rain. "But remember when I shared that dream I had about when I had the baby? When I woke up and I was in the hospital room and thought I saw a doctor and a nurse take my baby?"

"Oh, shit," said Yo-Yo. "You shared that at the meeting over by the ballpark. You told us the nurse licked all his features off his face. That was some disgusting shit."

"You're saying that's the same nurse?" asked Gay Bob, confused and visibly shaken.

"That was the first time I saw her," said Rain.

Yo-Yo frowned. "The *first* time . . . ?"

"Yes," said Rain, nodding slowly. "I've seen her hundreds of times since then."

"In porn videos?" asked Straight Bob.

"No. In real life."

"You're losing me," said Gay Bob. "You've been seeing her where? Is she in NA with us? Is she a local porn actress or something with a substance abuse issue? Is that who she is? Is that why you both have seen her?"

"I only saw her on the videos, and only recently," said Straight Bob.

"I don't know who she is," Rain admitted, "and what's worse, I don't know *what* she is. But I know she was here at this diner, sitting at that table over there last night. Remember the nurse getting into that old car when we were leaving? That was *her*. She was also one of the EMTs Yo-Yo and I saw taking the dead kid out of the building."

Gay Bob's eyes snapped wide. "Wait, wait . . . the Cadillac last night. Holy shit."

"What?" they all asked.

"I dreamed about it. And the people inside it. A doctor and a nurse, and some freak—maybe some kind of zombie—driving it."

"Did she have black hair and green eyes?" asked Yo-Yo.

He nodded. Sweat was beading on his forehead, and he looked around, his eyes wild. "Fuck me. What is this shit? Are you saying you, me, and Straight Bob are having some kind of visions of the same nurse?"

"The nurse and the doctor," said Yo-Yo, and they all looked at her.

"What?" croaked Rain.

Yo-Yo opened her purse and took out a folded piece of paper. "I wrote this last night, and I've been carrying it around with me all day." She chewed her lip for a moment and then handed it to Rain, who unfolded it. The first lines were unbearable.

Absolutely unbearable.

Doctor Nine
Is as thin as a bone.
He is a scarecrow
From a blighted field.

She flung the page away as if it had stung her and filled her with a deadly poison. Gay Bob caught the page. Read it. He sagged back, his face going dead pale.

"No," he breathed. "This isn't . . . this isn't . . ."

He was unable to finish. Straight Bob took the page from him and frowned. "This isn't about the nurse," he said. "Who the hell is Doctor Nine?"

Rain almost screamed to hear that name spoken aloud. Her parasite and all her inner voices *did* scream. And the chains on the Box of Rain groaned to the breaking point.

Gay Bob took the page back with a hand that shook so hard he dropped it, picked it up again, dropped it again, and left it lying there on the table.

"What's happening to us?" asked Yo-Yo. She sounded like a frightened little girl.

Straight Bob looked at Rain. "Maybe you'd better start from the beginning and tell the whole thing. Then the rest of you. Something's happening here, and we need to understand what it is. Now. Together."

Outside there was a flash of lightning and a deep bass boom of thunder. They all flinched, but Straight Bob actually grinned. "It's a dark and stormy night."

Rain licked her lips and tried to return his smile. "I guess that fits," she said shakily, "because I think what's happening is that we're all in a monster story. A real one."

They all nodded once more, but now no one was smiling.

Rain told her story.

CHAPTER SIXTY-FOUR

Monk recognized the young man. Rain's guy. Joplin. He was a wreck. Pale, shaken, hollow-eyed, confused. Monk walked him away from the dead man. The hall was otherwise empty. None of the other tenants had come out to see what was going on. The silence was oppressive.

"I . . . I heard a strange noise," said Joplin. "I came down to . . . to . . . you know . . ."

"You know who he was?" asked Monk. "His name?"

"Hoto. Don't know his first name."

"Any idea why he'd do this?"

"God . . . no."

Monk studied him but did not see any traces of guile. The kid was fried by this. "Look, I'm an investigator. Maybe Rain told you about me."

Joplin blinked, then nodded. "Monk?"

"Yeah. I'm going to go look inside Mr. Hoto's apartment. See if there's anything that might give me a clue as to why he did this."

"But—"

"I need you to call 9-1-1. Do not—and I need to be clear about this—mention my name or that I was here. I can't be tied up here for hours answering questions I don't have answers to. This might be tied to something else I'm working on. I need you to call this in, and then you're going to wait right here until the cops come. You found him, you called, and that's it. Okay?"

"Is . . . Rain in some kind of trouble?" he asked.

"I don't know," said Monk. "But maybe. If she is, I can't help her if the cops know I was here. Can you help me out here, or are you going to fall apart?"

That seemed to flip a switch in Joplin, and he wiped his mouth and straightened, nodding, blinking his glazed eyes clear. "Sure, sure. No problem."

Monk clapped him on the shoulder and walked over to the body, used his cell phone to take pictures, and then pushed Hoto's door open with his elbow. "Make the call," he said and went inside.

The apartment was small, cold, ugly, and nearly empty. A few Spartan pieces of furniture but no comforts at all. No TV or laptop. No art or framed pictures; however, there was a cluster of Buddhist iconography on the walls. And those same words, *Gomen'nasai*, written thousands of times on the floor, walls, ceiling, and even on the little futon in the corner. It was clear that Hoto was in some specific kind of hell that was tied up with guilt. *Gomen'nasai*. A profound apology.

Apology for what? Monk wondered. Apology to whom?

He saw something on the floor near the futon, and he squatted down to study it. A silver pocket watch and a coil of chain. It looked brand new, though the crystal face was cracked. He took a picture of it, then used a tissue from his pocket to turn it over so he could take a picture of the back, which had a key slot. There was no key around and no time to look for one. He stood, tucking the tissue back into his pocket. He'd touched nothing else. Monk took another two minutes, taking more than sixty photos of the apartment. Then he left.

Joplin, looking rocky and green, was in the hall staring at the dead man.

"Go down and wait for the cops in the foyer," Monk said. "I was never here, okay?"

Joplin nodded and followed him down the steps.

CHAPTER SIXTY-FIVE

Alyson Creighton-Thomas found the tiny windup watch on the table by the front door. It sat on top of the mail, shiny and pretty.

She picked it up, looked at the face, turned it over, and saw the keyhole, glanced around to see if there was a key, did not see one. It was not her watch. Maybe it belonged to the housekeeper. In which case it had no business being on top of the mail.

When Alyson went into the kitchen to get more ice cubes for her vodka, she dropped the watch into the trash can and never gave it another moment's thought. She limped back to the living room, sank back onto the couch, and took the dance videos off pause.

CHAPTER SIXTY-SIX

This time, Rain didn't hold back.

She broke all her rules and told them the name of the monster. All bets were off now that he knew Dylan's name. All bets were off now that she knew the monster was already in the lives of her friends.

"Doctor Nine," said Gay Bob, pronouncing it slowly, carefully. Cautiously. Tasting the words, marveling at them. Rain flinched to hear that name come from someone else's lips. It was different when Caster Bootey said it in her dream because that was only a dream; this was the real world. She braced her hands against the table as if expecting the floor to tilt and was surprised when nothing horrible happened to her friends.

Gay Bob told his story next. About the dreams he had and the stories he'd begun to write. He paused for a hard moment before telling them the rest of it. About the OxyContin tablets and how he had found himself perched on the windowsill, ready to jump. When he was done, he produced the Little Red Monster and placed it on the table. They recoiled from it as if it were a scorpion.

"Monster story," he said, and Rain nodded. They glanced at Yo-Yo.

"I wrote that poem," she said, "because I had to. It's how I deal with stuff. Ever since I was a little girl, I used to write poems when I woke up after a nightmare. It usually helps. It's like writing it down traps the nightmare on the page and keeps it from hurting me."

"Yeah," said Gay Bob, "I get that."

Yo-Yo shivered. "It didn't work this time. I . . . feel like I did something wrong by writing his name down. Something stupid. Something bad."

"I get that, too," admitted Gay Bob. "He doesn't like when anyone says his name. He doesn't even like us to write it down."

Rain wanted to cry. "All my life I've been afraid that I was crazy. Doctor Nine—wow, it feels so weird to say his name—I felt like he was my personal boogeyman. That's what he's always been."

Gay Bob and Yo-Yo nodded. Straight Bob did not.

"It's always the nurse," he said. "Just her. She's bad enough. But that name, Doctor Nine . . . it's familiar. It's in my head somewhere, in some bad place. Like maybe the same place where my addiction lives." He gave Rain a sheepish look. "Does that make any sense?"

"It makes a lot of sense," she said. "Remember a few months ago when I talked about that thing the therapist told me to build, the place where I put the stuff I'm afraid of?"

"Your Box of Rain," said Straight Bob.

"Right. When I have dreams of *him*, that's where I put them."

"Like my poetry journals," said Yo-Yo.

"And my short story files," said Gay Bob. " Safe places."

Rain shook her head. "No," she said slowly. "I don't think they're safe anymore."

They sat with that thought. With that truth.

The thunder rumbled again, closer now. It sounded like a growl of something big and hungry.

It was Straight Bob who finally broke the silence. "What's it mean?" he asked. "Is this some kind of shared psychic experience? Are we having the same dream?"

"No," said Gay Bob. "The dreams aren't the same. The stuff I've been dreaming is about Doctor Nine coming here. Of him maybe finding us. It's like I'm dreaming a kind of prologue to what's maybe happening now, if that makes any sense."

"I don't know how any of this makes sense," said Rain. "But right now, hearing this . . . I think that's exactly what you were dreaming. About how Doctor Nine came here."

"Is that what you've been dreaming, too?" asked Yo-Yo.

Rain shook her head. "Not exactly. I never had a dream about Doctor Nine coming here because in my dreams he's always been here." She paused, then gave another shake of her head. "No that's not right, either. I've had dreams where he's going somewhere else. *To* someone else. To the nurse, but when she was a little girl. I dream about how she called Doctor Nine to come find her. To *take* her. She was really crazy, and I think she murdered her sister when they were kids. Killed her because she wanted to know what murder felt like."

"Jesus God," murmured Gay Bob.

"I'm not sure if she was born crazy, like maybe a serial killer," said Rain, "or if Doctor Nine turned her bad. Maybe it's both. Like she was open to him and he reached into her head and did something. Made her bad. Or worse. Or something."

"Corrupted her," said Straight Bob, and after considering that for a moment, she nodded.

"There's more," said Rain.

"What do you mean?" asked Yo-Yo.

"Guys," she began, and faltered for a moment, feeling panic swirl like a dust devil in her chest. She summoned what little courage she could muster and told them about what happened in her apartment. About Doctor Nine coming to her in the flesh, about her accidentally letting him know Dylan's name. About everything. They sat in horrified silence for a long time.

"What's it mean, though?" asked Yo-Yo, breaking the silence. "So what if he knows your son's name?"

Straight Bob gave her a pained look. "In folklore, evil creatures like demons and such get power over someone once they know their real name. And, don't jump on me, I'm not saying this freak *is* a demon. I'm just . . ." His voice trailed as he looked at the expressions on everyone's faces. "No, I'm being pedantic and I'm talking too much because I'm scared. Forget I said anything."

Gay Bob said, "What matters is that he's real. Don't know how, don't know what that means, but he's real."

"Or we're all out of our damn minds," said Yo-Yo, "and somehow we're in each other's delusions."

"No, he's real," said Rain. After a moment they all nodded.

"You said his name again out loud," said Gay Bob. "Why risk that now? Is it because we're all having the same thing happen to us? Because we already know the name?"

Rain nodded. "I almost didn't say it because it scares me, but somehow, with you guys, I think I'm . . ." She fished for the word.

"Allowed," he suggested.

"Yes." She cut a look at the other people in the diner. "Not with anyone else, though."

"Yeah, okay," said Yo-Yo, "but what do we do? I mean, this isn't real, is it?"

"Not sure I understand what 'real' even means," admitted Gay Bob.

"I do," said Rain. "Until now, I thought this was all me and only me. I was thinking that I'm dead or in a coma and this is all a dream."

Straight Bob gave her a bleak stare. "How do you know it's not?"

"Oh, hell no," snapped Yo-Yo. "I'm not in anyone's damn dream. I'm me and I'm right here and so are all of us."

"Sure, but I could be dreaming that you're saying that," said Rain.

"I will be happy to kick both your skinny white asses to show you how real I am."

"No, thanks," said Rain quickly.

"Okay, okay," said Gay Bob, "let's cut that shit out. It's not helpful. If

207

this is a dream, then each of us is dreaming it at the same time, and as far as I'm concerned, it puts us in the same place. We still have to answer the same questions."

"Which questions in particular?" asked the other Bob.

"Well, first off . . . who or what is Doctor Nine? In my dreams, in the stories I write about him, he's arriving places. New cities, all over the place. Maybe all over the world. He's hunting, but he's following some kind of scent or call. Not sure what it is. What I do know is that my dreams go back a lot of years and he's not always with the same people," said Gay Bob.

"You mean the nurse and the—whatever it is who drives his car?" asked Rain.

"He's called the Mulatto," said Yo-Yo. "He's a zombie, but not like one of those *Walking Dead* flesh-eating kind. He's OG zombie, from Haiti. Voodoo and all that shit."

They thought about it. Gay Bob and Rain nodded.

"He used to have other people, though," said Gay Bob. "I can see them sometimes in dreams, but I can never make them out. They're like shadows. I think they used to be real people, but it's like . . ."

"Like they forgot how to be alive?" suggested Rain. "Or be human?"

Gay Bob nodded.

Straight Bob swallowed hard. "What about the nurse? Is she human?"

"No," said Yo-Yo without hesitation, then she looked surprised by the force of her answer. "I mean . . . she's not human anymore."

"Then what is she?"

No one had an answer to that.

"What do we know about her?" asked Straight Bob. "Let's start there and maybe we can figure out what she is from what she does."

"She likes to hurt," said Rain at once. "Not physically, but in other ways. Emotionally, psychologically."

"It goes a lot deeper than that, Rain," said Yo-Yo. "She's mean, or maybe *malicious* is a better word. She gets off on doing deep damage to people. Somehow she gets into my head and pushes all my damn buttons. The bad ones. The ones that want to make me do bad stuff."

"Like using?" asked Gay Bob.

Yo-Yo sipped her coffee and then held the cup, looking at it. "I . . . I have to tell you guys something. I don't want to, but I have to."

Rain tensed, knowing what was coming.

Yo-Yo was wearing a long-sleeved sweater and she slowly, painfully, pushed up her sleeve. There, tucked into the folds of her inner elbow, were several small black dots.

Track marks.

INTERLUDE FOURTEEN
THE MONSTERS AND THE BOY

They revealed the secrets of the windup pocket watch to him.

Every now and then, Doctor Nine would open one of the clocks, remove the crystal vial, and pour the stolen time onto his tongue. The doctor's eyelids would flutter shut, and he would moan the way the nurse did sometimes when the doctor did things to her on the boy's cot.

When he was nine, they offered him a taste.

"I don't want to," he said, and the nurse beat him with a big wooden spoon.

A month later, they tried again.

"Do I have to?" he asked.

The spoon again.

A month later, they tried once more. He realized that they would never stop. So he forced a shy smile onto his face, one he'd practiced by watching people on TV, and asked, "Will I like it?"

The doctor and the nurse smiled huge smiles. They glowed at him.

"You'll love it," said the nurse. "It's soooo good."

"It will change your life," said the doctor.

The boy nodded. "Okay."

The doctor produced a windup pocket watch, opened it, and removed the crystal vial. "This is a little drop, my boy. Not too much. Not the first time. A taste to whet your appetite."

The nurse took the boy's head and tilted it back and told him to stick out his tongue. He did, and for a long moment, he didn't think anything was going to happen. He'd never actually seen the stuff they put into the clocks. He never felt anything land on his tongue.

Then it hit him.

It.

Hit.

Him.

The boy's eyes snapped wide, but he no longer saw the basement or the TV or the chains. He did not see the doctor, the nurse, or the Mulatto. He didn't see anything that was part of his life.

He was inside the mind and the heart of a young woman in a filthy house in some part of Brooklyn. There were a dozen people there. Some of them were asleep. One might have been dead for all the movement the boy could detect. A few mumbled quietly to one another. One stood leaning on the doorframe, grinning and snatching at the front of his pants. A thin man with a rat face sat facing the woman. He had a vial, too, but it wasn't crystal. It was a small plastic vial filled with tiny crystals and he rattled it in front of the woman.

"What have you got to lose?" he asked.

It was exactly the wrong thing to say and exactly the right thing to say, and the boy could feel the sudden upsurge of emotion. There was real anger there. Or maybe it was outrage; he wasn't sure of the distinction. There was hatred, too, but it wasn't directed outward. Not entirely. Most of the hatred stabbed inward. It was a very specific kind of hatred that the boy instinctively knew was called self-loathing. The woman was at a crisis point. Take the vial of crack cocaine and finish her slide downward. She knew, as the dealer knew and the boy knew, that if she did this, then it would be the tipping point, and the weight of her own disappointment would send her crashing down through all the rotted floors in the tenement of her life. The boy understood this even though he was too young because he was in the woman's thoughts. There were flashes of her life before the drugs. There were flashes of real happiness. Of joy. Of passion. Of optimism. Those, however, were old and tarnished and fragile, and the weight of that vial would smash them beyond any hope of repair.

Beyond any hope.

The boy understood why Doctor Nine found this so delicious. It was not hope exactly that he craved. Hope was poison to someone like him. No, it was the last hope that was the drug. It was like the TV special the boy had watched about fugu fish. They were poison if prepared wrong but a delicacy if done just right. Hope *was like that. Doctor Nine craved that moment when a person's optimism failed and they were on the narrow ledge of their last true moment of hope.*

That's what the nurse caught as it fell. It's what the doctor stored away in his windup pocket watches. It's what fed him.

If he ate enough of it, then something bad would happen. A door would open?

That thought flicked in and out of the boy's mind, and he shoved it away for fear that the doctor and the nurse would somehow see it and know he thought it.

He was afraid, though. So very afraid. They were wise and they watched him, looking for thoughts like that.

Panic flared up in him. He knew he was onto something, but he had to play out the drama or lose his chance. The spoon would not be the consequence this time.

And so he took a great and dangerous chance.

He closed his eyes and let the dying hope dissolve on his tongue. He released all his resistance and let go.

And fell.

He fell so hard and so long and so deep. The boy fell further than he thought he would. He fell so far.

He fell all the way down.

The nurse and the doctor cried out with delight.

CHAPTER SIXTY-SEVEN

Monk tried to go back home to Manhattan a couple of times, but he couldn't manage it. Brooklyn kept pulling him back.

He drove past Joplin's building, past the police cars and emergency vehicles, and continued on to the Diner. He parked and was about to get out when he saw four familiar people framed in the window. Rain and her friends. He studied her profile. She was very pretty and very sad and right now looked like she was freaking out about something. Monk had no wife, no kids, no living family, but he felt an odd kinship toward her. Not a romantic or sexual thing. He wanted to help her, keep her safe. Or maybe it was deeper than that, he considered. Maybe it was about helping her find her power. It was there, he'd glimpsed it, but Rain had a lot of damage piled on top of it. He felt like she was in some indefinable way kin to him. Not in a blood way but on a deeper level. What Patty referred to as "spirit family."

He left the engine running for heat and sat in his car smoking a cigarette as he tried to make a picture of what was going on with too few puzzle pieces. Then his phone rang.

"Hey, Patty," he said. "You got something for me?"

"Hey, Monk," said the tattoo artist. "I do, but it doesn't make a lot of sense."

"That's pretty much in keeping with the day I've had."

"Why? What's going on? You sound wired as shit."

Monk told her about the boy's body being stolen from the morgue and incinerated, and about the Japanese man and the words tattooed on his body.

"Oh, my God!" cried Patty. "That's horrible! What's it mean? What are you into?"

"Trying to figure that out, Patty." He went to light a fresh cigarette and discovered the lit one between his lips.

"If that boy isn't the one you were hired to find," said Patty, "why are you getting all tangled up in this? It's weird, it sounds dangerous, and it's not your concern."

"I can't explain it, okay?" he said. "There's something about this thing that has its hooks in me."

There was a very heavy sigh of resignation on the other end of the call. "Then you're going to keep pushing at it," Patty said. "We both know what happens when you do that."

They did. Some of the ink Patty drilled into Monk's skin was there to hide the scars.

"It is what it is, Pats," he said.

"Then add this to the stew," said Patty Cakes. "I just got off the phone with Morty. He did a quick workup on the blood vial."

"And . . . ?"

"And it's not blood. Not exactly. Not completely. It had blood *in* it, but not a lot. Morty actually asked if you were playing some kind of joke on him."

"When's the last time you ever heard of me playing a joke?"

"Pretty much never. Which is what I told Morty," said Patty.

"Okay. So what is the stuff?"

"He said it was mostly water and a mix of electrolytes—sodium, potassium, and stuff like that. But there were also some proteins, carbohydrates, lipids, something called phospholipids, and urea, which is something produced in the kidneys that helps people pee. Or something. He tried to tell me all the chemistry, but I didn't want to know."

"I don't get it," said Monk. "What is that stuff?"

"He asked me if someone in the building where the kid died was pregnant."

"Why? What does that have to do with anything?"

Patty said, "Because the stuff in that vial was amniotic fluid."

"Wait—*what*?" barked Monk.

"He said that it's what you get when someone's water breaks."

PART THREE

IN CHILDHOOD'S HOUR

Children see magic because they look for it.

CHRISTOPHER MOORE
LAMB: THE GOSPEL ACCORDING TO BIFF,
CHRIST'S CHILDHOOD PAL

From childhood's hour
I have not been as others were;
I have not seen as others saw . . .

"ALONE"
EDGAR ALLEN POE

CHAPTER SIXTY-EIGHT

"I started using six months ago," said Yo-Yo. "The day after I had the first dream about Doctor Nine."

The others were quiet. Gay Bob held one of her hands; Rain had the other. Straight Bob's hands were folded on the tabletop and clenched into bloodless fists.

"I've been going to meetings all over Brooklyn," said Yo-Yo. "Haven't gotten up to talk much, and only then at meetings where there's no one I know. I *need* to share, because I'm afraid of what will happen if I don't."

"Did you use today?" asked Gay Bob, but Yo-Yo shook her head.

"But I got some stuff at home. Three fixes and some clean needles. My dealer has a way of getting the disposable kind. Always clean stuff."

"You need to throw that shit out, Yo," said Gay Bob. "You know that, right?"

"I don't know if I can."

"I flushed all those pills down the toilet," he said.

Yo-Yo pulled her hand free and flicked the Little Red Monster at him. "Fuck you did."

The pill bounced off Gay Bob's chest and landed back on the table. He stared at it and after a long moment gave a slow nod.

"I know," he said. "But I don't want to. And you know what? I brought it here to prove that it didn't own me, you know? Like a drunk with an unopened whiskey bottle on his desk? What bullshit."

The Little Red Monster sat there.

"Want me to flush it?" asked Rain, beginning to reach for it, but Gay Bob was so much faster. He snatched it up and closed his strong fist around it.

The moment held, with everyone looking at his fist and then up at him.

"Oh," he said, "God."

"This is him, isn't it?" asked Straight Bob. "Doing this to us. Giving us this stuff. I mean, Christ, you're sitting there holding that pill like you're drowning and that's a lifeline. You think that's any different than me jerking off until I bled? Doctor Nine and that nurse know us. They're in our heads and we, my friends, are totally fucked."

Gay Bob had fresh sweat on his face. He waved to Betty and called her over. As she approached, Gay Bob opened his hand and dropped the pill into his half-empty coffee cup. It vanished into the brown liquid.

"Betty," he said quickly, "can you dump this and get me a fresh cup? Please?"

Betty must have seen something in his expression, because she didn't ask any questions. She took the cup away. As soon as she left, Gay Bob sagged back, exhaling a ball of burning air from his lungs. He picked up his napkin and blotted the sweat from his face.

"That . . . that . . ."

He couldn't finish. Rain leaned over and kissed his cheek. "That was amazing, and I love you."

Yo-Yo touched Gay Bob's arm. "Will you come over to my place and help me, y'know . . . deal with that shit?"

"I'll try," he said.

"This is all real, isn't it?" asked Straight Bob.

"Yes," said Rain. The others nodded. "Whatever 'real' even means anymore."

"What are we going to do?" asked Straight Bob.

"We fight back," said Gay Bob. "I gave up that Oxy tab, and it was the hardest thing I think I've ever done. I'd never have been able to do it if you three weren't here."

"The point is," said Rain, "that you did. Doesn't that mean something? Doesn't it mean we *can* fight back?"

"Maybe," said Yo-Yo dubiously.

"Think about it—this is an attack. We've all been attacked in different ways. Either we fight back or we say fuck it and give up."

"Personally," said Gay Bob, "I'm leaning toward the 'give up' part. I'm tired of fighting."

Rain pounded the table with a small, hard fist. "Bullshit. I can't give up. I *have* to fight because Doctor Nine has my son."

"I thought you said he was dead?" said Straight Bob. "You saw him in the morgue."

Rain shook her head. "It wasn't him. That was someone—or something—else. Maybe it's going to be my son, but not yet. Not for a couple of years."

"What?"

"I've been working on a theory," she said, lowering her voice. "Look, I think Doctor Nine showed me what was going to happen to my son in the future. Don't ask me how because I don't know. This is what my gut is telling me. He showed me my son. Dead from suicide because of something that hasn't happened yet. Something either I do, or Doctor Nine does, or maybe something my son is going to do drives him over the edge and he kills himself. I think that's what I saw at the morgue. And I think that because he only looked like my son when I put on those glasses. They're the key. I started seeing him when I put them on when I was on the train. I saw him on the street and again outside of Joplin's place. Every time I see my boy, it's when I'm wearing the glasses. I think the glasses let me see the truth."

"Sure," said Straight Bob, "but seeing the truth isn't the same as knowing what to do."

Gay Bob held up a finger. "Right, but we skipped over some stuff. Like the fact that they have *supernatural* powers, or whatever it is. We don't. They can invade our dreams and influence our actions. They can—what's the word?—*manifest* things. The videos you watched, the pills I found, whatever the hell it was happened in Rain's bathroom. How exactly do we fight something like that? It's not like we can call the Ghostbusters."

"I guess we have to figure out what Doctor Nine is," said Straight Bob, trying to sound reasonable. "Is he a demon? Do we hire an exorcist? Is he a vampire? If so, do we go get holy water, stakes, and some garlic? I'll fight, Rain, as long as we have some kind of plan."

Yo-Yo said, "I know a guy who can get me a gun and—"

"Christ," said Straight Bob, "we can't go around shooting people."

"They're not people," said Yo-Yo.

"Wait," said Rain, "maybe I know where we can start. Those two guys I met. Sticks and Monk."

"Great," said Straight Bob, "a disabled veteran and a thug."

"Monk's tough and he has a gun," said Rain. "And Sticks might know how to find Boundary Street. If we can find that, maybe we can go to the Fire Zone. I think we can get help there."

"Whoa, wait . . . did you say Fire Zone?" gasped Gay Bob. "You didn't mention that earlier, but I *know* that name. I dreamed about that, too."

"Me, too," said Straight Bob, eyes wide. So had Yo-Yo.

There was an immediate burst of overlapping conversation as they each shared what they knew of the Fire Zone from dreams, old and recent. Some of the same names came up. Torquemada's, Unlovely's, and Café Vortex. The biker gang called the Cyke-Lones. Snakedancer and Caster Bootey. Other people, too, some of whom Rain recognized and some she didn't. Kamala Jane, Indigo Heart, Mr. Sin, Eyes, the Bishop, Europa, Brutal John, Dresden Blues . . . on and on. Strange affected names for people who had either left their real identities behind or had somehow transcended them. And the Music, which played everywhere and which was alive and aware but not safe.

Talking about the Fire Zone made them all smile until . . .

The smiles faded slowly.

Gay Bob said, "We're talking about a place we've all been to in dreams, but only in dreams. I don't know what that means, but it's not a real place, is it?"

After a moment's thought, Straight Bob said, "Not sure 'real' matters to the Fire Zone."

They all nodded.

"I think I was on the edge of it for real," said Rain. "That's where I met Sticks. Tomorrow we're going to try to find it."

"That sounds absurdly dangerous," cautioned Straight Bob. "For more reasons than I can count, but apart from any of the Doctor Nine stuff, there's the storm."

Rain glanced out the window at a newspaper being whipped and torn by the wind. "It's been raining off and on for weeks."

"No, he's right," said Yo-Yo. "They're screaming about it on the news. A big-ass nor'easter is going to hit tomorrow. They're closing schools and all. Supposed to be a motherfucker."

Gay Bob nodded. "Maybe you should wait until it's over."

Rain smiled. "Seriously? Wait? We're talking about monsters and magic and things that go bump in the night, and you're afraid of Mother Nature? I mean, guys, get real. Tomorrow I'm going to go looking for the

Fire Zone, and no matter what I find, I'm going to talk to Sticks and Monk Addison. The same gut that tells me about my son tells me that they're going to help me. Somehow. And, for the record, screw the damn storm."

As if in rebuke, the sky outside flashed an intense white that blinded them all and washed all the colors from the inside of the Diner, and a heartbeat later, there was a massive explosion of thunder that was so loud it seemed to shake the world. It was the loudest sound Rain had ever heard, and she cried out in fear and pain. The others reeled away from the window, covering their heads as if expecting the tortured glass to shatter. All the lights in the restaurant went out, and then the whole neighborhood went dark. Bang. Gone. Car alarms cried out up and down the street. When the rain began again, it was torrential.

"G-God Almighty," gasped Yo-Yo, and she crossed herself.

INTERLUDE FIFTEEN
MONK'S STORY, PART 1

I see dead people.

Make a joke. Go ahead; people do. Fuck 'em.

I see dead people.

Not all of them. My life would be too crowded. Just some. The ones who need to be seen. The ones who need me to see them.

Yeah. It's like that.

The diner's name is Delta of Venus. Most people think that's a pun of some kind, or a reference to Mississippi. It's not. The owner's name's not Venus. One of her girlfriends was. It's like that.

The Delta is one of a bunch of places where I hang out. Diners are good for street trash like me, and this one was close to Boundary Street. I had my spot. Corner of the counter, close to the coffee. Out of the line of foot traffic to the john. Quiet most of the time. I dig the quiet. Kind of need it. My head is noisy enough.

It was a Thursday night, deep into a slow week. The kind of week Friday won't make better and Saturday won't salvage. Me on my stool, last sip of my fourth or fifth cup of coffee, half a plate of meat loaf going cold. Reading The Waste Land *and wondering what kind of hell Eliot was in when he wrote it.*

World War I was over, and he wrote poetry like the world was all for shit. Like he'd peeled back the curtain and the great and powerful Oz was a sorry little pedophile and Dorothy was going to have a bad night. Depressing as fuck.

The coffee was good. The day blew.

Eve, the evening waitress, was topping off ketchup bottles and not wasting either of our time on small talk. Not on a Thursday like this. These kinds of days don't bring out the chattiness in anyone who's paying attention. Outside, there was a sad, slow rain, and most of the people who came in smelled like wet dogs.

Then she came in.

I saw the door open. Saw it in the shiny metal of the big coffee urn. Saw her come in. Watched her stand there for a moment, not sure of what she was doing. Saw her look around. Saw nobody else look back. Saw her spot me. And know me. And chew her lip for a moment before coming my way.

Little thing, no bigger than half a minute. Sixteen, maybe seventeen. Slim as a promise. Pretty as a daffodil.

Lost and scared. Looking for me.

People like her find me. I never ask how they heard of me. In my line of work, the referral process is complicated. I get most of my standard clients from asshole law firms like Scarebaby and Twitch. Yeah, J. Heron Scarebaby and Iver Twitch. Real names. Some people are that fucking unlucky and that dim that they won't use a different name for business. Or maybe it's a matter of rats finding the right sewer. Not sure, don't care. They hire me for scut-work. Skip traces, missing persons. Stuff like that. Pays the light bill, buys me coffee.

They hadn't sent her, though. I knew that much. She found me a whole other way.

I signaled Eve and tapped the rim of my coffee cup with the band of my wedding ring. Still wore the ring after all this time. Married to the memory, I suppose. Eve topped me off.

"Gimme a sec," I said.

She looked around to see what was what. Looked scared when she did it, which is fair enough. People are like that around me. Then she found something intensely interesting to do at the far end of the counter. Didn't look my way again. There were two other people in the Delta. A night watchman on the way to a lonely midnight shift, and Lefty Wright, who was always topping off his Diet Coke with liberal shots of Early Times. Neither of them would give a cold, wet shit if a velociraptor walked in and ordered the blue-plate special.

That left me and the girl.

I didn't turn, but I patted the red Naugahyde stool next to me. Maybe it was the color that drew her eye. I'm pretty sure it's the only color people like her can see. That's what one of them told me. Just red, white, black, and a lot of shades of gray. That's fucked up. The girl hesitated a moment longer, then she seemed to come to a decision and came over. Didn't make a sound. She stopped and stood there, watching me as I watched her in the steel mirror of the coffeemaker.

"It's your dime, sweetheart," I said.

She didn't say anything. I picked up the Tabasco sauce and shook it over the meat loaf to kill the taste. The Specials sign over the kitchen window doesn't say what kind of meat is in it, and I'm not brave enough to ask. I'm reasonably sure that whatever it was ran on four legs. Beyond that, I wouldn't give Vegas odds on it being a cow or a pig.

"You want to sit down?" I asked.

Still nothing, so I turned and saw why. Her face was as pale as milk. She wore too much makeup and clearly didn't know how to put it on. Little girl–style—too much of everything, none of the subtlety that comes with experience. Glitter tube top and spandex micro mini. Expensive shoes. Clothes couldn't have been hers. Maybe an older sister, maybe a friend who was more of a party girl. They looked embarrassing on her. Sad. She had one hoop earring in her right ear. The left earlobe was torn. No earring. No other jewelry that I could see. No purse, no phone, no rings. That one earring damn near broke my heart.

"You know how this works?" I asked.

Nothing. Or maybe a little bit of a nod.

"It's a one-way ticket, so you'd better be sure, kid."

She lifted her hand to touch her throat. Long, pale throat. Like a ballet dancer. She was a pretty kid, but she would have been beautiful as a woman. Would have been. Her fingers brushed at a dark line that ran from just under her left ear and went all the way around to her right. She tried to say something. Couldn't. The line opened like a mouth, and it said something obscene. Not in words. What flowed from between the lips of that mouth was wet and in the only bright color she could see.

She wanted to show me. She wanted me to see. She needed me to understand.

I saw. And I understood.

CHAPTER SIXTY-NINE

Light flashed through the dark, and Rain saw Betty standing there with a flashlight.

"Okay, folks," said the waitress, "looks like we're going to close up shop. Meals are on us 'cause the register's electric, too."

Someone gave a nervous laugh. No one else did.

"Hope you brought umbrellas," continued the waitress.

Rain and her friends got out of the booth and joined the other patrons filing toward the door. Everyone had an umbrella, but the winds outside promised destruction on any such frail devices.

"Guys," said Rain as they huddled for a moment under the outside awning, rain lashing them hard as blown sand, "let's meet at my place tomorrow at two, okay?"

She wrapped her arms around the others, pulling them all into a huge, tight, enduring hug. They broke apart slowly, kissing cheeks, squeezing hands. Gay Bob and Yo-Yo hurried off in one direction, and Straight Bob limped to his car. Rain lingered for a moment, watching them go, and then she hunched her shoulders, ducked her head, and ran for home. The downpour beat down with steady brutality.

Above them, the flocks of nightbirds crouched on the wires and rooftops, their ragged wings pummeled by the rain, watching, watching, watching. Then they launched themselves into the storm. A hundred ugly forms that struggled against the winds and followed the four friends.

INTERLUDE SIXTEEN
MONK'S STORY, PART 2

Later, after the dead girl faded away and left me to my coffee and mystery meat, I stared at the floor where she'd stood. There was no mark, no drops of blood. Nothing. Eve came back and gave me my check. I tossed a ten down on a six-dollar tab and shambled out into the night. Behind me, I heard Eve call goodbye.

"Night, Monk."

I blew her a kiss like I always do. Eve's a good gal. Minds her own business. Keeps counsel with her own shit. Two kids at home and she works double shifts most nights. One of those quiet heroes who do their best to not let their kids be like them. I liked her.

It was fifteen minutes past being able to go home and get a quiet night's sleep. The rain had stopped, so I walked for a while, letting the night show me where to go. The girl hadn't been able to tell me, but that didn't matter. I'd seen her, smelled the blood. Knew the scent. Walked.

Found myself midway up a back street, halfway between I Don't Know and Nobody Cares. Only a few cars by the curbs, but they were stripped hulks. Dead as the girl. Most of the houses were boarded up. Most of the boards had been pried loose by junkies or thieves looking to strip out anything they could. Copper pipes, wires, whatever. Couple of the houses had been torn down, but the rubble hadn't been hauled off.

What the hell had that little girl been doing on a street like this?

I had a pocket flashlight on my key chain and used it to help me find the spot. It was there. A dark smudge on the sidewalk. Even from ten feet away I knew it was what I was looking for. There were footprints all over the place, pressed into the dirt, overlapping. Car tire tracks, too. The rain had wiped most of it away, smeared a lot of the rest, but it was there to be read. If I looked hard enough, I'd probably find the flapping ends of yellow crime scene tape, 'cause they never clean that stuff up. Not completely, and not in a neighborhood like this. Whole fucking area's an active crime scene.

Doesn't matter. That's me bitching. I knelt by the smudge. That was what mattered. It was dried. Red turns to brown as the cells thicken and die. Smell goes away, too. At first, it's the stink of freshly sheared copper, then it's sweet, then it's gone. Mostly gone. I can always find a trace. A whiff. And it was hers. Same scent. If I were a poet like Eliot, maybe I'd call it the perfume of innocence. Something corny like that. I'm not, so I don't. It's just blood. Even the rain couldn't wash it away. I squatted there for a few minutes, listening to water drip from the old buildings. Letting the smells sink in deep enough so I could pin them to the walls of my head.

Back in the day, before I went off to play soldier, before I ditched that shit and went bumming along the pilgrim road trying to rewire my brain, smells never used to mean much. That changed. First time I didn't die when an IED blew my friends to rags, I began to pay attention. Death smells different than life. Pain has its own smell.

So does murder. I stopped being able to not pay attention, if you can dig that. I lost the knack for turning away and not seeing.

There was a monk in Nepal who told me I had a gift. A crazy lady down in a shack near a fish camp in bayou country told me I had a curse. They were talking about the same thing. They're both right, I suppose. A priest in a shitty church in Nicaragua told me I had a calling. I told him that maybe it was more like a mission. He thought about it and told me I was probably right. We were drinking in the chapel. That's all that was left of the church. They don't call them Hellfire missiles for nothing.

This girl had come to me. Couldn't say what she wanted because of what they'd done to her. Didn't matter. She said enough.

I dug my kit out of my jacket pocket, unzipped it. Uncapped a little glass vial, took the cork off the scalpel, and spent two minutes scraping as much of the blood as I could get into the vial. Then I removed the bottle of holy water, filled the dropper, and added seven drops. Always seven, no more, no less. That's the way it works, and I don't need to fuck with it. Then I put everything away, zipped up the case, and stood. My knees creaked. I'm looking at forty close enough to read the fine print. My knees are older than that.

Spent another twenty minutes poking around, but I knew I wasn't going to find anything the cops hadn't. They're pretty good. Lots of experience with crime scenes around here. *They even catch the bad guys sometimes. Not this time, though, or the girl wouldn't have come to me.*

The vial was the only thing that didn't go back into the case. That was in my pants pocket. It weighed nothing, but it was fifty fucking pounds heavy. It made me drag my feet all the way to the tattoo parlor.

CHAPTER SEVENTY

The streets were pitch black, and Rain had to slow down to keep from running into parked cars and walls. Puddles soaked her shoes, splashed dirty water halfway up her body. It was so cold. A deep, penetrating cold that made her bones hurt. She staggered on sore ankles, trying to be careful when care was impossible. A few cars hissed by, their lights blinding her. The darkness was filling with sirens, and someone was screaming far away.

Then lights behind her threw her own shadow into her path, transforming her silhouette into a capering goblin shape. She half turned and saw a car coming toward her. Driving very slowly. The rain was so heavy and the headlights so bright that she could not tell a single thing about the car except that it was big.

Was it him?

He's coming to get you, taunted her parasite.

"No," she murmured and quickened her pace.

The car fell behind for a few minutes and then it, too, accelerated. Not fast enough to catch up, but enough to keep pace twenty yards behind her. Rain heard a strange noise above—like flapping cloth—but when she tried to look up, the wind attacked her umbrella, snapping the thin metal struts and ripping the silk cloth. Disgusted, Rain flung the dead umbrella away, and it landed in the middle of the street, clearly illuminated by the oncoming headlights.

"Shit."

She started running again, and her block was up ahead, the line of tall, tired brownstones looking more welcome than they had ever been. The headlights painted her shadow on the wall of the apartment building on the corner, and she watched that ungainly figure diminish in size as she raced across the street. Joplin's building was sixth on the row, hers was eighth. The car was coming faster now. She heard its engine growling.

"Please, please, please," she panted as she sprinted toward her steps. She grabbed the rail and dragged herself up. Then she was through the door, turning to slam it shut, leaning on it, but also leaning close so she could see the car.

The car passed and Rain saw what it was.

A huge, black Cadillac cabriolet.

She whimpered and dropped to her knees, still pressing her hands against the door to hold it shut as if the very presence of it was a physical invasion of her haven.

The car vanished into the storm.

A second set of headlights swept the street ahead of another big black car. Rain stared at it wide-eyed. It was a battered old Jeep Wrangler.

"Monk?" she whispered.

The two cars were swallowed by the storm, and the darkness outside became absolute except for occasional flashes of lightning.

Rain got up, wiped water from her face and eyes, and then ran up to her flat, locked herself in, and shoved a chair under the door handle. Bug nearly turned herself inside out barking and jumping. The power was still out, so Rain used her phone to find a flashlight, candles, and matches. With the flashlight in one hand and her knife in the other, she checked the bathroom, the closets, under the bed. Nothing.

Doctor Nine was not there because the monster was out in the storm.

And Monk was following him. Why would he? How could he even know? Or was the strange detective with the monster?

INTERLUDE SEVENTEEN
MONK'S STORY, PART 3

"Hey, Monk," said Patty Cakes when she heard the little bell over the door.

"Hey," I said and dragged a stool over, and sat down. Patty and me go way back. She's one of my people, the little circle of folks I actually trust. We met the year I came back from Southeast Asia, and she spotted something in me from the jump. Bought me my first meal at the Delta.

I set the vial on her workstation. She looked at it for a moment, then got up, flipped the door sign to Closed and turned out the front lights. I stripped off my coat and shirt, caught sight of myself in the mirror. An unenamored lady once told me I look like a shaved ape. Fair enough. I'm bigger in the shoulders than most people, deeper in the chest, bigger in the arms. A lot of me is covered in ink. None of it's really pretty. It's all faces. Dozens and dozens of them. Small, about the size of a half dollar. Very detailed. Men and women. Kids. All ages and races. Faces.

She picked up the vial, held it up to the light, sighed, nodded. "Gimme a sec. Have a beer."

I found two bottles of Fat Pauly's, a craft lager from Iligan City in the Philippines, cracked them open, set one down on her worktable, lowered myself into her chair, and sipped the other. Good beer. Ice cold. I watched her as she removed the rubber stopper from the vial, used a sterile syringe to suck up every last drop, then she injected the mixture into a jar of ink. It didn't matter that the ink was black. All my tats are monotone. White skin, black ink. Any color that shows up is from scars that still had some pink in them, but that would fade away after a while.

I drank my beer as Patty worked. Her eyes were open, but I knew that she wasn't seeing anything in that room. Her pupils were pinpoints and there was sweat running down her cheeks. She began chanting something in Tagalog that I couldn't follow. Not one of my languages. When she was done mixing, she stopped chanting and cut me a look.

"You want the strap?"

"No," I said.

She held out a thick piece of leather. "Take the strap."

"No."

"Why do we go through this every time?"

"I don't need it," I told her.

"I do. Goddamn it, Monk, I can't work with you screaming in my ear. Take the fucking strap."

I sighed. "Okay. Give me the fucking strap."

She slapped it into my palm, and I put it between my teeth. She got out a clean needle and set the bottle of ink close at hand. She didn't ask me what I wanted her to draw. She knew.

I didn't start screaming right away. Not until she began putting the features on the little girl's face. We were both glad I had the fucking strap.

CHAPTER SEVENTY-ONE

Midnight came and went, and the storm pounded the whole region. The lights sputtered on piecemeal and, as the last of the darkness was chased back, the storm, too, abated, leaving Brooklyn battered and gasping.

Monk spent an hour driving around and finally found himself back on the same block as the Diner. It was still closed, so he parked outside and lit another cigarette. He debated whether to make the call or not and decided what the hell. He punched the number and waited until she answered.

"Hello?" The young woman sounded drowsy, as if she'd just woken up. Monk glanced at his watch and winced at the time.

"Rain? This is Monk Addison," he said. "Sorry to call so late."

"No, it's fine," she said thickly.

There was a bedsheet rustle, and Rain coughed to clear her throat. He heard a whimper, too. A dog. Small and scared.

"You okay?" he asked.

Rain snorted. "Oh, sure, life's a Disney movie."

"Sorry."

"I saw your car tonight," she said. "Outside my place."

"Yeah, I was driving around, running down some things."

"Were you following another car?"

"What other car?"

There was a beat. Rain said, "Never mind. What's up, Monk? Why are you calling?"

"You asked me to see if I could find out about the shower curtain."

"Yes," she barked, and all drowsiness was instantly gone from her voice. "Did you find out?"

"Yeah."

"God, what was on it?"

"Before I answer that," said Monk, "I have two things to say. Some information and a question. You steady enough to deal?"

"I guess so," she said with no trace of confidence in her tone.

"First, there was another suicide," he said. "Same place and same method the kid used. Not a shower curtain, but the same pipes."

"Oh, my *God*! Who was it?"

"Remember the old Japanese guy? Him." Monk described the scene and what was written on the walls and tattooed on the man's body. "Your boyfriend, Joplin, found him and called the cops. No, wait, don't yell. Joplin's fine. He's probably wrung out from answering a lot of questions he didn't have answers for. He'll probably tell you about it in the morning. And if you're thinking about going over there right now, don't. Detective Martini has the case. Might be best to avoid her."

"Okay," said Rain. "That's awful, though. That poor man."

"Yeah. Whatever's going on over there is now a pattern, and cops really hate patterns. I do, too. I mean, sure, it helps frame a case and gives them more to go on than a single incident, but at the same time, it proves the case is bigger and stranger. Maybe this is a murder suicide with the Japanese guy as the perp who did the kid and killed himself in remorse. That would fit the evidence, but I don't think that's what it's going to be. Don't ask me why I think that. Call it gut."

"That's so terrible."

"Yeah, and it's sad. And it pisses me off."

"Me, too," agreed Rain, and it sounded as if she meant it. "You said there was something else. A question?"

"It's about the shower curtain. Why do you want to know about the pattern? I need you to be straight with me, because right now, you've got a foot over the line into the suspect category. Martini will think that, and if you're clean, then you need to be totally straight with me. You know something about the boy we saw at the morgue. That's not a question, so don't give me any more bullshit stories about blogs or concerned citizen or any of that. You know something, and if you want my help, then you need to trust me."

"I never said I wanted your help."

"No? Cool. Then I guess I'm wasting my time with this call just like I wasted my time finding out about that shower curtain."

While he waited through a heavy silence, he lit a cigarette and blew smoke out into the wet wind blowing past his car.

"Okay," she said. "Remember I said that you wouldn't believe me?"

"Sure," said Monk. "Remember how I answered?"

"Yes," said Rain. "People say that, but they usually have limits on what they're willing to believe. No, it's more than that . . . people have limits on what they're even willing to listen to."

"Some people do," he conceded. "Maybe most. But let's go on the assumption that I've seen more weird shit than you have."

"I bet you haven't," said Rain.

"You'd lose that bet, kid. No matter what you've seen, I can guarantee you'd lose that bet."

He let her think about that. After a while, she said, "What if I told you that this might be something, um, different. Something strange. Stranger than—"

"For fuck's sake, Rain, you're walking all around the word. Just say it."

"What word?"

"*Supernatural.*"

He heard a sound that might have been a sob. Fear or relief—it was hard to say because sobs all sound the same. Especially this late at night.

"It's pretty dark out here," said Monk, "and I'm not talking about the time of day. Now, if you want my information, then it's tit for tat. Give me something."

"Over the phone?"

"Over the phone."

After a moment, Rain said, "I think monsters are after my son, Monk. I think they killed that boy as a warning. Or drove him to kill himself, I don't know. I think they're going to kill my son. Soon. I think I don't have a lot of time to find him."

Monk leaned back and pinched the bridge of his nose between thumb and index finger until fireworks burst in his eyes. "Give me more than that."

The wind turned once more to a gale, more goddamn rain fell, pinging and popping against the hood of his car. Monk did not say a word for the thirty minutes it took Rain Thomas to tell him her story. Not only her story but also the stories of three of her friends—the people he'd seen her sitting with in the Diner. Monk could tell she was abbreviating it, leaving some parts out, compressing others. That was okay. He was more interested in her tone of voice, in the nuances of pain and fear and panic that were cooked into every word. Monk was very good at reading people. His job and his life depended on it as much now, in the work he did here, as it did when he was a soldier hunting bad guys in the deserts and jungles of the world. Any hunter who can't read meaning, intent, motive, desire, and veracity was going to die. Especially at his level of the game.

She even told him about Doctor Nine, and that part was as terrifying now as it had been at the diner with her friends.

When she was done, Monk said, "Jesus H. T. Christ doing cartwheels."

"I know."

"That's some goddam story."

"I know," she said. "I *told* you that you wouldn't believe me."

Monk studied the burning end of his cigarette before he replied. "You were wrong about that then and you're wrong now."

"Wait, *what*? Why would you believe me at all?"

"But I need something else from you."

"What?" she asked, instantly wary.

"*You* to tell *me* what was on that shower curtain."

Rain paused for so long Monk had to look at the phone display to assure himself that she hadn't dropped off the call.

"Rain?"

"It was a print of Van Gogh's *Starry Night*. It's mine. I had one like it but Doctor Nine took it." She told him about what had happened in her apartment and Monk listened without comment. "That's the one the boy used to hang himself with, wasn't it?"

Monk flicked his cigarette out into the storm then rubbed his eyes, feeling old and scared and used up. "Yes," he said.

Beneath his clothes, the faces seemed to twist as if trying to shout something out to him.

INTERLUDE EIGHTEEN
MONK'S STORY, PART 4

It took her an hour to get it right, and I could feel when it was right. We both could.

I spat the strap onto my lap and sat there, gasping, out of breath, fucked up. I could see the pity in Patty's eyes. She was crying a little, like she always does. The light in the room had changed. Become brighter, and the edges of everything were so sharp I could cut myself on their reality. All the colors bled away. Except for red, white, black, and all those shades of gray. That's what I saw. It's all I'd see until I was done with what I had to do.

Sometimes it was like that for days. Other times it was fast. Depends on how good a look the girl got, and what I'd be able to tell from that look.

Patty helped me up, grunting with the effort. I was two fifty and change. None of it blubber. A lot of it was scar tissue. The room did an Irish ceili dance around me, and my brain kept trying to flip the circuit breakers off.

"If you're going to throw up, use the bathroom."

"Not this time," I managed to wheeze, then I grabbed my stuff, clumsied my way into my shirt and jacket, and stumbled out into the night, mumbling something to her that was supposed to be "Thanks," but might have been "Fuck you."

Patty wouldn't take offense. She understood. Like I said, one of my people.

The night was hung wrong. The buildings leaned like drunks, and the moon hid a guilty smile behind torn streamers of cloud. It took me half an hour to find my way back to where the girl was killed. My eyes weren't seeing where my feet were walking, and sometimes I crashed into things, tripped over lines in the pavement, tried to walk down an alley that wasn't there. It's like that for a bit, but it settles down.

Once I was on that street, it settled down a lot. I stood by the step where I'd found her blood. This is where it gets difficult for me. Victims don't usually know enough to really help, not even when I can see what they saw when they died. Like I was doing now. Half the time they didn't see it coming. A drive-by or a hazy image of a tire iron. The feel of hands grabbing them from behind.

It was kind of like that with the girl.

Olivia. I realized I knew her name now. Olivia Searcy. Fifteen. Even younger than I thought, but I was right about the clothes. They were her sister's. Shoes and push-up bra, too. She wanted to look older. No, she wanted to be older. But that was as old as she'd ever get.

I knew why she was there, and it was a bad episode of a teen romance flick. She was a sophomore in high school; he was a senior. Good looking, smart, from a family with some bucks. Good grades. A real find, and maybe in time he'd grow up and be a good man. But he was eighteen and all he wanted was pussy, and a lot of guys know that young pussy is often dumb pussy, which makes it easy pussy. So they come on to them, making them feel cool, feel special, feel loved. And they get some ass, maybe pop a cherry, and move on the instant the girl gets clingy. Fifteen-year-olds always get clingy, but there are always more of them. The boy, Drake, hadn't yet plundered Olivia. It was part of the plan for tonight.

They went to a party at some other guy's house a long way from here, in a part of town where stuff like this isn't supposed to happen, which is a stupid thought, because stuff like this happens everywhere. The party was fun and it was loud. They got high. Got smashed. He got grabby and she freaked. Maybe a moment of clarity, maybe she saw the satyr's face behind the nice-boy mask. Whatever. She bolted and ran.

She didn't know if Drake tried to find her, because she tried really hard not to be found. She was found, though. Just not by Drake.

For a little bit there, I thought I was going to have to break some parents' hearts by fucking up their pretty-boy son, but that wasn't in tonight's playbook. Drake hadn't done anything worse than be a high school dickhead. He got her drunk, but he hadn't forced her, hadn't slipped her a roofie. And, who knows, maybe if he'd found her in time, he'd have become Galahad and fought for her honor. Might have saved her life.

Probably would have died with her.

Or maybe the killer would have opted out and gone looking for someone else. A lot of serial killers and opportunistic killers are like that. They're not Hannibal Lecter. They're not tough, smart, and dangerous. Most of them are cowards. They feel totally disempowered by whatever's happened to them—abusive parents, bad genes, who the fuck cares? They hurt and terrify and mutilate and kill because it makes them feel powerful, but it's a lie. It's no more real than feeling powerful by wearing a Batman costume at Halloween. You may look the part, but you're a long way from saving Gotham City.

All of that flooded through my brain while I stood there and looked at the street through the eyes of a dead girl. Seeing it the way Olivia saw it right as hands grabbed her from behind. Right as someone pulled her back against his body so she could feel his size, his strength, the hard press of his cock against her back. Right as he destroyed her. Right as the cold edge of the knife was pressed into the soft flesh under her left ear.

I felt all of that. Everything. Her nerve endings were mine. Her pain exploded through me. The desperate flutter of her heart changed the rhythm of mine into a panic, like the beating of a hummingbird's wings against a closed window. I felt her break inside as he ruined her. I heard the prayers she prayed, and they echoed in my head like they'd echoed in hers. She hadn't been able to scream them aloud because first there was a hand over her mouth, and then there was the knife against her throat and those threats in her ear.

And when he was done, I felt the burn.

That line, like someone moving an acetylene torch along a bead of lead. Moving from under my left ear to under my right.

I felt her die because I died, too. Olivia drowned in her own blood.

Then there was a strange time, an oddly quiet time, because I was with her when she was dead, too. When he wrapped her in a plastic tarp and put her in the trunk. It was so weird, because while he did that, he was almost gentle. As if afraid of hurting her.

Fucking psychopath.

While the car drove from where she'd died to where he'd dumped her, Olivia slipped into that special part of the universe where the dead see one another. Certain kinds of dead. The dead who were part of a family. Victims of the same knife.

His people.

Olivia discovered that she was not the only one. Not the first, not the tenth.

She wasn't sure how many because he moved around so much. Had moved around. Not so much anymore. Not since he moved to this town. The victims she met were the ones who'd died here.

Twenty-six of them.

The youngest was eight.

I met those victims, too, because I was inside the memory. Like I'd actually been there. That's how it worked. I talked to them, and most of them already knew who and what I was. The first time I'd encountered that, it shocked the shit out of me. But now I understood. Not to say I'm used to it, because I'd have to be a special kind of fucked up to be used to something like that. No, it was more like I knew how to deal. How to use it.

Some of them had died just like Olivia. An attack from behind. Everything from behind. No chance of an identification. He varied it a little. One of those nearly patternless killers that the FBI have no idea how to profile. A knife across the throat, an icepick between the right ribs, a garrote made from a guitar string, a broken neck.

Most were like that.

Most. Not all.

There was one who fought. She'd had a little judo and some tae kwon do. Not enough, but enough to make him work for it. It was one of the early ones, after he'd moved here. The one that made him want to never bring them home again. She'd gotten out, and he'd chased her into the front yard and caught her before she could wake the neighbors. Single homes, lots of yard on all sides. Cul-de-sac. When he caught up to her, she spun around and tried to make a fight of it.

I saw every second of it.

The yard. The house.

Him.

I saw him.

I saw him block her punch, and then a big fist floated toward her face and she was gone. He was a big guy, and he knew how to hit. The punch broke the girl's neck, which made it easier on her, if easy is a word that even applies.

I stood there and watched all of it play out inside my head. No idea how long I was there. Time doesn't matter much when I'm in that space. I was there for every second of every minute of every attack. Beginning to end. All the way to when he dumped them, or buried them, or dropped them off a bridge.

Stack it all up and it was days.

Days.

Shotgunned into my head.

I wish I'd had the leather strap. Instead, I had to bite down on nothing, clamp my jaws, ball my fists, clench my gut, and eat the fucking pain.

It wouldn't save any of those girls. Not one. And maybe it wouldn't matter that I felt it all but didn't have to live it. Or die from it. I know that.

I couldn't help a single one of them. I couldn't help Olivia.

But as my skin screamed from the phantom touches and the blades and everything else, I swore that I'd help the next girl.

Goddamn son of a bitch, I'd help the next girl.

Because, you see, I saw the house.

I saw the number beside the door.

I saw the tags on the car parked in the driveway.

And I saw the motherfucker's face.

I went and sat down on the step next to the blood. Waited. I knew she'd be there eventually. It was how it worked.

Still surprised me when I looked up and there she was. Pale, thin, young, her face as bright as a candle. Eyes filled with forever.

"You can still opt out," I told her. "I can turn this over to the cops. Let them handle it."

She said nothing, but she gave me a look. We both knew that this guy was too careful. There would be no evidence of any kind. He'd been doing this for years and he knew his tradecraft. No semen, no hairs, nothing left for them to trace. The knife was gone where no one would ever find it. And he wasn't a souvenir collector. The smarter ones aren't. They could turn his house inside out, and the only things they'd find would be jack and shit.

Even if they watched him, he'd turn it off for a while. For long enough. Police can't afford to run surveillance for very long. They lose interest, even if they thought the guy was good for Olivia's murder.

I sighed. Actually, I wanted to cry. What she was asking was big and ugly, and it was going to hurt both of us.

She stood there with a necklace of bright red and those bottomless eyes.

She didn't say a word. She didn't have to.

The price was the price. She was willing to pay it because she was a decent kid who would probably have grown up to be someone of note. Someone with power. Someone who cared. Those eyes told me that this wasn't about her.

It was all about the next girl.

And the one after that.

And the one after that.

I buried my face in my hands and wept.

CHAPTER SEVENTY-TWO

Rain huddled in, gripping her cell phone with icy fingers. Bug snuggled in beside her, trying to share warmth. Monk Addison was still on the other end of the call. Still there, and that was something.

They talked about the shower curtain, trying to make sense of it, but Doctor Nine haunted the conversation. Somehow *he* had done it. He had taken the curtain and given it to the boy.

"It doesn't make sense," insisted Rain. "That boy hung himself with the curtain before it went missing from my bathroom. How?"

"How was the kid in the morgue an older version of your son, Rain?" asked Monk.

"I don't *know*."

"I sure as shit don't," he admitted. "But, listen, I have one more question to ask. Maybe it's another part of this. There was writing on the wall near where Hoto killed himself. Pretty sure it wasn't Hoto who put it there. Different handwriting. It said: *They are coming.* Do you know what that might mean?"

"I . . . don't know," said Rain, but she could hear the doubt in her own voice. "I've been seeing some things around town. Something I think may be connected, but I don't know how. Monk, have you ever heard of 'the Shadow People'?"

He said, "Heard of them, but not sure I can remember what I heard. Why?"

"It keeps coming up. I see it written on walls around town. I think maybe Doctor Nine and the nurse are Shadow People. Whatever that means."

Thunder rumbled far away.

"Monk," said Rain, "what's going on? I mean, seriously, what is this? What can we do about this?"

"We start by looking at this like a fight, kid," growled Monk.

"That's what my friends and I all said, but how do we fight something like this?"

"Maybe I can figure that part out," said Monk. "When I was in the military, I learned that a soldier is only as good as the intel he gets. You know that word? *Intel?* Intelligence? It means information that's gathered and analyzed. No matter how tough or scary the enemy is, if they're fighting us, then they have to be here, in our world. Maybe not ordinary flesh and blood, but bound by some of the same rules. We have some information already— what you've experienced, what your friends have been through, and some of what I've found. Now that we've compared notes, we collectively know more than we did individually. That's a strength. It makes it less scary."

"Not really."

"It does for me. It will for you," Monk assured her. "That's a start, but we need more, and I know who to call. I have a friend, Dr. Jonatha Corbiel down at the University of Pennsylvania. She's an expert in folklore, particularly the folklore of the supernatural."

"Wait, I know that name. She's black, right? Pretty? I think I've seen her on the History Channel. Those shows they play around Halloween."

"That's her. She's not just a talking head, though. Jonatha's a world-class expert. Think of her as my Van Helsing. I don't hunt vampires, but you get the gist. I'm going to tell her everything and see what she has to say."

"What if she doesn't know anything about this stuff?"

"Then we'll try something else," he said. "The point is that Doctor Nine's picked a fight. Fine. He's landed some good punches. Fair enough. He doesn't get to just roll over us, though. He's declared a war, so we give him a war. Our job is to make sure we go into that war armed with every scrap of intel we can get. We need to wise up and gear up."

"Okay," she said. It sounded very manly and bully-bully, but it was also a bit of a comfort. Rain stroked Bug's head. The dog was wide awake and listening because Rain had the speaker on.

Monk said, "The good news is now that we've shared everything, none of us are alone anymore. We got your friends, you, and me. That's a lot more than we had this morning, right? We may not be a full army, but we're a squad, a team."

"The Cracked World Society," she said and explained what that meant.

Monk laughed. "Yeah, that'll do. So it's the Cracked World Society against the Shadow People. Two sides. That makes it a war. Now we build our intel. I'm going to call Jonatha tonight and wake her up. She's used to that."

"That's great, Monk, and tomorrow, I'm going to go out with Sticks and try to find Boundary Street and—"

"You're going to find *what*?" Monk shouted it into the phone.

"Boundary Street. Wait, didn't I tell you that part of it?"

"No, you goddamn well did not. How the hell do you know about Boundary Street?"

Rain explained it to him.

"Listen to me," he said when she was done, "and don't freak out, okay?"

"You say that and I immediately want to freak out."

"Don't. This is good. Maybe it's good, I'm not sure. I know how to find Boundary Street," he said.

"You *what*?"

"This is going to sound crazy or it's going to make sense, but I think there's a Boundary Street in every town. Everywhere. I think there's always a Boundary Street."

"Sticks said that, too."

"He's right," said Monk. "The first time I found Boundary Street was when I was in Shanghai. And I found it again in Cairo and in Tehran. And a dozen other places. I always find it."

"Then you've been there."

"No," he said heavily. "I've never been there. I live down in the shadows along Boundary Street. Sounds poetic, but it's not. It blows. The kind of work I do doesn't get me an invitation to go up the hill. You say you've been *in* the Zone? Shit. That's pretty amazing. That makes me want to cry. Sticks has been there, too? Disabled vet? Maybe that's part of it. Maybe you have to lose something, or maybe you have to care for something or care *about* something, to be clean enough to go up that hill."

"But you're helping me, Monk," Rain said.

"I'm on your side, but don't make assumptions about me. You don't know the things I've seen. You don't know what I've done. If I go up that hill and stand in that light, it would all be there to see. And . . . I guess I don't want that. I'm not ready for that. I'm not one of the Shadow People, whatever they are, but there's this darkness that's down deep inside of me. I need it. It still has a purpose to serve, and as long as I need it, I think it's best if I stay down on this side of Boundary Street."

"Monk, I told you everything about what's going on with me. More than I've told anyone. More than I told my friends at the diner tonight. But you keep talking about your darkness and you aren't anywhere near as freaked out about all this as you should be. Why not?"

He cursed softly. "You really want to hear it?"

"I think I have to."

"It's going to scare the shit out of you."

Rain almost smiled. "I think it's too late for that."

And so he told her his story. It took a while, too. When he was done, Rain sat there, holding Bug, crying softly.

"I'm sorry the world's like this," said Monk. "For you, for your friends. For all of us. It's real dark out there, but you're not alone out here. Maybe I'm not, either. So believe me when I tell you we're going to fight this. Whatever it is, we're not going to just roll over and take it. That's not who I am, and I don't think it's who you are. Maybe before, but not now. Am I right?"

"Yes," she said.

"We're going to fight?"

"Yes." Rain did not wipe at her tears. "We have to. Not for me. For my son. His name is Dylan. It means 'ray of hope.'"

She heard a sound. Maybe it was a sob; it was hard to tell. The line went dead.

INTERLUDE NINETEEN
MONK'S STORY, PART 5

It took me two days to run it all down. The girl misremembered the license number, so that killed half a day.

Then I put the pieces together. Bang, bang, bang.

Once that happens, everything moves quickly.

I ran the guy through the databases we PIs use, and after an hour, I knew everything about him. I had his school records and his service record—one tour in Afghanistan, one in Iraq. Made me hate him even more. He was divorced, no kids. Parents dead, his only living relative was a brother in Des Moines. I figured there were bodies buried in Des Moines, too, but I'd never know about them. He owned three Jack in the Box franchise stores and had half interest in a fourth. Drove a hybrid, recycled, and had solar panels on his house. I almost found that funny.

I was in his Netflix and Hulu accounts, his bank account, and everything else he had. If there was a pattern there, or a clue as to what he was, it wasn't there. He was very smart and very careful. No cops were ever going to catch him.

I parked my car on the route he took to work and waited until I saw him drive past on his way home. Gave him an hour while I watched the sun go down. Twilight dragged some clouds across the sky, and the news guy said it was going to rain again. Fine. Rain was good. It was loud and it chased people off the streets.

Lightning forked the sky, and thunder was right behind it. Big, booming. One second, nothing, and then it was raining alley cats and junkyard dogs.

I got out of my car and opened an umbrella. I really don't give a shit about getting wet, but umbrellas block line of sight. They make you invisible. I walked through the rain to his yard, went in through the gate, up along the flagstone path, and knocked on the door. Had to knock twice.

The guy had half a confused smile on his face when he opened the door, the way people do when they aren't expecting anyone. Especially during a storm. Big guy, an inch taller than me, maybe only ten pounds lighter. His debit card record says that he keeps his gym membership up to date. I knew from my research that he'd boxed in college. Wrestled, too. And he had army training. Whatever.

"Mr. Gardner?" I asked.

He said, "What do you want?"

I hit him. Real fucking hard. A two-knuckle punch to the face, right beside the nose. Cracks the infraorbital foramen. Mashes the sinus. Feels a lot like getting shot in the face, except you don't die. He went back and down, falling inside his house, and I swarmed in after him, letting the umbrella go. The wind whipped it away and took it somewhere. Maybe Oz for all I know. I never saw it again.

Gardner fell hard, but he fell the right way, like he knew what he was doing.

Twisting to take the fall on his palms, letting his arm muscles soak up the shock. His head had to be ringing like Quasimodo's bells, but he wasn't going out easy.

He kicked at me as I came for him. A good kick, too, flat of the heel going for the front of my knee. If he'd connected, I'd have gone down with a busted leg, and he'd have had all the time in the world to do whatever he wanted. If he'd connected. I was born at night, but it wasn't last night. I bent my knee into the kick and bent over to punch the side of his foot. I knew some tricks, too.

In the movies, there's a brawl. A long fight with all sorts of fancy moves, deadly holds, exciting escapes, a real gladiatorial match. That's the movies. In the real world, fights are, to paraphrase Hobbes, nasty, brutish, and short. He had that one kick, that one chance. I didn't give him a second one. I gave him nothing. I took everything.

When I was done, I was covered in blood, my chest heaving, staring at what was left of him there in the living room. I'd closed the door. The curtains were closed over drawn shades. The TV was on. Some kind of CSI *show with the volume cranked up. Outside, the storm was shaking the world.*

Gardner wasn't dead. Mostly, but not entirely. That would come a little later. He wasn't going anywhere, though. That would have been structurally impossible. I went into the kitchen and found a basting brush. Slapped it back and forth over his face to get it wet, then I wrote on the wall. It took a while. I made sure he was watching. I wrote the names of every girl he had killed. Every one that I'd met there in the darkness of Olivia's hell. Gardner was whimpering. Crying. Begging. When I was done, I unzipped my pants, pulled out my dick, and pissed on him. He was sobbing now. Maybe he was that broken or that scared. Maybe it was his last play, trying to hold a match to the candle of my compassion.

Maybe.

But he was praying in the wrong church.

Gardner managed to force one word out. It took a lot of effort because I'd ruined him.

"P-please," he said.

I smiled.

"Fuck you," I said. The storm was raging, and I stood there for nearly an hour. Watching Gardner suffer. Watching him die. Judge me if you want. If so, feel free to go fuck yourself.

That night, I got drunk. Because it's the only reasonable thing to do.

Me and Patty, Lefty Wright, and a couple of the others. Ten of us huddled around a couple of tables in a black-as-pockets corner of our favorite bar. Me and my people. No one had to ask what happened. Patty knew, couple of the others maybe. Mostly not. But they all knew something had happened. We were those kinds of people, and this was that kind of town. We drank and told lies, and if the laughter sounded fake at times and forced at others, then so what?

It was nearly dawn when I stumbled up the stairs, showered for the third time that day, and fell into bed. I said some prayers to a God I knew was there but was pretty sure was insane. Or indifferent. Or both. My windows are painted black because I sleep during the day. Mostly, anyway. I had a playlist running. John Lee Hooker and Son House. Old blues like that. Some Tom Waits and Nick Cave in there, too. Grumpy, cynical stuff. Broken hearts and spent shell casings and bars on the wrong side of the tracks. Like that.

Stuff I can sleep to. When I can sleep.

Mostly, I can't sleep.

My room's always too crowded. They are always there. It's usually when I'm alone that I see them. Pale faces standing in silence. Or screaming.

Some of them scream.

I wear long-sleeve shirts to bed because they scream the loudest when they see their own faces. It's like that. It's how it all works. When I'm at the edge of sleep, leaning over that big black drop, I can feel the faces on my skin move. I can feel their mouths open to scream, too. Sometimes the sheet gets soaked with tears that aren't mine. But which are mine now.

Olivia was there for the first time that night. Standing in the corner, pale as a candle, looking far too young to be out this late. Thank God she wasn't one of the screamers. She was a silent one. She with her red necklace that went from ear to ear.

My name is Gerald Addison. Most people call me Monk.

I drink too much and I hardly ever sleep.

And I do what I do.

CHAPTER SEVENTY-THREE

Scot Joplin worked late into the night and deep into the new, dark morning. He was on his fifth chain-smoked joint and his seventh beer. Baked and boiled and all the way on the edge. Instead of mellowing him, the weed was scraping him raw and the beer was like salt in the wounds.

The canvas was wrought with stark colors that lunged at strange angles; colors collided with colors in improbable ways. With each slash of the brush, each cut of the palette knife, the painting seemed to groan. The image he was trying to bring to life eluded him, the composition failing even as he worked on it. Failed for no reason that he wanted to name.

His mind was a furnace.

First there had been the horror show of seeing the dead man hanging in the hall. That was bad; that would have been enough to drive his day off a cliff. Then that detective. Anna-Maria something. Treating him like he was a spitty place on the sidewalk. Making him feel guilty by the way she grilled him.

Then, when the body was gone and the cops were gone, after the blackout and the storm, there was the phone call with the man who owned Human Bean.

"Mr. Joplin?"

"Yes, Mr. Vick, thanks for calling. Sorry I didn't see you at the café."

"Maybe it's better we didn't, Mr. Joplin."

"Call me Scot."

"Mr. Joplin," Vick repeated, "let me come straight to it. I think it would be best if you arranged to come by and collect your paintings."

At which point Joplin almost laughed because he thought it was a joke, but after trying to find the punch line, he said, "What? Why?"

"Frankly, I think it was a mistake. Your work is, um, a little intense for our customers. We've had comments. Well . . . complaints, really."

"Complaints about *what*?"

"About the themes."

"What are you talking about? You said that you thought they were visionary. That's your word, Mr. Vick. *Visionary*."

"Well, now that they've been hanging, I suppose I've changed my mind. Please come and get them by Wednesday."

"I don't understand this. What's changed? Why are you doing this?"

Vick sighed impatiently. "Do you really want to get into this, Mr. Joplin?"

"Yes, I think I deserve that much. After all, you said—"

"I said you could hang your work because I'm friends with your sister, Lanie. It was a favor to her, and I regretted it as soon as I saw the work on the walls. I know something about art, Mr. Joplin. I *buy* art, and what you hung in my café is—and I'm going to be brutally honest—not very good. It's cheap and obvious, and it has a juvenile thread of obscenity in it."

"Obscenity? They're figure studies and cityscapes and—"

"And we both know what they really are, Mr. Joplin. I looked at them. Closely. At the brush strokes. I suppose you think you're being clever and subtle by hiding pornographic images within the brush strokes, but really . . . it's not actually all that subtle. People who *don't* understand art have noticed, and complained. At first I dismissed it, then I went and examined each picture. I am very disappointed in what I saw. Lanie spoke so highly of you that I expected something more than this. Something better. I'm sorry that I was so wrong about you, and I will have a talk with your sister. And if you're actually serious about making a name for yourself as an artist, stop with the juvenile tricks. A real artist would be more honest. Try opening a vein and bleeding a little. I know it takes courage, though, so maybe that's not what you're about."

There was more of the conversation, but that was all Joplin remembered. Joplin could not understand what the man had been talking about. Obscene images?

Not until he went and looked at the new canvases he had set aside to take to the Human Bean. Six canvases stacked against the side of the couch. He picked up the first one and studied it. A painting of two people dancing in the shadows of an alleyway, lit by a yellow bulb in a wire cage over a back door. A big green Dumpster in the background. The figures could have been struggling with each other, but to Joplin it had been a dance. There was tension to it, not any kind of sentimentality. No sweetness, but certainly nothing vulgar or obscene.

Except . . .

He frowned and turned the canvas so that the lamplight caught on the ridges of paint.

"What the hell?"

The composition told one story. The colors told a subtly different one. But the brush strokes, viewed at that angle, revealed a third story. It was not something you could see at all unless you looked at it in this way. And then it was all you could see. It shocked him. Chilled him. Terrified him. Formed entirely by contour but not by color or deliberately painted structure were two figures. A woman in what looked like a nurse's uniform but with her skirt hiked up around her waist, straddling a short, fat man with a swollen cock. Both of them had their heads thrown back and mouths open. The nurse looked like she was having an enormous orgasm. The man appeared to be screaming. Not in passion but in pain. Or terror.

Joplin dropped the canvas as if it had taken a bite out of him. He backed away from it.

"No!" he yelled. The canvas landed on the floor, and the angle showed nothing but two people dancing in the dark. He grabbed up a second one, held it this way and that, searching the landscape of brush strokes. Until he found it. This one was worse. A pregnant woman, her vagina exposed as she lay spread-eagle on a birthing table, her stomach cut open, and from her belly rose a tall, sinister figure dressed all in black. Eyes of flame and a smiling mouth, with a piece of raw meat hung around his neck like some obscene tie.

The third canvas was the worst of all. In those lines, revealed by the light, a child hung from the pipes, his throat squeezed to impossibility by a shower curtain.

Joplin had painted that canvas five days ago. Before the boy had killed himself in the hall.

His legs buckled, and he dropped slowly, inevitably to his knees and then bowed forward over the cramps in his stomach until his forehead was touching the floor.

CHAPTER SEVENTY-FOUR

Rain knew that she was not going to ever fall asleep again. Not after the call from Monk Addison. Not after all the things they had said to each other. Not after the ghosts, the masks, the blood.

Not after the message on the wall near where the boy and Mr. Hoto had both died.

She called Joplin's number but got voice mail.

On impulse, she put on the old lady's glasses and wore them while she looked around her apartment. Looking sideways out of the splinter hurt her eyes, but it made her see things she could not see without them. More of the maggots from before, hiding under rugs and between floorboards. Bug tried to eat them, but Rain pushed her away, dug the insects out with her knife, and stomped them flat. Bug continued to growl at the spots where the maggots had died.

Then she went into the bathroom and looked at the shower rod. There were smudges on it that she had not seen before. Like fingerprints, she thought, but when she stood on the rim of the tub and peered closely at them, she saw that there were none of the whorls and patterns of any normal fingerprints. Instead, the pattern was like a beaded mosaic, like lizard skin might make. She got Clorox and a rag and wiped everything down. Bug yelped and fled from the smell. When Rain was done, she stuffed the rags into a plastic trash bag, sealed it, and set it in the hall.

Looking for traces of Doctor Nine became an obsession, but she had to wear the glasses in order to see that kind of thing. Like the black spider crouching inside the left shoe she was going to wear tomorrow when she went out with Sticks. Like the roaches hiding under the fitted sheet on her bed.

No, sleep was going to be impossible.

Working like this made her feel like a soldier going to war. Doing something. Being proactive. It also gave her a measure of power while her inner voices screamed at her about what Monk told her.

They are coming.

Hours passed, and despite the cold, she was bathed in sweat. The apartment stunk of cleaning products and her head ached abominably. Not a full migraine, but close enough to sour her stomach and screw up her balance. She plunked down on the kitchen chair and closed her eyes to try to reset her brain. The small darkness behind her eyelids helped.

She never realized she was asleep until she saw *the flashing red hand outside of Torquemada's.*

"What?"

People were crowding into the place, and every time the door opened wide enough, the Music lunged out into the street. Bold and beautiful; dangerous the way the edge of the Grand Canyon is dangerous, the way a screaming tiger is beautiful. Rain saw Snakedancer and his disciples laughing and twirling as they ushered the crowd inside.

Rain saw Joplin go in, and Dylan was with them. They were holding hands and laughing. Joyful laughs, too. Behind them, dressed to kill, were Yo-Yo in a tight glittery sheath dress and towering spike heels, Gay Bob in a gorgeous tight shirt and black pants, and Straight Bob in a nice but old-fashioned business suit. They, too, were laughing. She saw an old Asian man behind them, and with a grunt of surprise, Rain realized that it was the monk she'd met in Central Park all those years ago, on the day Dylan was born. And in the same moment of clarity, Rain knew that the monk was the same person as Mr. Hoto, the latest victim of Doctor Nine.

"Hey!" she yelled, but no one turned toward her. The Music was too loud, and a moment later, they had all vanished inside.

Rain broke into a run and stopped at the edge of the crowd that was still squeezing through the doors. She couldn't see anyone she knew now, and the faces of the strangers there seemed slightly blurred as if they were moving at a different speed than she was. Only when she angled her head to see them out of the corner of the lenses could Rain see clearly. They were beautiful faces. Elegant, exotic, like the faces of angels in old paintings, or pharaohs from tomb walls. Everyone seemed taller than she was, fitter, stronger. They laughed and chattered in lovely voices, but none of what they said made sense to her, as if they spoke a language different from any Rain had ever heard.

She stood and watched until every single person had entered Torquemada's. The big doors swung shut, and the Music was gone. It stabbed her with grief not to hear it. Worse still, before the doors shut completely, she saw the dance floor. It was packed with people and bathed in rapidly changing colored light. The bodies all moved to the Music, turned and lunging and spinning with preternatural grace as if they did not dance to the rhythm but were actually part of it. One with it.

It hurt her to see it because Rain remembered dancing like that. On dance floors in schools and studios and on stages, Rain had danced like that. Part of something that was bigger and more profound than sound and motion, more important than choreography and timing. There was dancing, and then there was a level higher, deeper, better, more beautiful. She had been there, had been part of that, and when she was dancing, it made her more fully alive than anything.

Only once had Rain ever experienced anything as perfect.

It was that moment in the hospital when she had seen Dylan and he had seen her. That moment when she had given him his secret name.

After that, nothing was ever beautiful again. Doctor Nine and the nurse took Dylan away. Noah was already dead and buried. And the horror show of complications had stolen her ability to dance. Collectively, it had evicted her from a world like the one beyond those doors.

"Fuck this," she growled as she grabbed the door handles and jerked them open. They moved so much more easily than she expected.

The Music was there, waiting, crouching behind those doors, and it pounced on her, staggering her, driving her backward, but she still held on to one door handle. The other door swung closed, but Rain hauled herself forward against the tidal surge of Music.

Rain nearly died there. Right there in the doorway to Torquemada's.

Her legs wanted to collapse, and there wasn't enough air in the room or in her spasming lungs. She leaned against the inside wall and desperately tried to regain equilibrium. The hammering of the Music was only less explosive than the desperate insistence of her heartbeat. Sweat burst from her pores, and her fevered eyes jumped and twitched as she saw all the things that twisted and writhed within the club. It was like nothing she had ever seen before or even *imagined, and her reeling senses could not begin to comprehend it all. It was too much, and the overload bored holes in her head. Unable to resist, unsure if she wanted to, and yet terrified to let go, Rain stood shaking near the door. She felt more than heard the door slam shut behind her with ringing finality.*

"God save me," she whispered, but the Music beat all the tone from the plea.

Torquemada's was fantastically huge, much larger than it looked from without. The dance floor was a picture of mad infinity, stretching away beyond the reaches of perceptions. It was edged by a broad wooden apron, and the floor itself was clear acrylic. Looking down revealed images of Hieronymus Bosch—but alive and moving. The dancers themselves were insane, trapped within a musical force that was beyond definition: it caught them, spun them violently, drove them into dance steps that human limbs should not be able to perform. Yet faltering was impossible, for the Music held absolute command. With tentacles of force, the Music coiled around each body, probed every private place, discovered every secret; it kept moving, moving—always on the prowl for something deep, something rare. It writhed along the floor, forcing feet to move, buffeting sinuous bodies and making them gyrate in tune with its own pulsations.

In the throes of madness, the dancers were stretched and contorted like hot plastic, their bodies warping and changing according to the whims and demands of the Music. The fabric of material existence was altered so that the fingers of a stretched hand would suddenly fly off to the end of the room, but the stumps would not bleed. People exploded and became fragments of light. Off in one corner, a leg danced with itself, then grew a new body that was far different from the one it had lost. A man fell upward into the air and melted into the swirling plasterwork of the ceiling. These things—these mad things that Rain saw and felt—convinced her that her earlier guess had been right: she was either dead or insane, and this was all some kind of drug-induced nightmare.

Yet . . . the Music felt real, and the vibrations of the bass notes through the floor felt real, and the lights burned with stinging reality in her eyes. Rain tried to stand her ground, but her mind was already tumbling. Caught at the deadly edge of the whirlpool, she fought for balance but knew that she would be dragged down if she took even the tiniest step forward. Nothing she could do would prevent that. As she swayed, the rhythms pounded at her, tugged her, enticed her, cried out to her in siren voices, teasing her to succumb, to simply step off the precipice and plunge into the abyss that was the Music.

The Music closed itself as one song finished, and there was a trembling second of relief. Rain felt faint; her face was hot and running with sweat. She tried to concentrate, but the whole place seemed to be out of focus. Then the next song began, and it began with such intensity that Rain stumbled backward, crying out, gasping, and clutching at her chest as the first notes struck her above the heart.

Her back struck the door, and she fell outside into the cool air.

. . . jerked awake at the kitchen table.

The clock insisted that it was nine o'clock in the morning, but outside it was black as night. She started to get up and then saw something sitting on the counter beside the sink. Not one single thing.

Three things.

A crack pipe. A shooter, like the kind she used to have, with a small glass tube she'd bought at a liquor store in Jersey, fitted with a screen made from a copper Brillo pad.

A fat vial of beautiful crystals.

And a neatly folded shower curtain. Her curtain.

Rain screamed.

CHAPTER SEVENTY-FIVE

Alyson Creighton-Thomas sat on her couch in exactly the same place where she had been for eleven hours. She had twice gotten up to go to the bathroom, and twice more to get a bottle from the freezer. Otherwise, that couch was her throne, her electric chair, her place.

Watching the DVD. Watching the two little girls dance. They looked so much alike. Little Alyson and little Lorraine. Watching them touched that part of her that was still alive, still connected to life, to remembered joy. To hope.

But then other thoughts and feelings intruded. The babies. The one that had ruined her and the one that had ruined her daughter. When those feelings surged up inside of her, Alyson snatched up a Xanax or a Zoloft or an Amytal and washed them down with white wine or vodka. Or swallowed them dry if her bottles were empty and there was something happening on the screen she wanted to watch. The dance competition in Westchester. The recital in the arts center near the park.

Some of the video segments were as recent as eleven years ago. Some were as old as forty years in the remembered past. Two girls. So alike they could be twins. Two girls who looked more like sisters than mother and daughter. Dancing, dancing, joyful, elegant, talented, dancing.

The video ran all the way to the end, and Alyson restarted it.

She did not notice the birds on the windowsill. She did not notice the tall, thin, pale man in the dark suit standing behind her couch, his mouth carved into a jack-o'-lantern grin as he waited for tricks and treats. Even if she turned, she would not see him.

It wasn't time for that quite yet.

CHAPTER SEVENTY-SIX

It took Rain nearly an hour to cut the shower curtain into pieces so tiny that no part of the swirling star pattern was recognizable. She was deeply afraid of the sounds she made as the scissors went *snip-snip-snip*. She only stopped crying when the curtain was so badly mangled that there wasn't enough of it left to be used as a noose. That seemed to matter to her; it was an important early goal in this process.

As she worked, her eyes, her traitor eyes, kept darting over to the pipe and vial on the drainboard. Those things were so beautiful. Those things were so ugly. She wanted them so badly.

Snip-snip-snip.

She cut the curtain into pieces and cut the pieces into confetti. Rain would have flushed them if she wasn't positive they would clog the toilet.

Snip-snip-snip.

Listening to music way too loud for this early so that she could not hear the storm. Heard the storm anyway. Mentally begged the phone to ring. It refused.

The pipe whispered to her. Not in the voice of her parasite. Not anymore. It had tried that before, and Rain cursed it to silence.

Nor did it whisper in *his* voice. The pipe knew better.

Instead, it whispered in the voice of her son. In Dylan's voice.

It's okay, Mom. Go ahead. You can't save me anyway, so smoke some rock. It'll help. You won't be able to hear what Doctor Nine does to me. I promise. The smoke loves you as much as I do.

Like that.

On some level, Rain knew that she was framing the argument. It had her overblown sense of drama. She also knew that it was saying all the right things.

Caster Bootey sure as shit did not show up to help her out. As figments of her imagination went, he'd turned out to be as useful as a baseball bat to the back of the head.

Snip-snip-snip.

The last pieces of the curtain fell to the floor, and there was nothing left big enough to cut.

Rain chewed her lip for a moment, considering what else to do with the scissors. Bad things. Very bad things.

She got up and forced herself to put the scissors away. The debris littered the floor, and tiny pieces clung to her sweat. Rain opened a drawer and rooted around until she found a meat tenderizer. An item she had never once used for cooking because she was a lousy cook. It was a pretty good hammer, though.

The pipe stood on the drainboard.

Rain raised the tenderizer so that the overhead light cast its mallet shadow across the pipe and the vial. She had no idea at all how long she stood there, poised to strike, still as a statue.

The phone rang.

The hammer was clutched in her hand when she went over to the table to answer the call.

"Rain?" asked Sticks. "I'm downstairs. Are you ready?"

She hefted the tenderizer and looked at the pipe and vial. "Almost," she said. Her voice sounded way too normal. Scary.

She fed Bug and spread out some newspapers on the floor in case she'd be home late. Then she picked the dog up and held her so tight for so long, burying her nose in the little animal's fur.

"Be good," she whispered as she kissed Bug and set her down. "Mommy loves you."

Bug whimpered softly but wagged her crooked tail. The innocence and trust in the little dog's eyes came close to breaking Rain's heart.

Five minutes later, she left her apartment. The vial and the pipe stood there, untouched, waiting for her return. Certain that she would come back for them. Come back to them. Come back.

CHAPTER SEVENTY-SEVEN

Doctor Nine reached out his hand and pushed against the skin of the world.

"Almost," said the nurse.

His smile dimmed, though. "No."

She looked at his hand. All she could see were his long, thin fingers and black fingernails clawing at the empty air inside the car. Bethy could never see what he saw. Not even now. Not even with all that had changed for her and in her and of her.

She was greedy for more. She was greedy for all of it, and she rubbed her hands on his arm and along his thighs.

"Tell me," she begged. "Make me feel it."

But Doctor Nine withdrew his hand, his smile still gone but his eyes burning. The window was open and rain whipped into the car. Nightbirds perched on the frame, dripping dirty water onto the upholstery. Doctor Nine bent and kissed the closest one. Kissed its black head and licked the length of its neck.

"I'm hungry," he murmured. "Bring me something delicious."

With a cry like a beaten child, the nightbird twisted away and threw itself into the storms. The other birds—the ones on the car and the dozens perched on rooftops and wires—followed. The beating of their wings was like drums of war.

Doctor Nine's pale hand snaked out and caught a vicious handful of the nurse's hair and pushed her head down toward his lap. She was willing, eager, and tried to show him by moving quickly, but he pushed her faster.

At his speed. In his way. She fumbled for his zipper while he clenched his grasping hand into a fist and blood ran from her tortured scalp.

Behind them, in the trunk of the car, the sound of a child weeping drove them both to madness.

CHAPTER SEVENTY-EIGHT

The Red Rocket idled at the curb, smoke curling from the tailpipe, the red paint burning in the light drizzle. Steam rose from the hood as if the big car had driven straight out of a furnace. It crouched there, powerful and threatening, but not to Rain.

It made her smile.

She got in, buckled up, and looked at Sticks. He frowned.

"What's wrong?" he asked at once.

Rain smiled at him. "Everything. Let's go."

He studied her for a moment longer, then nodded and drove away, heading toward the city. However, when they stopped at a light, Sticks said, "Look at me. Let me see your eyes."

"Why?"

"I want to see your pupils."

"Fuck you," she snapped. "I'm not high."

"Look at me anyway." She did. After a long moment, Sticks nodded and pulled out of the loading zone. "If you expect me to apologize for that," Sticks said, "don't hold your breath."

"No," replied Rain with a protracted sigh. "It's all good. It was a bad night, and I have a lot to tell you."

"Guess I have some things to tell you, too," he said. "You first."

Rain went over it all again. After having shared with the Cracked World Society and Monk, she felt more free to talk about these things, but she still stumbled when she mentioned Doctor Nine. She told him Monk's story, too. All of it. They were in Manhattan before she finished.

Sticks's hands were tight on the steering wheel, and that had nothing to do with the traffic. He kept giving her frightened sidelong looks. "Jesus Christ," he said, over and over again.

"Yeah," said Rain. "I know."

They drove in silence. "Before I get to my stuff, let's figure out what we're doing, okay? We're looking for Boundary Street, and we're both hoping that we can actually drive to the Fire Zone, right?"

"That's the plan, I thought."

"I'm wondering, though, what exactly we're hoping to accomplish here."

"What do you mean? We both know the answers are in the Zone."

"Do we, though? I mean, which actual answers are we talking about?"

"To what's happening," she said.

"No," countered Sticks, "which specific answers. A lot of weird shit's been happening over the last few days. This monster who's after you, this boogeyman of yours, he seems to be messing with a lot of folks. Now we're going to a place that maybe exists only in dreams. This ain't going to be on Google Maps, I can tell you that."

"I asked Monk about that. He said—"

"Right. Keep making random turns until I get lost. Wow. Nothing like laser-precision guidance."

"What was your plan, then?"

Sticks mumbled something.

"What was that?" asked Rain.

"Keep making random turns," he said but only a fraction louder.

"That's what I thought."

They drove.

Rain tried not to look at street signs, afraid that if she marked her location in her mind, it would prevent them from getting lost, and she thought getting lost was the only way they would find where they were going. Once she saw a figure standing in the doorway of a closed-down fabric store. Small, too thin, with a scuffle of brown hair whipped by the wind. She scrambled to put her glasses on and to try to look out of the corner of the cracked lens, but by the time she managed it, they were too far down the street.

"Go around the block!" she cried. "I think I saw—"

And a huge green-and-orange recyclables truck came barreling through a red light and smashed into the side of the Red Rocket. Rain had a brief flash image of the driver flailing his arms at the storm of ragged black birds filling his cab.

Then she was smashed out of the world.

CHAPTER SEVENTY-NINE

Dr. Jonatha Corbiel worked for the University of Pennsylvania as a professor in the folklore department. She was the author of more than forty nonfiction books, most of which dealt with myths, legends, cultural beliefs, and religious accounts of the supernatural. She was a very popular talking head on the History Channel and National Geographic for shows dealing with vampires, werewolves, ghosts, demons, faeries, and other creatures belonging to what she called the Larger World.

Monk Addison knew her as a drinking buddy from before his time in the military. They'd dated once upon a time, and it got heated for a while, but then it became clear to both that they were friends making love rather than lovers making love. They fell out of touch when he fell off the world, and when he'd come back to the world and looked her up, Monk learned that she was married, a mother, and a celebrity, at least as far as a folklorist will ever be.

She was one of the handful of people who knew about Monk. His "condition," as she called it, fascinated her, but so far, she hadn't found a corollary in folklore. Certainly not in medicine. It was not unusual for Monk to call her with challenging problems. If the matter was ordinary—in terms of what they both considered ordinary—he would handle it himself, because Monk understood a lot about the Larger World. It was his world, after all.

She was in her office grading papers from one of her graduate programs when he called.

"You alone?" he asked. He was in the back booth of Eve's, and there was no one within earshot. His heavy .45 Navy Colt automatic was under his hoodie, cold against belly flesh, the magazine loaded with hollow points. Two spares were in his left front pocket. He had a fighting knife in a belt holster and a silver strangle wire threaded through his belt loops. Both weapons had been dipped in holy water he'd obtained from a priest who drank at the same bar Monk did. He wore a Hamsa hand on a chain around his neck and had a pair of brass knuckles in his back pocket that had a crucifix, an evil eye, a lotus flower, and an upright pentacle welded to the front. He was taking no chances.

"Yes," said Corbiel. "And hello to you, too. I'm fine, thanks for asking."

"Sorry," said Monk, "it's not a social call, and I got a feeling there's a clock ticking on this."

"How much time is left on that clock?"

"Hell if I know. Could be years; could be five minutes. I really don't know, and that's part of the problem. I got something that's totally outside of anything I know or anything I've been within pissing distance of, but people are getting hurt. Couple of people are dead, there's a kid that's maybe in real trouble, and whatever's going on, I think it's about to break bad."

"Well, then," she said, sounding calm, but he knew she was faking it. "You'd better tell me."

He told her. When he was done, there was a pregnant silence. Monk finally broke it with a simple, hard question. "This Doctor Nine . . . what *is* he?"

"Well," said Dr. Corbiel, "he's not human."

"Oh, gosh, thanks a lot, Jonatha. That explains everything. So glad I called you for your expert opinion."

"First off, don't be a smart-ass," she said. "I'm trying to answer your question, but we have to be structured in our thinking. The last thing you ever want to do in these matters is be imprecise."

"Yeah, you're right. Sorry. Go ahead. I'll zip it." He waved at the waitress to bring him fresh coffee.

Jonatha cleared her throat. "In the movies, there is a pretty obvious difference between the various kinds of monsters. A werewolf is a werewolf, a demon is a demon. That's pop culture. In folklore and in religious beliefs around the world, the lines are much less clear. In fact, it's more common for supernatural beings to possess elements and aspects of more than one. There are ghosts who are also vampires, demons who shape-shift like werewolves, vampires who are also witches. Thousands of variations throughout the world and back through history."

"Swell."

"I'll give you some examples," she said, clearly excited by her topic. "The *soucouyant* is a skin-shedding vampire from Dominica in the Lesser Antilles. As the sun goes down, the *soucouyant* shucks her disguise—that of a helpless old woman—and rises into the air as a ball of fire that swoops down on the unsuspecting, knocking them to the ground and feeding on their blood. Sunlight doesn't kill her but makes her need to put her skin back on. However, if someone grinds coarse salt into her skin, she won't be able to put it back on and will ultimately starve and die."

"That's a vampire?"

"It's one kind. There are hundreds of them, and they're all different. Actually, the closest vampire to the Hollywood version of Dracula is the *jiangshi* of China, but most vampires are really exotic. The word *vampire* is imprecise. The *tlahuelpuchi* is an Aztec vampire that attacks infants and young children for their blood. This vampire is a shape-shifter that can become a cat, dog, bird, but their preferred shape is a turkey. Birds are the most common."

Monk thought about the flocks of ugly black birds he'd been seeing lately and asked about them.

"Sure," said Jonatha, "if they're supernatural birds, then they could be nightbirds. They're a kind of familiar, but not true animal familiars. The nightbirds are embodiments of corrupt people, lost souls. They are usually in the service of a greater power."

"Like Doctor Nine?"

"Maybe. If so, they are his eyes and ears. They aren't real birds, though. Their bodies are composed of dust and rot and shadows."

"Jesus, Jonatha."

"You asked."

"How do I fight these things? A hammer and stake?"

"You watch too many movies." She took a breath. "Look, your thinking is polluted by pop culture. Just say this is a vampire we're talking about, okay? Sake of argument. How would you kill it?"

"Well, offhand," said Monk, "a cross, sunlight, and mirrors. Oh, and they can't come in unless you invite them, right?"

"Fine, so if this was one of the more than ninety different kinds of European vampires, you'd be dead."

"Why?"

"First," she said briskly, "it's a crucifix, not a cross. Catholic iconography is in play in the novel *Dracula*, which is where the cross was first introduced, and it's there because the author, Bram Stoker, was Irish Catholic. The crucifix is the ultimate symbol of religious purity because Christ died to wipe away the sins of the world. His sacrifice proved also that he was sinless, or above sin. Stoker implied that this level of purity would be anathema to anything evil, because evil is representative of a stained and impure soul. The cross, on the other hand, is more often used by Protestant churches to symbolize the resurrection. However, neither the crucifix nor the cross was ever used to stave off a vampire. Not in folklore, anyway. There are plenty of vampires who were believed to rise from graves or crypts in churchyards, which by their nature imply sanctified ground. Stoker put holy objects in his story because he was tapping into his personal beliefs in order to amplify the backstory of a novel."

Monk touched the shape of his brass knuckles in his pocket, tracing the outline of the crucifix. "What about sunlight? That turns vampires to dust."

"In the movies. Dracula actually walked around in daylight in the novel," said Corbiel with a laugh. "Sunlight became part of the vampire pop culture mythology after the silent film *Nosferatu*. Now people think it's always been there. Stakes, too. Stakes were never used to kill vampires. They were like spears used to hold a vampire down so that the head could be cut off as part of the ritual of exorcism."

"Well . . . shit."

"My point is that if this Doctor Nine or his nurse are really vampires and you armed yourself with crosses, stakes, and a flashlight with a UV bulb, you wouldn't have a chance. It would be like fighting a fire by eating a bowl of chicken soup. The cure has nothing to do with the problem."

Monk fished for his cigarettes, glared at the No Smoking sign nailed to the wall, cursed, put the smokes away, and sat there fuming. "Shit," he said.

"That's all going on the assumption that we're dealing with vampires," said Corbiel, "and I don't think it's as simple as that."

"Fighting vampires would be simpler?"

"Figure of speech," she amended. "What I mean is that each of these monsters has very specific powers and very specific limitations. Fight one the wrong way and you die. Underestimate them and you die. Take the wrong precautions and—"

"I die. Got it. Lots of variations have me being dead. Tell me something that keeps me and Rain Thomas alive."

He could hear her drumming her fingers on a wooden desk or tabletop. She did it very slow, one finger at a time. He imagined her doing it. Jonatha was six feet tall, very pretty, very dark skinned, devastatingly intelligent, and extremely married. Her husband was a short, dumpy little writer who'd had a string of bestselling novels, several of which had been made into box office smash films. He wrote about vampires and other monsters, too, but unlike Jonatha, her husband made everything up.

Or, at least, that's what he said in the press. Monk had his doubts.

"Monk," she said, "I want you to go through it all again. Every detail. Everything you know, everything Ms. Thomas told you, everything you can remember. Give me your thoughts and guesses, too."

"There's a lot, and I'm not allowed to smoke where I'm sitting."

"Good. Those things will kill you."

Monk gave a single, sharp, harsh laugh. "Not sure I'm going to live long enough to die of cancer."

CHAPTER EIGHTY

Alyson Creighton-Thomas made herself get up from the couch and go into the bathroom. The floor tilted under her with every step, and when she reached for the doorknob, it pulled away. She stumbled, tried to catch herself, hit the door, and fell through because it wasn't closed all the way. She struck her cheek on the closed lid of the toilet and landed hard on the cold tiles.

She sagged down, hurt but not damaged, embarrassed in her own eyes because there was no one else to stare in disapproval. Standing up seemed like too much work and required more engineering skills than she currently had.

So she sat up, turned slowly and awkwardly until her back was against the cabinet under the sink, and then smoothed down her robe and silk pajamas, tucking her legs modestly beneath her.

The apartment was big and cool and white and silent.

Alyson fished in her pocket for the folded letter that she had been carrying around for days now. It was there, folded into a neat, precise square, and she opened it to read for the hundredth time the summary of the months-long surveillance report that had cost her many thousands of dollars. There was a longer and more detailed version of the report on her desk. Two hundred and eighteen pages of it, including photos.

Lorraine looking like a starved street person.

Lorraine coming out of some man's apartment in the middle of the night.

Lorraine telling god-awful stories in front of a bunch of complete losers.

Lorraine sitting in diners with junkies and homosexuals.

Lorraine spending her money on junk food, because junkies always craved sweets.

Lorraine showing up a day late for a simple job interview.

Lorraine falling further down. Sliding down. Plummeting.

Lorraine being Lorraine.

Lorraine.

Alyson wished that she could cry, but she wasn't sure who the tears would be for. That was a moment of clarity that made her ache for the vodka that was sitting cold and delicious and welcoming back in the living room. It was the kind of awareness that made her very angry. It was the kind of introspection that she had tried hard to excise from her life. It was vulgar and obvious.

She closed her eyes for a moment, and when she opened them, she was back on the couch. Her robe and pajamas were stained and they smelled, but Alyson did not choose to pay attention to that.

The vodka was there. And the lovely pills. And the video.

CHAPTER EIGHTY-ONE

When Monk had gone over it all again, Jonatha said, "The Shadow People . . ."

Leaving it there, letting it hang.

"What about them?" demanded Monk. "Talk. If you know something, Jonatha, you have to tell me right damn now. Are they real?"

"Yes," she said, "I think they are."

The storm was getting bigger, wetter, louder. Monk thought of Rain somewhere out there in all of that, and it scared the hell out of him. He signaled the waitress for his check. "Then what are they?" he asked Jonatha. "Are they some kind of demons?"

"If they're anything, Monk," said Corbiel, "they're closer to vampires, but not really that, either. They're a kind of predatory spirit called an *essential vampire*. They don't feed on blood, and some of them don't have actual physical bodies. They're a presence. In a lot of cultures, vampires are closer to ghosts than what you see in Dracula movies. You've heard the word *nosferatu*? You know what it means?"

"Sure, undead."

"No. That's a mistranslation used in pop culture," she said. "*Nosferatu* means 'plague carrier.' They are spirits of disease and pestilence. The Shadow People are like that, except that they feed on things like life energy or psychic energy. Modern vampire cults talk a lot about psi-vampires, but they think it's a lifestyle choice. The Shadow People are real, and no one in their right mind would choose to invite them in. There are some that feed on dreams, others that consume sexual energy—"

"Like a succubus?" said Monk. "And what's the male version? The incubus?"

"Yes. They're more common. But there is another kind, a much more dangerous kind that feeds on subtler emotions, like pity, self-confidence, optimism, and, most of all, hope."

"Hope? Why that most of all?"

"Why not? Think about it, Monk," said Corbiel. "Imagine being crushed down by sickness, or debt, or heartbreak, or even injury in battle and then losing all hope. It's unbearable. As long as you have hope, you have some measure of courage and strength. You'll try to survive. You may sacrifice yourself for someone else. You will move mountains. But *without* hope, there's no optimism. Hopelessness is what fuels the blackest kinds of depression. Without hope, when it's running low or run out, you have no imagination."

"Can't be. There's a million tortured artists out there and—"

"And they still have hope. They're heartbroken, but heartbreak by itself is self-indulgent. It's mired in injury to the self, but it isn't the absence of self-love. A tortured artist longs to be in love again or to reclaim a lost love. If hope dies, truly dies, they don't care about art, or love, or anything. Their emotional batteries are dry, dead."

"How's a dead battery feed a vampire?"

"It doesn't. It's that last tiny drop of hope that excites them. It's like a super distillation of all the life's energies, all the juices boiled down to a tiny drop. It's sweet and subtle, and it is so precious because once it is consumed, the victim is like a zombie. Not a flesh-eating type but genuinely dead inside in every way that defines us as human. They are like living examples of entropy, winding down to total spiritual inertia."

Monk touched the Hamsa hand he wore. "God Almighty. Do you think that's what these Shadow People are?"

"I think that's what Doctor Nine may be. He seems to be pushing everyone in the direction of whatever's going to ruin their lives and push them over the brink. He'll feed on that last bit of hope before it winks out."

"Christ," said Monk and realized the waitress was right there. He shook his head, took the check, dropped too much money on it, and got up and headed for the door.

"Doctor Nine is preying on recovering addicts who, according to what your friend told you, are all losing their battles with sobriety. He's inside their dreams, nudging them toward the kinds of decisions that will weaken their resolve. Maybe each of them is on that critical last rung. One push and they'll fall for good this time. Who knows, maybe that's what drew them together as friends in the first place. They recognized some kind of spiritual kinship in each other. It's sad, but it fits. And maybe Rain would be Doctor Nine's most treasured victim. She gave up her son. She believes herself to be responsible for ruining her own mother's life. She's lost the love of her life. She can't follow her own dreams of being a dancer. Monk, when she told you about her life and you told me, it's pretty clear that she's dancing right at the edge of a long drop. She's dancing right toward Doctor Nine."

Monk said, "Let me call you right back."

He hung up, ran for his car, got in and tried Rain's number. It rang but it didn't even go to voice mail. That was weird. He tried again and got the same nothing of a response. It frightened him. Monk started the car but then turned it off. He had no idea where he wanted to go. Rain and her army vet friend were out looking for the Fire Zone. Monk had never been closer than Boundary Street, but he really doubted he could find them.

What to do? He knew the nicknames of Rain's friends, but not who they were or where they lived. Then he realized that he had a lead and restarted his car. Joplin. He redialed Dr. Corbiel, and she answered right away.

"I can't get in touch with Rain. Something's wrong," he said. The rain was the heaviest it had been in days, which was saying a lot. Walls of it seemed to march down the street. Monk started the engine again, but then he sat there, uncertain where to go. "What about the graffiti I saw and the messages Rain got? The '*They are coming*' stuff."

"That might refer to Doctor Nine and his Shadow People being ready to take physical form. Remember, Monk, essential vampires don't have ordinary bodies. Not usually, anyway. But under the right circumstances, they can manifest one. It takes an enormous amount of power to do it, though. They would have to consume mass quantities of their special food. Wait, wait," she said, "there was something you said. Something Rain told you about when she had her baby. Hold on." Monk heard her tapping at her keys, probably doing a word search. "Here it is. It was about the monk she met in Central Park. The monk said that her baby was special. That he wasn't the flame but he would strike the match."

Monk started driving, heading toward Rain's neighborhood. "What about it?"

"I heard that before. Let me think. It was a while back, something I read or a lecture I . . . wait! Shit!" Corbiel cried, suddenly very excited, "Rain named her son Dylan? That's what she told you?"

"Right. She kept the name a secret until accidentally saying it out loud to Doctor Nine. Cat was out of the bag, which is why she told me. What about it?"

"Well . . . that's classic, isn't it?"

"What is? Make a little goddamn sense."

"Dylan means 'ray of hope.'"

"And my name's Gerald, which means 'rule of the spear.' So what? A name's a name."

"Not to the spiritual community it's not. Since the middle 1980s, there's been a lot of talk and, God, a ton of books published about a new ascended master coming into the world to bring positive change."

"You're losing me here. The fuck's that got to do with essential vampires and some kid a junkie gave up for adoption?"

"There have been a lot of people looking for this new master. Not just in America but all over the world. He is supposed to start a movement away from the polarizing cynicism that's torn everyone apart."

"Like a new Jesus?"

"He's supposed to be a spiritual being, not a religious figure. There's a difference. Hold on, I have something here on it, from a book published in 2000. I'm quoting a foreword written by the Dalai Lama: 'Hope is coming to this world. Believe it. It will not be a vague conceptual thing but actual hope, embodied in the physical, with a voice that will be heard across all political lines. He will speak and be heard. He is not the flame, because the flame lives in all of us, though it has burned low or, in the case of so many young people these days, has not yet been kindled. When *he* comes he will not be the flame itself. He will come in simplicity, in humility, and with quiet ways that will not call attention to himself. But he will be the match that starts a great and holy fire. It will burn brightly in the dark times that we all know are coming. Many will not know his name because he won't be the face of the movement. He will be its spark. He is coming, my friends. Those who have eyes, let them watch very carefully. Those who have ears, let them listen for a whisper. He is coming, and he will raise a match to the kindling of our hope.'"

Monk stared out the window at the heaviest downpour he had ever seen in his life, and he had endured monsoons. "Yeah, that's interesting as all hell. So?"

"If you believe in this sort of thing, Monk, then this is a big deal. I mean, let's face it, the world *has* been spinning in some bad directions. Religious extremism, political polarization, governments being turned inside out, wars, and global financial meltdowns. The last election doesn't even seem real, and the people making decisions over our lives clearly don't care."

"Okay, sure, Jonatha," said Monk dubiously, "but that's the kind of thing that makes people crazy. Protestors, hate crimes—that's all pretty intense emotion."

"Sure, but not everyone's out yelling in the streets. Fewer than half the population voted in the last election. A lot of people didn't come out to vote because they simply didn't think it would have done any good. They've lost faith in the system, and that's another pathway to hopelessness. And a lot of those who *did* vote and lost feel that they're simply screwed. They feel run over by events and do not feel that they have any control. Believing that creates a moral and social lassitude that's—"

"Hopelessness, yeah, I got it. Christ almighty . . . is this what Doctor Nine's all about?"

"If what your friend told you is true, then yes."

"Jeee-zus."

"The universe is not naturally chaotic, Monk, and it's not naturally benign. It seeks a balance of those two forces. Individual entities fight to throw things out of balance because it serves their desires and their hungers. With the world tipping toward despair, there's a certain logic to the universal forces, call them the 'powers that be' if you want, to attempt to restore balance. Throughout history, ascended masters have appeared when the scales have tipped too far toward negativity, just as—one could argue—the universe chucks out a Hitler or Napoleon when things become too benign. If that's the case, if any of this is true, then this child, this Dylan, is crucial. Without him, the balance could tip radically toward chaos. Toward destruction."

A homeless man, screaming and dressed in plastic trash bags, staggered in front of Monk's parked car. He turned, pounded on the hood of the Jeep, and yelled, "*They are coming!*"

Then he shambled away into the storm.

Monk sat there, staring after him.

"Monk," continued Corbiel, unaware of this, "for the last couple of decades, writers, channelers, prophets, visionaries, and other notable people in the various global spiritual communities have been talking about the coming of the bringer of hope. They have names for him. Asha in Hindi, Xīwàng in Chinese, Espérer in French—"

"So what?"

"You want to take a guess what the name is in English? Begins with a *D*."

Lightning shattered the sky and painted the world in stark blacks and whites.

"Fuck me," said Monk. "Look, Jonatha, this is pretty goddamn esoteric."

"Really? Ghosts hire you to solve their murders, and you wear their faces on your skin."

Monk said nothing. He was trying not to believe in this, but his heart was racing out of control.

"Monk," said Corbiel with fresh urgency in her voice, "if Doctor Nine is an essential vampire and if he has figured a way to destroy the hope in Dylan, then he is going to break out of the shadow world and into ours. I don't know if I believe in hell, but I think that would qualify as hell on earth."

"What can I do?" he said weakly.

"Find Rain Thomas. Protect her, because I think she's in mortal danger. I'm not joking. And, if you can, help her find her son. Get him away from Doctor Nine, or help his mother do that. Protect them both from Doctor Nine."

CHAPTER EIGHTY-TWO

Rain expected to wake up dead. Or something like that. In hell or purgatory or limbo, and with a padlock on the door to paradise.

She woke up with a scream that pulled her out of the darkness and into the white-hot now. She thrashed and smacked at things before she could see them, trying to knock away bits of broken metal, windshield glass, jagged pieces of the Red Rocket. Her flailed hands cut through empty air, and the motion overbalanced her, and suddenly Rain was falling. She cried out, expecting the fall to go on forever, once more down into the bottomless dark where she had fallen twice before.

Instead, she crunched against concrete and cool grass.

Rain opened her eyes. She was in a park.

The park. The clock tower rose above her, but Caster Bootey was nowhere in sight. His ladder was there, and his toolbox, but not the wizened old repairman.

She heard it then. The ticking sound.

Less like a clock and more like a time bomb from a James Bond movie. *Tick-tick-tick*. The minute and hour hands seemed frozen at four minutes to midnight. Only the second hand, which had not even been on the clock before, moved, counting off seconds in a jerky, awkward, painful way, as if it had to chop through heavy resistance to advance toward its goal. She lay there and watched it go all the way past six, to nine, and then to twelve, but the minute hand did not follow in the perpetual dance. It remained at four minutes till.

Sitting up took effort; it was like jacking up a truck. Every part of her body hurt. Her bones, her skin, but when she looked, when she touched the places that hurt worst, there was no trace of damage. Nothing visible.

Time seemed broken, and Rain wondered if that was a good thing. What would happen when the minute hand finally moved? What was going to happen when time caught up to itself? Was she dead on the other side of that minute? Were those the wounds that killed her?

She looked around, but the Red Rocket was nowhere in sight. Nor was Sticks.

Oh, God, she thought. *Sticks!*

The truck had hit his side of the car. She could clearly—horribly—remember the flat steel bumper crushing the car inward, splintering and exploding the windows, shoving the engine off its mounts, buckling the door, compressing the space around Sticks into nothing.

"Sticks?" she called, posing it as a question, hoping that he, too, was safe on this side of midnight. Or noon. Or whatever hour it was. Rain couldn't remember if it was day or night. It was always night here in the Fire Zone.

She used the bench to pull herself up, but standing was too much, so she plunked down on the seat, winded, weak. The park seemed different, and with a gasp of alarm, Rain realized that there was no sound. No Music. There were no colored lights or fireflies dancing in the air. Turning, she looked down the street to see if the red hand still flashed outside of Torquemada's.

It did. That motion of color, of bright red light and utter darkness, was the only motion in the world. That and the *tick-tick-tick* of the clock. She looked down and saw that the glasses still hung around her neck. There were cracks in both lenses now.

Rain took a breath and then lifted them and put them on.

Suddenly, all the colors of the Fire Zone were back, more intense than ever, and Rain stared with slack-jawed amazement. Lights burned in every corner of the broad street that bordered the park; they glowed from every wrought iron post, glimmered atop tall buildings, and flashed in the very air around her. On the glittering sides of the buildings, neon tubing and LED lights twisted and retwisted before her eyes, forming works and acts and thoughts and images faster than Rain's mind could absorb them. Straight lines of iridescence shot upward along the sides of buildings to the rooftops, raced along balconies, and then plunged insanely downward to the streets again, dragging her goggling gaze with them, dizzying her with the rush of color and speed. There was no looking away—the lights were everywhere, bursting like fireworks in her brain, even detonating beautifully behind the veil of closed eyes.

And then the Music spilled out into the madhouse streets, washing the avenue and drenching everything with sweet sounds. Footsteps clicked along in time to every drumbeat, hands clapped with the resonant bass notes, fingers popped with guitar riffs, and voices were raised in song to match the powerful voice of the Music itself. The Music rose above the street, taking elements from every individual song and blending them with the countertempo of thousands of beating hearts; it stirred them, seasoning them with magic, and brewed one single song, one ultimate and unique song. It became *othertone*—the ultimate state of sound, the purest aspect of the Music itself, hovering a tone above perfection.

Rain didn't even realize she had risen from the bench and was swaying to the beat, slapping her thighs in time to the drums; completely lost in the inrush of things her senses could barely accept and only partially contain. She was not sure if she was awake or even alive. One small part of her mind that was not totally caught up in the moment wondered if she was dead on the street, curled with Sticks in a tomb of gleaming red metal, and all of this was a dead woman's dream.

It was okay, though. If being dead meant that she was allowed to be here, then dying was a small price to pay.

Maybe Noah was here somewhere. The thought made her heart race. Was that it? Had sweet Noah somehow done all of this to save her from the burning house that had been her life? Was he here in the Fire Zone, waiting for her all this time?

Another thought followed that one, and it almost stopped her heart.

Was Dylan here, too?

Tick-tick-tick, said the clock, trying to reach midnight.

You're so close, whispered a voice. Caster, maybe. Or Dylan. Or possibly her own voice. *You know almost enough now to make sense of it, Rain.*

"You're not making sense," she said aloud, her voice strident and jarring.

The repairman's words came back to her as clearly as if he stood beside her. *As long as you think this is a mystery, then it'll be a mystery. As long as you think this is a war, then it's a war. As long as you think that you're helpless, then you'll be helpless. That's how it's always worked.*

Rage suddenly surged upward from her gut, past the trembling heart, and out into the night. "No more fucking riddles!" she screamed. "Just fucking tell me what's happening!"

Instantly, the Music warped into a discordant screeching, the laughter of the dancers became the bray of donkeys. All the colors were stained, and she squeezed her eyes shut against the glare. Pain flared in her head, and she reached up to take off the glasses.

Did not, though.

Through the fractured lenses, she saw a figure step out from behind a tree not twenty feet away. The sight of him yanked on the leash of time and jerked it to a juddering stop.

It was a boy around thirteen years old. He was dressed in cheap Salvation Army thrift store clothes. Seedy, dirty, badly mended, stained, and ragged. His hands were dirty, too, and his face. He was so thin. Malnourished to the point of starvation, with the belly swell that happens when gas is released as the starving begins to feed on itself. His nails were bitten to the quick, and his hair hung unwashed and lank across his face.

"Dylan?" she breathed, and it came out as a question.

The tree behind which the boy had been hiding seemed to ripple, but not with wind. When Rain peered at it, she realized that it was not heavy with leaves. It was completely covered with dark birds. Small and large, standing on every branch, every twig. Hundreds of them. Thousands. Nightbirds. *His* birds.

"Dylan?" she asked again,

Dylan it was, but not the beautiful boy she had imagined all these years. Not even the feral child she had seen running in the glimpses she'd gotten. This boy was wild, ugly, unhealthy in every way that mattered, and sickness shone in his dark, wary, calculating eyes. When he smiled at her, she saw yellow teeth and receding gums and a hunger that was so deep, so bottomless that it transcended a need for food. He was hungry for something else. Ravenous.

"Mommy," he said slowly, tasting the word. Enjoying it. "I've been looking everywhere for you."

CHAPTER EIGHTY-THREE

"Dylan?" whispered Rain.

The boy moved toward her, walking with dangerous delicacy, the way a jungle cat does. "Mommy," murmured the boy. "I've been looking for you for so long. Why did you leave me? Why did you let them take me away?"

"Dylan, I . . . I'm so sorry. I made a mistake. I was stupid, and I should never have let them take you." Her heart wanted her to run forward, to embrace her son, even if he had become the thing that stood beneath the tree filled with nightbirds, the thing that smiled. Her body backed another step away.

"You gave me away, Mommy," said Dylan. His smile never wavered, but there was hatred and hurt in his dark eyes. "You couldn't wait to do it."

"No . . ."

"What did I ever do that was so bad that you had to throw me away like I was trash? I was a *baby*. I didn't even have a chance to disappoint you, and bang. Gone."

"I'm sorry," she whispered, and the tears began to fall.

"We could have been together all this time," he said. There was a plaintive need in his voice that was at odds with the rapacious grin. "We could have played together."

A vagary of wind brought a snatch of the Music into the park. As it blew past Rain, it was lovely, elegant, complex, wonderful; but as it wafted toward Dylan, it changed, became cheap and obvious and vulgar. He raised his head and sniffed at it like a dog, then he gave her a sly look.

"We could have *danced* together, Mommy." He leaned on that word, giving it so many layers of meaning, good and bad. His voice was wholesome, innocent; his smile was infinitely vile.

The boy took another step forward.

Rain took two steps back. "Don't!"

He stopped. One of the nightbirds fluttered down and landed on his shoulder. Something thick and red dripped from its beak and spattered on the front of the boy's shirt. Rain took several quick backward steps.

"You're *not* my son," she said, trying to shout but managing only a frightened whisper. "You're not my little Dylan."

The boy bent forward and snapped at the air between them. "Not yet, but I will be. Oh, yes, Mommy dearest, I will be."

And then, like a ravenous wolf, he leaped at her and drove her to the ground.

CHAPTER EIGHTY-FOUR

Monk had no good idea where to start.

He had a bad idea, but it scared the hell out of him. It hurt him just to think about it.

He sat in his car and punched the steering wheel until his fists ached.

"No," he said to the night. "This isn't my goddamn fight. This isn't mine to fix."

The storm raged around him.

"Please, no," he begged. "I don't want to do this."

He tried calling Rain's phone one more time and still got nothing. His heart was hammering now.

Monk started his car and drove away.

CHAPTER EIGHTY-FIVE

Rain fell backward with Dylan on top of her, but she landed well, the way she had learned in dance class, tucked her chin, rolled backward over her left shoulder. The motion turned her into an axel, and it threw Dylan over her. He smashed upside down into the trunk of a tree.

Rain scrambled to her feet and started to run, stopped because it looked like Dylan was hurt. She even took a step toward him, reaching out, ripped in half by mother's need and woman's survival. But Dylan swiveled his head around and leered at her, blood running from between his lips and up his chin.

"He said you wouldn't fight," said Dylan. "He said you were empty of everything. I'm so glad he was wrong." He spat blood onto his hands, looked at it, then licked it off. "This is going to be delicious, Mommy dear."

He oriented himself and slowly began getting to his feet.

"Why are you doing this?" Rain demanded. "I never meant to hurt you. I gave you up because I couldn't raise you like you deserved."

"You didn't even try," he said with real pain in his voice.

"I was *sixteen*!"

"So what? How's that an excuse, Mommy dear? I heard Jesus's mother was only fifteen. She did okay. You really think being sixteen is an excuse for throwing me away?"

"I thought you'd be adopted by good people."

He spat at her. "Good? *Good?* You gave me to the boogeyman. I lived in a cellar my whole life. Do you want to know how many times I was beaten? Want to know the things they did to me down in the dark? Do you want to know how I learned about pain? Do you want to know how I learned how to eat that pain the way *he* eats hope? It was my food, and they kept me very well fed." Tears broke and rolled down his livid cheeks. "Do you want me to . . . to tell you what you did to me?"

"I'm so sorry."

"Sorry? *Sorry?*" His voice disintegrated into a sob but then swelled with immense fury and turned into a roar that shattered the world.

Rain screamed, whirled, and ran.

Dylan stood panting, fists balled, giving her a chance. Letting her run, the way a cat would. The way a monster would.

Rain crashed into bushes and through hedges. Skeletal fingers of sapling trees plucked at her like beggar children. The nightbirds flapped noisily overhead, jeering and diving to tear at her cheeks and scalp and arms with their razor-sharp beaks. One of them tried to land in her hair like a bat, but Rain grabbed it with both hands, tearing it free and losing hair as she did it. It tried to bite her hands, but she gave its neck a savage twist, delighted and disgusted by the snap of hollow bones. Rain let the bird fall and ran, and all around her the other birds cried out in fury.

The boy gave a huge, mad laugh and launched himself in pursuit, his body hunched so far forward, that he ran sometimes on all fours like a dog.

That's not my son. That's not my Dylan! Those words banged around inside Rain's head.

"*Moooommmmmeeeee!*" cried the thing that pursued.

Suddenly, a form rose up in Rain's path, making her skid to a stop. Dylan was nowhere in sight, maybe circling her. The figure was short, crooked, broken. An old Japanese man wearing the saffron robes of a Tibetan monk. His head was shaved, and his eyes were filled with fire. He stood with his head canted too far to one side and there were vicious rope burns around his throat. He reached out to her and tried to speak, but his voice was a raspy croak as words tried to claw past all the damage in his throat.

"*Gomen'nasai,*" he wheezed.

Rain did not understand Japanese, but Monk had told her what those words meant. He was apologizing, and she realized that she knew why. This man had tried to warn her, but sixteen-year-old Rain was too scared, bullied, and confused to understand. He had wanted her to do what was best for Dylan by keeping him. It had been something vitally important to Mr. Hoto, and Rain had misread his warning and done exactly the opposite.

"It's not your fault," Rain said. "It's me. You tried to help, but I didn't listen."

Tears glittered in his dead eyes. He tried to apologize again, but his throat would not make anything more than a hoarse croak. A shudder swept through him, and he dropped down to his knees. Past him, just outside the last row of trees, Rain could see the tall white edifice of Torquemada's. The flashing red hand winked on and off, throwing the color of blood onto the night. The monk turned his body stiffly to point that way.

He tried to say something else, but then a howling shape came crashing out of the bushes and slammed Hoto to the ground. The monk screamed as Dylan, foam flying from his mouth, tore at him with fingers curled like claws. Then the flock of nightbirds dove down, crashing into the monk, tearing at him. Tearing him apart.

"Stop it!" screeched Rain, bashing at the birds, grabbing at Dylan's shoulder. He spun at her touch, quick as a cat, and bared his teeth at her. But not teeth. Not really. Not anymore.

His mouth was filled with long, pointed, red-smeared fangs.

Dylan was more than insane. He had become a monster.

CHAPTER EIGHTY-SIX

Monk pulled his car to a squealing stop, one tire up onto the curb. He was out and running across the pavement and up the steps, crashing through the door, and ran up the stairs. He stopped on the third floor and stared at the hall, half dreading to see yet another body swinging from the pipes. The hall was empty, though. Yellow crime scene tape hung limp around the ladder.

Monk went over to Hoto's apartment, tried the door handle, found it locked.

"Fuck it," he said and kicked it in.

The place was a mess, proof that the crime scene people and detectives had been through every inch of it. They hadn't cleaned anything up, though. The words were still on the walls, and the blood was still spattered on the floor. Monk knelt, removed a vial from his pocket, used his knife to scrape some of it up, then took his small bottle of holy water from his kit and added the seven drops. He replaced the stopper, shook it to mix the contents, and put it away.

Then he left the apartment, pausing only long enough to wipe his fingerprints from the doorknob.

He started toward the steps to go back down, then glanced up. The mailboxes downstairs listed Joplin as being on the fourth floor. Maybe he would have information about how to contact Rain's friends in the Cracked World Society. He went up, found the right door, and knocked.

"Joplin!" he yelled. "Open up. I'm a friend of Rain's. I need to find her. Open up."

There was no answer. On impulse, he tried the knob, and it turned. Monk leaned in and was about to call out again. And stopped.

There was a big canvas on an easel in the center of the room and several other canvases scattered around like they'd been blown by a wind. Or hurled. Paints covered everything. The canvases, the floor, the walls, the furniture, the ceiling. Everything was covered in fresh paint. Not random spattering but images. Artwork. Rain was there. Beautiful as an angel, lying sprawled in a chair made from blocks of color. Her eyes were the most realistically painted part of her, and they were unfocused and dead. Not merely junkie's eyes but eyes that had lost the ability to see even the narcotic light inside drugged dreams. They were dead eyes in a living face. And Monk had seen that before. In the eyes of slave children in third-world countries. In old women who had outlived husbands and children. In child soldiers in Africa and Asia. It was a hopelessness so acute that it stabbed him.

The other faces on the walls were strangers to Monk, but probably not to Joplin. Two of them might have been parents; a pretty woman might have been a sister. Others. Their faces were animated as if talking, laughing, living; but in each of them the eyes were dead.

And so were the eyes of the young bearded man who sat in the overstuffed chair that was positioned in front of the canvas. He sat there, pale and still, eyes open and empty, and all his colors leaked from the deep cuts torn in Joplin's wrists.

Monk exhaled slowly and squatted down beside the chair, unable to bear his own weight of grief. He put his face in his hands and listened to the screams in his head.

Six seconds later, the phone rang. He did not recognize the number.

"Yeah," he said.

"I'm calling for Gerald Addison," said an officious female voice.

"Speaking."

"Are you a friend or relative of a Miss Lorraine Thomas?"

Monk's heart went cold. "Why? Has something happened to her?"

"I'm an emergency room intake nurse at Mount Sinai Beth Israel Hospital in—"

"I know it. What happened to Rain Thomas?"

"Your business card was on her person. This is the only number we had. Miss Thomas has been in a serious accident," said the nurse. "Do you know if she has any family in the area?"

On impulse, Monk said, "I'm her family."

He said it as he was running for the door.

CHAPTER EIGHTY-SEVEN

Dylan slammed into Rain and drove her down with such force that the whole world flickered. For one split moment, she was not in the park in the Fire Zone—she was on the street, covered in glass and blood. Sirens filled the air, and the flashing of the red hand was replaced with the blue and red of emergency vehicle lights.

Pain owned her in both worlds.

Hands were on her in both. She could feel the clawing, grasping animalistic hands of her ruined son; but she could also feel the strong, kind, desperate hands of firefighters and EMTs trying to pull her from the wreckage of . . .

Of what?

She tried to turn her head to see, and there was a microflash of the Red Rocket crumpled around her, torn and dead, with smoke curling up and fluids leaking out. She turned to see Sticks crushed inside a fist made of torn steel, his eyes open and empty.

Then Dylan grabbed her throat, and she was snapped back to the darkened park, on cold grass, being murdered. His fingers were like bands of ice around her throat, and she tried to bash them away, twist them, tear at them. It was like fighting a statue. His muscles were rigid, and he was on top of her, using his weight—however meager—to push his hands down, to crush the life from her.

"Dylan . . . please . . . don't . . ." Each word came out faint, choked to a whisper.

The words seemed to hit him like slaps. His eyes cleared for a moment, with the insanity being replaced by something else. Hurt.

"You threw me away like trash," he said in the coldest voice Rain had ever heard. "Junkie whore has an inconvenient little piglet and throws him to the dogs. Fucking bitch."

"No!" she cried. "No, I—"

He let go with one hand and struck her a savage blow across the face. Blood and broken teeth sprayed onto the grass.

"You gave me to the monsters," he said in a fierce whisper, bending low to spit the words at her. "Do you have any idea what they *did* to me?"

He hit her again.

"My whole life?"

Hit.

"Raised by monsters."

Hit.

Rain sagged down, bleeding heavily, trapped in a world of pain. There was something wrong with her left eye, then she realized that the glasses were still on, though the side pieces were twisted out of shape and the sharp end of the temple piece gouged into her brow. The cracked lens was shifted over, and now she was forced to look through the fragment and to see the world more fully—in all its horrible reality. She saw the face of this version of her son. Not the Dylan of her dreams, and not the terrified boy on the train. Not the shifty-eyed version glimpsed on the street in Manhattan or the sad-eyed Dylan she'd seen outside of Joplin's apartment. This version of her son was older, definitely closer to thirteen. Now she could see the facial bluing of adolescent beard and the harder lines of his face. He was much more like Noah, except a Noah driven mad by all that he had experienced, driven to the edge of hope and then over into personal darkness. Rain could see all that now. This was what her son would become; it was the impact point along the line of trajectory his life had taken since she'd given him up. This was truly the monster version of him. Corrupted, broken, emptied of optimism and love. A shell, a golem made of nothing but dirt and hatred. His face was the face of the boy in the morgue.

Nightbirds flapped around the boy as he raised his fist one final time, ready to kill her and by doing it, kill them both. Then the air was shattered by the roar of a car engine.

Doctor Nine is coming, thought Rain's dying brain. *He's here. My boy is bringing him through. This is my fault. I failed and this is all my fault.*

Her inner voice spoke in the same voice as the parasite, and in a moment of clarity that was coming too late to save her, Rain realized that there was never any difference between them.

The car engine suddenly roared louder. Too loud. Headlights smashed across the scene, turning skin white and blood black. Dylan turned, a smile of dark triumph blossoming on his hard mouth, as if to say, *See what I've done, Doctor? See what a good boy I am?*

"Rain!"

A man's voice called her name. Dylan's smile faltered, and Rain looked past her son's cocked fist to see the grille of a huge car. Blood red with yellow lines running along its sides and the words *The Red Rocket* painted in fiery letters. The car slewed to a stop six feet away, and the driver's door flew open and Sticks stepped out.

Sticks.

Tall and powerful, his brown skin unmarked by burns, his legs strong and his arms corded with muscle. Sticks, whole and young and alive.

Come to save her.

CHAPTER EIGHTY-EIGHT

Monk called the hospital and said that he was Rain's older brother. The nurse took his information and, using the kind of careful verbiage they're trained for in sensitivity classes, told him that she was in critical condition and invited him to come and "be with her."

They never put it that way when things were good. Or even carefully optimistic.

Monk did not go to the hospital. Instead, he drove to the tattoo parlor to see Patty Cakes. The vials of blood rattled in his pocket.

CHAPTER EIGHTY-NINE

"Leave her alone," said Sticks, his voice stronger than Rain had ever heard it. Confident, filled with power and command.

Dylan raised his head and studied Sticks.

"Stickssssssss," he hissed, drawing it out like a reptile. "I know you."

"You don't know shit."

"Oh, yes," said Dylan, his voice strangely old. "I remember watching you burn."

Sticks paused, his face registering surprise. "What?"

"What?" said Rain at the same time.

Dylan grinned like a jackal. "Oh, yesssssss. I remember watching your black skin bubble and blister. I saw it run like tallow as the fire danced along it."

It was almost Doctor Nine's voice, but not quite. The voice of one of his creatures. A shadowy voice, starved and awful.

"Sticks . . . what is he talking about?" asked Rain.

Dylan looked at his mother and back to Sticks. His eyes brightened. "You didn't tell her, did you?"

"Shut up," said Sticks.

Through the cracked lenses of the reading glasses, the driver looked at least ten years younger, a man of twenty or so. A pair of silver dog tags hung around his neck.

Dylan touched his own face, placing his fingers beneath his eyes. "I have my father's eyes," he said. "Ask my mom. I can see everything my father ever saw. I saw what you did."

"Shut up," Sticks repeated. "You don't see shit."

"Did you think that by finding my mother and being her friend you could atone?"

"I didn't go looking," said Sticks, his voice losing its edge. "I was called. I . . . just found her there."

"Tell her the truth," said Dylan.

"Sticks," asked Rain, "what's he saying? What's he mean?"

"Tell her, Corporal Alexander Stickley," taunted Dylan. "Go ahead and tell her what my eyes have seen. Go ahead and tell her about the last thing my father's eyes ever saw."

Rain looked at her friend. "Sticks?"

Sticks said nothing, but as he stood there, he changed again. His skin turned a dark red and then began to bubble as blisters rose all along his arms and face. The blisters swelled and popped, seeding the air with a fine pink mist. His hair melted away, and he staggered back, reaching for support as his legs twisted and withered and died.

As he fell, a shape rose around him. It was not quite real, not solid, but Rain could see all of it. It was a vehicle, an army Humvee. Fifteen feet long, tan, with heavy armor plates. As soon as it appeared, it lifted on a balloon of explosive force, crashed over on its side, and burst into flames. The troops inside tried to escape, but the doors were jammed shut. Their screams rose to ungodly howls as the fire from the land mine touched them with yellow fingers and turned them each into a blazing torch. One man, the driver, crawled out of the vehicle, his skin and clothes on fire, his legs shattered and melting. He rolled over and over in the sand to try to douse the blaze.

Inside the Humvee, visible for a moment through the window, was a young man with kind eyes filled now with terror, and brown hair that flickered like a candle. He screamed and screamed and beat on the window for as long as he could, until the smoke and flames consumed him. The Humvee burned and burned, and then it faded, leaving the air smudged with soot and cries. The driver was all that was left, and he lay on the ground where Sticks had fallen. One and the same.

Dylan turned to Rain. "You didn't know, did you? Didn't even suspect?"

All she could do was shake her head as she stared down at Sticks.

"You just happen to meet a veteran who was burned when his vehicle ran over a mine. A coincidence? And he knew about the Fire Zone? He found you on Boundary Street? All of that a coincidence? God, Mom, I'm only a kid, but I'm not *that* stupid."

"No . . . it's impossible . . ."

"Impossible died when you gave me up," sneered Dylan. "Now everything is possible, and that means all the bad things, too. You gave up on me and on everything and invited Doctor Nine in, Mommy, and he brought with him all his favorite shadows."

Sticks appeared even worse than he had at the diner. His burns were raw and glistening, and Rain realized this was how Sticks looked when he was first injured. It was awful to see. And yet she did not move to help him. The things Dylan said battered her with all the uncompromising force of truth. This man had *known* Noah. He had driven the Humvee that terrible day. He had rolled over an IED. He had crawled to safety while the other soldiers burned. While Noah—beautiful, kind, gentle Noah—had burned.

While her son's father had burned and screamed and died.

"As attempts at redemption," said Dylan, still speaking with a voice beyond his years, "this one was pathetic. No actual plan. Certainly no skills. A crispy-critter cripple in a big, shiny car. There's not even a country-western song in that." He leaned over and spat on Sticks. "Because of you, I never had a chance, did I?"

Unable to wipe the spittle away, Sticks looked up at the boy-thing. "I . . . I'm sorry."

Dylan kicked him in the face. Hideously fast, brutally powerful, the whole side of Sticks's face collapsed, and teeth flew through the air.

"No!" screeched Rain, lunging forward to get between them.

Dylan backhanded her, mashing already torn skin, dimming the lights. She reeled against the grille of the Red Rocket.

"Oh, don't worry, Mommy. I haven't forgotten about you. Your moment is coming. *Our* moment is coming. But first I need to—"

Sticks suddenly darted out a hand and clamped scorched fingers around Dylan's ankle. The boy yelped in surprise and pain, and steam rose from the dying driver's grip. There was a sound like sizzling flesh, and the cuffs of Dylan's dirty jeans began to blacken.

"Let me go!" cried Dylan.

"R-Rain," gasped Sticks. "Run."

Balancing on his trapped leg, Dylan raised his other foot and kicked Sticks over and over again.

Rain pushed away from the car, turned to run.

Almost ran. Took a step.

Did not run. Instead, with a howl of grief, she flung herself at Dylan and wrapped her arms around him. Unbalanced and surprised, Dylan fell. Rain held on as they fell. Sticks did not let go, either. The three of them were caught in a strange and terrifying dance. The blackened trousers popped with yellow fingers of fire and they raced along the material so fast it was as if Dylan were doused with accelerant. His legs blazed, and still Rain held on. Dylan screamed and thrashed, and still Rain held on. He head-butted her and bit her with his fangs, rending her, and still Rain held on. He spat at her as the flames marched over his clothes and dug down into the skin beneath, and still Rain clung to her son. Even when the flames spread to her body, her clothes, her hair, she never let go.

And they all burned together.

CHAPTER NINETY

"You're insane," said Patty. "I won't do it."

Monk sat on a stool, stripped to the waist, face still running with rainwater. The two vials lay on his hard palm.

"You're telling me all kinds of stories," she growled. "Crazy shit. The kid's little, then he's ten, then he's a dead thirteen-year-old? How's that work?"

"Fuck if I know," Monk admitted. "Rain thinks they're all the same kid. Her kid."

"Who's only supposed to be ten years old right now."

"Yes."

"So how's he a thirteen-year-old in the morgue?"

"*Was* in the morgue."

"Oh, right," she said, "someone stole his body and burned it. That makes it all make sense."

"Look," said Monk, "this is some mystical bullshit. Not sure how the time thing works with the kid, but I believe Rain's right. This is her son. He's alive now and he's going to kill himself in two or three years."

"Uh-huh."

"Closest I can come to a theory is something Jonatha Corbiel said," he explained. "If this Doctor Nine is an essential vampire who feeds on hope, and if Dylan was born to be some kind of spiritual leader, what she called an 'ascended master,' who reignites hope when it's burning out of the world, then Doctor Nine wouldn't just want to kill him. No. If he's had the kid all these years, then it would make more sense to ruin him, corrupt him, but also break his heart. Who knows, maybe he's been force-fed a lot of propaganda about his mother abandoning him. Maybe the kid's Hannibal Lecter Junior by now. Maybe, but I don't think so. He started showing up in Rain's visions as a younger version of himself and maybe as he is now. The older version is the one who killed himself, so it would seem that we're getting close to the point where maybe Dylan loses hope in himself. Or in his mom. Or in everything. Not sure. If he killed himself, or if he is going to, then we can suppose he bottomed out, right?"

"And you believe all this?" asked Patty. "It doesn't make sense. It can't be real."

Monk touched one of the faces on his chest. "Does this? Does what you do? Or me?"

Patty picked up the first vial. "Still not all blood, though."

"Maybe there's enough."

"Even if there is, wouldn't that trap the kid? Let's face it, Monk, the ghosts who 'hire' you," she said, using fingers to make air quotes, "don't exactly pass on to eternal peace. They're stuck with you and you with them. Is that what you want for the kid?"

"The kid's still alive, Patty. Maybe it won't work like that. And we have Hoto's blood, too."

"You don't know that, Monk. You can't."

He gave her a bleak stare and a smile without a trace of humor. "What choice do we have?"

CHAPTER NINETY-ONE

Rain burned, but she did not die.

The flames hurt so badly, so insanely badly, but if this was what Noah felt in his last moments, then she would bear it and die and become ash. Like he was ash. Like her life was ash. Dylan thrashed wildly, but the fires seemed to burn him worst of all. His skin withered and melted and flickered to the night. She held him. All the time she did, as they burned together, mother and son, she whispered the same thing over and over again. Not an apology. There had been enough of those to bury them both under a mile of dead rock. No. As they died, she kissed her son's charred flesh and said the only words that could be heard through the roar of fire.

"I love you," she said. They burned and burned.

And then the flames flicked and faded. Sticks was gone, leaving only a smear of ash. Dylan lay within the iron circle of Rain's arms. He was so frail now, weightless. The fires faded out, and Rain lay there, bleeding from where she had been beaten but not burned. The fires had raged, but they had not consumed her.

It was Dylan who was gone. He was there only for a moment longer, a pale shadow made of hate. Then he crumbled into hot ashes in her arms and the winds blew every trace of him away. Rain put her hands over her eyes and begged to die.

She heard a sound.

A long, insistent, frantic *beeeeeeeeeeeeeeeep*.

And a voice, a stranger's voice, said very clearly, "We're losing her. I need a crash cart."

What a funny thought, mused Rain. *How can they lose me when I'm already lost?*

288

CHAPTER NINETY-TWO

Rain opened her eyes up and expected to see nurses and doctors clustered around, fighting to save her life.

She did not. Instead, she looked up into the gentle eyes of Caster Bootey. He was sitting on the park bench, and she lay with her head on his thigh. Her skin felt hot, though, and she looked down to see that she was covered with ash.

"Oh . . . my . . . God."

Caster lifted her into his arms, held her as she bucked and sobbed.

"My dear young woman," he said softly, "be strong. You are so close to understanding everything. I know it's hard for you to believe me. It's hard to hear through the pain."

"Dylan!" she wailed. "I've lost him!"

"No," he said, "you have not."

Rain pushed off and looked up at him. "What?"

"That wasn't your Dylan, and you know it."

"It was!"

"No," said Caster, "it will be. It may be. Things are running fast in that direction, but that boy, that animal of a thing with Dylan's face, is years away. He is not yet born. Not into that life. Doctor Nine owns that creature, but he does not yet own your son."

"I . . . don't understand."

"Then listen while I whisper a secret to you."

She tried to listen. She tried so hard.

But someone yelled, "*Clear!*"

And a huge white bomb blew her out of the world.

CHAPTER NINETY-THREE

"Mrs. Creighton-Thomas?" said the nurse. "I'm calling from . . ."

There was more. Alyson listened to it without comment. The accident. The condition of her daughter, the damage done. It was all about damage done. She listened and sipped her vodka and stared at the child dancing on the TV screen.

"I think you should come to the hospital to be with her," said the nurse. "She is—"

Alyson hung up the phone, reached out a languid hand, and scooped the five white pills from the end table, put them into her mouth, swallowed them with vodka.

There were five more. And there was more vodka. The phone rang again, but she did not care to answer it.

She did not care.

CHAPTER NINETY-FOUR

Rain stood on the street.

No park bench, no park. No Caster Bootey, no Sticks. No birds. No Dylan. Only her, standing outside of Torquemada's. The heavy doors stood ever so slightly ajar, enough to allow a whisper of the Music to seep out and fill the darkness around her. She thought she knew the name of the song even though she'd never heard it before. The Music was like that. It shared so many things with people who listened the right way.

Rain felt that something in her had changed. She could hear more levels of the Music than she had in any of her dreams. *That's because you're dead*, whispered her parasite.

If that were the case, then this level of awareness might be worth it.

The door handles wanted to be touched, to be pulled, to yield to her need. The doors wanted to open and let her in. The Music and the dance floor waited just inside. Beautiful, mad, swirling, hungry. Hers. If she took that step.

She had a thought. It isn't a light people follow when they die. It's the Music. That was true, she considered, but not completely true. She did not yet have the whole thing worked out in her head. Was the Fire Zone heaven? No. That seemed wrong. Too shallow an answer. Too corny. Was it even an afterlife, maybe a secular one? No, not that, either.

The Fire Zone, she decided, was the Fire Zone. Complete in itself, requiring no more specific a definition. She touched the glasses she still wore. They were no longer damaged from the fight. Rain turned her head and looked through the crack, then turned around and looked out at the Fire Zone behind her. It was not the Fire Zone at all. She was in a crowd scene. Nurses, doctors, people yelling, machines whining. She tried to speak, but her mouth was blocked.

There were three other people in the room with the medical staff, but no one seemed to notice them. Or maybe it was that the hospital staff could not see them. The trio stood apart, unnoticed, unmoving. The Japanese man, Mr. Hoto. Sticks. And Dylan. Not the thirteen-year-old Dylan but a younger one. Eight or nine, dressed in baggy clothes and standing with a skateboard tucked under his arm.

The problem was that she could see right through all three of them. Like they were ghosts. Or maybe that's what she was becoming. Maybe only the dead could see the dead.

Something moved outside, and she turned to look out the window. A black bird landed on the outside sill. Ugly and dirty and dead.

"Oh, God," she breathed. "They're coming."

CHAPTER NINETY-FIVE

Monk stared at himself in the mirror. He was stripped to the waist and pasted with sweat and blood. His torso and arms were covered with faces, including the new one on his chest.

It was not exactly a face, though. It was faces. Two of them, overlapping, merging, and yet retaining their identities. Patty had cell phone pictures to work from. A dead boy in a morgue. A dead man hanging from a rope. Her needle drilled the ink into Monk's skin, in that one empty place over his heart where he once told her he would never get a tattoo. A place he'd been superstitious about ever covering. The ink was cold, but it still burned. It felt like frostbite.

He tried to take a step toward the chair where he'd left his shirt, but his knees buckled and he went down hard.

"Help . . . help me up," he gasped. Monk was a big man, Patty Cakes was a small woman, but they managed. When Monk was back on his feet, Patty pushed him against the wall so he wouldn't fall. She dabbed the blood away and then helped him pull on his T-shirt and zip up his hoodie.

"You should rest," she said.

"I can't," he wheezed.

"I know," said Patty. She rose to tiptoes and kissed him gently on the lips. He took her in his arms and held her with all the strength he had, burying his head in the soft cleft formed by her shoulder and neck. Then he staggered away from her. His eyes were glazed, unfocused, filled with pain.

"You can't drive like this," she said, then she recoiled from him as his expression changed. First to amazement, and then to awe, and then to a mingled mask of horror and anger.

He pushed past her, his words blurred into a cry of inarticulate madness as he blundered out into the storm.

CHAPTER NINETY-SIX

A nurse came in, saw that Rain was awake, asked inane and ordinary questions, then ran off to find a doctor. A cute Pakistani doctor who looked like he was sixteen came hurrying in. He asked the same questions and Rain gave the same answers.

Then she asked, "My friend was driving the car. His name is Sticks. Alexander Stickley?"

She let it trail off because their faces became wooden.

"I'm so very sorry," said the doctor, "but Mr. Stickley did not survive the accident."

Rain closed her eyes, and there was a tiny flicker of satisfaction that the man who had killed Noah had died the same way. Burning in a crushed metal box. It was an ugly thing to be happy about.

"How bad am I?" she asked.

The faces remained wooden, and it took the young doctor a while to decide how to break the news. Rain braced herself, knowing it was going to be bad. It wasn't. It was worse.

He talked and she listened, and it was a description of how her life, as she knew it, was done. Multiple fractures—pelvis in five places, left femur, both tibias, right fibula, ribs, various and assorted smaller bones. Damage to liver, spleen, and right kidney. Damage to lower intestine. Damage to uterus. Heart failure.

He kept reciting the list. The nurse looked like she wanted to flee.

Rain listened to it all and did not weep. She did not scream or protest. Maybe that was the drugs in her system. Maybe she had reached a point of acceptance where having her body destroyed was not only inevitable, it was appropriate. With enough damage, maybe it would finally be okay for her to simply cash it in, buy a ticket for the night train and see what the next incarnation had to offer. Had to be something better than this. Besides, dying here was still better than dying in a crack house.

Rain took a chance. "Has anyone called my mother?"

"Yes," said the nurse, though her eyes slid away.

"Is she coming?"

"I'm not sure. I'll, um, check with the intake nurse. But . . . your brother said he was coming over."

"My brother?"

"Sure, Gerald?"

"Oh," said Rain. "Fine. That's fine."

Then the nurse brightened. "Oh, and you'll be happy to know the EMTs were able to salvage your glasses. The lenses are cracked, but not bad. They're in pretty good shape. We can have someone contact your optometrist to get a new pair." She opened a drawer in the bedside table. "Do you want to put them on or . . . ?"

"Yes," said Rain. "Please."

The nurse helped her because Rain's hands were swollen into angry red sausages. The nurse and doctor said some more useless things and left. The door swung shut on silent hinges. As it closed, it revealed a figure who had been waiting for them to leave. It was a little boy of about ten. He was thin and dirty, but beautiful. He smiled at her.

"Hello, Mommy," said Dylan.

CHAPTER NINETY-SEVEN

Monk knew that he had no business operating heavy machinery in his condition. He could barely see the streets, and it wasn't because of the rain. The tattoos on his skin had begun to come alive, and there was a war going on inside his head. Or his soul. He had never been able to determine which it was.

Before, starting back when he got the very first face inked onto him, it had been a very personal thing. One ghost. One set of memories. One need for some kind of justice. Not vengeance. Justice. He never accepted the cases from ghosts who simply wanted payback—that kind of thing was a dead-end proposition with no way for anyone to win. Stopping serial murderers, though, that was why Monk took the risks he took, even though the cost was a real prick.

This time, though, the rule book had been doused with lighter fluid and set to burn.

There were two ghosts in his head, and neither of them had asked for his help. Hoto and the Dylan-to-be. One was mad as a hatter and consumed by guilt; the other was a soulless monster.

Neither of them wanted to be in the same headspace, soulspace, whateverspace with Monk Addison. For his part, he could think of ten or twelve thousand things he would rather be doing. Getting kicked in the balls with an iron boot was on that list. So was being eaten by rats.

Too late, asshole, he told himself as he drove.

He drove badly and way too fast.

CHAPTER NINETY-EIGHT

"Oh, Dylan," said Rain. Now the tears came, and now she felt pain that even the best drugs could not mask. Something ruptured deep inside her heart, and the ache was unbearable. She tried to raise her arms, wanting—needing—him to come to her; desperate to hold this version of her child.

He took a few steps closer, but he did not reach for her.

"Please, baby," she begged.

"I can't yet, Mommy," he said. His eyes really were like Noah's, but also like her own. The best and brightest parts of each of them. The happy parts. The alive parts.

"Please."

"Mom," said Dylan, "listen, we have to go."

"Go? Go where?"

"To the Fire Zone."

"But . . . but I can't. My legs—"

"Just get up," he said. "All you have to do is want to and you can."

Rain looked down at the ruin of her body. Casts and splints, wires suspending shattered limbs, mountains of bandages. "I'm ruined," she said.

"You're not," said Dylan. "Not yet."

He fished in a pocket and took out a small clock and held it up by its silver chain. She recognized it as the one that had been in her mailbox.

"How . . . ?"

"There's still time," said Dylan. He took a delicate silver key from another pocket, inserted it into the back of the clock and gave it a tiny twist. "He's coming. He'll be here any second. We have to hurry."

"But I can't," said Rain.

Then she realized that she was sitting up. Kind of.

She was sitting up but also lying there. It was as if part of her, a version of her, was rising from the broken body. It was like seeing a special effect from a movie—with a ghostly astral form rising from the physical body.

Her spirit rose from the bed and turned to look at what was left of Rain Thomas. There wasn't much. "I don't understand," she said.

"It doesn't matter," said Dylan quickly as he pulled the door open. "He's almost here. We have to hurry."

Rain took an experimental step. There was pain, but it was faint. The ghost of pain. Or maybe she was a ghost. When she looked at her body, she did not see her chest rise and fall. Even the machine noises were muted.

"Am I dead?"

"No," he said, showing her his clock. "We're between heartbeats, but time is trying to catch up."

He went out into the hallway, and Rain followed. Even as a ghost or spirit or astral form—she didn't know the right word—her legs felt weak, damaged, wrong. They hurried down the hall, and not one person turned to look at them, though Rain noticed a few people shivered as if touched by a cold and unexpected breeze.

Rain realized that she still had the glasses on, but she wasn't sure how that worked. She wore clothes, too, but they were the clothes she'd worn when she left this morning to meet Sticks. Not her hospital gown.

Dylan ran, and every time she glanced at him, she wanted to grab him, pull him in, hold him. Love him and never, ever let him go. Behind them a door banged open, and they jerked to a stop for a moment to witness something absolutely impossible.

There, in the middle of the hallway, was the Cadillac. It filled the whole corridor, its doors scraping the walls. The Mulatto sat behind the wheel, and he looked exactly as Gay Bob had described him. Dead. Withered. A husk with hungry eyes. He revved the engine, and the roar filled the air. It was clear that the staff did not see the ghostly car, but they all jerked their heads around, looking for the sound.

"Oh, God!" cried Dylan. "He's coming through!"

The car lurched forward, tearing at the walls, crushing medical apparatus, knocking handles off doors, cracking windows. Rain was not sure if the staff could see the damage, but they all heard the noise. A few stepped toward the sounds, but most of them were frozen in place, confused and frightened.

"No," murmured Dylan. "It's too soon. Too soon."

The engine growled and roared, and then the car began accelerating toward them. One of the nurses was in its way, and the car slammed into her—and through her—leaving her spinning in place. In a movie, it might have been comical, but she staggered and suddenly vomited all over the wall. The young Pakistani doctor was clipped by the car and staggered, blood suddenly spouting from his nose.

"Run!" screamed Dylan. "Mom—run!"

CHAPTER NINETY-NINE

Doctor Nine's car was gaining.

It ripped its way down the hall, and when Rain and Dylan turned a corner, it turned, too. The physics were impossible, but that did not seem to matter to anyone anymore. People were screaming, and a deafening alarm began buzzing out, then another that was more of a bell. Both too loud. The hospital fire control system suddenly kicked in, and ceiling-mounted sprinklers began whip-hissing as they sprayed everything with icy water.

He's breaking the whole world, thought Rain as she ran.

Her legs blazed with pain, and fires kept erupting inside her nerves. It was worse than when she was being burned in the Fire Zone. It was a different and more intense pain, because unlike the pain of fire, the nerve endings in her astral form did not die. Instead, they seemed to come more fully alive, and she could feel everything that had been done to her real body during the crash. Every single thing. She could actually feel the broken bones. Each and every one of them. Her stomach and chest hurt, and she knew that it was the mess that was her liver, spleen, and kidneys. And her heart.

Dylan kept running ahead, outpacing her, then turning to wave her on. Several times he almost—almost—reached out to take her hand, to pull her, but each time, he snatched his own hand back. Clearly afraid of something. No—terrified.

"Through there!" cried Dylan, pointing to the wide double doors at the end of the hall. It was maybe twenty yards but looked like it was a mile away. Rain was stumbling now. Her body felt heavy and ready to collapse. She wondered what all of this was doing to her body—was the stress of running undoing all the surgeon's work?

Yes, whispered the parasite. *You're dying, and he'll feed on your soul.*

She ran anyway.

Behind her, the car was cracking the walls of the hospital. Acoustic tiles fell from the ceiling as the aluminum frames twisted out of shape. Fluorescent lights exploded, showering Dylan and Rain with sparks. Nurses and doctors ran screaming, hysterical because they could not see what was causing it. Maybe they thought it was an earthquake or a terrorist attack. Rain knew that either of those things would have been a mercy compared to what was really happening.

The Mulatto gunned the engine again, and now it was a monster roar so loud that windows shattered, filling the air with a storm of glittering shards. Rain felt them razoring into her, but she did not—or could not—actually bleed. They slashed through Dylan's hoodie, and he staggered, crying out, and fell to his knees with such force that he slid forward ten feet. Rain screamed and staggered over to him, but he waved his arm frantically to fend her off.

"Don't!" he cried. "If you touch me now, it'll break the spell!"

"What? Are you . . . are you a dream?"

He actually smiled. Or maybe it was a wince. "I'm real," he said, "but you're not."

The car was moving slowly but inexorably down the narrow hall, and the whole building was cracking open like a walnut.

"C'mon, Mom, we need to get through those doors," he gasped as he climbed back to his feet. He was bleeding from a dozen small cuts, and there was one long gash on his forehead that sent lines of bright red blood running like tears down his face. The water from the sprinklers washed it to a pink paleness. "Please . . . the second is almost up."

Rain forced herself to move.

The car was destroying the hospital to catch them. Maybe it was destroying the world. Rain did not know and could not understand what was happening. He was no longer coming for her. Doctor Nine was here.

The Cadillac seemed to bound forward as it broke past another doorway. It bucked and lifted and the bumper struck Rain in the back with all the force of a runaway train. It broke something inside. More than just bones. She felt her spine explode within her as she was lifted and hurled.

She hit the door with shocking force.

If the door had been one that opened inward toward the hall, it would have ended right there, right then. Finally. All hope crushed beneath those wheels.

The big double doors yielded to the force of her impact and swung outward on silent, well-oiled hinges. As Rain hurtled like a rag doll through the doors, she saw, there, unmistakably on the wall of the hospital, a huge, red, flashing neon hand.

CHAPTER ONE HUNDRED

Monk Addison drove through the storm with a carful of ghosts.

Mr. Hoto sat in the back seat, his face turned away, hands over his eyes, weeping. Thirteen-year-old Dylan crouched in the shotgun seat beside Monk, teeth bared, face and hands covered with new burns, his clothes singed and blackened.

"Doctor Nine will eat your soul for this," snarled the teenager.

Monk believed him. He had no choice. When the tattoos had been finished, the connection between Monk and the dead was made. He had not only relived the sad, desperate death of Mr. Hoto, but he had been inside of the mind of Dylan, and there was so much to see. To know. Too much.

All of those years with Doctor Nine and the nurse. The lessons and cruelty in the basement prison. The abuses heaped upon innocent flesh. The torture of the pure mind of a child in an attempt to subvert the emergence of a new ascended master. It was all so big. Bigger than Jonatha had said, because it wasn't merely preventing the world from shifting back to some kind of balance. This was going to tip things all the way toward chaos. It made the lines of an old poem ring with new and terrifying meaning.

Things fall apart; the centre cannot hold;
Mere anarchy is loosed upon the world,
The blood-dimmed tide is loosed, and everywhere
The ceremony of innocence is drowned . . .
And what rough beast, its hour come round at last,
Slouches towards Bethlehem to be born?

Maybe this was what Yeats was seeing when he wrote those words a century before. Not the coming of an antichrist but the coming of Doctor Nine. It was not the Beast who would launch a war against mankind and challenge heaven itself. No, Doctor Nine was subtler than that. And much more dangerous. He was the enemy of hope itself. It was like the devil tempting Jesus during his trial in the desert, but instead of offering him riches and power, he put him in a Nazi concentration camp. Like that.

The boy had been broken beyond repair. That much was evident. The version of Dylan that had attacked his mother remembered his torture and hated Doctor Nine and the Shadow People for it, and yet he was now complicit in the goals of that experience. His hope had died so thoroughly that the light of mercy had gone out of his life as well, leaving only a hungry thing that believed his nourishment could come from feeding on his mother's life force.

Was that how essential vampires were born? By crumbling under the weight of their loss and clutching at something to fill their void? Monk thought so. He wondered, then, how Doctor Nine came into being. The

Mulatto, the nurse, all the Shadow People who had fallen under Doctor Nine's spell had been human. Had the doctor ever been that?

Or was he something older and stranger? Some kind of elemental force that was beyond any definition of humanity? Monk did not know, because the answers were not in the memories of either Hoto or Dylan. The old Japanese guy believed that Doctor Nine was some kind of dark god. Dylan though he was a demon. Monk could not tell if either of them was close to the mark.

One thing the two of them agreed on, though, was that if Doctor Nine fed enough, he would become flesh. He would become fully alive in this world. At first Monk thought that this was an opportunity. Flesh can bleed, and in his experience, a bullet to the brainpan tended to settle the hash of pretty much everyone.

His gun was in his waistband. He had his knife, brass knuckles, strangle wire, and a lot of hard-earned know-how about killing. He did not enjoy it, but he was good at it. That's why he had eventually dropped out of the world all those years ago. He'd floated off in a river of blood spilled by his hands.

Doctor Nine, though . . . if he was a god or demon made flesh, maybe it would take more than a bullet. Fine. Monk would try everything. Hell, he'd burn down the whole hospital if that's what it took.

The boy, reading Monk's face, grinned. "He will feast on your—"

"How about you drink a nice fresh cup of shut-the-fuck-up, okay?"

The boy laughed. A high-pitched jackal's laugh. Mr. Hoto began banging his head against the car window. Monk tried to tune all of that out as he fished inside the boy's memory for information. For anything he could use.

And it was there.

Memories from three years ago. Or . . . from now, from days ago. Time was broken, and Monk had to force himself not to get hung up on it. Three years ago from the teenager's perspective; now from the perspective of the Dylan who was still alive in this world. The ten-year-old, wherever he was. The memories were hidden behind walls of hatred, but they were there. A kid on a skateboard with a backpack filled with pocket watches. Handmade clocks, built in a dark cellar when Doctor Nine and the nurse were not paying close enough attention. Devices constructed in secret, using the twisted science of the lord of the Shadow People. It was how the doctor stole time from people, stole the last moment of hope so they would plunge into personal darkness. The boy had learned the skills like an apprentice, and the thirteen-year-old would certainly have used those skills to do the same unkind, unholy work as the doctor.

Except . . .

He had not done that. Instead, he had taken great risks. Instead, he had escaped—as he had many times, knowing that he would be caught. Before he was taken back to the cellar, though, he had done something with those clocks. And Monk knew what it was.

Monk turned onto a street and headed toward an apartment building. The teenager's malicious grin froze as he realized where Monk was going. And why.

"No," he said.

Now it was Monk's turn to smile.

CHAPTER ONE HUNDRED AND ONE

Rain nearly died there. Right there in the doorway to Torquemada's, on the edge of the dance floor.

Dylan, bleeding and panting, dropped to his knees near her.

"Mom," he said. It was all he said.

She looked around her. The club was monstrously huge, with walls that soared up to a ceiling that was either painted to look like the Milky Way or it was that great sweep of the galaxy in fact. Pillars rose around the central floor, but they seemed to vanish into the upper darkness. Starlight and neon light mingled and danced, and, as they had on the streets and in the park, colors burst out of nowhere in the air and then vanished into memory.

There were people in the club. Thousands of them. Some were dressed like her, like ordinary people. Others were in elaborate costumes from different cultures, different times, maybe different dimensions. It was impossible for Rain to tell where reality and affectation ended and impossibility began. Everyone was in motion. Everyone was dancing. The force of all that motion was like a fist, though, that drove the air from her lungs and made her collapse against the inside wall. The hammering of the Music was only less explosive than the desperate urgency of her heartbeat. Sweat burst from her pores, and her fevered eyes jumped and twitched as she saw all the things that twisted and writhed within the club. It was too much, and the overload bored holes in her head. Unable to resist, unsure if she wanted to, and yet terrified to let go, Rain stood up, shaking near the door. She felt more than heard the door slam shut behind her with ringing finality.

"God save me," she whispered, but the Music beat all the tone from her plea. Was this real, or had her mind finally and completely snapped?

Her son was nearby, down on hands and knees, panting and bathed in sweat. His head bobbed, though, as if nodding in answer to a question. Or maybe to the beat of the Music.

Yet . . . the Music felt real, and the vibrations of the bass notes through the floor felt real, and the lights burned with stinging reality in her eyes. Caught at the deadly edge of the whirlpool, she fought for balance but knew that she would be dragged down if she took even the tiniest step forward. Nothing she could do would prevent that. As she swayed, the rhythms pounded at her, tugged her, enticed her, cried out to her in siren voices, teasing her to succumb, to simply step off the precipice and plunge into the abyss that was the Music.

The Music closed itself as one song finished, and there was a trembling second of relief. Rain felt faint, her face hot and running with sweat. She tried to concentrate, but the whole place seemed to be out of focus.

The door behind her burst open.

And Doctor Nine came in.

He was there. In the flesh. Fully real, and Rain knew it. Tall, thin, dressed in black, smiling with triumph. He still wore his sunglasses, but there was a hellfire glow behind the dark lenses.

The nurse was with him, her uniform stained and torn, unbuttoned to show too much cleavage. The Mulatto, tall and lugubrious, stood on the doctor's other side, his skin dried to leather. Behind them were other shadows, less clearly defined. His people.

Doctor Nine pointed a finger at Rain. "Mine."

CHAPTER ONE HUNDRED AND TWO

And another voice rang out.

"No. She's *mine.*"

Doctor Nine turned. They all did. All the thousands gathered there. All of them looking as Dylan rose to his feet, bloody and small and starved, and he stood in front of his mother, arms held protectively wide.

"She's my mom, and you can't have her."

The doctor laughed. The Shadow People laughed. It was an ugly sound, like rat feet over old boards. A flock of nightbirds flew in through the open door and swept upward to circle the dance floor.

In the absence of the Music, the club seemed oddly frail, like it could crack open as easily as Doctor Nine's car had shattered the hospital walls.

"You called me here, sweet Lorraine," said the doctor.

"No, I didn't," cried Rain. "That's bullshit. You're lying."

Doctor Nine leered at her. "Why would I lie? Why would I need to? You begged and wept me into existence."

Like a magician conjuring an illusion, he swept his hands upward, and a figure appeared in front of him. Noah. Whole and alive, as he was the last time Rain had seen him. Alive and happy, giving her a brave smile as he stepped onto the bus to head to join his unit for the long trip across water and sand.

Then the Humvee was there again. Whole one moment, bursting and burning the next. The screams of all those men rose in a hellish chorus, and like a conductor, Doctor Nine extending a single finger to silence everyone but a single shrieking voice. It was the sound of Noah burning to death.

"Stop it!" cried Rain. "Stop it!"

"I'm trying to, Lorraine," said the doctor. "That's exactly what I've always been trying to do. You think I'm a monster, but I'm not. I don't steal your dreams or your hope. I am the drug that stops you from caring about what you lost. I've always been there for you, through the long years of long nights. Who else was ever there for you? Your mother? That hag? She's with me now."

One of the shadows behind Doctor Nine coalesced into the form of her mother. Alyson Creighton-Thomas stood there, dressed in a white silk bathrobe, leaning on her cane, her eyes unfocused and empty, her mouth turned down into its usual frown of disapproval.

"Mom?" said Rain, stepping forward. Dylan shifted to block her, and she stopped.

"She was in pain for so many years," said the doctor, "but now, see? No pain. No jealousy. She is purified of all of that."

Her mother stared with a terminal vacuity that was unbearable. Rain did not know if this meant that her mother was dead or if she had become transformed into a shadow creature. Like the nurse. Like the version of Dylan who had tried to kill her.

"Oh . . . Mom . . ."

The dead eyes blinked, and then her mother looked at her.

"All I ever wanted to do was dance," she said. It was something Rain had heard before, but back then, there had always been a wistful quality to it, even if it was painted over with bitterness. Now it was an empty comment, devoid of passion.

"I know, Mom," said Rain, bowing her head. "I'm sorry."

For a moment, the whole room pulsed, the lights fading to blackness and then coming back on.

Dylan spun around. "No! It's one minute to midnight. You can't say things like that."

The watching crowds, still and silent until now, like mannequins in a store display, turned, and several stepped back to let a figure walk out onto the dance floor. Thin, old, with grizzled hair and a gentle face, dressed in soiled work clothes. The Shadow People recoiled from him, but not Doctor Nine.

"You have no say here," said the doctor.

Caster gave him a weary smile. "This is the Fire Zone; everyone has a say. I bet even your dusty friend there," he said, nodding to the Mulatto, "could find his voice here. If he wanted to."

Doctor Nine took a challenging step toward the old man but pointed to Rain and Dylan. "This is mine to do. She is mine. The boy is mine."

"Not yet."

"The clock is running out, the hour has come, and they are both mine."

Caster looked at him, his face troubled, then he turned to Rain. "Tell me, my girl, what is it you want?"

"I want my son."

She said it without hesitation. Dylan looked at her, and there was an expression on his face that she had never before seen on those features. Not on his actual face.

There was love.

"I love you, Mom," he said.

She dropped down to her knees in front of him. "If I could go back," she said, "if I could undo it all, I would. I'd never give you up. I'd keep you with me. You and me, Dylan. We'd be together; we'd be amazing. That's what I always wanted. No matter what else happened. Even if we had nothing at all, we'd have that."

Doctor Nine began clapping, slowly, mocking her words, sneering at her. "And the Academy Award goes to—"

"Shut up," growled Rain.

Caster Bootey came over and bent to whisper in her ear. It was the same thing that had been written on the fortune cookie the other night. He said, "Life's too short to spend so much of it on your knees."

She shook her head. Too much of her hurt, too much was broken, and even though Dylan was inches away, she wasn't able to touch him. "I can't."

"You haven't tried," said the old man.

"I'm broken. This isn't really me. I'm in a hospital bed, and I'm broken."

"The clock hasn't struck midnight yet, child," he said gently. "There's still time."

"Time to do what?"

It was Dylan who answered. "It's time to dance, Mommy."

She shook her head. "I can't."

"No," said Doctor Nine, "you can't."

She nodded, accepting it.

Caster squatted down and hooked a finger under her chin, lifting her face. "Listen to me," he said. "Your personal midnight is almost here. You're correct, your body is elsewhere and it's broken, but your spirit is here. Don't you even understand what the Fire Zone is?"

Rain shook her head.

"The Fire Zone is possibility," he said. "It's potential. It's intention. It's hope. Right here. All around you. You are inside a place made up of pure source energy. Everything you see was born in someone's dream. Every sound you hear, the smells, the floor beneath your feet, the stars above us, are all dreams from the head of a dreamer. They wished it into being and it has existed, in one form or another, forever, and it will burn with a wonderful heat forever. Look around, Lorraine. Look at these people."

She turned to see the thousands of faces watching in silence.

"They are dreaming of you as you are dreaming of them. As Doctor Nine is dreaming of you. As your son is. Life is what you dream it is."

Rain shook her head again.

"You wanted to be a dancer. Being a mother took that away, but did you ever try to get it back?"

"My leg . . ."

"Is a leg. You've dreamed that it won't ever lift you like a bird or sail you like a swan across a stage. Do you think a dancer is defined by a standard of perfection as fragile as that? No. A dancer dances. A singer sings. A writer writes. Believe that. Go further. A child imagines being an adult, and he becomes one. A prisoner closes his eyes and walks free. A dying woman walks through a door and is born again."

"Does that mean I have to die?"

"No," said Dylan.

"Yes," said Doctor Nine.

"Hush," said Caster to both of them. "It means that if you want to dance, you can dance. Don't impose a need for perfection. Dance for the joy of it. Dance for your life, Lorraine."

He rose and held out his hand to her.

"Stay down, my sweet," said the Doctor. "Stand and you will fall. Try and you will fail. There is only more pain for you. There is nothing but defeat if you walk out onto that dance floor."

"Stay down," said her mother in a listless voice. "Be sensible."

Dylan stood, too. He walked out on the floor, past Doctor Nine and the shadows. He stopped and turned. "Come on," he said, looking back. "Come on and dance with me, Mommy."

Doctor Nine stepped onto the floor, too. "I promise you this, Lorraine Thomas, that if you do this, you will die. Come with me and you live. You and your mother will be together. It will all be fine. No more pain. No more worries."

"No joy," said Caster, but Doctor Nine laughed.

"Joy is fleeting, and it's a lie."

Rain looked at Dylan.

"This is a dream," said the doctor. "So what if you dance here? Your body is dying. In fact, if you do this, I will have my nurse cut your throat."

He snapped his fingers, and the Shadow People vanished. The nurse, the Mulatto, all the others. Only Rain's mother remained, gray and silent.

"They are at the hospital," said the doctor. "They are going to kill you. They *will* kill you, and no one here can stop them. Not even Caster can stop them, because that's the real world and this, as he so rightly said, is a dream."

It was easy to stay down. It hurt less. She felt her heart breaking.

But she took Caster's hand. It took so much effort to stand. Dancing was going to be impossible, and she stood there, swaying, in agony, feeling her heart beating in all the wrong ways.

Even so, she turned to Caster and smiled. "Life's too short to spend so much of it on my knees," she said.

It was Doctor Nine who answered. Three small words. Cold and filled with bottomless promise.

"So be it."

The Music began to play.

Rain limped toward the dance floor but stopped at the edge of the apron. Other people were moving out to dance as the Music swelled. It was a song she did not know but felt she should know. A kind of synth pop but with classical undertones in the bass line. Deceptive, intriguing, but fast and dangerous. The other dancers were immediately caught up in it, and Rain lost sight of her son. The last fleeting image she had of him was of Dylan moving. To run or to dance? There was no way to tell.

Doctor Nine stood only a few feet away, and Caster was on her other side.

"Dance, Lorraine," murmured the old man, his voice nearly lost beneath the Music. "Dance as if your life depends on it."

Rain shook her head, and yet one rebellious foot—too weak to resist any longer—stepped off the wooden apron, and she was instantly dragged along into the sound and the fury.

CHAPTER ONE HUNDRED AND THREE

Waves of Music slammed into Rain, and she staggered, gasping, but the beat mastered her and she was held upright, dominated entirely, completely in its thrall. Her battered legs did not collapse under her. In fact, they moved with surprising freedom, carrying her deeper into the press of dancers. Her pelvis swung around, and she arched back. Rain felt like a surfer crouched atop a heavy roller that was swelling, gathering big chunks of the ocean as it raced toward the shoreline. The Music soared upward from the floor, and she rode it shakily, fighting for control.

The Music settled into a pattern now, and Rain was able to dance. She danced by instinct, by reflex, her muscles remembering how to move to rhythm and beat even if her body was too badly injured to do it with grace. She felt as if she were still caught in that tidal wave and was beginning to be afraid of what would happen when it smacked down on the beach. Or maybe it was more like a river speeding onward to a waterfall. Would there be jagged rocks down there? Would she sink down in waters infested with biting sharks? Or would there be something more monstrous, something as alien as this place? Were the Shadow People lurking within the song, waiting for her to make a false step so they could take her? Or would there be some resolution to this madness, some solution beyond imagination? There was no way to tell.

Something brushed against her shoulder, and she turned. It was Doctor Nine. He gave Rain a slow, lascivious wink.

She recoiled, her stomach churning, a shriek caught in her throat.

Laughing, the doctor vanished into the crowd, but his passage had torn open a hole in Rain's brain, spilling out the memories she had long ago locked. Memories of loss and pain, of failure and descent into addiction. Memories she could not afford and certainly could not face right now, not with all the madness boiling around her. Everything that she had smashed down into the bottom of her Box of Rain was fighting to be let out, let loose. She reeled across the dance floor, careening into other dancers, but even her screams became part of the Music.

"Help me!"

The piercing squeal of a child, her son, in terrible pain silenced her own cries and made her whirl, but there was nothing behind her except the wildly thrashing dancers. The screams rose again; and they went on and on until they blotted out even the Music. "Oh, God! No! Please don't! Mommy . . . please . . . help me!"

Rain stared in horror even as she realized that this was some kind of trick. Like a recording of what her son had endured, played back to torture her now. In her mind, the Box of Rain creaked threateningly, straining against the locks and chains she'd placed around it.

"No!" she said as much to herself as in denial that the voice of her screaming child was real. "Goddamn it! No!"

"Please, help!" The tone of the scream was caught and blended with a guitar note that rose and warped and vanished into the next progression of distortion-heavy guitar chords. The illusion, the trick, was ended. What would Doctor Nine try now? she wondered.

"I need to get air!" she cried.

All time and reality went sideways. The bass rhythms of the Music shook her like thunder; lasers flashed like lightning and stabbed Rain repeatedly through the heart. The floor canted, and she felt herself sliding, shoes scuffling on the Lucite as the pit tried to suck her down into despair. Pain flared in her sides as she dragged in air, and she wondered how she could have become so terribly exhausted in mere minutes on the dance floor. Surely it was well past midnight now. Surely her time had all run out.

"*No!*" she cried, then she cringed, feeling terribly exposed and vulnerable. She tried to match her own heartbeat to the pulse of the Music, sensing somehow that this might save her, that this was what she was supposed to do if she wanted to survive this. Rain opened up, stretched out, let the

Music in so she could match it note for note. The pain flared as the Music invaded her completely. .

"No . . ."

In the dark niches of consciousness, Rain heard the whispering voice of the Music. It asked her terrible questions; it revealed to her awful truths. It held before her eyes the key that would unlock the Box of Rain and let out all her demons. Failure and addiction and need and loss. Inside was the proof that she was rotten, ruined, worthless. Already dead.

"No!"

The sound of her voice was instantly blended with the backbeat, an unexpected but useful note, percussing and concussing with the drums. She prayed desperately that it would peak soon. Peak, and be over, even if it meant that she would die with it—just so that it would be over. Failure was better than suffering, right? That had to be a truth. She thought that even the fatal plunge downward to destruction would be a foundation on which she could somehow stabilize herself.

Twitching and stumbling to the beat, she found it almost impossible to feel her body. Rain was aware only of a proportionless cloud of pain and fear. Only the Music's raw and commanding force kept her spinning like a marionette on wildly jerking strings; without its power, she would have collapsed in a boneless heap on the plastic floor that looked down on hell. She staggered after each note, hands reaching and fingers clawing, knowing by the grace of some alien instinct that if she could survive just a few notes longer, she'd be safe.

"Nonononononononononono," she mumbled insanely. In confusion, she pulled the glasses from her face, hoping that without them the world would lock back into place, that things would make sense. The glasses hung from their chain, and she kept screaming.

The song galloped toward its climax. Just a fistful of notes hung between her and salvation as the song burned its way to its explosion. Rain tensed as she moved, waiting and craving for the last note that, once resolved, would save her. Left unresolved, she knew she would be as good as dead, or perhaps dead in fact. The Music was not a wave anymore but a vast mountain rising between her and survival. The notes climbed the jagged cliff of the crescendo, and her sanity climbed after. The notes burned themselves into her mind. Rain's sanity clung to the need to hear that last resolving, sanctifying, redeeming note.

The penultimate note slashed at her and she drew in breath, ready to scream. The gap between the notes sizzled in the air, and time stretched as she willed—no, begged—that last note to play.

Then the Music stopped.

Ice cold.

Unresolved by that single, final note.

"*Noooooooooooooooooooooooooooooooooooooo!*"

The scream was ripped out of her, out of soul, torn from body and mind. She tottered on the very edge of the precipice, arms flailing. A desperate shiver shuddered through Rain's soul. This was the point of greatest danger, the splintered fragment of time between survival and total, perpetual failure. The universal clock was poised to tick past this moment, and if it did, she would never stop falling. In a moment, the echo of that previous note would burn away and be gone forever.

So would she.

Already she began to feel insubstantial.

And then . . .

Then she heard the note.

That last, glorious note. Not blasting at her from the speakers but breathing gently against her face like the first breath of a golden dawn. It sighed across ruined nerves; the most soothing and healing balm possible. It flowed into her, into lungs and into veins, a musical elixir vitae.

Trembling, weeping as hands touched her sweaty and tearstained face, she sank to her knees. The floor was solid beneath her, cool, real; she bent and touched her cheek to it. A schoolkid giggle bubbled out of her chest. Then Rain threw back her head and laughed for the sheer joy of being alive. For having danced.

A second later, her mind was jolted by a revelation that was more powerful than the sound of that last note.

She knew, all at once and with total certainty, that no band had ever played that final note. Her ears had never actually heard it. That single, delicious, saving note had come from within her own mind, from within her own soul. It had come from some deep place in consciousness, blossoming from need to hear it, created by some part of essential self in which beauty dwelled and thrived despite the ugliness in life.

Of all the skills and knowledge she possessed, that one quality had saved her. She had danced herself out of hell. Beauty—understanding of beauty had brought her through the fire.

She was alive. She felt whole. Strong. Free of pain.

Rain rose to her feet and looked around. The other dancers backed away from her, clearing the center space. Some of them nodded to her. She knew which ones they were. They were the Invited. They were the ones who had dreamed the Fire Zone into being. She, in turned, bowed to them. A dancer's curtsy. Not perfect, but perfect enough.

Rain looked at the crowd.

"Where is my son?"

CHAPTER ONE HUNDRED AND FOUR

It took Monk two hours to do everything he needed in Brooklyn and get to the hospital. At least he thought that's how long it took. His dashboard clock seemed to have stopped at 11:59.

"What time is it?" he said aloud. Neither of the ghosts answered him.

But Gay Bob said, "Almost midnight."

"What I thought," said Monk as he pulled into the turnaround in front of the hospital.

They all got out. Monk, a tall mixed-race woman named Yo-Yo Jablonski, a fat guy they called Straight Bob, and a big bruiser of a man called Gay Bob. Each of them held a small silver windup pocket watch in their hands. They looked at the hospital. The two ghosts stood to one side, both wearing expressions of doubt.

There were sirens blaring and people screaming.

"What exactly are we doing here?" asked Straight Bob.

"Saving the world," said Monk. Only half meaning it.

Above them, the sky was filled with rain and thunder and nightbirds.

"Come on," said Monk, "we're running out of time."

CHAPTER ONE HUNDRED AND FIVE

The other dancers once more moved back and there, in the center of the dance floor, was a sight that tore a cry from Rain.

Dylan was there. So was Caster Bootey.

Doctor Nine stood there, still smiling.

In front of him, squatting on the floor, brought to terrible reality, was the Box of Rain.

Real.

Iron bound and wrapped in heavy chains, stained with a decade of bitter tears and innocent blood.

Waiting for her.

CHAPTER ONE HUNDRED AND SIX

Monk Addison rode an elevator with three drug addicts and two ghosts. The addicts could not see the ghosts, but they knew they were there. He'd told them. The three members of the Cracked World Society crowded into one corner, looking frightened and confused.

These were the three people who were closest to Rain. Each of them had been given a windup pocket watch. Monk understood what the clocks were, why they had been created, though he did not yet understand how to activate them. He had a theory, though. If he was right, they had a chance, however slim, of surviving the next few minutes. If he was wrong, there were going to be a lot more ghosts.

He wondered, not for the first time, what would happen if he died. Would the ghosts who haunted him be released? Or would he join their ranks as souls trapped forever in a world of pain and sorrow? No one with whom he'd ever shared his secrets, not even the mystics who had offered him sanctuary all those years ago, had a clue.

The teenage ghost seemed able to read his emotions, and he mocked him, laughed at him. Mr. Hoto was no longer weeping, but he stood apart, watching and praying. The elevator dinged, and they stepped out onto the ICU floor.

And stepped into madness.

As they exited the car, they heard a scream and they turned to see Dylan—a younger version of the teenager who stood beside Monk—come tearing down the hallway. And staggering behind him was Rain Thomas.

Which was not possible, because when Monk had called for a report on the young woman, it was clear she was critically injured. Broken legs, internal damage. There was no way this was happening.

He reached out to touch her shoulder, to catch her, to warn her of what was happening. But as his fingers closed around her arm, Rain passed straight through them. It made him jerk backward, scared out of his mind, and for a moment, he did not know if she was a ghost or he was.

Yo-Yo and the two Bobs called out her name, and they tried to catch her, too. Rain did not see them, but she threw a confused look behind her, missed her footing, fell, scrambled up again, and kept running.

Which is when the doors blew open at the end of the hall and a big fucking Cadillac came roaring forward.

They all screamed and flattened against the wall. Teenage Dylan laughed his jackal laugh.

However, Mr. Hoto stepped out into the path of the car and stood there. His face had been filled with despair and sadness before, but now he set his chin and held out his hands as if he could somehow stop the car.

It hit him.

It hit him real damn hard, smashing him backward.

Monk saw Hoto's thin arms break and collapse like a ruptured accordion, but something else happened at the same moment. *The car slowed.* The wheels spun on the linoleum floor, kicking up clouds of smoke. The driver kept stamping on the gas, but the car's speed was reduced to a fraction because Hoto was still there. Pushing back. His arms were smashed, his chest crushed, but he pushed back. His head still hung sideways on its broken neck, but he pushed back.

"What's happening?" demanded Yo-Yo.

"A tough fucking little ghost is what's happening," said Monk, filled with wonder. "Holy shit."

The hospital staff were yelling, looking wildly around, seeing damage happen around them as something tore at the walls and shattered equipment, but it was clear to Monk that none of them saw the car.

"This is nuts," he said. Then he saw teenage Dylan bolt to the left and go running up the hall toward an ICU room whose door stood open.

"Shit," Monk growled and pelted after him. He heard the others following.

They reached Rain's room, and there she was. Monk jumped forward to position himself between the feral teen and the woman who was nearly lost in a maze of splints, bandages, and tubes.

"Oh, God!" cried Yo-Yo, covering her mouth with both hands. "Rain!"

The others flew toward her, surrounding the bed, touching her with tentative fingers to convince themselves of her reality. Gay Bob bent to study the monitors.

"Christ, her blood pressure is really low."

"So's her pulse," said Straight Bob.

"Is she in a coma?" asked Yo-Yo.

"I think so," said Straight Bob.

"She's dying, you assholes," said Dylan, but only Monk heard him. "The doctor is winning. He's killing her right now, and you can't do anything to stop it."

"Shut up," said Monk. Straight Bob cut him a look, then followed the line of Monk's gaze and shivered.

"Which ghost?" he asked.

"Little dickhead."

"Hey," said the ghost, "fuck you."

For some reason, that made Monk smile. He went and leaned over Rain. "Hold on, sister. We got you."

"How exactly do we have her?" asked Gay Bob. "What are we here to do?"

"We're too late to do anything," complained Straight Bob, and Yo-Yo nodded.

Monk looked at them and he grinned. "No," he said, "the clock hasn't struck midnight yet."

It was a phrase he'd pulled from Dylan's mind. It had also been echoing in Mr. Hoto's thoughts. Midnight had nothing to do with the time in any physical clock. Not the bedside clock or Monk's cell phone clock. Midnight was the moment when the greatest chance for hope died. It was almost here, the seconds ticking away differently from ordinary time.

"You guys all have your clocks?" They did; they showed him the tiny windup timepieces. Monk nodded. Then he pointed to what they saw as the emptiness at the foot of Rain's bed. "Dylan is right there. You can't see him because he's dead. But here's the thing—he won't be dead for three years. If we don't stop Doctor Nine, if we can't save Rain, then at midnight, the version of Dylan who is still alive somewhere in the world is going to break. He'll have failed to save his mother and save himself and maybe save the world. His hope will die, and from then on, he'll be a husk of a person, dead in every way that matters. From one moment after midnight, Dylan will begin sliding into darkness. He'll fall for three years, and during that time, he will be Doctor Nine's lapdog, his fetch dog. Then he'll bottom out and hang himself outside of the apartment of the man, a former Tibetan monk, who had failed to properly warn Rain and in fact helped convince her to give up her baby. That's the long-story-short version of this. But here's the kicker: Dylan—the real one—took a big risk. He created these clocks. They don't just tell time; they store it."

Straight Bob looked at his, turning it over to study the face and the back. "What's that even mean?"

"Each of you has lost time recently," said Monk. "Rain lost a whole day."

"She lost Friday," said Yo-Yo.

"You each did, too."

"I—" began Gay Bob. "I lost a couple of hours the other day. Maybe more. I kind of blanked out,"

"Me, too," said Yo-Yo. "I went to a meeting, and then bang, it was gone. All the time I was speaking. Maybe more."

Straight Bob nodded. "I've been losing minutes and hours for days now."

Monk reached out and tapped his clock. "It's in there."

"How?" demanded Yo-Yo. "Are you saying Doctor Nine stole our time?"

"No," said Monk, "I'm saying that Dylan stole it."

He dug a hand into his front jeans pocket. "I have Dylan's memories of the last few days. I explained how that works."

"It's freaky as shit," said Gay Bob.

"Preaching to the choir, brother," said Monk. "Point is, that's how I know about the clocks, and it's how I know where Dylan hid the keys."

"Don't do it," warned the feral ghost. "He will kill you for this."

Monk did it anyway. He removed his hand and held it out, palm upward, to show what he had. Three small, delicate silver keys.

"So, yeah," he said, "we have time. We have your own time."

"No," said a cold voice from the doorway, "you're all out of time."

They turned. Dylan clapped his hands in dark delight. The doorway was filled with people.

The Shadow People. The nurse smiled with red, red lips.

CHAPTER ONE HUNDRED AND SEVEN

Caster Bootey touched Rain's arm. "Everyone has places in which they hide the things they don't want to look at. You're not alone in that. It's human nature."

"I was told to hide away the things I can't bear," said Rain. "To keep me safe."

"And are you safe?"

"No," said Rain. "Not even a little."

"Sometimes things can stay hidden in the back closets of the soul," murmured Caster. "Sometimes these things die back there and become a useless and harmless part of the past."

"And . . . sometimes they don't."

"No. Sometimes they don't."

They faced each other for a long moment. Rain said, "Sometimes they feed off the darkness and get bigger and stronger, don't they?" she asked, but it was rhetorical. "Sometimes these things get so strong that they fight to get out."

The old man nodded.

"Caster?" Rain asked.

"Yes?"

"I . . . I kind of understand that somehow it was you who did all this, brought me here, helped me . . ."

"Some of it."

"Why? I mean . . . why bother? Who am I to you?"

Caster shrugged. "I have my reasons, Lorraine. And before you ask . . . they are my reasons, and I don't choose to share them with you. Just accept that I did what I did out of love."

Rain had nothing to say to that, so she nodded and dabbed at her eyes. Then she turned to Dylan. "I want to hold you, baby. I want so much to hold you and never let you go."

"He is lost," said Doctor Nine. "He is mine and—"

"Lorraine," interrupted Caster gravely, "there is still one thing left for you to do tonight."

She had avoided looking at the Box of Rain, but now she turned and faced it. The thing stood a dozen paces away. Too close. Way too close.

"Oh," she said, understanding filling her like ice water.

"Turn your back on it and take my hand," said Doctor Nine. "Come with me and you will never feel pain again. Touch that thing and pain is all you'll ever know. You will lose your son as you've already lost your lover and your mother."

She chewed her lip. The box rattled as the demons inside fought to get out. She touched Caster's sleeve. "I . . ."

"No, child," said Caster. "No more words. Just go and do what you have to do. Go and do what you came to the Fire Zone in the first place to do."

Across the battlefield of the dance floor, Doctor Nine gave her a look of pure murderous hatred. "Be damned, then."

CHAPTER ONE HUNDRED AND EIGHT

Monk pivoted and tossed the keys to Gay Bob, who stood closest. "Wind everyone's clocks. Hurry!" he yelled.

"And do what?"

But there was no time for Monk to answer. A towering, leathery figure pushed past the nurse and lumbered toward him. Monk knew from Dylan's memories that this was the Mulatto. A zombie of some kind. Old, with a withered black heart. The zombie reached for him with leathery hands, and Monk ducked the grab and shoulder-rammed the creature in the gut, driving it back against the other creatures filling the doorway. The Mulatto slapped his hands against the sides of the doorframe and kept on his feet, then charged again, but Monk had bought himself enough time to take the brass knuckles out of his pocket and slip them on. It was a solid pound of steel set with symbols of spiritual protection. He stepped into the reach, bashed the arms to one side, and hooked the zombie in the ribs. Dry skin tore and bones broke as a great rush of stale, dusty air shot from the thing's open mouth.

The nurse pushed past them and rushed the bed, drawing a long, slender knife from her pocket. Straight Bob threw his clock across the bed to Gay Bob.

"Here!" he yelled, then he tried to block her, but the nurse slashed him across the face, opening a red line from his left eyebrow to the right corner of his mouth. The blade cut through Straight Bob's nose and blood exploded as he fell back, clutching his face and screaming. She cut him again and again, ripping his face apart, trying to get his throat.

Yo-Yo threw her clock, too, then growled as she grabbed the nurse's hair and jerked the woman sideways, slamming her head into the side rail of the bed. The nurse cried out in pain, but, cat quick, she turned and drove the knife deep into Yo-Yo's stomach.

The clocks fell onto the floor, and Gay Bob dove for them. The Shadow People changed from vaguely human forms into the clearly defined shapes of nightbirds. They flew across the room and covered him, stabbing at him with razor-sharp beaks, slicing his face, his throat, his hands.

Monk heard the high-pitch cry of pain, but he was too busy to do much about it. Even hurt, the Mulatto was incredibly strong. The zombie caught Monk by the throat and lifted him completely off the ground, then slammed him into the wall. Monk was a big man, and what the zombie was doing was virtually impossible. Monk hammered at the arm holding him, but without effect, so he kicked the Mulatto in the chest, the shoulder, the face as the crushing grip began to collapse Monk's neck vertebrae.

Dylan laughed and danced and tried to fight, but his ghostly fists passed straight through Gay Bob, who was backing away from the fight, fiddling with the keys, dropping them, scooping them up, trying each one to find the one that unlocked any of the clocks.

The other Shadow People, formless and malevolent, began pushing into the room.

CHAPTER ONE HUNDRED AND NINE

The Music held itself in check, letting silence provide the score for Rain's approach to the box. However, the silence seemed to hum with unleashed power.

Licking parched lips, Rain took the first step forward. She did not say anything because she did not want to hear her voice crack and break.

She took a second step. A third. With each step, she seemed to hear an echo or see a shadow of things that had brought her to this moment. Her first dreams of the Fire Zone. The old woman on the train and those damned glasses. Seeing her son. Seeing Dylan running and screaming.

Step.

The news about Noah coming on the same day she learned she was pregnant and how those two things stretched her apart and broke her into pieces.

Step.

Sticks. The man who killed her life when he rolled over that mine with Noah in the back seat. Sticks, who lied to her and hid his guilt from her. Sticks. Dead and burned. How she hated him. Except . . . he had come to save her in the park, hadn't he? Was that some kind of penance?

Step.

The little monk in Central Park. Mr. Hoto. Trying so hard to warn her about the choice she was making. Being so destroyed when he realized that he had failed.

Step.

The actual birth. Dying. Being shocked back to life while her baby was still inside of her. Had it been his life force or the electrical jolt that had given her a direction in which to swim in all that darkness? Did it matter?

Step.

The drugs. The beautiful, horrible, delicious, disgusting, delightful, dreadful, wonderful drugs. The Void that took her to other worlds and maybe warped so much of her mind that she now thought this was actually happening. The crack cocaine that lifted her on its sweet smoke. There was a crack pipe waiting for her at home. Someone was going to find it. Her mother, her father, the landlord, the cops, her friends. She would not be going home from the hospital anytime soon. Whoever found that stuff would make the obvious guess.

Step.

The shower curtain, too. That was there. Maybe cut into pieces, but there. What would the police make of that? Of her trying to destroy the evidence of a questionable suicide? Someone had stolen the body from the morgue. Would Detective Martini be waiting for her with a warrant and handcuffs when she got out of the hospital? If she ever got out.

Step.

Her friends in the Cracked World Society. Each of them had been haunted by Doctor Nine. None of them had dreamed of him before they met Rain. Their pain was her fault. Maybe their slide downward toward using again was on her. Sure. It was on her. More crimes on her personal rap sheet.

Step.

Dylan. Poor little Dylan. Named for a ray of hope, but now that hope was fading. He was going to commit suicide and Rain—the real-world version of herself—was in a hospital, broken beyond repair. She could not go looking for him. She would never find him in time. All she could hope for was to wait to die so that she wouldn't have to live with the knowledge that she had failed her son in every single way. All the way to the end. Even if Doctor Nine lost control of him, Dylan was lost, and he would fall. His heart would break, and the light inside of him would finally and completely go out.

Step.

Now she stood only a few feet away from the box. Her Box of Rain. Filled with all these horrors and so many more. It contained all the memories of everything she had done during her years of addiction, of need, of doing whatever she had to in order to guarantee her next high. And the next. And the next.

Step.

Doctor Nine came and stood in her way. Rain thought she could hear sobs in the air around them. Lost and broken people grieving for their own dreams, their own possibilities. He slowly removed his sunglasses, and Rain recoiled from him. Hellish fires burned in the doctor's eyes, and Rain could actually feel the heat emanating from them. Sweat ran in rivulets down her body, and she could feel it pooling at the base of her spine.

Doctor Nine licked his lips with a long, black tongue. "Are you going to stand there and tell me that you finally got the spine to face the thing you've been running from your whole life?"

Rain tried to swallow, but there was nothing but ashes in her mouth. "I . . . have to," she said weakly.

"No," said Doctor Nine, "you don't. Leave the box closed. Keep it chained. Let it be and I promise you peace."

"Go to hell," she said.

She stepped around him and approached the box. The Box of Rain. Pandora's box. Same thing. Same set of problems. Same horrors lurking inside. After all these years. It squatted there with menacing solidity, no longer a concept in her mind but a devastating reality, and its presence here struck Rain solidly in the gut. Her knees wanted to buckle, her heart hammered in her chest, and she wanted to scream just at the sight of it. She could feel the eyes of all those people watching.

"My God," she said, and that caused Doctor Nine to laugh. Rain turned to him.

"Yes," sneered Doctor Nine, "that is your God. Everybody always talks about how God is something so big and powerful that they fear him. It. Whatever. Well, this is something big and powerful, and your life's been wasted because you fear it. That thing has moved worlds for you. Maybe this is your God, after all. Go ahead—bow to it. Crawl on your belly before it."

"Just . . . shut up." Rain wiped her mouth with the back of a hand, and she was aware that the hand was shaking badly.

She forced herself to move closer until she stood within touching distance, then she turned and walked in a slow circle around it, examined it from every side, marveling at the detail that she had created, impressed despite herself at its apparent reality. No, she corrected herself, not apparent—that was too dodgy a way of thinking about it. No, she was impressed by the reality she had imposed upon it, by the reality she'd forced out of it, and by the solidity she'd forced it to accept.

Yes, she thought bitterly, *that was it.*

In that box were whole parts of herself that she had roughly cut away with a bloody scalpel or snapped off in desperate haste. She'd used the heat of fear to forge the iron for the metal bands and the chains that held it. With crafty skills learned over years of self-deception, she had constructed the lock and snapped it shut through the links of that chain, trapping and containing all the demons she had conjured. The demons strained continually against the chains, their strength indefatigable—not just to get out, but to drag her inside.

Now it was here, and this was the moment. She had no weapons left with which to fight. All she had with her was the windup pocket watch and the glasses that hung around her neck. Two things that might not even be real.

She accepted that as somehow appropriate.

Rain finished her slow circle and once more stood in front of the box. Then she knelt and reached out a tentative hand, touching the iron bands, feeling their cool, rough surface. She trailed fingers along the wooden sides and then ran them over the knobbed contour of the chain until she reached the steel arch of the lock's shackle.

"I did a pretty good job on you, didn't I?" she said quietly. She gripped the combination lock and gave it an experimental tug, but despite the rust and scarring, it was still solidly locked. But nearness, perhaps presence, sent a tremble through the box, and the huge box rattled heavily against the floor as the demons fought to escape. Or maybe they shuddered with hungry expectation. Rain sat back on her haunches for a moment, giving herself time to gather thoughts and courage.

She looked at the digits on the lock and closed her eyes for a moment. It required a combination. A set of numbers. Rain already knew what they were. Or thought she did. She dialed them in. Dylan's birthday, month and year. And pulled.

The lock held fast. She grunted, and Doctor Nine sighed with real pleasure.

Rain tried it again, the same numbers but reversed. Year, month, day. Nothing. Another try, this time with Noah's numbers. The lock did not open. There was another huge pulse in the room as the clock hand ticked off the last second. It was midnight.

Then Rain understood. It was so simple. So *obvious*. This was her box of horrors. Not Noah's, not Dylan's. Their memories were in here, but it was her own private box.

And so she dialed once more as the clock struck the hour.

Her numbers. Year. Month. Day. This was her box, after all.

And the lock opened with a soft *click*.

CHAPTER ONE HUNDRED AND TEN

Gay Bob beat the nightbirds back, but he knew that he was hurt. Badly hurt. One eye was blind and the other was veiled by red. Blood poured from a hundred cuts, many of them terribly deep. Through the haze of pain, he saw Straight Bob sinking down to his knees, both hands clamped around his throat in a futile attempt to stanch the sprays of bright arterial blood. The nurse loomed over him, the bloody knife in her fist, her mouth curved into a jack-o'-lantern grin of red triumph.

By the door, Monk Addison brought the brass knuckles down once, twice, three times, and the dead hand holding him shattered. He dropped to the floor, but the Mulatto grabbed him with his other hand. Monk kicked him, driving him back into the doorway, trying to block the other shadows.

Even so, Gay Bob stabbed the key into the back of the clock and turned it. There was a small click that was almost lost beneath the screaming and the screeching of the nightbirds. All of this happened in the single tick of a second. It happened as he turned the key and unlocked someone's stolen time. He wasn't sure whose it was.

There was a terrible high-pitched scream, and he turned to see Yo-Yo, bloody and pale, the front of her clothes drenched with blood, collapse backward over Rain's still form. But standing a few feet behind the nurse . . . was *another Yo-Yo*. Now there were two of them. One dying, one not. One bloody, one not.

With a feral snarl, the second Yo-Yo snatched up a visitor chair and swung it with all her strength at the back of the nurse's head. The metal legs crunched through all those black curls, and the nurse crashed sideways into the bedside table. Yo-Yo threw a wild look at Gay Bob, raised the chair, and swung it again.

"Holy shit," gasped Gay Bob as he fished for a second lock and a second key. He turned it, and Straight Bob was there—whole and alive—behind the Mulatto, looking surprised but not stunned by it. He jumped up and wrapped his arms around the zombie's neck and yanked him violently backward. Monk staggered away, coughing and gasping. He looked at Straight Bob and then over at the other version of the man that was crumpled and still in a corner.

"This is totally nuts," said Monk.

Gay Bob felt himself fading, going away, becoming nothing. He fumbled for the last of the clocks and clumsied the key into place. With his last ragged breath, he turned it.

A second Gay Bob rose up beside him, snatched up a blood pressure stand, and went charging into the fight.

CHAPTER ONE HUNDRED AND ELEVEN
THE FIRE ZONE

Despite all the years of rust, the lock clicked open immediately.

The trembling and rattling of the box increased to a frantic level. Steeling herself, Rain took hold of the chain and pulled the shank through the links, considered the lock for a long moment, then tossed it behind her. The lid jerked up ferociously against the chain, but she held it in place with a knotted fist and all the strength she possessed.

"Please," she whispered softly, "please, God."

The whole box jumped and banged; the lid hammered upward against the chain. She took a deep breath and then let go of the chain. There was a single violent wrench against the lid. Then the ends of the chain clattered down and hung limp. The lid did not tremble. The box did not shake. There was total silence in the vast dance hall of Torquemada's. Rain's eyes were fever bright as she reached out and pushed the chain through the restraining ringbolts and let it rattle down to the floor. The lid was held down by nothing more than its own weight. Rain took another breath and took hold of the hasp, pulled it up, and braced herself to lift the lid. A shadow fell across the box, but she didn't turn.

"What do *you* want?" she asked coldly.

"You sure you want to do this?" said Doctor Nine in a reptilian voice.

"I've come this far."

"You can still lock it back up again. You don't have to face the demons yet. Numb is better. Numb is safe. Life hurts."

Rain gritted her teeth. "Go away, asshole," she said in a voice that was as hard and sharp as the edge of a knife. "You're standing in my light."

The shadow wavered for a moment and then receded.

Rain set herself again, took one last steadying breath, and then lifted the lid of her personal Pandora's box. The lid was heavy, but she had the strength to raise it, and she swung it up and over and let it fall away. The colored lights shone down into the box, revealing the contents.

There was only one thing inside the box.

And it made her scream.

THE HOSPITAL

The fight raged on around the body of Rain Thomas.

Screams and blood. People fighting to save a life that might already be lost. Fighting to save their own lives, knowing that the versions of themselves from the past would catch up to the present, and in the present, they were dying. Or doomed.

They fought anyway.

Hope is like that.

The ghost of Mr. Hoto stood on one side of Rain's bed, praying for her. Praying for them all.

The ghost of Dylan stood on the other side of the bed. Watching the fight. He was breathing as hard as if he had run up twenty flights of stairs. He looked from Monk and the Bobs and Yo-Yo to the nurse and the Mulatto and the others. To the Shadow People, who were his kin now. He looked down at his dying mother, at the splints and drains and breathing tubes. She was so close to the edge now. If he could only do something.

He reached out and touched the morphine drip. His fingers passed through it, but the machine suddenly beeped, and the monitor indicated that a dose had been released.

Dylan stared at the screen, then down at the woman who had abandoned him. He smiled a cruel little smile and reached again for the drip.

THE FIRE ZONE

Rain reached into the box and lifted the object out. The thing was heavy, more than an inch thick, and a foot square, edged by a heavy frame of some dense, overly ornate wood that had been covered with countless layers of cheap paint. Rain rose with it in her grip, feeling its weight, turning it over in her hands and then back again so that she could stare at the face in the frame. It was the face of the person she hated most in the whole world. The person who had profoundly and comprehensively disappointed her and ruined everything. The face of her enemy. She took two wandering-sideways steps and then caught her balance, but only just; clutching the frame in sweating, trembling hands. Here at last was the truth. The monster she most feared, the one who had done all this harm, framed for her to see.

She stared at what she held, at what she always suspected was the chief demon in her Box of Rain.

She stared into a mirror.

That was all it was. A mirror.

Only that.

But it was a mirror whose glass was warped and imperfectly made so that its reflective surface was irregular—concave in places and convex in others, cracked here and there, and covered with dust. Rain gazed down at her own distorted reflection and beheld the face of her enemy.

She opened her hand and just let it go. The mirror fell from her fingers, struck the ground, and shattered into a million fragments.

THE HOSPITAL

Dylan's ghost brushed through the monitor, and there was another beep as more morphine dripped into the IV tube. On the bed, Rain moaned in her troubled sleep. The other monitors recorded the jump in heart rate and blood pressure as the drug did its work and found a welcoming and familiar home.

THE FIRE ZONE

Rain suddenly staggered and cried out, clutching her chest. Sweat burst from her pores.

"What?" she asked. "I broke it . . . I understand . . . I beat the clock . . ."

Doctor Nine burst out laughing. "You stupid cow, do you think you ever had a chance? It's midnight, and that is my hour."

Rain dropped to her knees, gasping as fireflies seemed to ignite all around her. Not the pretty ones from the park but the ones that burst inside her eyes. Far away, she could feel her body twitching. Her real body, the physical Rain. Something was happening to her.

She was dying.

"Mom!" cried Dylan, rushing to her but still not touching her. Still unwilling to break the spell, even now. "Mom, I'm sorry."

Her sleeping body in the hospital came awake. Not all the way. Enough to see the thirteen-year-old Dylan swipe his hand across the morphine drip.

Again.

And again.

Flooding her with the deadly narcotic. Getting her high once more.

One. Last. Time.

Rain fell forward onto the dance floor, surrounded by the shattered fragments of the mirror. She could see herself reflected in a thousand different ways. Daughter, dancer, lover, mother, friend, addict. She saw one fragment reflecting her true self back in the hospital. Rain made the lips of her real body speak. Not to beg for her life. But to say something, one last thing, that she needed to say.

She said, "Dylan . . . I love you."

And then she closed her eyes.

And for the fourth time in her young life, Rain Thomas died.

CHAPTER ONE HUNDRED AND TWELVE

Rain Thomas felt the breeze on her face.

She opened her eyes slowly and stood there, trying to understand.

People walked past her, laughing and talking, following the winding footpaths in the park. The sky directly above was a startling blue, but there were gray storm clouds peering with bad intent over the eastern skyline. The breeze was damp with the promise of rain.

A colored streamer caught her eye, and she turned to watch it flutter. It was one of several that unwound across the sky, twisting like dragon tails, painting the day in colors of saffron and red and white. Each stream was attached to a tall bamboo pole that swayed above the trees.

She looked down at the immense belly that strained against her maternity blouse.

"What?" she asked.

It was then that she heard a voice speaking or chanting in a low, almost inaudible mumble. A bass voice, and the sound of it rolled through the air and changed the texture of the moment. She moved toward the sound, knowing what it was going to be. In a field, seated on colored mats or embroidered cushions, sat a hundred people in postures of meditation. They were arranged in a half circle around a group of five men in reddish-yellow robes.

"No," she said, realizing what day it was. Knowing that this was some kind of cruel reset that was going to make her relive everything. Her water was going to break, then she would be in the delivery room. Dying. Being dead. Being alive again. Giving away her baby. Again.

All of it, all over again.

That was a stab through the heart, and sick in soul and body, Rain spun away from the crowd and the monks, needing to escape somehow.

And she bumped into another monk who stood a few feet behind her. The monk stepped back, bowing, smiling. "Pardon, miss," he said.

She stood there. Unable to speak for a moment. She remembered her lines, her script. Every part of that drama was burned into her memory. She forced herself to say nothing, to delay the inevitable.

The monk nodded to indicate her stomach. "Soon."

She said nothing.

The monk seemed uncertain, as if he had rehearsed for this but the play had changed. He cleared his throat and nodded at her stomach again. "This is a special one," he said.

Rain just looked at him.

"He is important," continued the monk. "He is not the flame, but he will strike the match." He paused and he studied her. "Do you understand?"

"Yes," said Rain.

The monk's smile tried to return, flickered, faded. "Listen to me, little sister," he said. "You are his mother. You must do what is best for him."

Rain forced herself to speak. She glanced over at the people sitting in meditation, all of them here to be part of something. Maybe to be part of this.

She said, "Thank you, Mr. Hoto."

The monk's eyes widened, and he stepped back. "How . . . ?"

"I know my baby is special. Or was. Or maybe will be. I don't know. All I know is that I love him. And I will do what's right for him."

"Y-yes . . ."

"So . . . thank you. You're a good person."

She walked away as fast as she could, nearly running, wheezing and crying and growling as she headed for the nearest exit. Rain looked over her shoulder to see if the monk was following, but the man stood there, looking shocked and horrified, one hand raised as if he was about to call after her. She quickened her pace because there was nothing else he could say. He'd already said enough.

Then she suddenly stopped and looked at the pavement in front of her. There was a small lift of one block of concrete, its edge pushed up by a tree root. Ten years ago, she had tripped over it and someone caught her.

Rain turned around, and there he was.

The tall man in the dark suit, with sunglasses and too much of a bad smile. His hands were already starting to reach out as if he knew he would catch her.

"Hello, Doctor," she said.

Doctor Nine withdrew his hands. "What?"

"What was it you said to me? Babies. A blessing and a curse. Am I right?"

Doctor Nine's smile faded. "What are you talking about?"

"I told you once, you bastard," she said quietly. "Go to hell."

Rain turned and walked away, left the park, crossed the street at West Ninetieth, and did not look back again. When she reached the corner of Ninetieth and Columbus Avenue, Rain stopped and took her cell phone out of her purse. She punched in a number and waited through four rings before it was answered.

"Mom," she said, "I made my decision. I know you'll hate me for it, but I'm not giving him up. I'm not giving Dylan to anyone. I'm going to keep my baby."

It was then that her water broke.

. . . and then she was back in Torquemada's. Back on the dance floor. Awake. Alive.

She sat up and heard some of the crowd gasp.

Rain crossed her ankles under her and rose to her feet. Doing it easily on dancer's legs. She turned gracefully, rising onto the ball of her foot. Making it a dancer's turn. There was no pain in her body. There was no weakness. Death did not own her.

Doctor Nine stood staring at her in slack-jawed amazement. "You . . . cannot . . ."

"Yes, she can," said a strong young voice.

Doctor Nine whirled with a snarl, then froze. The boy who stood there was ten. He was neatly dressed in new jeans and a T-shirt with a picture of the earth on it. He was a strong boy. Fit and tall, with dark eyes that were filled with mischief. He wore a silver chain around his neck from which a small silver windup pocket watch was hung.

"How?" demanded Doctor Nine.

Rain smiled a smile that was as bright as all the light in the world. "Go on," she said to her son. "Tell him."

"I stole a day from my mom," explained Dylan. "I gave it back to her. Only it wasn't the same day. I let her pick which one she wanted."

"That's the funny part," said Rain as she walked over to stand next to her son. "That's the part you never understood. It doesn't have to be the same time you steal. It just has to be the *time* that matters. Guess what day my son gave me?"

She took a step toward him.

"Dylan is alive. I'm alive," she said with quiet ferocity. "You've lost. Go to hell, or go back to whatever shadow you call home. Never come near me or my son again. If you do, we'll *burn* you." She took a small, definite step forward, and there was fire in her eyes. "And I hope you believe me. I really, really hope so."

Doctor Nine tried to stare her down. He tried. But the fires in his eyes could not compete with the blaze in Rain's. His fires dwindled and went cold. His flesh changed, fading to darkness, and then all the lights in the dance hall flared bright, and there was nowhere for his shadows to hide.

Rain stood there with her son. Clean and whole. And alive.

The crowd erupted into thunderous applause. They cheered and screamed and yelled, and then the Music started again. Louder, better, cleaner.

Rain spun in a circle, throwing her hands into the air and laughing aloud for the sheer joy of it. She saw Caster Bootey grinning and nodding.

And then someone took her hand. A small, strong hand.

"Come on, Mom," said Dylan. "Let's dance."

EPILOGUE

1 The paintings were all about leaving. About loss.

Rain moved around the café and examined each one. Taking her time. There were twenty canvases, large and small. Each with a crisp white card that gave the title and a price tag. In one, a sailboat leaned to starboard as it swung into the outgoing current, away from a wooden dock. In another, it was a train moving through steam as it left the station. A car driving away from a remote country farmhouse, mourners walking away from a grave. Like that. However, in each case there was a solitary figure left behind, sometimes lifting a hand in farewell, other times turning to walk the other way. The figure was often a woman. Because the paintings were impressionistic, the figures were often blurs of soft colors, with mood being suggested by color and brush stroke.

One picture was different from the others. In this one, the solitary figure was in the foreground while behind her a group of others filed out through a rear door. The artist had used warm colors for the wooden floor and soothing blues and whites for the long mirrors. The remaining figure stood facing the mirror, freeing her wavy brown hair from its ponytail.

A boy came and stood beside Rain. He was twelve but tall for his age. Handsome, with beautiful brown eyes. He was dressed in clean jeans and a sweatshirt with a flowing Hindu om symbol stenciled over the heart.

"She looks like you," he said.

Rain nodded.

Dylan took his mother's hand. "He doesn't know you anymore, Mom."

"I know."

And yet in the painting, the face was hers. Both of them. The one in the mirror was cast differently, with shadows changing the expression into one of pinched fear and suspicion. The eyes of that mirror image were untrustworthy and afraid. However, the face of the real-world woman was bathed in clear light from the window. She looked a little older, calm, aware. And happy, though there was a bittersweet quality to the shape of her mouth. She did not look with disapproval at her mirror image; instead, there was sympathy.

They looked at the painting. Rain touched the scrawled signature in the corner. Joplin. It was nearly two years since that night on the dance floor at Torquemada's. Two years, and another life.

"He shouldn't be able to remember you," said Dylan, touching the edge of the frame. "He never met you."

There was doubt in his voice, though.

Rain bought the painting.

2 Later, Rain used her Lyft app to call for a car, and when an old 1957 Chevy glided smoothly out of traffic to pull up in front of the café, her heart skipped a beat. Dylan squeezed her hand.

"That's the one you told me about?" he asked.

"Yes," she said.

"He knew Dad?"

"Yes."

Dylan nodded. "He didn't mean to—"

"I know, baby. None of it was his fault."

As Rain reached for the door handle, Dylan whispered, "He won't remember you, either."

"I know," she said again. "It's nice to see him, though."

It was nice. The last time Rain had seen Alexander Stickley was on the day he died.

Sticks turned around in his seat. "Going to Brooklyn?"

"Yes. You have the address?"

"Sure. Buckle up."

Rain saw that Sticks was wearing his veteran's cap. She thought back to how much she had hated him when she learned he had driven the Humvee in which Noah was killed. That hatred had burned briefly, but it had left a scar on her. She reached over the seat and touched his shoulder.

"Thank you for your service," she said softly.

"Thanks," he said, but he caught her eye in the mirror. His gaze lingered, and he wore a puzzled expression. "Have I driven you somewhere before?"

She almost said yes. She almost said that he picked her up once in an alley near Boundary Street. Almost. Dylan took her hand, squeezed it, and gave her a tiny shake of his head.

"I don't think so," said Rain.

"You look familiar," he said as he turned away and started the car. "You famous?"

"I dance," she said.

"What kind?"

"Ballet," said Rain.

"Oh," he said, and there did not seem to be anywhere for the conversation to go. He pulled into traffic. Rain had no idea if Sticks understood their karmic connection in this version of the world. It did not matter. She asked him for his card in case they needed him again. Sticks drove them away from the big apartment near Central Park that Rain shared with her son. It was in the same building where her parents lived. It had taken her a few years, but her mother had come to accept her daughter's child, and now she doted on Dylan. The boy made her laugh.

They laughed a lot.

During the drive, Rain almost started a conversation with Sticks, but she did not know where to begin. The conversation would be awkward, maybe even hurtful.

The trip was long because the traffic was heavy. Rain said that she wanted to hire the car for a few errands. She said she'd pay cash. Sticks shrugged and said it was okay by him.

They parked for a while across from a row of brownstones.

"You used to live there?" asked Dylan quietly.

"I did."

"Wonder whatever happened to your dog."

"I don't know. Someone else adopted her, I expect. Whoever did, they'll fall in love with her. Sweet little Bug."

Rain dabbed at her eyes.

"Hey," said Dylan, "can we get a dog? A rescue, like Bug?"

She kissed his head. "The shelter is six blocks from here."

He hesitated. "It won't *be* Bug, though. You get that, right?"

"I know."

She caught Sticks giving her an odd look in the rearview mirror.

Rain asked the driver to take them to a different address. Once there, they stayed in the car. Watching.

The big church across the street looked old and run-down, but there were people clustered around a side door. Talking. Being together. Being there for each other. To one side stood a cluster of three people. Two men—one tall and fit, one short and round—and a very tall mixed-race woman. They were all laughing at some shared joke. Then they crossed the street and walked into a diner. They were still laughing when the door closed behind them.

"Okay," said Rain. "Let's go."

They drove back to the city, and the car dropped them outside of the Koch Theater at Lincoln Center.

Where Rain would be dancing that night.

Tomorrow they would go to the New York Society for Ethical Culture on West Sixty-Fourth, where twelve-year-old Dylan would give another talk.

3 Rain got a call late on a Tuesday night seven months later.

Dylan was asleep, and the city looked like it was fashioned from silver and diamonds. She stood at one of the big windows, a glass of white wine in one hand, the other touching the pane.

When her phone rang, Rain looked at the number, and her heart stopped. Just for a moment. It was a number she remembered from a long, long time ago.

She put down the wine and picked up her cell from the table by the couch. As she raised it to her ear, she glanced at the painting on the wall. It was one of eleven she now owned, all by the same artist. She knew the artist now, too. Sometimes he came over to spend the night. The whole night. Sometimes he stayed for days.

Rain pressed the Call button. "Hello?"

"I remember," said Monk Addison.

It took her a long time to find her voice. "How?"

"The tattoo," he said. "I still have it."

"God . . ."

"Mr. Hoto never killed himself, you know. Neither did the kid, but I guess you know that," said Monk. "But I still have the tattoo."

"What can I do?" she asked.

"Do? Nothing. It's okay. They never died, so they don't haunt me. That tattoo . . . sometimes it makes the other ghosts go quiet. I can sleep at night. Not always, but sometimes."

Rain said nothing. Two tears fell down her cheeks.

"I wanted you to know," said Monk. "I remember. And if you ever need me—someone like me—call, okay?"

"Yes," she said.

"But, Rain?"

"Yes?" she whispered.

"I don't think you ever will," he said. "You won't have to. I think you're going to be okay."

The line went dead.

Rain picked up her wine and looked out at the night. There were clouds in the sky, but there were no storms at all in the forecast.

Sara Jo West

JONATHAN MABERRY is a *New York Times* bestselling author, five-time Bram Stoker Award–winner, producer, and comic book writer. His vampire apocalypse book series, V-Wars, is a Netflix original series. His young adult postapocalyptic zombie series, Rot & Ruin, is in development by Alcon Entertainment and is now a Webtoon. He writes in multiple genres, including suspense, thriller, horror, science fiction, fantasy, and action; and he writes for adults, teens, and middle grade. His works include the Joe Ledger thrillers, *Dead of Night*, *The Wolfman*, *The X-Files Origins: Devil's Advocate*, the Pine Deep series, and many others. His comics include *Black Panther*, *Pandemica*, *The Punisher*, *Captain America*, and *Bad Blood*. He lives in Del Mar, California. Find him online at www.jonathanmaberry.com.

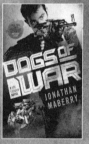

Don't miss out on the first
in a brand-new series featuring
JOE LEDGER AND ROGUE TEAM INTERNATIONAL

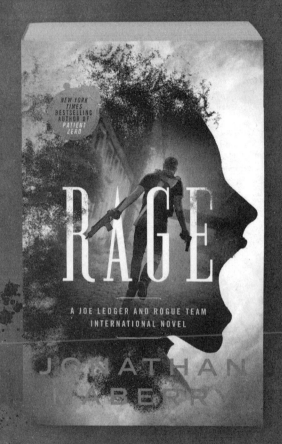

NEW YORK TIMES BESTSELLING AUTHOR OF *PATIENT ZERO*

RAGE

A JOE LEDGER AND ROGUE TEAM
INTERNATIONAL NOVEL

JONATHAN MABERRY

"A master of his craft."
—Rachel Caine,
bestselling author of the Great Library series

Available Wherever Books Are Sold

 ST. MARTIN'S GRIFFIN